VOODOO, LIES, AND MURDER

an Amber Fox mystery

SIBEL HODGE

**Here's what critics are saying about
Sibel Hodge's books :**

"Hodge created a lovely chick-lit/thriller storyline that reminds me of Charlaine Harris' Lily Bard mysteries that I love to eat up."
 - The New Podler Review of Books

"This is one of the best self published books I've read yet. There were just so many over the top and lol moments that it made me fall in love with Amber. It's been a long time since I've enjoyed a mystery this much."
- A Buckeye Girl Reads

"A witty well-paced romp, full of energy and with plenty of satisfying twists and turns."
- Romantic Novelists' Association

BOOKS BY SIBEL HODGE

Amber Fox Mysteries:

Fashion, Lies, and Murder
Money, Lies, and Murder
Voodoo, Lies, and Murder
Chocolate, Lies and Murder

Other Works:

Fourteen Days Later
My Perfect Wedding
The Baby Trap
How to Dump Your Boyfriend in the Men's Room (and
other short stories)
It's a Catastrophe
The See-Through Leopard
Trafficked: The Diary of a Sex Slave

Non Fiction:

A Gluten Free Taste of Turkey
A Gluten Free Soup Opera
Healing Meditations for Surviving Grief and Loss

"The truth is rarely pure and never simple."
OSCAR WILDE

CHAPTER ONE

———

When everything in your life is going amazingly well, do you ever get the feeling that something bad is about to happen? It's kind of like in the back of your mind you don't think you deserve to be happy, and something, or someone, is going to turn around and bite you on the ass to spoil everything. Like the world as you know it is going to suddenly go *bang!*

That was the feeling I had that moment as I lay in bed, staring at Brad. Brad, who was once my fiancé, then my ex, then my boss, then my fiancé again. Are you confused yet? I know I'd spent a long time being confused over my love life, but now everything felt right, and I was feeling pretty damn good about life, so this feeling I was getting of a doomsday cloud hovering over my head was très bizarre.

I propped myself up on my elbow, my eyes wandering with appreciation over Brad's face. Closed eyelids with sexy, long lashes hiding his blue-gray eyes that changed color depending on his mood. A smile that could melt an iceberg. Sensuous lips that could…well, that would be telling! My eyes wandered farther, toward abs that Mr. Universe would be proud of. Lower. Mmm. I licked my lips. Yep, Brad was Hot with a capital H.

Six months ago, I'd ended up moving in with Brad after Vinnie Dawson delivered a gazillion spiders to my apartment in an attempt to stop me asking questions about him. Call me strange, but there were much better things I wanted as a present. A lifetime's supply of Chunky Monkey ice cream, perhaps, or that sporty Mercedes I'd seen in a car showroom recently. Plus, I had a big phobia of spiders. No, that was putting it mildly. They scared the pants off me, and even though my apartment had been fumigated, I couldn't bring myself to move back in case one of the little creepy-crawlies was still lurking around in there somewhere, waiting to freak me out in the dead of night. Vinnie's little stunt didn't shut me up, though. I've got a big mouth and I'm not afraid to use it. Anyway, after that, Brad had asked me to marry him (again), and I'd never actually left his three-bed barn conversion since. Everything had been going perfectly. Better than perfectly, actually, so why did I have this weird brain-hovering thought that something bad was going to happen?

I pushed back the duvet, padded to the bathroom, and hot-blasted myself in the shower with some lemon shower gel until my skin was pink. When I returned to the bedroom, Brad had his hands laced behind his head, dozing, so I pulled on some black skinny jeans and a black T-shirt, and ran my fingers through my curly mane to try and tame it so I didn't look like I'd had a bad electric shock in the night.

Downstairs, my ginger cat, Marmalade, greeted me at the kitchen door, meowing and rubbing his head against my leg. I wasn't the only one who preferred Brad's place to my old apartment. Marmalade loved it, too. Hell, what wasn't to prefer? Brad's house had lots of wooden beams and rustic character. It was spacious, he had constant hot water, and one of those huge fridges that could store more chocolate than Cadbury. It backed onto empty fields and the views were incredible. Since Marmalade was the new boy on the block, he'd been outdoors more than usual, chasing mice and getting lots of extra pussy attention. Actually, since I moved in, so had I—minus the mice, of course.

"Hey, boy." I picked him up and gave him a quick cuddle, then grabbed two mugs from the cupboard, along with a French press, and switched the kettle on. I was scooping some fresh-roasted coffee into the press when Brad crept up behind me, sliding his arms around my waist.

"Agh!" Surprised, I spilled the coffee grains onto the granite worktop.

"I've still got the knack." He grinned as I turned around.

"Stop creeping up on me all the time." I playfully swatted his shoulder and looped my arms around his neck. Brad had learned a lot in his days in the SAS, but he'd get ten out of ten for stealth maneuvers every time.

"You want breakfast?" he drawled in his Australian accent, grinning suggestively and kissing me full on the lips.

I raised an eyebrow. "What are we talking here? Food or something else?"

"Food. Otherwise we'll be late for work. Tia just phoned and said something urgent's come in."

When Brad left the SAS he'd started Hi-Tech Insurance. When I wasn't being sexually harassed by my boss, I was his insurance investigator.

I unlooped my arms and turned my attention to clearing up the coffee as Marmalade growled at me and sat on my foot in protest at the lack of kitty chow heading in his direction. He swished his tail, slapping it on my ankle, telling me to get a move on.

"I'll feed him." Brad grabbed Marmalade's bowl and poured the stinky biscuits into it. A side order of milk and Marmalade was in feline heaven.

As I made the coffee, my eyes followed Brad rolling up his shirtsleeves, pulling a frying pan from the cupboard and whisking some eggs for an omelet. He was good with his hands. In the kitchen and *definitely* in the bedroom.

"So, Tia said on the phone she can't wait for you to set the wedding date because she's dying to get her bridesmaid dress," Brad said casually as he fried off some mushrooms.

"Uh-huh." I took a sip of coffee and gave him a look to show he wasn't fooling me. "You mean *you* can't wait for me to set the date." I was tempted to smile at his not-so-subtle hint, but I squashed it before he got any more ideas about the wedding.

"Well, why wait any longer?" He poured the egg mixture into the pan. It sizzled and bubbled in the olive oil.

"Marmalade, what do you think? Meow once for 'yes' and twice for 'no.'" I glanced down at my ginger fur ball. Okay, yes, so I talk to my cat. Sometimes I also ask him to make decisions about my life. But in my defense, before you call me completely nutso, a lot of the time he gave better answers than some humans I'd met.

Marmalade glanced up from his food bowl and meowed once.

"See?" Brad grinned. "Even Marmalade can't wait for you to set the date."

"Okay, okay!" I leaned my elbow on the breakfast bar, watching him work. He was always calm and relaxed, like his body was a perfectly tuned machine and motion was completely effortless for him.

Since I'd moved in everything had been domestic bliss, but was it all too good to be true? Was it about to come crashing down on me?

There it was again, that horrible, niggling feeling that something bad was about to happen. I shook my head to clear it of negative thoughts, and sipped my caffeine fix.

"What's the urgent thing at the office?" I skillfully deflected the conversation away from wedding dates, or the lack of them.

"Not sure. Tia was babbling on about psychics and voodoo and a missing girl." He shrugged. "You know Tia. I hope she hasn't been doing spells at the office again." He rolled his eyes.

I hoped so, too. Tia was the office receptionist, who was psychic and did weird spells. Usually she made me do them, too, and something always ended up breaking. She was the daughter of American fashion designer Umberto Fandango, and her dress sense could only be described as screamingly loud. She'd ended up working for Hi-Tec after I'd investigated the suspicious disappearance of her dad.

"Psychics and voodoo and a missing girl?" I pondered this. Since Tia was going out with Hacker, who also worked at the office, maybe it was something to do with him. He was from Haiti and knew all about voodoo stuff. "Has Hacker got himself in trouble with something?"

"No, Hacker's fine. Apparently, a woman called Chantal Langton has gone missing." Brad handed me a plate with half the omelet on it. I took it, wishing it were a big bowl of Coco Pops. Since I'd moved in, Brad was trying to break my addiction to junk food and wean me on to healthy stuff. Yeah, good luck with that. I mean, if junk food was really so bad for you, why did it taste so good?

I forked in a mouthful. Brad was a great cook, but a lack of chocolate and sugar in the mornings? Come on! How was a girl supposed to function properly? Oh well, I'd just sneak in a chocolate bar when he wasn't looking. Or a whole box, even. The way I saw it, a nice box of chocolates could provide all your daily caloric intake in one place. How handy is that? Or maybe I'd stop for donuts on the way in. Donuts! Ooh, I was salivating at the thought. In fact, if I had an apple donut and a banana muffin, plus a box of chocolates that included orange creams, lemon creams, and strawberry creams, they'd easily count as my five fruit and veg a day.

"Who's Chantal Langton?" I asked.

"She's insured with Hi-Tec, although I don't remember her name so I'd need to check the file. Tia says Hacker's got some info for us about the voodoo angle."

"Voodoo?" I shuddered. Okay, yes, I had a growing list of people I'd like to do voodoo on, but Hacker wouldn't oblige. He said if you dished it out, you got it back three times over. Bad karma and all that. And even though everyone on my voodoo-to-do list totally deserved it, the thought of voodoo dolls, turning people into zombies, and human sacrifices kind of freaked me out. Eeek!

* * *

An hour later, Brad and I arrived at the plush Hi-Tec office. Tia was on the phone as we entered reception, her blonde ringlets bobbing up and down with animation as she spoke. She caught sight of us and hung up, bounding around the reception desk toward us. Tia had—how can I put it?—an odd dress sense. Today she had on a pair of lilac boot-cut trousers, a clashing yellow fitted shirt, and an orange tie. Where did I put my sunglasses?

"Omigod!" Tia said, her American accent even more pronounced when she got excited. "Chantal Langton's gone missing." She handed me a file.

I took it, flicking through.

"Her mother's the famous voodoo priestess Nicole Langton and her father's the big property developer James Langton. All three of them have life insurance with us in excess of five million pounds, plus house and vehicle insurance," Tia babbled on. "Nicole Langton used to have her own TV show a few years ago. Did you ever see it? She's sooooo psychic, it's amazing!" Tia nodded knowingly. "I went to see her about five times. She always gets everything right about people. She goes into these trances and connects with the spirit world and then tells people in the audience about friends and relatives trying to get in touch with them. She's, like, totally awesome."

I glanced up, unable to concentrate on both the file and Tia-babble at the same time. I knew what sort of show she was talking about. I'd seen them before, although never with Nicole, but I didn't believe in all that mumbo-jumbo and thought it was all faked for the cameras. "Tia, those shows aren't real. They're just staged." I handed the file to Brad for him to look at.

Tia gasped, a hand flying to her chest, as if she'd been mortally wounded. "They are real! I can prove it. Chantal told me things about my mom that she couldn't have known."

Sadly, Tia's mum died when she was young. If Tia wanted to believe it was real, then who was I to burst her bubble? I let it go. "Okay, I've never heard of Chantal or Nicole, but I've heard of James Langton."

"Langton Developments is one of the biggest development companies in the country," Brad said. "Shopping plazas, huge housing developments, hospitals—you name it, they've built it."

"When did Chantal go missing?" I asked.

"Five days ago," Tia said.

"Have Nicole and James reported her disappearance to the police?" Brad asked, skimming the file.

"Uh-huh." Tia nodded. "But Nicole said the police don't take adult missing persons seriously until it's been a week, so they're not really doing much. And she heard Amber is the best investigator around, so she wanted her to get involved in trying to find Chantal." Tia grinned proudly at me. "She's offering a big bonus to find her daughter."

Brad raised an interested eyebrow. "What sort of bonus?"

"A million pounds," Tia said.

Brad whistled.

"Wow. I hope she doesn't broadcast that at the moment." I shook my head. "She'll have all the nutters coming out of the woodwork claiming to have seen Chantal."

"Nope. The bonus is only for you, Amber." Tia stared at me, wide-eyed. "Hacker has some more information for you about her. Apparently, he knew Nicole back in Haiti. Oh, and there's a present on your desk."

Oh, crap. "It's not spiders again, is it?"

She shook her head.

"Or a fox's nose?" I took a deep breath in. Yep, I got all the best presents!

"Nope. You'll like these." She grinned at me and followed as Brad and I took off down the corridor.

"Yo," I said to Hacker as I dumped my bag on my desk in the office I shared with him.

Hacker glanced up from a mass of screens and keyboards surrounding him. He was a computer whiz kid and had more electronic equipment and a bigger backup system than Houston. He was the spitting image of the rapper Snoop Dogg, complete with plaits and gangsta rapper hoodies. Today he wore one with *Rap Is Not Dead* plastered on the front in gold lettering.

"Yo." Hacker finished doing a few keyboard strokes, then glanced up at Brad and me.

Brad nodded back. "Hacker."

Hacker and Brad went back a long way, having met when Hacker was serving in Brad's SAS unit.

"Agh! The chocolate éclair fairy's been," I squealed, eyeing the open box on my desk. Six delish-looking éclairs with thick icing, oozing cream. Now that was what I called breakfast!

"Told you you'd like the present." Tia grinned.

I could've kissed her. I would get my choccie fix after all. Hurrah! I picked one up and offered the box around. Since Hacker and Brad were obsessive about health food, they didn't take one. Tia grabbed one and tucked in.

Brad perched on the edge of my desk, arms folded, shaking his head at my éclair.

"What?" I asked. "Chocolate comes from cocoa, which is a bean, and everyone knows beans are healthy."

"So, what's the story with Chantal?" Brad asked Hacker, ignoring my weird woman logic.

Hacker leaned back in his chair and clasped his hands behind his head. "Okay, I knew Nicole and her sister Marie back in

Haiti. Everyone in Haiti knew the La Fru Fru sisters. Both of them are *mambo*—voodoo priestesses."

Visions of sacrificed chickens and freaky rituals with snakes popped into my head. Knowing my luck, someone would be sending me snakes as a present next. Not that they bothered me at all. Well, unless they bit me. Agonizing pain and being paralyzed to death weren't exactly on top of my wish list.

"Around twenty-five years ago, Nicole La Fru Fru met James Langton and she married him and moved to the UK," Hacker carried on. "Marie soon followed. Both of them have been here ever since. Chantal is twenty-five and the only daughter of Nicole and James. Five days ago, Chantal vanished without a trace."

"Has she ever disappeared before?" I asked.

"Apparently not, and in order to find out what happened to Chantal, you might have to look into the voodoo angle." Hacker gave an ominous pause.

"Go on." I nodded at him.

"How much do you know about voodoo?" Hacker glanced at us all.

"It's a religion, much the same as Catholicism," Brad said.

Hacker nodded. "True. Voodoo is a form of worship and spirituality like any other religion. In fact, there's a lot of Catholicism mixed up in voodoo. If you mention voodoo to people, most of them will think about black magic, and there is an element of that, because, like any religion, there are people who use it for bad things instead of good, but that's not what voodoo should be about. Voodooists believe that nothing happens by chance. Everything happens for a purpose, and that purpose is determined by the many spirits that surround us. In order to appease these spirits and make sure bad things don't happen, we perform rituals or consult a mambo like Nicole to restore harmony."

Back to the dead chicken thing again. Ew. "Like animal sacrifice rituals?" I pulled a face.

Hacker clutched the dead chicken's foot he wore round his neck for protection. "Animal sacrifice is a part of it for some spirits, yes. But there are many rituals, such as simple offerings, prayer, spirit possessions, and dance ceremonies."

"That's what Nicole did on her psychic show on TV," Tia breathed with excitement. "She gets possessed by spirits who have messages for people."

"Uh-huh," I said skeptically.

"Well, *I* think she's genuine." Tia poked her tongue out at me.

I poked mine back. Childish, I know. "Okay, so if she's psychic, why doesn't she know where her daughter's gone, Miss Smarty-Pants?" I grinned at her.

"I told you before—it's not like you can just turn it on and off at will." Tia scrunched up her nose. "Sometimes you get psychic visions and feelings and sometimes you don't. You can't control when it's going to happen."

Brad glanced over at me thoughtfully. "I'm having a great psychic vision about something that's going to happen tonight."

My temperature shot up a few thousand degrees just thinking about it. I broke smoldering eye contact with him and turned back to Tia. "So if you can't turn it on and off at will, how come she gets possessed by these psychic spirits at the exact time her TV show airs, hmmm?"

"The show is pre-taped, not live," Brad said. "Maybe if the spirits aren't calling that day, they won't record it."

I gave him a disbelieving look. "Is being psychic a part of voodooism?" I asked Hacker.

"Not in the sense of having a TV show, no. In that respect, Nicole is an oddity. But in ceremonies a mambo is often possessed by the spirits, also known as loas, who will give prophecies on the future or advice on how to help with certain problems or situations."

"So she may or may not be a fake psychic?" Brad asked.

Tia shook her head so hard I was surprised she didn't get whiplash. "Not a fake," she said through a mouthful of éclair.

"I've seen Nicole do things back in Haiti that shouldn't be possible," Hacker said. "Things that have no explanation other than voodoo power. She's definitely not a fake priestess. "

"Okay, what else?" I asked him, starting to think we'd be here all day debating the finer points of psychics.

"In voodoo, there is one supreme god called Bondye who reigns over the whole universe. Since we can't communicate directly with him, there are hundreds of other spirits called loa that we have to make sure are happy."

"Wowzer. That's fascinating." Tia stared up at Hacker with loved-up goo-goo eyes.

"So, basically, it's all about rituals that are designed to protect you and show respect to the spirits or give thanks to them?" I asked as I finished my third éclair (I know, I know, slightly piggish!). I wiped my hands on a paper napkin. "You'd better take this away before I eat the whole box." I shoved it in Tia's direction.

Hacker sat forward in his chair, making his plaits wobble. "Yeah. Voodoo focuses on respect and peace. Most voodoo beliefs center around love and support for your family and community, generosity, and helping each other. Greed and dishonor are traits that should have no part in our lives. And there's a big healing element involved, too. Often mambos will perform healing rituals using spells and herbal remedies."

"See, I told you spells were good." Tia grinned at me.

I rolled my eyes at her. "Don't even think about it. I told you after the last time I'm never doing one of your spells again."

"Getting back to Nicole's sister, Marie," Hacker went on, "mambos don't normally practice left-handed voodoo, what we call black magic or bad voodoo, using this to curse or harm other people. But where there is good in the world, there's also evil. A bokor is someone who uses voodoo to cause misfortune or injury, even death. These people are extremely powerful." Hacker clutched the chicken's foot so tight his knuckles paled. "At some point after Nicole and Marie arrived in the UK, Marie turned her back on good voodoo and became a bokor." He paused for emphasis. "Since then, Nicole hasn't spoken to Marie or had anything to do with her."

There it was again. That horrible, burny feeling somewhere deep inside that something bad was going to happen. In the days that followed, I wished I'd listened to it more closely.

CHAPTER TWO

———

"Can I come with you to see Nicole?" Tia's huge blue eyes pleaded with me. "Purleaaase."

"I knew it! Those éclairs weren't a present at all, they were a bribe! You're busted."

Tia had the good grace to look sheepish, and chewed on her lower lip.

I was about to protest but then I figured, why not? If Tia could get some psychic vibe about what was going on then it might make my job easier. Not that I was exactly hopeful about it, but maybe Tia would connect with Nicole on some heebie-jeebie level.

"Go on." Tia bumped me with her shoulder. "She gave me a message from my mother at one of her psychic shows. The least I can do is return the favor if I get any feeling about where Chantal is."

"Okay. But don't touch anything. You know what happened the last time you came on an investigation with me."

When I was looking for her dad, Tia had insisted on tagging along and we'd inadvertently blown up a washing machine and a warehouse building. But even though she seemed like a quirky, head-in-the-clouds kind of girl, she wasn't afraid of anything, and all this talk about voodoo was making me feel spooked. It would probably be a good idea to have someone watching my back. And maybe Tia's screechingly loud clothes would frighten off any freaky spirits and stop them from turning me into a zombie.

"Great!" Tia clapped her hands together.

I grabbed my rucksack, which contained all kinds of practical investigatorish tools, and we headed out to my Toyota with Tia clutching the Langtons' file close to her chest.

"Where do Nicole and James live?" I cranked the car into gear and sped out of the Hi-Tec car park.

"Farnham House," she answered without looking at the file. When it came to office stuff, Tia seemed to have a photographic memory.

* * *

Farnham House wasn't really a house. According to their house insurance file, it was a humongous twenty-eight-bedroom mansion. An impressive winding drive through perfectly manicured lawns went on for a mile before we even got a glimpse of the whitewashed walls and entrance pillars.

It had been used as a hospital in World War II. Spooky. If Nicole really was psychic, I bet she saw lots of people floating around in white sheets.

"Wowzer!" Tia gasped, staring at the sheer size of it.

James Langton was a successful property developer, so I would imagine they'd be rolling in it, but I wondered how much of the money had come from Nicole's voodoo priestess sideline. Hacker said mambos were like healers, helping out the community with health issues or problems going on in their lives. I thought James Langton would be the sort of person who wouldn't be too impressed at waifs and strays turning up here at all hours asking Nicole to do a spell because their unemployment check hadn't arrived yet, or for Nicole to cure them of some infectious disease.

I knocked on the heavy wooden door and it was opened by a young black woman wearing a black and white maid's outfit, complete with a white cap.

"'Ello?" she enquired in heavily accented French.

"We're here to see Nicole and James Langton. It's about Chantal," I said.

"I spoke to Nicole earlier," Tia butted in eagerly.

"Oui. Of course." The girl nodded timidly. "Come in." She stood back and let us into the large hallway that could've contained my entire old poky apartment. "Follow me, please." She hurried across flagstone floors, passing impressive floral displays of white lilies resting on antique tables, and numerous carved wooden doors that were closed.

At the end of the hall, she knocked on a door and said something in French that I didn't understand. The only two things I remembered from my French class at school were a couple of emergency phrases we'd learned for a French exchange holiday—"I've got my period" and "I've got diarrhea." Probably not too helpful in this case, and strangely enough, I'd never actually used them since.

I caught a muffled "Oui" from behind the door and the maid let us in.

The room was dark, despite the sunny day outside. Heavy and expensive-looking curtains were drawn, covering most of the large windows, giving it a creepy feel.

More French from Nicole and the maid drew the curtains back as Nicole stood to greet us.

I'd been expecting someone with a snake wrapped around her neck or a goat's skull on top of her head, wearing a black smock with white skulls and bones on it, but Nicole looked pretty normal. She had black skin that was so smooth it looked like melted chocolate, oval-shaped, slanted brown eyes that were puffy from crying, and regal cheekbones and jaw. She carried herself with great posture—shoulders back, spine straight, chin jutting upwards slightly. I suspected she was in her fifties, but she could easily have passed for a woman twenty years younger. Maybe they should be bottling secret voodoo potions for anti-wrinkle cream. They'd make a fortune. I tried to work out if she'd had Botox or not. Nope, didn't look like it. Maybe drinking goat's blood was the key to her flawless skin.

"Hi, I'm Amber Fox." I held out my hand to shake hers. "This is my assistant, Tia."

Nicole took my hand in hers and then placed her other one over the top, grasping tightly. "Oh, thank you so much for coming. I don't know what to do."

Her hands were warm. Hot, almost. When she removed them to shake Tia's I could still feel her palms against mine.

"I'm so happy to meet you again. Last year you gave me a message from my mother," Tia gushed, then seemed to remember the situation and slapped a hand over her mouth to avoid blurting out anything else.

Nicole managed a smile, patting her hand. "I'm so glad I could help you."

Tia's sealed mouth didn't last for long. "You see, I'm psychic, too, and I wanted to return the favor for you if I can."

Nicole grasped her hand tighter. "Are you getting any kind of feeling? Do you know what's happened to Chantal?" Nicole's eyes glistened with tears. "I can't seem to see anything spiritually or psychically that will help."

Tia shook her head sadly. "Not yet, I'm afraid. Sorry."

Nicole deflated, her shoulders slumping. After wiping her eyes, she composed herself again. "Where are my manners? Would you like some coffee?"

I nodded and smiled. "Coffee would be good." *As long as you don't put any animal blood in it.*

More French to the maid, who nodded and disappeared, closing the door behind her with a soft click.

Nicole gestured to an embroidered gold sofa. "Please, have a seat." She perched on the edge of an ornate gold chair opposite.

"I understand Chantal has gone missing," I said. "Can you tell me what happened?" I pulled out a pad and pen from my rucksack, ready to take notes.

She took a deep breath. "Five days ago she just disappeared. She's never done this before, just left without a word. I know something's happened to her. I can feel it. Inside my heart." A hand flew to her chest. "She'd been staying with James and me for the last few months. She has an apartment in town but she's been"—she searched for a word—"well, very withdrawn lately. You see, six months ago her best friend Liza Bennet disappeared. The police have never found out what happened to her." She took a deep breath, blowing it out through her nose as if trying to calm herself. "Liza's disappearance affected Chantal deeply, and she was becoming very depressed. I was concerned about her and asked her to move back in with us until she was feeling more like herself again. That way I could keep an eye on her and try to help her. Chantal couldn't sleep; she couldn't concentrate on anything except trying to find out what happened to Liza. She kept asking the police if they had any leads but they always said no."

"So Liza has never been found?" I asked.

Nicole shook her head. "It's so sad. Her parents are devastated."

I let that sink in for a moment. Two girls missing in the past six months. Could it be just a case of a spoilt little rich girl running off with her friend, searching for some adventure, or was there something far more sinister going on? My mind wandered through all the possibilities I'd come across while investigating missing persons as a police officer. "Was Chantal on antidepressants or any other medication?"

"No. She didn't want to take antidepressants. I tried to get her to talk to our family doctor, but she refused."

"Did Chantal take anything with her? Clothes, passport, money?"

"I don't know about clothes. She has so many clothes at her apartment I can't keep track of them. She could easily have taken some. Her passport is still there. And as for money, she works for my husband so he pays her wages into her bank account. The bank won't tell me if she's taken anything out."

That wouldn't be a problem to find out. I'd yet to meet a computer system Hacker couldn't get into.

"But she has a trust fund set up that pays her three million pounds when she reaches twenty-six. James and I set it up when she was a little girl." She rubbed at her sternum, as if she were in pain.

"And when's her twenty-sixth birthday?" I asked.

"In ten days," Nicole replied.

Tia gasped. I glared at her to keep quiet.

Hmmm. Interesting. "I hate to ask this, but I need to know who the money goes to if something happens to her." That could be one big reason for Chantal's disappearance right there.

"It reverts to James and me."

Maybe not so interesting, then. If they were the ones who set it up in the first place, what would they have to gain now if she was dead? "What can you tell me about the day she disappeared?" I asked as the maid returned with a silver tray bearing a jug of coffee, cream, and assorted biscuits.

"It was a Friday. She'd been at home in the morning, even though it was a workday. Chantal hasn't been at work much lately because she can't seem to concentrate on anything since Liza disappeared."

The maid handed us all china cups of steaming black liquid. I added cream and avoided looking at the biscuits in case I ate them all.

"What kind of work does Chantal do for your husband?"

"She's an architect. She's been working on a big new project of James's—the City Park Complex. But she'd only been going in to the office lately to get the project sewn up. She hasn't even been interested in work since all this business with Liza, which is so not like her." Nicole took another deep breath and continued. "Chantal told me she was going to meet a friend in the afternoon. She left in her car about two p.m. and never came back."

"Did the police find the car?" I asked.

Nicole took a sip of coffee and nodded. "It was at the local train station. The police made enquiries, but there was no trace of her buying a train ticket to anywhere."

I made a note to find out if the CCTV cameras caught anything from the car park or surrounding areas. "What else have the police found out?"

She shrugged. "Nothing, and that's the problem. They're not going to take it very seriously until she's been missing a week, but anything could happen in that time. They've made a few preliminary enquiries but they have no leads." She reached out and clutched my arm. "I can't just sit here and wait for them to do something. I read in the newspapers that you helped Umberto Fandango and I wanted to get you involved as soon as possible." Her watery eyes pleaded with me. "If anyone can find Chantal, it's you."

I smiled and placed my hand over hers, giving it a quick squeeze. "I'm going to do everything I can to find her."

She visibly relaxed with relief. "Thank you." She let her hand fall from my arm as if now embarrassed by her display of fragility. "I spoke to all of her friends and they all said they didn't meet her that day, so I don't have any idea where she was really going. The police told me they made some enquiries in the area around the station and no one remembers seeing Chantal. It seems like she's just vanished."

I frowned. No one just vanishes. There's always a trail left somewhere, and despite my reservations about the voodoo side of things, it was up to me to find out where that trail led. "What can you tell me about Liza's disappearance?"

"Do you think it's connected to Chantal?" Her eyes widened, as if she hadn't yet considered that possibility.

"It sounds like it could be." I finished my rich coffee and set the cup back on the tray.

"Liza and Chantal have known each other since they were five years old. They went to school together and were inseparable. When Chantal went to university to study architecture, Liza was studying journalism at the same campus. They couldn't bear to be parted from each other. Of course, we knew Liza's parents extremely well, too." She sat back with a wistful look in her eyes, as if remembering happier times. "Liza's parents, Jeff and Val, always took Chantal along on family holidays with them down to Dorset, and we'd take Liza abroad with us, too. Even in the summer holidays Chantal and Liza couldn't stand six weeks of not seeing each other."

I wondered about that for a moment. If the girls were inseparable, no wonder Chantal was depressed about her disappearance. Had Chantal discovered what had happened to Liza, and if so, had it got her killed? Or was Chantal involved in Liza's disappearance somehow? It seemed unlikely, but I couldn't rule anything out. Was that why Chantal had been so withdrawn and depressed, because she'd done something to Liza? Or was she just genuinely upset because she wanted to find out what happened to her friend? The questions rattled around in my brain.

"So Liza was a journalist?" I asked.

Nicole nodded. "She worked for the *Post*."

The *Post* was a national newspaper. Lots of big exposé stories. Maybe she'd been working on a story that someone didn't want printed. "What kind of story was she working on at the time of her disappearance?"

Nicole sniffed and dabbed at her eyes with a white handkerchief. "Apparently, no one knew what Liza was working on."

"What do you mean?"

"Liza wouldn't tell anyone what she was working on before she disappeared. Even her editor didn't know. Liza kept it a big secret."

Uh-oh. Alarm bells clanging. A secret story? "And the police haven't managed to find any clues about what happened to Liza?"

Nicole leaned forward in the chair and clutched my arm again with amazing strength. "No. Please don't let Chantal and Liza end up as some empty file on the police's cold case list." Her brown eyes darkened with emotion. "You have to find them."

"I'll do everything I can to find them, I promise," I reassured her again.

She finally released her grip and nodded. "I'm willing to offer you a one-million-pound bonus if you find her, or find out what happened to her. I don't want to be like Liza's parents, living in limbo, not knowing what's happened to their little girl. I need to know the truth."

"A reward isn't necessary," I started, but she cut me off with a raised hand.

"What good is money to me if my daughter is missing?" She laughed, but there was no joy in it. "The police couldn't find out what happened to Liza. I don't want it to be the same with Chantal. You're the only one who can help me find her, I just know it."

I nodded. "I understand you're a well-respected voodoo mambo. Can you explain how that works?" I asked. "It may have a bearing on what's happened to Chantal."

Her eyebrows raised in surprise for a moment. "You've done your research already."

I smiled. "It's my job."

"Plus, I told her about your psychic TV show," Tia piped up. "And Hacker's from Haiti so he knew about—"

I glared at Tia to shut her up.

Tia bit her lip and clamped her mouth shut.

"It's true, I am a mambo, but voodoo is not sinister or disturbing like it's portrayed in the movies. It's actually very misunderstood. We worship spirits like any other religion. And these spirits guide us in the physical journey of life. Voodoo is much like Christianity, in that we both believe one god created the earth. But since we cannot communicate directly with our god we must communicate through lesser spirits we call loa. Not all loa are good, of course. If a certain loa is treated with disrespect or ignored, they can inflict illness or pain or cause bad things to happen. This is why we must keep the spirits happy, to stop bad things happening in the world. As a mambo, I use my power for good. I perform rituals, spells, potions, and healing for people so the spirits will guide and protect them. I hold religious ceremonies to invoke the spirits. And, as in my TV show, I let the spirits possess me so they can pass over messages or guidance to their loved ones. In voodoo, death is a substantial part of the religion, which is why it may be so misunderstood. We communicate with the spirits of our dead ancestors or leaders, too, for comfort and guidance. We believe signs of death shouldn't be feared but cherished for the protection they give us, and we want to honor them." She paused. "We have many different spirits that control the universe. Spirits for love, war, healing, rivers, agriculture, forests, everything."

"Is there much call for a voodoo priestess in the UK?" I asked her skeptically. I mean, obviously Nicole wasn't short of a few quid, but was that from her husband's money or hers? Tia had said her TV show had been top of the ratings a few years ago.

"Around sixty million people in the world practice voodoo. Obviously, the United Kingdom is a melting pot of cultures, so there are voodoo worshippers here. But most of my clients don't necessarily believe in voodoo, they believe in healing and protection, and that is what I give them, along with advice about love, relationships, health, work—anything that affects people's daily lives. I also do voodoo readings to predict the future with spirit guidance, and I connect with people's dead ancestors for them. I have some very high-profile clients."

"It's not that different from people having their tarot cards read and seeing a medium," Tia said to me. "And look how many people do that."

Okay, yes, she had a good point. "But what about left-handed voodoo or black magic?"

"I don't practice that." She shook her head hard, her eyes darkening with emotion.

"I know that, but your sister Marie does, doesn't she?" I asked.

Nicole's forehead crinkled with despair. "Do you think Chantal's disappearance has something to do with Marie?"

Definitely no Botox going on.

"I don't know yet, but I have to look at every possible angle."

"I haven't spoken to Marie for about twenty-six years because she decided to use her powers for evil instead of good." She leaned forward in her chair. "I met James before he started his business. He was taking a year off to travel the world after he finished university. He's always been fascinated by different cultures, and when he came to Haiti, he was interested in the voodoo religion and the role of high priestesses. Because Marie and I were the most sought-after mambos, he wanted to meet us, and…well, it was a whirlwind romance, and the rest is history. We fell in love, I moved here, and we got married. Marie and I were always close, so when I left Haiti, we missed each other, and she decided to start a new life here as well. She met a man and had a brief fling and a son. Both of us carried on with our mambo rituals here, but she became tempted by the bad things that left-handed voodoo could give her—money and power. When she became involved in the darker side of our religion, I couldn't bear to have anything to do with her." Nicole sighed. "I know the evil things left-handed voodoo can do, and I didn't want any part of it. I cut off all ties with her back then, which was just before Chantal was born. Marie never even met Chantal so I can't see how she has anything to do with this." Her voice came out forceful.

"I will still need to speak to her," I said, not exactly relishing the thought. I was too young to be turned into a zombie. Plus, I was supposed to be getting married at some point in the future and I had my eye on a dress. A sexy little Vera Wang number wouldn't exactly go with gray, flaky skin and yellow teeth, would it? "I really need to question all family members when someone disappears."

"I don't even know where Marie is."

"I'm sure we'll be able to track her down," I said. "Do you have a list of Chantal's friends? I'll need to talk to them, too."

Nicole rose from the chair as if she were balancing a book on top of her head. She moved elegantly, like a dancer. "I already drew up a list for the police." She went to a small bureau in the corner of the room, retrieved a piece of paper, and handed it to me.

I scanned the list. "Did she have a boyfriend?"

Nicole nodded to the list. "Steven Shaw. His name is down there. They used to go to school together and were childhood sweethearts, but after Liza went missing, Chantal broke it off with him. They were still friends, but I got the impression he wasn't happy about the situation. He still texted her and sent her gifts, and he was trying his hardest to get her to change her mind and come back to him."

Could it be a crime of passion? Jilted lover kills ex? I'd just have to find out. "Is your husband here? I'll need to talk to him, too."

"He should be here soon. He had some things at the office that needed his urgent attention."

"Do you have a photo of Chantal?"

"Of course, how silly of me." She shook her head softly to herself, trying to keep her composure as she rose to her feet again. She walked with purposeful steps toward a fireplace. Above were several pictures in ornate frames. As if in slow motion, she reached out to touch one, delicately stroking the face of a young woman. She picked it up and clasped it to her chest, walking back to us. Handing it to me, her eyes filled with unshed tears.

Chantal was stunningly beautiful. A mixture of black heritage from her mum and white from her dad. She had long, thick curls and the same almond-shaped eyes as Nicole, but lighter brown, full lips and cheekbones to die for. She could've been a model.

"What else can I do to help?" With delicate fingers, Nicole wiped away the tears that snaked her cheeks.

"I need to have a look at her bedroom here. And if I could have a key to her apartment, I'd like to check there, too."

"Of course. But the police already checked and they didn't find anything that could help."

"They may have overlooked something." I'd been a police officer for seventeen years; I knew things often got missed. Plus, if the police weren't convinced she'd really gone missing and not just run away of her own accord, it was likely they didn't do a very thorough search.

"Follow me." Nicole rose and she guided us back through the hallway to a stairway with an ornate banister. Upstairs, we passed more closed doorways until we got to one at the end of a corridor. God, the place was huge. Did they really need so much space for just Nicole, James, and Chantal? It seemed kind of lonely to me. I liked cozy with a hint of clutter. Okay, more than a hint, but I liked to have my stuff around me. Stuff was good, although since Brad was such a neat freak, I was trying to be more clutter-free since moving in with him. Was this house more of a status symbol? Big developer equals big house. Maybe he had short-man syndrome and was trying to make up for it.

Nicole paused and took a deep breath. "I won't go in with you. I keep expecting to see her there, and I can't stand it. I'll wait downstairs." She retraced her steps, leaving us to it.

With the eerie voodoo conversation reverberating in my head, I half expected to walk in and find Chantal there, too. No such luck. Although I could smell a hint of perfume in the air.

Chantal was either a neat freak, too, or the maid had won the National Dusting and Tidying Championships. The police wouldn't have left it this tidy after searching it, so I was guessing the maid had put everything back in the same position as Chantal would've left it. The double bed had a gold satin duvet cover on it with perfectly plumped pillows. More scatter pillows in dark brown satin covered the bed, along with a tatty white teddy bear that looked old and worn, and was probably a much-loved toy in Chantal's childhood. Heavy dark brown velvet curtains were open at the window that led onto a balcony, overlooking the well-cared-for gardens. A large white dressing table with gold edging sat in an alcove on the other side of the room. One wall housed floor-to-ceiling cupboards. Lots of them. Cupboard heaven.

"Awesome room," Tia said, opening one of the cupboard doors.

Chantal had more clothes than Tia, which was saying something, since Tia's dad was always giving her his latest creations. Still, at least Chantal's clothes were more of the non-glaringly bright variety. If she had this many clothes here, even though she'd only moved back a few months ago, how many did she have in her apartment?

I wandered into an en suite bathroom. Brown fluffy towels, spotlessly clean and unused. A variety of normal girlie stuff—makeup, tweezers, moisturizer, expensive soap, a bottle of perfume. I took the lid off and sniffed. Yep, it was the same brand I'd smelled in the bedroom. While Tia looked around, I rummaged in a cupboard under the sink. Nothing interesting in there. Nothing that screamed CLUE in loud neon. No map with an X to mark the spot where Chantal was. And no smoking guns to make my job easier.

Big fat bummer.

It seemed like Chantal had a fairytale upbringing. Privileged, not wanting for anything, possibly spoilt. What had happened to her? Had she run away? That seemed out of character for her. Been kidnapped? And if so, why? For a ransom? Nicole hadn't mentioned anyone contacting them for money. Abduction for some other, more sinister reason? Possibly.

"What am I looking for?" Tia asked.

"I don't know." I shut the cupboard door and headed back to the bedroom.

"Well, how can we find it if we don't know what we're looking for?" Tia's eyebrows knitted together.

"We don't know what might be important until we find something."

Tia scratched her head, frowning, as she opened the drawers on the dressing table, and I went to work on the cupboards, going through pockets, handbags, and boxes of shoes. "Make sure you look underneath and behind the drawers. There may be something hidden."

"Ooh, what about this?" Tia swung around to me, a snow globe in her hand. "I used to have one of these when I was a kid."

Bless her. She meant well, but I'd never make an investigator out of her. I'd have to double-check the drawers when she'd finished, just in case. "That's just a snow globe."

"Omigod!" Tia exclaimed. "I'm getting a feeling about Chantal."

"What sort of feeling are you getting?" I raised an eyebrow. When I was looking for her dad, Tia had a weird feeling he was being held hostage in a pasta shop. While the shop part wasn't true, there *was* a pasta connection—only it didn't really help me much in tracing him. What would she come up with this time? A bubblegum factory?

Tia closed her eyes, holding the snow globe to her chest. "I'm just getting this feeling that she's alive." Her lids flew open again and she smiled.

"Well, I'm glad about that, but maybe you shouldn't mention it to Nicole just yet, in case it gets her hopes up." I turned my attention back to the cupboards, running my hands along the top shelves.

Nothing hidden. Damn.

I glanced around the room.

"You don't believe me, do you?" Tia said, a hurt expression settling on her face.

"I do believe you," I fibbed. I didn't want to hurt her feelings, and what was a little white lie between friends?

"Don't."

"Do."

"Don't."

"D—" My gaze hit the teddy bear on the bed. The rest of the room was in keeping with a mature young woman—elegant, tidy, modern, expensive. But the bear was tattered and old. Its fur had once been soft and thick and now it was balding and worn. One of its ears was practically falling off, and it was a grubby shade of brown. I glanced around the room. There were no other childhood mementoes here, so why had Chantal kept the bear around?

I strode toward the bed and picked it up. I squeezed it. The stuffing had been squashed over the years so it felt lumpy and was out of shape.

I turned the bear over and found a zip underneath its round tail.

Undoing the zip, I reached my hand in.

There was something inside.

CHAPTER THREE

———

"What is it?" Tia peered over my shoulder.

My hand connected with some paper and cardboard inside the teddy bear. I pulled them out onto the bed and sat down.

The first thing that caught my eye was a pregnancy test box—the kind that holds two plastic wands. I opened it up. There was only one tester left in the box.

There was a business card that read *Dr. Andrew Scott— Second Chance Clinic* with an address and phone number. On the back of the card, two words were scrawled in black biro: *Holbrook Clinic.*

The last item was a folded-up note, written in different handwriting to the words on the back of the card:

Chantal

I am extremely sorry you won't return my calls. That night was never a mistake for me, you have to believe me. I've loved you for a long time, and I will continue to love you, no matter what.

I promise I will not pressure you into anything. I am here for you when you need me.

Lovingly yours

X

"Nicole said Chantal had broken it off with her boyfriend, Steven." I re-read the letter. "They went to school together so they would've been around the same age, but this letter doesn't sound like the kind of love letter a young guy would write."

"No. This definitely reads like it's from an older guy."

"And as far as Nicole knew, Chantal wasn't seeing anyone else. It sounds like this night the letter refers to was a one-night stand. So, what? She gets pregnant and runs off to have an abortion?" I asked, more to myself than Tia. "And if so, why hasn't she come back?" A horrible thought popped into my head. Had something bad happened to her during a termination?

"Omigod." Tia's eyes widened, then she shook her head. "No, I'm definitely getting the feeling she's alive."

"I hope to God you're right." I stuffed the pregnancy test, note, and business card in a plastic bag and popped it into my rucksack, and we finished searching the room. When nothing else of value turned up, we descended the stairs and met the maid on her way up.

She avoided our gaze, nodding at us but glancing down at the carpet as she tried to scurry past.

"Excuse me," I said.

She stopped, back rigid.

"How long have you worked for Nicole and James?"

She glanced up at me. "Five years."

She looked like she was almost the same age as Chantal. Did they share secrets? "Were you close to Chantal?" I asked.

"Not really," she whispered. "I mean, we spoke to each other, of course. She was always polite to me, but we were not friends. I am just the employee, I know my place." She chewed on her lower lip, eyes darting around the hallway.

"So Chantal didn't confide anything in you? Anything that might help us find her?" I asked.

She shook her head, lip biting getting more pronounced.

Now, I don't want to blow my own trumpet, but over the years I've become a bit of an expert on body language. Especially when people are lying. There are a million little hints that give it away. Some of them are involuntary reflexes that people aren't even aware of—tiny movements that the untrained eye wouldn't notice. While I was pretty sure she wasn't actually lying, I was convinced she knew something.

"And you never found anything in her room that was odd? Anything that could help me find her?"

Another shake of her head.

"Was Chantal acting strangely before she disappeared?" I asked.

"Well, she had been very depressed because of her friend disappearing. Sometimes she would not talk for days. Lately, she had been saying that she was going to find out what happened to Liza because the police could not come up with anything."

I noted her French accent again. "Are you from Haiti, like Nicole?"

"Yes." She jutted out her chin with pride.

"Is James Langton here yet?" I asked.

"Yes, I will take you to him." She rushed back down the stairs as if she were happy for the reprieve from my questions.

Back in the same room as earlier, Nicole was sitting by the window, staring out into the expanse of lawn, wiping her eyes with an embroidered handkerchief.

James Langton sat opposite her, legs crossed, a crystal tumbler of what looked like scotch in his hand.

I checked him out as we walked toward him. Mid-fifties, expensive suit, light brown hair, graying at the temples and swept back, a small scar on his right eyebrow.

He stood and shook our hands, forehead wrinkled with worry. He towered over me. Definitely not a case of short-man syndrome going on there.

"Nicole told me she'd spoken with you, but if I can offer any other information…" He waited for me to speak.

"Did you find anything that could help?" Nicole stood, balling up the handkerchief in her hand.

Before I could say anything, Tia took hold of Nicole's hands and blurted out, "I think Chantal's still alive."

I glared at her.

Nicole gasped. "What makes you say that? Do you know where she is?" Her eyes darted from Tia to me and back to Tia again.

"I'm just getting a psychic feeling that she is." Tia blushed, realizing she shouldn't have said anything.

"We found a few things but I don't know how or if it will help, or exactly what it means at the moment," I said, observing James as he ran a hand through his hair.

"I'm getting very skeptical that anyone's psychic abilities can bring back my daughter safely. I need to deal in hard facts." James's eyes narrowed in Nicole's direction, and I got the impression they'd probably argued about her psychic/voodoo connections many times before. Maybe the original fascination with voodoo and Chantal's exotic heritage that attracted him to her all those years ago had worn off. "And the fact is, at the moment, the police have no leads and their investigation is going nowhere, which is why we wanted to get you involved. Do you think Chantal is still alive? I've heard that the forty-eight-hour period after someone goes missing is crucial, and if they're not found by then…" His voice cracked.

"I'm afraid it's too early for me to say," I said.

He stared at me intently, as if assessing my ability to investigate the case. "Do you have any children, Ms. Fox?"

"No."

"If you don't have children, I'm sure you can't appreciate how anxious we are to find Chantal."

"I was a police officer for seventeen years, Mr. Langton. I investigated many high-profile cases, including missing persons, and I can assure you that I know exactly how anxious you're feeling at the moment." I turned my attention back to Nicole. "You said Chantal had split up with Steven Shaw after Liza's disappearance. Was there any other man in her life?" I asked.

"Not as far as we knew," James said.

"You're obviously a wealthy businessman. Have you received any threats lately? Has anyone approached you demanding a ransom?" I asked.

"You think this could be a kidnapping?" His eyes darkened.

A sharp breath escaped from Nicole's lips.

"It's possible." I nodded.

"Obviously, there are some people who are not happy with certain developments my company is involved in."

"Such as the City Park Complex?" I tilted my head, waiting for an answer. Lately, Langton Developments had been granted planning permission to build an eighty-story luxury apartment block on a piece of formerly protected land in the middle of a historic residential area. The locals weren't happy about it at all, and neither were the Heritage Department, who'd been slamming the council's decision.

"Yes, there's been some opposition to it, but we've been granted planning permission now and the project will go ahead. I've received no threats to my family because of my business."

"And Chantal worked on that project?"

"Yes, she was the architect for it."

"It can't be a kidnapping." Nicole shook her head. "If it was a kidnapping, someone would have contacted us by now for a ransom."

I didn't want to tell her what I was thinking. If it was a kidnapping that went wrong, maybe Chantal was already dead. Maybe that was why there was no ransom demand.

CHAPTER FOUR

———

Call me weird, but ever since I was a kid, bad news always made me hungry. By the time we left James and Nicole's mansion, my stomach was shouting at me to feed it.

"KFC or Burger Land?" I asked Tia, who was a girl after my own heart and loved junk food almost as much as me.

"Burger Land sounds yum."

I was almost salivating at the thought of a juicy burger and crispy fries. Oh, and a chocolate shake. Or strawberry. No, chocolate. Maybe both.

"What about Hacker and Brad?" Tia asked.

The pair of them were health freaks. Go figure! I don't think a Burger Land or KFC had ever passed their lips. Didn't they know what they were missing? "We could get them an apple pie. Apple's healthy." In fact, I might get myself one and it could count as one of my five a day. I wasn't entirely sure where I was going to get the other four from since I hadn't got a box of chocolates or a packet of donuts and muffins, but it was a start.

Luckily, there was no one in the queue for the drive-through.

"Can I take your order?" a muffled, tinny voice said through the microphone as we scanned the menu sign.

"I'll have a cheeseburger and a strawberry thickshake," Tia told me.

"Sorry? I can't hear you?" the voice said.

"Two cheeseburgers, two fries, and two strawberry thickshakes, please," I said.

"Do you want cheese on that?" the voice said.

Well, duh! "Only on the cheeseburgers."

"Do you want half-fat thickshakes or full fat?"

"Full," I said. Half fat didn't sound anywhere near as tasty.

"Do you want gherkins on that?"

"Only on the cheeseburgers."

"Do you want to eat in or to go?"

I frowned at the microphone. *Hello? I'm in a drive-through!* "To go. And can we have two apple pies as well, please."

"Shall we get the boys a drink?" Tia said to me.

"Pardon, what was that?" the voice said.

I nodded at Tia. "Do you have any green tea?" I said to the mic, wondering how the hell they could prefer green tea to a scrummy thickshake.

"Erm...hold on a minute, please." Muffled static. "The packet's green, does that count?"

"What does it say on the packet?" I asked.

"Tea."

"Right. Better make it two waters, then, please," I said.

"Anything else?"

"No thanks."

"Please drive to the next window," the voice said, followed by an ear-splitting screech from the speaker.

I drove to the pickup window and came face to face with Dad. "Dad! What are you doing working in Burger Land?"

"Sssh!" He pressed a finger to his lips, glancing around behind him.

"What are you doing here?" I whispered.

"I'm on a job," he whispered back.

Dad had been a dedicated police officer for forty-five years. After he retired, he didn't know what to do with himself and formed a neighborhood watch committee. He'd been on a one-man mission to stake out local crime areas and catch the bad guys (and girls, of course, don't want to be sexist here), until Mum had got fed up with all his disguises after he was roaming around like a homeless tramp for weeks, complete with dirty clothes and homeless, trampish smells. It had put a big strain on their marriage for a while. At least he was dedicated, though. I wasn't the only one in my family who lived for their job, or, for that matter, was slightly nuts. But Mum had been a cop widow all these years, and she'd been looking forward to spending some quality time with him after he left the force, so a while ago he'd promised to give up the neighborhood watch after it started taking up all of his time. They'd been having a second honeymoon period together ever since. So what was he up to now?

"I thought you promised Mum you weren't going to do the neighborhood watch stuff anymore," I whispered.

Tia shook her head at him. "Oooh, she won't be happy with you."

"I'm going mad stuck in the house all day. I need to do something. I've promised her it won't take up as much of my time as before."

"Uh-huh." I nodded, not believing him. I was exactly like Dad—a workaholic. It wouldn't be long before he was out of the house fulltime, trying to rid the neighborhood of crime. "And what are you doing at Burger Land?"

He glanced around slowly, making sure none of the staff could hear him. "Someone's stealing from the till. The manager asked me to work here so I can catch who's responsible."

"Right." I nodded as a girl who looked about fifteen, with bright pink hair and a pierced nose, appeared behind Dad and handed him a brown paper bag of food.

"Here you are, madam. That will be seven ninety-nine, please." Dad handed me the bag.

I gave him the money as another car drove up behind me. "See you later. Good luck with the till thief," I whispered.

* * *

I plonked myself in front of my desk and handed Brad and Hacker the water and apple pies. Tia had disappeared off to do some office paperwork.

They looked at the pies like I'd just given them a big lump of rat poison to eat.

"Gross." Brad exchanged a look with Hacker, who nodded his agreement.

"What?" I said. "Don't tell me you don't eat apples. They're healthy!"

"Not when they're coated in ten tons of sugar, refined flour, and hydrogenated vegetable oil." Brad parked his gorgeous behind on the edge of my desk.

I wagged a finger at him. "I've told you a hundred million times not to exaggerate."

"Good job I brought my own lunch." Hacker pulled out a fork and a plastic box of some weird couscous concoction from his desk drawer. He handed another box to Brad. "Here. I made you one, too."

Goody goody.

I tucked into the cheeseburger, my stomach doing an appreciation gurgle. "This is soooo yummy." I did an exaggerated smile. "You don't know what you're missing." Taking a big slurp of thickshake, I filled them in on what had happened so far.

"So there are a few possibilities," Brad said. "Kidnapping, abduction, runaway, possible medical procedure that went wrong. If she's been depressed you could also include suicide." He ticked them off on his finger.

I nodded. "There was no suicide note, though. She may have been pregnant and gone for a termination at this Second Chance Clinic or Holbrook Clinic and something might've happened to her." I handed Hacker the card. "I need you to find out what you can about these clinics and this doctor, Andrew Scott."

Hacker nodded and took a sip of water.

"According to Nicole, Chantal had split with her boyfriend, but I found this love letter from someone." I handed Brad the note. "It seems like they had some kind of one-night stand. The guy says he's loved her for a long time but won't pressure her into anything. It could be from Steven, but the tone feels like it's written by an older guy."

Brad studied the note. "Maybe it was more than a one-night stand. We don't know when the note was written, so they could've had a relationship since then. Maybe this guy is married and didn't want his wife to find out he was having an affair with Chantal, and his bit on the side's pregnant, so he kills her."

"Maybe." I nodded. "But her friend Liza also disappeared six months ago in suspicious circumstances, and Chantal was apparently trying to find out what happened to her." I paused for a thickshake hit. "It seems likely that Chantal's disappearance is connected to that, so I need to look into it."

"If it is a kidnapping, there's no ransom demand. Unless something went wrong and she's already dead," Brad said.

"You think this has anything to do with voodoo?" Hacker asked.

I thought about that for a moment, head on one side. "At this stage, no. It seems like Nicole is just the equivalent of a psychic and healer, although I will need to go and see her sister who does the freaky voodoo. Can you come with me for that?" I asked Hacker. "If she puts a hex on me or something, I want you to turn her into a zombie."

Hacker clutched his dead chicken's foot again. "Okay." Although he didn't look too thrilled by the possibility. "But I can't do any bad voodoo on her. I told you before, if you do bad things, you get it back three times worse. Plus, as a bokor, any voodoo she can do will be a lot stronger than mine."

Brad gave me a lopsided grin. "I thought you didn't believe in all that stuff, anyway. Spells, potions, hexes."

"I don't normally, but I've seen that James Bond film. What was it called?"

"*Live and Let Die*," Hacker said.

"Yeah, that one." I shivered. "And the thought of black magic voodoo is a tad creepy."

"We'll both go with you," Brad said.

"James Langton is a big property developer, so it may be that someone who doesn't agree with one of his developments has a grudge against him. There's been a lot of opposition to his City Park Complex going up." I glanced at Hacker. "There was an article in the paper a few weeks back about a guy who was running a campaign to try and get the development stopped. See if you can find out more about him. Maybe he's taken things one step too far and abducted Chantal as payback, or leverage for his cause. Some of these environmentalists can get a bit excited about things."

"Sure." Hacker nodded.

"I also need to know if Chantal has used her bank accounts since she went missing, and see if you can hack into the train station's security system and check the CCTV. Chantal's car was abandoned there." I scribbled the registration number on a slip of paper and handed it to Hacker. "And check her mobile phone number to see if she's made any calls." I finished my cheeseburger, screwed up the paper wrapper and threw it in the bin. "The other interesting thing is that Chantal had a trust fund. On her twenty-sixth birthday, in ten days, she was due to get three million pounds from it."

Brad whistled. "Not exactly small change.

"No. In the event of her death, it reverts to Nicole and James, who set it up, so I can't really see what kind of motive there would be to kill her for the trust fund." I shrugged. "But see if you can get into the financial records for the fund and Langton Developments," I told Hacker.

"Shouldn't be a problem." Hacker grinned and his front gold tooth shone back at me. He cracked his knuckles, ready for action.

I pulled out the list of Chantal's friends that Nicole had given me. "Can you make enquiries with these people?" I asked Brad. "And here's the key to Chantal's apartment. If you could see if there's anything else hidden there, that might help us."

He took a last mouthful of couscous slop and nodded. "Sure."

I sucked up the rest of the thickshake, making sure I'd got every last drop. "I'm going to talk to the ex-boyfriend, Steven Shaw. I also need to find out what I can about Liza Bennet." Which meant I'd need to call my ex, Romeo, who was a police officer, and see what info I could get from the police file. I hadn't spoken to Romeo since I'd officially broken it off with him six months ago. It was complicated. I still loved him, he was a genuinely lovely guy, and I hated hurting him. The trouble was, I was in love with Brad more.

I grabbed my rucksack and headed past reception, waving at Tia as I went.

"Pssst!" she said, head bobbing around to make sure no one was looking.

"What's up?" I stopped.

She held her finger up. "One second. I've got something to show you." Her head disappeared behind the reception desk and I heard the clunk of drawers opening and closing. She rushed around to the front of the desk, a magazine pressed against her chest with one hand, and pulled me into the toilets with the other.

"Oh, God. You're not going to try and make me do one of your bloody spells again, are you? Because I told you the last time—"

She cut me off by holding the magazine up in front of me, grinning from ear to ear.

Haute Couture Wedding Dresses by Umberto Fandango stared back at me from the cover.

"Dad's doing a line of wedding dresses now." She jumped up and down, squealing as she thrust the magazine in my hand. "Isn't that soooooo awesome? Especially since you need a wedding dress!"

"Shush!" I put my finger to my lips to emphasize I didn't want all and sundry to hear it.

She stopped jumping and cocked her head. "Why? If I was getting married I'd want the whole world to know." Her voice cranked up a few decibels again. She pulled the magazine out of my hand and started flicking through it, showing me the gorgeous dresses. On a scale of fabulousness, these were fabulicious. Previously, I'd lusted after a Fandango handbag and Tia had very kindly given me one as a present. In some ways, I wish she hadn't shown me the magazine because now I was severely lusting after the dresses, too.

A small sigh slipped out and I tried to ignore the pictures on the pages. Pretty hard, since if she shoved them any closer the whole magazine would be up my nose. "It's complicated."

She rolled her eyes at me with exaggeration. She'd got that little maneuver from me. "How complicated can it be? You love each other; you're getting married. Where's the complication in that?"

When you put it like that, it didn't sound complicated at all, but it was. "What if getting married isn't the right thing to do?" I asked her.

"Are you nuts?" She did her signature snorty hyena-like giggle. Loudly. In fact, they probably heard it in France.

"Shush!" I said again.

"Of course it's the right thing," she whispered back, finally getting the message to keep her voice down.

"What if it doesn't work out?" I rested my hands on my hips. "What if it's just a fairytale and the reality is we get married and then end up getting divorced? What if we don't really love each other, we just *think* we do? What if we end up hating each other? What if we lose what we have now? What if he disappears again and breaks my heart?" The problem was, I felt like I'd been going round in circles with Brad for years, and part of me was worried that even though we'd been through so much to get back to this point, what if our marriage didn't work out and then I'd have to admit it was finally over between us?

"Aha!" She held up a finger. "That's the main problem, isn't it? You're worried about him disappearing and leaving you again."

"Well…" I shifted on my feet, staring at the ground. "Yes, but all the other things could happen, too. Call me old fashioned, but when I get married I want it to be forever, so what if he does disappear, or anything else on my list happens?"

She threw her arms around me in a giant bear hug. Tia was surprisingly strong for someone who looked so fragile. "I've never met someone who over-analyzes everything so much."

"It's what makes me a good investigator," I said into her hair.

"And a crappy bride-to-be."

Okay, I wouldn't have put it so bluntly, but maybe she had a point.

She finally released me and thrust the magazine back toward my nose. "Promise me you'll look at them."

If I didn't promise, God knows what she'd do next. Probably a wedding spell in the middle of the high street for me. "Okay." I crossed my fingers behind my back.

"Did you have your fingers behind your back?" She gave me a knowing look.

I faked surprise. "Of course not!"

* * *

I dialed Romeo as I slid behind the wheel of my Toyota. It rang five times and went to his voicemail. "Er…hi, it's…Amber. How've you been? I hope you're okay. I…I need some help on a case I'm working on and wondered if we could meet. I'm investigating the disappearance of Chantal Langton and it might tie in to her missing friend, Liza Bennet. All righty, then. If you could…er…call me back, that would be great." I hung up and let out the breath that I hadn't even realized I was holding.

Next, I phoned Steven Shaw.

"Hi, Steven, I'm Amber Fox from Hi-Tec Insurance. I'm investigating Chantal's disappearance and I need to ask you some questions. Can we meet?"

"Er…sure. The police already asked me all sorts of stuff, though."

"I know. Her mum wanted me to look into it, too."

"Oh, okay, then. I'm at work at the moment. I've been trying to keep busy since…you know, since she went missing. I can't just sit at home and think about it all the time. Why don't you come here?"

"Where are you?"

"Burger Land. I'm the regional manager, but I use the office at the branch in town."

Oh, God, Dad would freak if he saw me in there again! Still, it might be an excuse to get another apple pie in. That would be number two of my five a day. "I'll be there in fifteen minutes."

As I pulled up in the car park, Hacker rang. "Yo," he said.

"Yo. What you got for me?"

"Okay, the CCTV at the train station is a no-go. The cameras in the car park weren't pointing in the direction of Chantal's car so you can't see who left it there."

"Bummer."

"Chantal took out five hundred pounds from her back account the day she went missing."

I thought about that. In the scheme of things, five hundred wasn't much. If she were running away, she'd want more than that. Judging by some of her clothes, I figured she could probably blow five hundred on one item, which meant it was highly unlikely she'd been running away of her own accord. "That's small change for her."

"She made one phone call the day she went missing to a phone number that's an unregistered pay-as-you-go phone. She's made no calls since."

"What's the number?" I rummaged around in my rucksack for a pen and pad. "Hang on." Had I left the pad at the office? I opened the glove box to find something to write on. A CD case?

Nope. A chocolate Easter bunny that had melted into the shape of a heart that I'd meant to throw away ages ago. A map! Aha! I grabbed the map. "Fire away." I scribbled down the number he gave me.

"And the guy who's running the opposition group to City Park Complex is Alfie Cross. He's sixty-two, a retired security guard. He and most of his neighbors don't want a modern apartment complex in the middle of a street full of historic houses. He's already been cautioned by the police for vandalizing a sign outside Langton Developments' office."

"Interesting. What kind of vandalism?"

"He spray-painted the words *Profit Over Heritage!* on the sign at the entrance to their car park."

Hmmm. Hardly violent threats, but it was worth talking to him. Maybe some simple threats had escalated into something else. "Does he have a criminal record?"

"Yes. He had a fight with a guy in a pub about ten years ago. Broke his jaw, apparently. The court was lenient with him, though. If he completed an anger management course, he could do community service instead of jail time."

"Very lenient," I agreed.

"Then Alfie was on his way to the anger management course one day and got arrested. Apparently, a guy ran into Alfie's bike with his car and knocked him off. Alfie lost the plot, dragged the guy out of the car, and punched him a couple of times in the face."

I could just imagine the newspaper headlines: *Man hits someone on the way to anger management course!* "Great course, then. What a waste of taxpayers' money."

"Yep."

"Chantal was the architect on the City Park Complex project. Maybe Alfie held an extra-special grudge against her. Okay, what else?"

"I checked out the Second Chance Clinic on the web. It's a free clinic for birth control. They also carry out terminations."

"So maybe Chantal was going there to get rid of her pregnancy."

"I checked their computers. There are no records of any appointments in the name of Chantal Langton."

"If something did happen to her during a procedure, they could easily cover it up in their computer records. I'll need to pay them a visit."

"You remember that *Holbrook Clinic* was written on the back of the business card you found in Chantal's room?"

"Uh-huh. Do they also carry out terminations?"

"I don't know what the hell they do. I checked out their website and it doesn't tell you much at all. Apparently they carry out 'unique treatments, tailor-made to suit qualified clientele.'"

"Huh? What's that supposed to mean?"

"Exactly. It's some kind of private clinic that does who knows what."

"It sounds a bit of a wide spectrum from a free clinic to this Holbrook Clinic. I mean, Chantal could afford to use a private clinic for a termination, so why did she have the card for a free clinic?"

"I don't know. I'll keep digging and see what I can come up with."

"Cool."

"Yo." That was Hacker's way of saying hello and goodbye. Maybe it was a Haitian thing.

"Yo." I hung up and made my way into Burger Land.

At the counter, I asked Pink Hair to get Steven Shaw. I saw Dad in the kitchen area behind, flipping burgers. When he spotted me, his eyes grew wide and he dropped a burger on the floor. He bent down to pick it up, and by the time his head popped up again, Pink Hair had led me to an office upstairs. I seriously hoped he wasn't going to serve up the burger to anyone.

"Here you go," she said, in between chewing gum so loudly it made my teeth cringe.

"Thanks," I said as she disappeared back to the restaurant floor.

I knocked on the door and went in.

Steven Shaw was tall and skinny. Gangly, like he was all arms and legs. He had delicate features and strawberry-blonde hair. Not ginger enough for him to be teased at school and not blonde enough to be considered cool. He wasn't the kind of ultra good-looking guy I'd imagined as Chantal's boyfriend. In fact, he was bordering on effeminate.

He stood up and leaned over his desk, giving me a weak handshake.

"Amber," I said.

"Steven…but then you…uh, know that already." He glanced around the room, blushing.

I sat down. He followed suit.

"What can you tell me about Chantal? I heard you two were going out but that she broke it off after Liza went missing."

"I loved her." His face paled and his eyes moistened with tears. "I wish I knew what had happened to her."

It didn't escape my attention that he'd referred to loving her in the past tense. Did he know something or was it just a slip of the tongue?

"We went out for two years and everything was going really well. I was…I was going to ask her to marry me." He pursed his lips together. "Then when Liza went missing, Chantal was just too upset about everything. She broke up with me a few weeks afterwards. She said she couldn't handle being in a relationship anymore. I tried to get her to come back, but she wouldn't."

"Did you see her at all after you broke up?"

"We met up for coffee a few times but it wasn't like a date or anything, unfortunately." Tears fell from his eyes. He quickly wiped them away.

"Had you seen her recently?"

"No." He averted his gaze from me and glanced down at the desk. His mouth gave an involuntary twitch.

Oooh, lie alert! "Not at all?" I prompted him.

He shook his head, eyes cast downwards, hands fiddling in his lap.

"Do you know if she was seeing someone else?"

That got his attention pretty quick. He looked up at me with wounded puppy-dog eyes. "No! She couldn't—I mean, she wouldn't. She told me she still loved me but she couldn't be with me until she knew what happened to Liza. She was down, depressed, but she wouldn't have got involved with someone else, I know it!" His breathing got faster, more agitated. "I just know it."

"Did you write her any letters?"

"No. I texted her, but I didn't write any letters."

"And you don't know what could've happened to her?"

This time he carried on holding eye contact, but his hands were trembling slightly. "No, I don't know."

"Did you know Liza Bennet?"

"Of course." He sniffed. "She was Chantal's best friend."

"Any idea what might've happened to her?"

"No."

"Do you know what sort of story Liza was working on when she disappeared?"

Trembling stopped abruptly. Full eye contact. "No."

Okay, that part was the truth.

"Can you think of any other information that might help me find Chantal or find out what happened to Liza?"

He shook his head.

I stood. "Okay, thanks for your time."

He stood, too, looking pretty relieved the questions were over.

On the surface, it looked like Steven was a sensitive guy. A gentle giant who wouldn't hurt a fly.

But what was lurking underneath the surface?

CHAPTER FIVE

———

Romeo phoned as I was leaving Burger Land. "Hey, Amber."

"Hey back. How are you?"

"Pretty good. Busy with work. You?"

"Yep, I'm good. I—"

"You want to know about Chantal Langton and Liza Bennet?" Straight down to business. But then, what did I expect? I'd dumped him for Brad, and I still felt like a prize bitch.

"Yeah."

"Can we meet?" he asked.

"Tell me when and where and I'm all yours." Oh, God, why did I say that? It sounded like I was coming on to him. "Er...not literally, of course."

He ignored my faux pas. "Starbucks. Ten minutes?"

"I'm on my way."

Starbucks was like my second office, and I could find my way there blindfolded. I was the first one to arrive so I ordered a mochaccino, heavy on the whipped cream and chocolate sprinkles, and a latte for Romeo. I eyed the double-choc muffins with lust, then decided I'd probably eaten enough junk food for one day. At this rate, I wouldn't even be able to get into a wedding dress. I seriously needed to stop eating crap if I wanted to look good for the wedding. *Right, that's it. I'm going on a no-junk-food diet.*

Oh, shit! How was I supposed to tell Romeo I was getting married? Not that we'd actually decided on a date yet, although Brad kept pressing me to set one every chance he got. I wasn't the kind of girl who wanted a fairytale wedding. After everything that had happened between Brad and me and Romeo and me in the last few years, I was exhausted with it all, really.

Okay, long story short—the last time Brad and I had been engaged, he'd disappeared on a secret SAS mission for three months without a word. As I sat there worrying about what the hell had happened to him, he was in some sweaty country, saving the world as we know it. Trying to get a message to me would've compromised his mission and his men, although I didn't know that at the time, and I spent those three months worrying myself sick. When he finally came back, I didn't want anything to do with him. I wouldn't see him or even talk to him. Eventually, after a lot of heartache, I'd got involved with Romeo, and he helped me get myself back together again—until the point when I was fired from my job as a police officer for shooting my boss in the ass (she so deserved it!), and Brad offered me a job as his insurance investigator. Brad had made it clear he'd stop at nothing to get me back. And now we were engaged again and…and what? Well, I guess I was worried history was going to repeat itself. So part of me wanted to just elope one day so I knew it would really happen. I didn't want all the months of planning and organizing a wedding, only to worry constantly about something getting in the way again and it not happening. The truth was, I had so many doubts and fears about getting married that it was hard to choose a single one that was the main reason for stopping me naming the date.

Romeo sat down at the table in front of me, jarring my thoughts back to the present. The sight of him took my breath away. Tall, sexy. Cinnamon skin and green eyes from his Spanish/Irish parents. Plus, he was one of the nicest guys in the world. We'd both worked on the Special Operations Team on the force, and before we'd got together romantically, we'd been great friends. I hadn't realized how much I'd missed him until now.

"Hey." He gave me a killer smile.

"Hey yourself." I smiled back, but it wobbled a bit on my face. "So…how've you been?"

"Pretty good. Work's crazy." He gave me a you-know-how-it-is shrug. "You?"

"Same."

"I've missed you." He pierced me with his eyes.

Okay, maybe I'd just wimp out and not tell him about my wedding. I know, I know, but how could I hurt him all over again? So what if I'd missed him, too? I still loved Romeo, I mean, it's not like you can just turn off your feelings like a tap, is it? But I loved Brad more, and deep down I knew I was meant to be with Brad.

"Sorry." He glanced away. "I shouldn't have said that."

I reached out and touched his hand. "I'm the one who should be sorry. You know—"

He held up the hand I'd touched to stop me, shaking his head. "Don't say anything. It's better that way." He took a sip of latte. "So, you're investigating Chantal's disappearance?"

I nodded, relieved for the change of subject. "What have the police found out so far?"

He shook his head. "As you probably know, her car was abandoned at the train station but CCTV didn't catch anything. It was parked in a blind spot of the camera. CCTV inside the station wasn't working at the time, and none of the staff remember her buying a train ticket. Apparently, she was supposed to be meeting a friend the day she disappeared, although we questioned all of them and none had arranged to see her." He sat back in the chair, stretching out his long legs in front of him.

"What did you think of the ex-boyfriend, Steven Shaw?"

"He seems pretty harmless. He was working the day she disappeared."

"He lied to me about not seeing Chantal recently," I said. "He definitely knows more than he's telling."

"Interesting."

"James Langton's a wealthy guy, but since there've been no ransom demands, it doesn't seem like a kidnapping," I said. "Unless it went wrong."

Romeo nodded. "A kidnapping doesn't feel right to me. As you can imagine, Langton's made a few enemies over the years with members of the community opposing his developments. Quite a few people are pissed off with his latest City Park Complex project. They don't want their sleepy, quaint street turned into a vast housing complex."

"Which brings me to Alfie Cross. He organized an action group to try and stop the planning permission being granted.

Maybe he held some kind of grudge and took things a bit further than a spot of vandalism to Langton's sign."

"We spoke to Alfie. He's a bit aggressive when it comes to saving his community, but I don't think he would've done anything to Chantal. He did some prison time for a couple of assaults in the past, but his alibi checks out. He was at a yoga retreat for two days when Chantal disappeared."

"A yoga retreat?" I snorted. "Aren't people who do yoga supposed to be all calm and Zen-like? Vandalizing property and assaulting people doesn't sound very calm."

"He's apparently turned over a new leaf since he did his time for assault." He paused, thinking. "Another development company, Sage Development, was originally supposed to be buying the plot that's going to house the City Park Complex, but James Langton beat them to the punch, upping his offer for the land to a ridiculous figure. Sage Development weren't too happy about it."

"Are there any other business rivals not happy with Langton?" I spooned the froth from my mochaccino into my mouth.

"No, but there's a rumor that Langton Developments have lost a lot of money recently. With the recession going on in the last few years, they were overextended on some big developments. They've slashed all the prices on sales for their housing developments, but people just aren't buying new houses anymore. So with all the delays in cash flow, Langton Developments could be in some serious financial trouble if they don't pull something out of the bag in the next few months."

"So where did he get the money to buy the City Park Complex plot and build it if they're in trouble?" Which brought my thoughts back to Chantal's trust fund. If James Langton was short of cash and needed some to finance a new project that might save the company, three million quid would come in mighty handy. The timing of Chantal's disappearance was suspicious since she was due to get the money in ten days, and if something happened to her…well, the money reverted to Daddy Langton.

Romeo shrugged. "At the moment we have no cause to look into any of his possible financial problems, but I'm sure Hacker would be able to." He raised an eyebrow.

I filled Romeo in on the trust fund. "Hacker's working on James Langton's financial accounts at the moment."

"So, what, you think James killed Chantal to get his hands on the money?"

I shrugged. "It's possible. If his business really is in trouble, a three-million-pound cash injection could be just what he needs. But I think there's more going on." I showed him the love letter. "You can keep it, I've got a copy."

"Bloody search officers missed this." Romeo read it, shaking his head.

"And I think she could've been pregnant." I told him about the pregnancy test, the card for the Second Chance Clinic, and the Holbrook Clinic's name written on the back.

"Maybe Steven lied to you about not seeing her lately because they were still having sex and she got herself pregnant. The Second Chance Clinic works with a lot of prostitutes," Romeo said. "They offer birth control, STD screening and treatment, and terminations. I've never heard of the Holbrook Clinic."

"Well, from what Hacker dug up on their website, it's not clear exactly what kind of procedures they carry out."

"I'll look into it, too." He read the letter again. "So, who's the guy?"

"I'm going to get Dad to check out Steven's handwriting to see if it's from him."

"Does your dad know him, then?"

"He's doing a neighborhood watch stakeout at Burger Land. Apparently, someone's stealing from the till." I rolled my eyes at him.

"I bet your mum's pleased." He grinned. "Not."

"Hmmm. Still, at least it's stopping him from getting bored."

"Somehow, I can't see Chantal having an abortion at this Second Chance Clinic. Maybe she was just getting advice."

"Or maybe she wanted to go somewhere no one recognized her because she didn't want her parents finding out, or the wife of her one-night stand, if he was a married guy." I downed the rest of my drink and licked my lips. "And I don't know how her being pregnant ties into this yet, if at all."

Romeo gazed at the lip-licking with a lazy grin.

I stopped abruptly in case I gave him any ideas. "What about the disappearance of Liza Bennet? Chantal was obviously upset about it and had started trying to find out what happened to her. Do you really have no leads on it?"

Romeo sighed. "I wasn't working her case, but I looked into it. Liza's an investigative journalist. Apparently, she was working on a big story, but her editor and colleagues didn't know what it was. She left the office one day to meet a so-called source and was never seen again."

I sat back, fingers tapping the table, thinking. "She just vanished? Like Chantal? It has to be something to do with the story she was working on."

"Liza kept all the notes for her stories on her laptop, which has never been found, either."

"And she never told anyone what she was working on?"

"No. She was paranoid about someone else stealing her scoop."

"Maybe Chantal managed to find out what happened to her."

"Seems likely. We checked Liza's phone records. Most of the numbers checked out okay, but there was one number she called on the day she disappeared that we couldn't trace an owner for. It's a pay-as-you-go mobile so it could belong to anyone."

My heart did a little tap dance. "What was the number?"

He told me.

It was the same number I'd got from Hacker that Chantal had called the day she'd gone missing.

"Have you tried ringing it?" I asked.

He nodded. "Loads of times. It just rings and rings. No answer and no voicemail."

"Damn."

"Exactly."

"So we now have two girls who've disappeared in suspicious circumstances and they both called the same mobile number," I said, knowing there was no way we could ever trace an owner for a throwaway phone. "You know Nicole is a voodoo priestess?"

He nodded. "From what I can gather, it's much like any other religion."

"Apart from the animal sacrifice bit." I pulled a face.

"Well, yeah."

I leaned forward, elbows on the tables. "What if they were into human sacrifice, too?" A horrible feeling crept over me, chilling me to the core, despite the sun streaming in through the windows. "Nicole's sister, Marie, apparently does left-handed voodoo—black magic. What if Liza and Chantal were sacrificed for some weird ritual?" My brain started hearing *dodododododododo* from *The Twilight Zone*.

"The thought crossed my mind, but I don't think it's likely. Nicole and Marie hadn't spoken in years. Chantal had never met Marie, so I think it's unlikely she's got anything to do with her disappearance."

I seriously hoped so, because the possibility was way too scary. "Did you question Marie?"

"Yes, and while she's—how can I put it?—incredibly weird and creepy, she tells the same story, that she's never seen Chantal. Marie and Nicole had a falling-out before Chantal was born and they haven't been in touch with each other since. So far, there's nothing to link them to each other at all. According to the file I read, some officers also questioned Marie's son, Andrew, and he says he's never seen her either."

Hello! My ears pricked up. "Andrew? Is his surname Scott?"

"How did you know that?"

"Andrew Scott was the doctor listed on the business card for the Second Chance Clinic, and now you're saying that Marie has a son called Andrew. It just seemed like too much of a coincidence for my liking. And, as you know, I don't believe in coincidences. I didn't make the connection before because he must've taken his dad's surname, not Marie's. If Chantal had never seen Andrew or Marie, like Nicole said, then how come she had his business card?"

"Good question."

My mind started sprinting out of control, remembering a case from 2001 where the torso of an unknown African boy had been found in the Thames. He'd been murdered in a voodoo-style ritual killing, and the case was never solved.

What the hell had Liza and Chantal got themselves into?

CHAPTER SIX

———

I was convinced that whatever led to Chantal's disappearance was something that had been going on long before she went missing, and the clue must be in what happened to Liza. I needed to talk to Liza's boss, so I got the number of the *Post* from Hacker and called Sarah Simpson, editor of the biggest national paper, and arranged a visit.

As I entered the busy office, phones were ringing off the hook, reporters were scurrying around the open-plan room trying to stick to deadlines, and the hum of keyboards clattering filled the air.

"Hi. Have a seat." Sarah waved a hand toward a chair piled high with newspapers as I entered the office. "Oh." She noticed the papers and added, "You can put them on the floor. Sorry about that."

I scooped them up and put them in a corner of the floor that wasn't already covered with yesterday's news. Sitting down, I said, "Thanks for seeing me."

She shook her head. "Anything I can do to help." She leaned her elbows on the desk. "We're all so shocked about Liza."

"Apparently no one knew what story she was working on? Is that right?"

She nodded, glancing out through the glass windows into the busy office. "Investigative journalism can be a cutthroat business sometimes. No one wants to do all the hard work only for someone to scoop you at the last minute. A lot of my reporters don't tell me what they're working on until a story's ready to go to print and I give it the yay or nay. Liza had had a story stolen from underneath her before, and she was probably more paranoid than most about letting anyone know what she was investigating."

I leaned back in the chair, sighing. "What kind of stories did she normally write?"

Sarah tipped her head to the side. "Liza was mostly into human interest stories. Abuse of power, women's rights, trafficking, war crimes, slavery, atrocities like what's happening in Darfur, that kind of thing."

"That's a pretty intense list." And a list that could spark off a lot of heated feelings from someone who wanted things kept quiet.

"Exactly. She could've been writing anything." She shook her head again. "I don't have the first idea how to try and work out what. It seems like the police couldn't find out, either. If they'd found her laptop, it would've been on there. I just feel like I'm partly responsible." She rubbed at her forehead. "She was working for me, after all. I'm going to have to make it a new policy that all my journalists tell me what they're doing from now on to avoid anything as horrible happening again. They're a secretive lot, though. As I said, it comes with the territory of protecting their stories and sources."

"What about scandalous stories? Politicians fiddling their expenses? Actors having affairs? Did Liza work on anything like that? It sounds like that wasn't something she'd normally work on, but I guess with investigative journalism, you have to go where the story is, right?"

She was silent for a moment. "True. She did a story once, early in her career, about a politician who was having a homosexual affair, but she didn't say anything about that kind of story to anyone here recently. Like I said, she went more for the gritty, tear-jerking kind of media."

"Did she mention whether she'd had any threats?"

"No, she never said." Sarah's phone rang. She picked it up, yelled into it something about not being able to extend a deadline, plus a few expletives, and hung up. "Sorry about that."

"Was Liza especially close to any of her colleagues?"

Sarah shook her head. "No. Liza was a bit of a loner at work. Head down, work your ass off, and get on with the job was Liza's motto. You're welcome to talk to the staff but, honestly, none of them knew what she was working on."

Damn. I felt like I was taking one step forward and two frustrating steps back all the time. "Liza's best friend, Chantal, has also now gone missing. I'm pretty sure that they're both linked somehow."

She gasped. "That's terrible."

I handed her a business card. "If you think of anything else, please give me a ring."

"Of course."

I shook her hand, pondering what she'd said. Liza might not have told her editor, and she obviously hadn't told her friends, since Chantal seemed to be trying to find out as well—but what about her parents? Would she have told them? Only one way to find out.

* * *

Even though it had been six months since Liza had vanished, her parents were in pretty much the same state as Nicole and James Langton. I doubted you could ever really get over the loss of your child, especially when you didn't know what had happened to them. Could you ever get any kind of closure in those circumstances?

Jeff and Val Bennet were in their late fifties. They were pale and gaunt and moved in slow motion, as if they'd had the life sucked out of them.

"Can I get you something to drink?" Val asked me.

"No, thanks." I smiled and sat down opposite them on a hard-backed sofa. "I'm really sorry to hear about Liza."

Val sucked in a breath at the mention of her daughter's name. Jeff's gaze drifted to some pictures on top of a stereo system. "Is that Liza?" I followed his gaze.

He nodded blankly.

I stood up and wandered to the pictures. Liza was the opposite of Chantal. Blonde, blue-eyed, pale skin, but still very attractive. One picture showed her as a little girl on a swing, missing a couple of front teeth. In another, a young Chantal and Liza were grinning at the camera, arms wrapped around each other in front of a gray-stone house. In a more recent one, Liza was holding up an award to the camera, an ecstatic smile on her face.

I picked up the one of Liza with the award. "What did she win?"

Val smiled with pride. "It's funny, ever since she was little she knew she wanted to be a journalist. She always got het up about injustices going on in the world. That picture was taken at the National Media Awards last year. She won Best Human Rights Story about a piece she did on sex trafficking."

"What an amazing achievement. A girl with a conscience—a great quality to have." I replaced it and picked up the one with Chantal and Liza together.

Val pointed at the picture. "That was taken at our summer house in Dorset. Every single school holiday we'd take Chantal and Liza down there. They loved it. They had a great time playing at the beach. I could never get them off there when it was time to go home. I had to bribe them with ice creams." She stared out of the window at something I couldn't see, a distant memory in her mind. "When they got too old to want to go away with us, they would still go down there sometimes for a girls' weekend to get away from everything."

Jeff stood up abruptly. "That will never happen again, will it?" He looked accusingly at me, as if somehow it was my fault. "I keep expecting her to walk through that door any minute, but she's never coming back."

"We don't know that for certain yet, Jeff. She could be anywhere." Val reached for his hand, but he brushed it aside.

He shook his head, his eyes bulging. "Of course she's not coming back. It's been six months. Don't you read the papers? Don't you know what goes on in the world? If she hasn't come back by now, something terrible has happened to her," he spat, directing his anger toward Val now.

"Then he pressed his clenched fist to his mouth and rushed from the room.

Val closed her eyes briefly. When she opened them she said, "I'm sorry about that. It's hard. It's just so unbelievably hard not to know where she is or what's happened to her. In some ways…" Her voice caught in her throat. "In some ways it would

be better to find a body. Then at least we'd know for certain."
She turned anguished eyes on me. "Does that sound terrible?"

I sat next to her and patted her hand. "They're perfectly
normal emotions to go through when a loved one goes missing.
It's like you're in some kind of limbo until you can find out
exactly what happened. I know you don't want to think about the
worst. You try to cling onto hope, but you need an answer. I
promise you I'm going to try and do everything to find that out. I
need to ask you some questions, though. Are you up to it?"

She nodded, fresh tears appearing in her eyes. She
rummaged around up her sleeve, grabbed a tissue, and dabbed at
her eyes.

"Did she tell you what story she was working on recently?" I
asked.

"No. The police asked me that as well. I've been trying to
think if something she said in conversation could give us a clue
as to what it was, but she was keeping it under her hat, just like
she always did."

"She won the award for the Best Human Rights Story. You
must've been very proud."

"Yes. Liza liked getting involved in the stories that could
make a difference to people's lives. She'd covered all sorts of
things, from the lack of women's rights in the workplace to the
sex-trafficking industry and child abuse in children's homes."

"Did she ever receive any threats about any of the stories she
wrote?"

Val took a minute to think. "No. At least, she never told us if
she had."

"And she didn't mention anything about voodoo?"

"Voodoo?" Val's eyes widened with fear. "Do you think her
story was about voodoo?"

"I'm not sure yet. It's possible."

She clasped her hands together in front of her face. "Oh my
God. What did she get herself into?" It was more a statement
than a question so I didn't reply, and besides, I didn't have the
answer to that yet.

I glanced back at the photo of Liza and her award. "She
must've been very dedicated."

"She was. If there was something terrible going on in the world, she wanted to write about it and let everyone know." Her eyes watered. "I can't believe Chantal's gone missing now, too. They were very close. More like sisters, really. Is Chantal's disappearance related to Liza, do you think?"

I nodded. "I think so. I think somehow Chantal found out what Liza was working on and something happened."

A hand flew to a slim gold crucifix around her neck. "That's terrible. I know how Nicole and James must be feeling at the moment. The anger and frustration. The worry and hopelessness." She fingered the cross. "I keep praying that they'll both come home safely," she whispered.

"Apart from the story she was working on at the time she disappeared, was there anything else going on in her life? Did she have a boyfriend? Did she have any problems?"

She was silent for a while, seemingly struggling to cope with her grief. Finally, she said, "No, she had no problems that I knew of. She lived for her career and it was going really well. She didn't have any financial problems, either. And she didn't have time for a boyfriend, but she was happy with that at this stage in her life." Val turned anguished eyes on me. "She had everything to live for."

Yes, it seemed she did, but someone else apparently didn't agree.

* * *

I was just pulling up outside my parents' house when Dad swung his battered Land Rover onto the drive.

He opened the door, grinning, holding up a bag stuffed full of Burger Land food. "Amber! Three times in one day! Want another burger?" He waved the bag at me. "A perk of the job."

I grinned. "No, I'm trying to give them up."

He slammed the door with a loud thud and frowned in amazement. Me refusing food, especially junk food, was unheard of.

"I don't want to put weight on for the wedding."

He nodded. "Ah. So you've set the date, then?"

"Nope."

"Don't tell your mother. She's been dying to buy a hat for ages." He let us in the front door.

Sabre, their nutso ex-police German Shepherd, came bounding out of the kitchen and jumped up, launching his front paws onto my shoulders, slobbering all over my face.

"Yuck! Sabre!" I tried to push him away, but he wasn't budging.

Dad wafted the Burger Land bag under his nose and ran into the kitchen. That got Sabre's attention pretty quick. He let out a noise that sounded like *yum* and hurtled after Dad. As I rounded the corner of the door, I saw Sabre's claws trying to get a grip on the slippery tiled floor. He skidded to a halt in front of a cupboard and bashed his head on it. Then Sabre did something that sounded like a sigh and passed out.

"He's always doing that," I said. "No wonder he's got a screw loose if he keeps banging his head."

"He'll be okay in a minute."

Sabre opened his eyes and sat up, staring at the Burger Land bag in Dad's hand with longing.

"He's not allowed any. He's supposed to be on a diet, too," Dad whispered, as if Sabre could understand what he was talking about. "The only way to get him off people is to give him a doggy treat, so he's been piling on the pounds."

Now he mentioned it, Sabre was looking a little porky. "What are you going to use instead to get him to behave?"

"Celery sticks."

"Celery sticks? What, and he actually eats them?"

"He loves them. I came up with that little idea," he said proudly.

"Amber!" Mum came into the kitchen and gave me a hug. "Want some cake? I've just made a nice coffee and walnut sponge."

"Oooh, yeah." Then I remembered the diet. "Er...actually, I'll pass."

She looked at me like I'd just walked in covered in dog poop. Her jaw dropping open, she put a hand on her hip, tilting her head and examining me with a frown. "Okay, what's wrong? The only time you ever stopped eating is when you broke up with

Brad." She gasped. "Oh no. You two haven't broken up again, have you?"

"No. Relax. I just want to make sure I can get into the wedding dress I've got my eye on, so I'm cutting out junk food."

Another gasp. "You've picked out the dress! Fantastic." She clapped her hands together. "Can I buy my hat now? I've seen this really beautiful one on sale. It's peach with a little flower arrangement on the side and it would look perfect with the peach silk dress I've seen. And—"

"No. We haven't set the date yet." I cut her off before she got more carried away and sat down at the shaker-style island in the center of the kitchen.

She rolled her eyes at me. "You mean *you* haven't set the date. If it were up to Brad, you would've been married months ago. What's the problem, honey?" She sat down next to me. "I know you want to, so what's stopping you?"

I shrugged. "I just don't want history to repeat itself. What if we get married and *then* we split up?"

"You won't." She wagged a finger at me. "This time it's for keeps. He loves you. You love him. Now set the date and let me buy that hat." More finger wagging.

"Anyway, Dad, I wanted to ask you something about Steven Shaw." I masterfully changed the subject. Go me!

"Oh, yes, I meant to ask why you were at Burger Land today seeing him." Dad switched the kettle on. "You want coffee, or have you given that up, too?"

"I'm never giving up coffee."

"You've never given up cake before," Mum butted in. "So if you're giving it up you must be subconsciously thinking about setting the date." She gave me a you-can't-fool-your-mum kind of grin.

It was my turn to eye roll. She wouldn't let up when she got her teeth into something. Maybe she was right and my subconscious had made my mind up for me, but if my conscious mind kept thinking about it, I would just worry myself to death and go round and round in circles like I'd been doing for the past few months. Probably better just to not think about weddings and concentrate on the case. Yep, that was it. No more thinking or talking about weddings at all. There. Banished from my mind. *Subconscious, are you listening?*

"What do you think about Dad doing surveillance at Burger Land?" I asked her, steering the conversation away from my love life again.

"Actually, we've reached a compromise. Which is what *marriage* is all about." She glared at me when she said the M word. "Your father can do his neighborhood watch stuff during the day, as long as we get to spend quality time together in the evenings and weekends." She smiled at him.

"Plus, you get lots of free food." I eyed the Burger Land bag on the kitchen worktop and something seemed to click in Sabre's head. He leaped up, grabbed the bag, and ran out of the room with it.

"Sabre!" Dad ran after him, closely followed by Mum and me.

Sabre legged it through the open patio door in the lounge and out into the garden, bounding around the lawn in a figure of eight as we chased after him. After a few minutes of tearing about, panting (Sabre *and* us), Dad managed to grab his collar, holding on for dear life, but Sabre wasn't having any of it. He bucked Dad's hand off, causing Dad to lose balance and fall slap bang in the middle of Mum's vegetable garden. Sabre, sensing he could make a clean getaway with the distraction, disappeared into the house.

Mum's hands pressed onto her cheeks. "My vegetable patch! That bloody dog!"

"So the celery sticks really seem to be doing the trick, then." I grinned at Dad.

Dad frowned, dusting himself off. "I need to rethink my game plan." He shook his head as we followed a trail of ripped-up Burger Land bag and crumbs back into the kitchen.

Sabre sat there like butter wouldn't melt, licking his lips and staring innocently at us while his tail wagged, whipping on the floor with loud thuds.

Dad pointed a finger at him. "That's it! No dinner for you tonight."

I swear Sabre gave us a look as if to say, "Am I bothered?"

"So, anyway, back to Steven Shaw," I prompted Dad. "Did you know him before he asked the neighborhood watch program to help?"

"No." Dad poured instant coffee into three mugs, topped them with water and milk, and stirred while simultaneously glaring at Sabre. "He didn't want to report the thefts to the police. He wanted to deal with it internally, so he asked if I could do some surveillance there." He handed Mum and me a mug, grabbed one for himself, and sat down at the island. "So far I haven't seen anything suspicious going on."

"And what do you make of him?" I asked. "I think he knows more about Chantal's disappearance than he's letting on."

"The day after she disappeared he was at work and the police came to question him. I was trying to listen in on the conversation, but he took them up to his office. When he came back down, he was pretty shaken up. He's been very quiet and withdrawn ever since."

"Has he talked about Chantal to any of the staff?"

"No. They're all avoiding him because they don't know what to say to him."

I pulled out a copy of the love letter from my rucksack and handed it to Dad. "Can you rummage around in his office and find out if he's got the same handwriting as this letter? I need to know if he sent it or not."

Dad took the letter and read it. "No problem." He took a big mouthful of coffee and swallowed, thoughtfully. "So, what's Nicole Langton like? I heard she's into voodoo. Do you think it's got anything to do with Chantal disappearing?"

"I'm not sure yet." I told him about Liza Bennet's disappearance, too.

"God, their mothers must be worried sick." Mum shook her head. "Poor things."

"I've got a feeling that Nicole only uses her spells and potions and stuff for good things, but her sister Marie apparently does black magic."

Mum did a mock shiver. "Like sacrifices?"

I nodded. "Maybe."

Dad glanced out the window, a look of concentration on his face. "You remember that boy that was found mutilated in the

Thames in 2001 in some kind of black magic killing? They never found out who he was. He was known only as Adam. Since then there've been a lot more ritual killings. All of them unsolved."

I nodded, swallowing back a lump in my throat. It was too horrible to even think about.

"Nicole said Chantal hadn't had anything to do with Marie, but I found a business card for Marie's son, Dr. Andrew Scott, hidden in Chantal's bedroom, so they had some kind of connection."

"Well, if you need any help, just ask," Dad said as someone rang the doorbell.

Sabre ran out into the hall and started barking at the front door.

"Why does Sabre always assume it's for him when someone rings the bell?" I asked Mum.

A few minutes later, Dad came into the kitchen with my sister Suzy, closely followed by Sabre, who was sniffing her ass.

Suzy was a psychiatrist who always tried to overanalyze everyone. She was so serious it was unbelievable, which was so weird because Mum, Dad, and I weren't like that at all. In fact, if you could take a degree in seriousness, Suzy would have a double honors. I secretly thought that she must've been the milkman's or switched at birth. Immaculately dressed, as always, in a beige trouser suit, she rested her Gucci clutch bag on the island and smiled at us all one by one. "Hello, I was just passing and thought I'd pop in." She twisted around to Sabre, whose nose was still attached to the back of her trousers, and tried to swat him away. "Sabre! Stop it!" she yelled, grabbing some kitchen roll and wiping off the slobber from her clothes.

Sabre's ears pricked up and, for once, he sat obediently. I wondered if she spoke to her patients in the same way.

Bumping her shoulder with mine, which she hated, I said, "Hey, sis, how's it going?"

She glanced at her shoulder and wiped that as well. For a psychiatrist, she had some major issues going on. Mind you, how could you be around all that craziness and not have it rub off on you?

"Not too bad, thanks. How about you?" She studied me carefully. "Working on a new case?"

I nodded.

"Anyone trying to kill you yet?" She tilted her head.

"Not yet. I'm kind of missing that. It's makes life so boring." I grinned.

"You actually like it when people are after you?" Suzy said. "I don't understand you at all."

"Hey, that makes six of us, then," I said.

"Six?" Suzy asked.

"Yep, me and the five other voices in my head."

"I was just telling her to set the wedding date," Mum butted in.

Extraordinary eye rolling by me.

"Yes." Suzy raised a quizzical eyebrow. "Let's talk about that."

"Let's not," I said.

"I hear what you're saying." Suzy raised a perfectly arched eyebrow. "You're scared of committing to Brad in case he runs off and leaves you again, and you get hurt so badly for a second time."

"That's weird, because I'm sure I didn't just say any of that."

"You don't need to say it. I know you."

"Oh, God, here we go with the psychoanalyzing babble," I groaned.

Suzy rested her hand on her hip. "You know, there's a famous saying: 'Do not dwell in the past, do not dream of the future, concentrate the mind on the present moment.'"

"Nice." I nodded. "Who said that, Oprah?"

"*Buddha!*" Suzy sighed. "It means—"

"I know what it means," I said. "There's another famous saying, too: 'Eats, shoots, and leaves.'"

"That's a book," Suzy said.

I shrugged. "Whatever." I looked at Dad to help me get her off my back.

He just raised his eyebrows sympathetically. If Suzy was doing her psycho stuff on me, it meant she wasn't doing it on him.

I pointed at Dad's Burger Land uniform. "Look, Suzy, what do you make of Dad working in Burger Land?"

Suzy turned to Dad. "And how does that make you feel?"

Dad glared at me.

"Anyway, must dash. I think I left a salad in the oven," I said, grinning back.

"Amber, be careful, honey." Mum squeezed my arm.

I nodded. The only problem was that being careful didn't solve cases.

* * *

It was dark by the time I got back home. As I opened the door to the smell of garlic and spices, Marmalade trotted up to greet me.

"Hey, boy." I dumped my rucksack by the door, kicked off my boots, and scooped him up. "What did you get up to today?" I rubbed his head with my chin, wandering into the kitchen.

Marmalade yawned.

"Busy day, huh?"

He purred in response.

"Catching mice or stalking pussy?"

He meowed.

That could mean either.

"Hey, Foxy." Brad turned his attention from a pan of pasta he was stirring and grinned. It was the kind of lopsided, sexy grin that made me want to ravish him on the spot.

Whoa—down, girl!

Marmalade jumped out of my arms at the sight of some chopped-up bacon in his food bowl, tucking into it like he'd never been fed before.

"You're spoiling him. He'll get fat."

"The way to a woman's heart is through her pussy." He smirked.

I curled my fingers into his shirt and pulled him close. "Ooh, I like that idea." I reached up and kissed him. Pretty soon we were involved in some heavy-duty tongue action and the pasta made slopping noises as it bubbled over.

"Hold that thought." Brad winked. "Dinner first, bedroom after."

"I love it when you talk all forceful." I smiled, pulling out bowls for the pasta and pouring a couple of glasses of red wine.

"But what a shame you cooked. I was so hoping to do the cooking tonight."

Brad gave me a disbelieving look. "The only thing you know how to cook is a frozen pizza, and even then you cook the plastic tray with it and melt it to the grill pan."

I feigned shock, even though I knew he was right. I could even manage to burn boiled eggs. Still, I considered that quite an achievement. It's not everyone who can do that. "No, that's not strictly true. I did attempt to cook you that chicken-liver casserole last month."

"Yes, which gave us both food poisoning."

I shrugged. "Well, it's the thought that counts."

"Exactly, so don't even think about it." Brad dished out spaghetti and carbonara sauce, sprinkling fresh parsley on top.

We sat at the breakfast bar and tucked in.

"So, I checked out the list of Chantal's friends. None of them have seen her in months." Brad expertly twirled some spaghetti around his fork and spoon. "After Liza went missing, she broke off contact with them. They said she started acting weird. She was withdrawn and depressed. They tried to get her to go out, and tried to cheer her up, but she wasn't interested."

"That ties in with what everyone else has been saying." I cut up my pasta into bite-sized pieces. Sod the twirling thing, it took too long. Plus, I'd end up with it all down my top. "Apparently, Liza was working on some big story when she went missing, but no one at the paper knew what it was. It's sounding more and more like Chantal must've found out something about what happened to her."

Brad nodded. "Sounds likely. I've got something to show you." He rested his fork and spoon on the side of his plate and walked out to the lounge. When he returned, he had a piece of paper in his hand. He placed it on the breakfast bar in front of me. "What do you make of this?"

There was a list of letters and numbers in the same handwriting that had scrawled *The Holbrook Clinic* on the back of Andrew's business card I'd found in Chantal's teddy bear:

MP - 28/01
DL - 15/02

CT - 01/03
EJ - 27/03
LS - 07875567893

"The numbers look like they could be dates. The letters could mean anything." I picked up my glass and swirled the wine around thoughtfully.

"I found it hidden in Chantal's apartment under a loose floorboard. There wasn't anything else of interest there."

"Codes for projects she was working on for her Dad? Passwords for something? People's initials?" I could go on forever. It could mean anything. "If it was hidden, then it had to be something pretty important. And I'm guessing it was to do with Liza." Then I had a light-bulb moment and did a mental head slap. "Wait a sec." I retrieved my rucksack from its resting place by the front door and brought it into the kitchen. Pulling out my notes, I read through them, then double-checked them against Chantal's list." I pointed to the number on the last line. "This is a phone number. Both Chantal and Liza phoned this number the day they disappeared."

"Interesting." Brad raised an eyebrow.

"Maybe this was one of Liza's sources for her story?"

"Maybe. Give the list to Hacker. He's good at cracking codes."

"Romeo said that the police examined Liza's phone records and all the people she called checked out apart from this number, which, as Hacker said, is an untraceable mobile. If Chantal listed that phone number next to the letters, maybe this is a list of people's initials. I think we need to get Hacker to check Liza's phone records, too, and see if we can compare it to this list."

A muscle in Brad's jaw pulsed at the mention of Romeo. "Good thinking. So what else did you find out?"

I filled him in on my day. "Steven Shaw is hiding something. He lied to me."

"You think he's involved in Chantal's disappearance?"

"Maybe. Dad's going to find out if the love letter is the same handwriting as Steven's." I paused for a bite of spaghetti. "Romeo told me that Alfie Cross, the guy running the opposition campaign to City Park Complex, didn't seem like the type of guy who would do anything physical to Chantal. He thinks painting slogans and organizing protest rallies is as far as it goes. His alibi checks out, too, so I guess we can cross him off our list of possible suspects. And apparently, Langton Developments are having financial troubles due to the recession. Another company, Sage Developments, were due to buy the plot for the City Park Complex and build apartments on it, but James Langton made a ridiculously high offer for it and beat them to it. Maybe there's some kind of rivalry thing going on."

"I heard that plot sold for four million pounds. A hefty price in this current climate," Brad said. "If he was having money problems, where did he stump up that kind of cash from?"

"My thoughts exactly. How's Hacker getting on looking into Langton's bank accounts?"

"He's still working on it. He's been trying to get into the Holbrook Clinic's computer system to find out what they do there, but their computers don't have much on it. It seems like they keep their files on a secure server elsewhere. He's still trying to crack it."

"Tomorrow I need to see Nicole's sister Marie and visit Andrew Scott at the Second Chance Clinic." I told Brad my thoughts about the unknown boy in the Thames and the escalation of weird ritual killings in the UK. "I'm not looking forward to it. What if she puts a hex on me and makes all my teeth fall out or something?" Maybe someone had already put some kind of love curse on me, which was why my love life was always such a big drama.

"You'd still look sexy to me." Brad grinned, reaching out and touching the corner of my lip. "You've got a little spot of carbonara sauce. Want me to lick it off?" He tilted his head, radiating heat like a furnace.

Hell yeah! I was feeling pretty hot myself. I didn't need asking twice.

CHAPTER SEVEN

_____

"Morning!" I said to Hacker as I breezed into the office the next day. "Where's Tia?"

Hacker glanced up from one of his vast array of computer screens. "At the chemist."

"Is she okay?" I dumped my rucksack on my desk and plonked my ass in my chair.

"She's got a cold, but she's convinced someone's put a voodoo spell on her. She's dosing herself up on Beechams and paracetamol."

"Well, I've come up with a plan so that when I go and see Marie she doesn't put one on me."

"Go on." Hacker gave me a look, as if to say this should be interesting.

"Okay, Brad and I will go and visit her for a voodoo reading of our future. Then I'll just sneak in some questions about Chantal very casually. That way she won't know we're actually looking into Chantal's disappearance, just that we're concerned citizens or nosy parkers."

"Oh, she'll know."

"How will she know?"

"Some of the things I've seen black magic bokors do in Haiti, you wouldn't believe."

"Well, that's the point, isn't it? Don't you have to believe in voodoo to get hexed? If I don't believe it, then she can't hex me. Right?" Well, that was what I was trying to convince myself of, anyway.

He shook his head gravely. "It doesn't matter. I've seen people who didn't believe in it die slow, painful deaths after they were cursed by a bokor. Deaths that had no explanation for them other than voodoo. She'll know everything you're thinking and everything about you."

I started to ask him exactly what kind of things had happened and then I clamped my mouth shut. Maybe it was better if I didn't know. Anyway, I didn't believe in all that mumbo-jumbo.

Yeah, right, Amber. Remember Live and Let Die*!*

Shut up! I don't believe in voodoo.

Do.

Do not.

Do.

Not.

The sensible part of my brain had the last word. Zombies? Making people die of curses? Impossible.

Still, I wasn't taking any chances, which was why I'd come up with my plan.

I handed Hacker the notes Brad found in Chantal's apartment. "I think this is a list of people's initials. This phone number is the one you found yesterday that Chantal called the day she went missing. Liza also called the same number the day she disappeared. I've been trying it but there's no reply." I pointed to the numbers on the list. "These look like some kind of dates. Can you see if you can crack this and find out what it means?"

"Sure. I love a good code." He rubbed his hands together and rolled up the sleeves of his purple hoodie that said *Gangsta Rappers Do It Better*, eager to get started.

"And can you get me a printout of the other calls made by Chantal and Liza from their phones?"

He handed me a stack of papers. "Already done."

"Cool." I shoved them in my rucksack.

"I'm still trying to get into the server with the files for the Holbrook Clinic. What kind of medical facility doesn't store any files on site? Strange, huh?"

"Very strange." Thoughts started going through my mind as I chewed on the end of my pen. Some kind of medical research? Nope, that didn't really fit with what it said on their website. Experimental treatments that weren't approved by the medical board yet? Maybe. Cloning? Stem-cell treatment? Rehab programs for the rich and famous? Sex addiction clinic? It could be anything. And how did it tie in with what had happened to Chantal and Liza?

"Let me know as soon as you find out what they're up to. Have you got anything else for me?"

"You'll like this." He leaned forward on his elbows. "Langton Developments is on the verge of bankruptcy. The only thing that's going to save it is the new City Park Complex, but with all the delays in getting the plot and planning permission, it was going to be touch and go as to whether they'd be able to save the company. So, what does James Langton do in the meantime?"

"Steals from Chantal's trust fund?"

"Damn. How did you know that?"

Hey, was I good, or what? I gave him a huge smile. "Because I'm a shit-hot investigator."

"The hot part is definitely right." Brad crept up behind me. I swear in a past life he was the Invisible Man.

"Don't creep up on me!" I play-punched his arm. "I hate it when you do that."

"You didn't complain last night." He raised an eyebrow.

Okay, so there was a bit of role-playing going on in the bedroom that involved creeping up on me. It was…oh, never mind, you'll just have to imagine.

I blushed. "Let's get back to the trust fund, shall we?"

"Out of the three million in trust fund, there's only pocket change left," Hacker said.

I tapped my lips with a pen. "And in nine days, Chantal and Nicole would've found that out."

"So he kills Chantal to cover it up?" Brad crossed his arms and perched on the edge of my desk.

"Possibly. Was he the executor of the trust?" I asked Hacker. "Yes."

I glanced at Brad. "I need to pay James Langton another visit."

Tia came in with a bright red nose and streaming eyes. "Morning," she said through a blocked-up nose. She thrust a box of donuts toward me. "Want one? They're cinnamon. Apparently, cinnamon is good for a cold." Which came out more like,

"Dey're (sniff) dinnamon. Apparently, dinnamon is good for a (sniff) cold."

My eyes lit up. "I lurrrrve cinnamon donuts." I reached out to take one and then stopped, remembering my resolve to keep slim for my wedding dress. "Er…no, I'm okay, thanks."

Three pairs of eyes looked at me like I'd just told them I'd had a threesome with an alien and a cyborg.

"No donuts?" Brad tilted his head. "Are you ill, too?"

I sat up in my chair, acting nonchalant. "No. I just don't fancy one, that's all."

"You don't fancy a donut?" Hacker snorted. "Pull the other one."

Tia put the box down on the desk in front of me. I was good, too—I didn't even peek at them.

"You're worried you might not be able to get into one of the wedding dresses you've seen in Dad's collection, aren't you?" Tia grinned, blowing her nose. "Awesome. That means you're going to set the date. Ooh, I can't wait to be a (sniff) bridesmaid. I've never been one before!" She leaned closer toward me conspiratorially.

I backed away in case I got cold/flu germs.

"Go on, tell me which dress it was (sniff). Was it the one with the diamante straps? Or…oooh, I know, don't tell me. It's the one with the fitted bodice and sheer sleeves, isn't it? Oh, that one is *so* you! Achooooooooooo." Her hand flew to her mouth as she let out an almighty sneeze.

I rolled my eyes at her. Okay, so maybe she was really psychic. I'd only ever got the magazine out in the privacy of my locked bathroom at Brad's, like a secret porn addict, so how could she have known I'd seen the one I wanted? "No!" I fibbed, avoiding Brad's gaze. If Brad knew I was thinking about the wedding dress, then he'd be putting even more pressure on me to set the date, and then I'd have to think about all the what-ifs again when I'd only just managed to squeeze them out of my head.

"I told you I was psychic." Tia grinned, looking pretty pleased with herself.

"Okay, Miss Smarty-Pants, if you're psychic, why can't you see anything useful that's going to help me solve the case?" I said, hand on hip.

"I told you, it doesn't work like that (huge sniff). I can't control when the feelings happen and what they're about. They just come to me."

"Right." I said in a disbelieving tone.

"But I'm still getting the feeling that Chantal's alive." She nodded at me. "Achoooooooo." She wiped her nose with a tissue.

I wasn't so sure about that. James Langton had a three-million-pound motive to kill his daughter. And that was without all the voodoo stuff, a missing friend, a jilted boyfriend who knew more than he was saying, and a possible pregnancy thrown into the mix.

"Are you going to see Marie?" Tia asked.

I nodded.

"You have to do a spell for protection. Someone's already put a bad spell or curse on me to give me flu." Tia's eyes grew wide with worry.

"It's just a cold," I said, but the neurotic part of my brain was wondering. Did I really have a love curse?

Brad looked at Tia with an amused smile.

"No. I've been cursed." Tia shook her head. "Oooh, I shouldn't do that." She stopped shaking. "My head's too stuffy to shake."

"I told you before, I'm never doing another one of your spells again."

"Well, you didn't want to do the last one and it got you and Brad back together." Then she slapped a hand over her mouth. That was supposed to be a secret, and she'd only roped me into it because she wouldn't take no for an answer and I was humoring her. I didn't believe it was what had really got Brad and me back together. Not in the slightest. At all. Seriously, I didn't.

"Oh, so you were doing a love spell to get back with me, were you?" Brad grinned at me.

"Tia made me do it," I said.

"Maybe you can help me do a spell to get her to set the date," Brad said to Tia.

"You don't believe in spells either!" I said.

"Who says?" Brad carried on grinning, which was getting a bit annoying now.

"She should so totally do a protection spell, shouldn't she?" Tia's head swung between Hacker and Brad, looking for their approval to her harebrained idea. "Ouch, remind me not to move my bunged-up head."

"It's not a bad idea," Hacker said to her.

"The trouble is, getting her to do anything she doesn't want to is a complete nightmare," Brad said to both of them.

"Hello? I'm right here!" I threw my hands in the air. "Why are we talking about spells when we've got work to do?"

"If you don't want to do one of my spells, get Hacker to do a voodoo one to protect you from Marie." Tia reached out and grasped my hand. "Please, for me. I don't want anything to happen to you."

"Oh, for God's sake, okay!" Giving in seemed the only way to get them off the subject.

* * *

Two candles alight, one chicken's foot being waved around, a few stones placed on the desk, and lots of mumbling in French later, Hacker's spell was complete, and Brad and I were on our way to Marie's house.

"Let me do the talking," I said as we pulled up outside her terraced three-bedroom house in Brad's Hummer.

"Why do you get to have all the fun?" He raised an eyebrow.

"Because I have a plan." I gave him a smug grin.

"If she's really psychic like Nicole, she'll see through your plan, anyway."

"I don't believe in psychics," I said, studying Marie's house: paint peeling from the doors and windows, rough end of town, overgrown garden. Nicole had said the lure of money and power had got Marie into left-handed voodoo, but judging by her house and the area of town she lived in, obviously the black magic voodoo didn't pay as well as the good voodoo. Maybe she did it because she was just genuinely evil. I shuddered at the thought.

"Don't let Tia hear you say you don't believe in psychics."

"I've told her loads of times, but she always ignores me." I snorted. "Are you sure you want to leave the Hummer here?" I spied a gang of teenage boys with spiky hair and multiple ear and face piercings farther up the street. One of them had a tattoo of a spider's web on his neck. Even though the spider was just on a tattoo, it still creeped me out. The gang were kicking a bottle around and eyeing the Hummer like it was the best thing since the hoodie was invented.

We opened the doors and got out.

"Wait here." Brad walked toward the boys as I leaned against the cool black metal, arms folded, watching.

As he approached, the boys puffed their chests out, oozing cockiness. Spider's Web jutted his chin in the air. He was obviously the leader. Since Brad had his back to me, I couldn't see what he was doing, but after a few minutes, the boys' demeanor became more wary. Scared, almost. They glanced at each other with worried eyes. Spider's Web's lips moved quickly, like he was dying to say something and get out of there quick. Five minutes went by and Brad came back, grinning.

"What did you say?" I asked.

"I just politely asked them to keep an eye on the Hummer for me." Brad's eyes danced with amusement.

"Or what?" I tilted my head. I had a pretty good idea. Brad was trained to kill with his bare hands, and he was pretty protective of his possessions and his friends. He'd killed someone to save my life a while back. I was sure the boys got the message loud and clear about what would go down if anything happened to his Hummer.

Brad shrugged. "Let's go and see Marie."

We walked up her narrow path covered with moss and weeds and knocked on the door. The house would've been painted white at one time, now it was a kind of grayish-brown.

I half expected the door to swing open on its own and loud, suspenseful music to start playing, like in the horror films.

"Yes. I'm coming," a croaky voice yelled from inside.

I glanced at Brad, feeling nervous. He glanced at me, not giving anything away, as usual. Cue suspenseful music.

The door swung open and I jumped.

For God's sake, Amber, get a grip, girl. There's no such thing as voodoo black magic. You don't believe in it.

Marie was the opposite of Nicole in every way. She looked like she'd taken a nosedive from the ugly tree and hit every branch on the way down. Hunched shoulders; wrinkles galore that gave her skin a sundried tomato appearance, only not quite as red; wispy black hair with a thick streak of white at the front that made her look like a malting badger; narrow eyes so dark they looked almost black. She looked at least two hundred years old, possibly three. Maybe she'd been a hot babe when she was younger, but I seriously doubted it.

"Er…hi. I booked an appointment for a voodoo reading," I said, not wanting to stare at a big, hairy mole on her cheek but finding it impossible to tear my eyes away. It was huge. A mouse could be hiding in all that undergrowth and no one would notice.

Her penetrating gaze went from me to Brad and back to me again. Then she clicked her tongue and said, "You'd better come in."

We entered a depressingly dingy and dark hallway where books and boxes were piled up either side. A white cat sat at the end of the hall, watching us as if trying to work out if we were friend or foe. Even the cat looked ugly and scary. Its head was too big for its body, and if I didn't know better, I'd think it had an evil glint in its eyes.

She led us past a few closed doors. A painting on the wall made the hallway seem even more disturbing. It had a black canvas with patterns of red and white that looked like hundreds of bloody skulls. In the center, a young, beautiful woman danced around a bonfire. In her hands she held what looked like human bones.

The hairs on the back of my neck rose.

Yikes! Don't look at the picture. Don't look at it. It might curse you!

At the end of the hallway was a cluttered, dated kitchen. Every surface was covered with stuff. I mean, don't get me wrong—as you know, I like stuff and clutter, but this was way over the top. The kitchen worktops had rows upon rows of jars containing what looked like bits of dead animals, rotten leaves, stones, sticks, and various funny-colored potions. Something foul smelling bubbled away on the hob—a cloying scent of things decaying and rotten.

"Have a seat." Marie nodded toward a small wooden table covered with a red cloth in the corner of the room. Four rickety wooden chairs surrounded it. In the center of the table were a pack of cards, stones, and half burnt-down candles.

Next to the table were French doors that opened into an equally overgrown back garden. They were ajar, but they didn't do anything to disperse the smell of…God, what was it? It smelled like road kill with a hint of infected dog's ear and rotting rubbish.

We sat down opposite Marie.

"You want some tea?" she asked.

"No thanks," Brad and I said in unison.

If that was what she was boiling up on the hob, I'd rather drink liquefied fish eyeballs.

Marie sat back in her chair, eyes narrowed. "Why not? I make it special. Special tea for a special couple." She grinned, revealing crooked teeth. "What's wrong with my tea?"

"Er…nothing. I'm sure it's lovely," I said. I didn't want to piss her off by refusing her tea, but who knew what the hell would be in it? What if it was some weird kind of potion that turned me into some kind of half-human, half-chicken woman?

"Everyone who has a reading must have tea. It's part of the ritual so I can tune into you better." She stood up, went to the boiling pan, and gave it a quick stir. Then she poured it into two teacups. As she carried them toward us, some of the dirty green liquid sploshed onto the saucers. "Here." She set them down in front of us.

It looked like iguana piss. I stared at it, then picked up the cup as she watched me. It smelled even worse close up. I tried hard not to heave, and quickly placed it back on the table out of sniffing range. No way was I drinking that.

"Something wrong with the tea?" She tilted her head.

"Looks lovely," Brad said.

"Lovely." I nodded my head in agreement. "It's probably a bit hot. I'll wait for it to cool down." I gave her my best smile.

"So, you want to know what the future holds for you?" Marie asked, sitting back and studying us both carefully like she could see into our souls.

I nodded. "We want to get married soon, but we've both been married before and we want to make sure we're doing the right thing."

Out of the corner of my eye I saw Brad glance up at me sharply at that little fib.

"Give me your hand," Marie said to me, holding out her callused one.

I obliged and she stared at my palm for a few minutes.

"You will have a long and happy life." She roughly dropped mine and took Brad's. "You will travel and have good fortune," she said to him.

What? Wasn't that what all supposedly psychic people said? She was definitely a fake. What had I been so worried about?

Marie stood. "Let me get my cards. I'll be back in a minute."

As she shuffled out of the room, I looked around for somewhere to pour the foul-smelling tea. The kitchen sink was out of bounds as it was already piled high with clothes, soaking in washing powder, so I sprang over to the French doors, yanked one open, and swiftly poured the contents of mine and Brad's cups into a nearby giant rhododendron bush. The bush made a loud screeching sound as Marie's cat shot out of its depths, dripping from whiskers to tail in green liquid.

My eyelids flipped open in surprise.

The cat flew into the kitchen like Concorde, closely pursued by me. I put the empty cups back on the saucers and looked around frantically for a cloth to wipe the cat, and then spied some kitchen roll.

"Foxy," Brad hissed. "What the fuck are you doing?"

"Shush!" I undid a whole bundle of kitchen roll and crept toward the cat that was now crouched under the table. A loud, throaty growl stopped me in my tracks.

"Here we are." Marie wandered back in the room. "Oh! Snowy, what's happened to you?" She bent down, picked up the cat and sniffed its fur. Then her eyes flickered slowly in my direction. "Strange, smells like tea." She peered at the lump of kitchen roll in my hand.

I gulped. *Uh-oh.* I was going to get a humongous curse for this!

"Er...I...the cat went to jump up on my lap and knocked the tea out of my hand." I bit my lip. "I'm really sorry. It was an accident."

"That's funny, Snowy's never sat on anyone's lap before. He hates it." She did the narrow-eyed thing again. It didn't do much to enhance her good looks. "You're very accident prone, aren't you?"

I figured it was a rhetorical question, so I didn't answer.

She put Snowy back on the floor. He gave me a filthy look then went into a fur-licking frenzy. "You should be careful. One day an accident might be dangerous." She emphasized the word "dangerous."

A cold shiver danced up my spine. My neck gave an involuntary twitch.

"Let's do the reading. I haven't got all day," she said gruffly, and we sat back down again. "I need to call upon my spirit guides." She closed her eyes and her head flopped forward onto her chest, her hands clasped tightly together. Then her eyelids sprang open, her eyes rolling into the back of her head. She threw her head back, her lips distorted with weird moaning noises coming from deep in her throat. This carried on for a few minutes.

I glanced at Brad, whose face was expressionless, taking it all in. I mouthed the word *fake* to him.

Then, in a manner that I can only call miraculous, she relaxed again and started acting normal. Well, as normal as she could for a creepy black magic woman, I suppose.

She passed me a set of cards, but these weren't the usual kind of tarot cards I'd seen before. These had numbers on them made out of skulls.

"Shuffle them," she ordered.

I shuffled the cards and handed them back to her.

She took a card from the top of the deck and placed it on the table.

Ten of skulls.

"Happiness will soon come. Either something pleasant or joyful will happen, or a situation will come to a happy conclusion." She laid out another.

Eight of skulls.

"Beware of a new path, as it may lead to misfortune or danger." She glanced up at us both, making sure we were taking it in.

I eyed the cards warily.

She laid out another one.

Six of skulls.

She tapped the card. "A festive atmosphere. This card could signify an enjoyable social gathering."

Yeah, yeah. Blah, blah, blah. She wasn't fooling me. She was definitely a fake.

She was just about to lay another card down when I felt Snowy nudge his head against my leg. I glanced down and he looked at me all cute-faced and purring. Oh, bless him, just because he looked ugly and was owned by an evil voodoo priestess didn't mean he wasn't a nice cat. And I felt really bad for chucking that disgusting tea over him. I reached my hand down to stroke his head, keeping my eyes on Marie. Then I felt something hot and wet on my right leg and boot.

"Agh!" I glanced under the table to find Snowy spraying on me. I pushed him away with my foot and he glared at me, growling.

Marie looked at Snowy and chuckled. "He doesn't like you."

No kidding.

"Have you got a piece of kitchen roll I can use to wipe this off with?" I asked.

"I think you used it all up. Ain't karma a bitch?" She grinned at me, and the hairs on her mole twitched. "Back to the reading." She barked and laid out another card.

Sixteen of skulls.

"This card represents loss. This could be in the form of losing someone you love, a friendship, a financial loss, a job, or a home."

Well, that pretty much covers everything.

"Even death," she hissed.

The way she said it made my skin scrawl. I fought the urge to scratch myself.

"I'm going to read the asparagus now." She stood up and went to the fridge.

Brad and I exchanged a confused glance. Did she just say asparagus? Nah, she couldn't have.

She came back with a bunch of asparagus spears.

"You're going to read…asparagus?" I stifled a laugh.

She looked up sharply, clucking her tongue at me. "Yes, haven't you heard of veggiestrology? I'm also an asparamancer. You can read the future by seeing the pattern they form when they land."

"How…interesting." I raised an eyebrow as she threw the spears on the floor.

Brad and I leaned over the table to get a look.

She studied the spears on the dirty carpet thoughtfully. Then she pointed at me. "You can't make up your mind."

That part was true. Still, she'd just made that up. She couldn't really predict the future.

She tilted her head, examining the spears again. "Troubles you've been having in the area of love and happiness should be lifting soon."

Brad elbowed me and mouthed, *Set the date!*

I rolled my eyes at him.

"You will find something that's lost," she said.

I nearly snorted at the vagueness of it. That could mean anything. Keys, mobile phone, biro, the socks that always get sucked into a giant abyss at the back of the washing machine, never to be seen again.

I'd had enough of listening to her rubbish. "I heard on the news your niece, Chantal, went missing," I said, faking wide-eyed innocence. "I'm sorry to hear that."

Marie glanced up sharply. "Yes. It's bad news."

"Do you know where she is? You and all the family must be so worried," I said.

She nodded. "I'm sure they are." She picked up a piece of asparagus in her hands, turning it round and round, not answering the question.

"I mean, if you can see into the future and all that, can't you tell what happened to her?" I waved a hand around casually.

"You don't always get to see the things you want." She studied me once again like she could see into my soul.

Goose bumps rose on my skin.

"Can't you see anything about her disappearance at all?" I pressed her.

Her eyes flashed with anger. "You ask a lot of questions, don't you, missy?"

"If we wanted something bad to happen to someone, could you do it with your voodoo?" Brad interrupted.

She cocked her head in Brad's direction, interest piqued. "What sort of something?"

Brad leaned forward conspiratorially. "Well, we weren't exactly honest with you earlier."

"Really?" she said in a sarcastic tone of voice.

He paused for a moment. "You see, my girlfriend here is already married and her husband won't give her a divorce. Could you arrange for something bad to happen to him to get him out of the picture?"

Marie sucked her lips for a few minutes, eyes summing up Brad and me. "You don't need me for that. I can see you've killed before." She stood up, giving us a glare that could've seared through glass. "Now get out of my house and don't come back," she spat in a voice loud enough to raise all her zombie mates from whatever in-between world they were living in.

Ooooh! Grumpy knickers!

Wait a sec, how did she know he'd killed before? No, she couldn't be genuine, surely. Could she?

Brad and I strode back down the hallway to the front door. Snowy was sitting on a pile of books, watching us leave. I gave him a wide berth in case he decided to aim his pop-up lipstick in my direction again. This place was freaking me out.

I breathed in gulps of fresh air as we strode to the Hummer. Spider's Web and his gang were sitting on a wall next to it. Brad nodded at Spider's Web. Spider's Web nodded back, then the gang all wandered up the road.

"Well, that was fun." I got in the passenger seat. "Ew, she is one creepy woman." I did a mock shiver and looked down at my smelly, wet foot.

"If she knew I'd killed people before, what else did she know about us?" Brad put it into gear and screeched off down the road like he was freaked out, too. Not much scared Brad, but I had a feeling Marie had got under both of our skins.

"I think she knew exactly what we were doing there. Hacker was right about her." I sighed, snorting in fresh air through my nose. I couldn't get the rotting smell of decay out of my nostrils. "So much for my plan. She didn't give anything away about what might've happened to Chantal. Maybe we need to break into her house to see if there's any evidence Chantal was there. We might find some kind of altar inside with human sacrifices."

"I know Chantal was there." Brad glanced at me.

I turned to face him in my seat, ears pricked up. "What? How do you know?"

"Those lads who were so kindly looking after the Hummer in our absence. I showed them Chantal's picture and persuaded them to tell me if they'd ever seen her go into Marie's." He paused for dramatic effect. "A couple of weeks ago, they saw her on the doorstep, ringing the bell. They remembered her because they thought she was pretty hot."

"Did they see her go in?"

Brad nodded. "Marie let her in."

"Then we definitely need to break in and have a look around."

"I'll get a guy to watch the place. As soon as we know the coast is clear, we'll check it out."

"In the meantime, I need to change." I pulled a face at my stinky foot. "Then I'm going to pay a little visit to James Langton."

My phone rang as we pulled into Hi-Tec's car park. "Hey, Dad. How's it going?"

"If I have to ask 'Would you like fries with that?' one more time, I'm going to scream!"

I chuckled.

"But I managed to check out Steven's handwriting and compare it with that love letter to Chantal."

"Yes?" I breathed with excitement.

"It's not a match. Steven didn't write it."

So the questions was, who the hell did? And how, exactly, did it contribute to Chantal's disappearance?

CHAPTER EIGHT

———

I headed back home to grab a new pair of jeans and boots. Marmalade greeted me at the front door with a dead mouse in his mouth, looking pretty pleased with himself.

"Hey, boy. Catching lunch?"

My stomach growled at the thought of food. With everything going on I'd completely forgotten it was that time of day.

He dropped the mouse, narrowing his eyes at me accusingly, like he'd had to resort to a spot of mouse killing because I never fed him. He sniffed the air, then crept closer to smell my UGGs. He narrowed his eyes, glared at the offending item, and hissed at it. Was that a reaction to Snowy's pheromones or a sixth sense about Marie and her bad voodoo? They said animals were extra sensitive to things, didn't they? Often I'd catch Marmalade staring at things I couldn't see. What could he see now that might help me crack this case?

One pair of jeans, a backup pair of UGGs, and a generous squirt of perfume later, I was in the kitchen, devouring a ham and cheese toasted sandwich, silently praising whoever invented the toasted sandwich maker.

I pulled out the lists Hacker had given me for Chantal and Liza's phone records and studied them as hot, melted cheese dribbled down my chin.

In the last few months, Chantal had phoned the number for the Second Chance Clinic twice. Liza had also called them. They'd also both called the Holbrook Clinic. I looked closer at Liza's calls. A couple of months before Liza vanished, she'd phoned someone called Emily Jacobs.

I finished the sandwich, fed Marmalade some scraps of ham, and wondered why that name was sending alarm signals in my brain. Emily Jacobs. I hadn't come across it before.

Then I had a mental head-slap moment.

I pulled out the list of initials and dates that Brad had found in Chantal's apartment:

MP - 28/01
DL - 15/02
CT - 01/03
EJ - 27/03
LS - 0787 5567893

Questions buzzed around in my head. Could the EJ on the list be Emily Jacobs? And if so, what did she have to do with all this? Was the big story Liza was working on to do with the Second Chance Clinic and the Holbrook Clinic? What had the two girls discovered? Where were Liza and Chantal? Were they dead? Was this anything to do with voodoo sacrifices?

I reached for my mobile and dialed Hacker as Marmalade jumped onto my lap and licked the crumbs off my plate. "Yo," I said when he picked up.

"Yo."

"Any luck in cracking the code from that list?"

"Not yet."

"I think the initials EJ might relate to an Emily Jacobs. Can you see what you can dig up on her?"

"I'm on it." He paused. "I heard you had fun at Marie's house earlier."

"Uh-huh. I'm pretty sure she knew what we were doing there."

"I hate to say I told you so, but..."

"Yeah, yeah. We're going to poke around inside her house when she's out to see if there's any trace of Chantal or Liza."

"Rather you than me."

"I'd rather swim with sharks or spend the weekend at Guantanamo Bay than go back there again." Next time I went I'd make sure I was wearing my Wonder Woman knickers. Not sure if they held the same kind of powers as the original ones, but I wasn't taking any chances. "You come up with anything on the Holbrook Clinic yet?"

"Still working on it."

"Okay."

"Yo."

"Yo back atcha!" I hung up and glanced at a blob of cheese that had fallen onto my plate and gone hard. It was in the shape of a ring. A wedding ring, in fact. Maybe it was a sign? Was my toastie trying to give me a message?

I shook my head to myself. A sign from a toastie about whether to get married or not? I was going nuts. Well, more nuts than I already was.

* * *

Next stop, Langton Developments. The imposing glass building was announced by a new, undamaged silver sign that was so big and shiny it was hard to miss. The place gave off an air of success and wealth, hiding the fact that the business was in trouble. I wondered just how far James Langton would go to save his company. Would he kill his daughter?

Langton's secretary, Oliver, met me at reception and we rode the glass lift to James's office. Oliver was a tall, skinny guy, mid-thirties, with thick glasses that magnified his eyes about a squillion times. In fact, he was so skinny his Adam's apple looked the size of a melon in his scrawny little throat. He had a habit of squinting his right eye after he answered a question.

"How well did you know Chantal?" I asked him.

"Oh, just through work. We didn't socialize or anything—apart from work parties, of course." Squint. "It's terrible that she's disappeared. She was a lovely girl." Squint, squint. His voice was high-pitched and, like Steven Shaw, he was very effeminate in his mannerisms. I was pretty sure Oliver was batting for the other side.

"How did she seem to you before she disappeared? Was she depressed? Worried? Anxious?" I squinted back at him. Damn, he had me doing it now.

"Well." He rested a hand on his hip and leaned toward me, as if letting me in on a big secret. "In the last few months she wasn't here much. She only came in to work on getting the planning permission completed for the City Park Complex, which we finally got two weeks ago. Mr. Langton thought she could do with some time off to…" He paused, searching for how to put it. "Well, to get her head together again. Of course, you know about her friend, Liza, disappearing as well?" He carried on without waiting for me to answer. "Poor Chantal was devastated about that. Devastated." Big squint.

"Did Chantal ever mention that she knew what happened to Liza?" I said as the lift doors pinged open and we walked down a long corridor with large potted palms.

He shook his head. "No. She never said anything to me."

"Do you know if she was seeing anyone?"

"I'm sorry, I can't help you there. We didn't share our private lives with each other." He paused. "But now that I think about it, she did get a delivery of flowers here a few weeks back, so she obviously had some kind of admirer."

"What about people who didn't admire her? Is it possible someone she worked with had a grudge against her?"

He paused for a moment. "Not against Chantal, no. She was a sweet girl. But…" He glanced around to make sure no one was looking and lowered his voice. "James had to make some redundancies recently. What with the global recession going on, Langton Developments is suffering just like everybody else. One of the other architects, Philip Gates, was made redundant and he didn't go quietly."

"What do you mean he didn't go quietly? What happened?"

"Well, Philip kind of threatened James."

"In what way?"

"Philip had just had a little baby girl and he was obviously worried about being able to provide for her and his wife if he was made redundant and couldn't get another job. He told James that he'd 'show him what it felt like.'"

"Are those the exact words he used?"

Oliver nodded and squinted at the same time.

I let that sink in, wondering what he could've meant. *I'll show you how it feels to worry about your daughter? I'll show you how it feels to be so useless that you can't help your daughter? I'll kidnap Chantal to prove a point?*

Oliver knocked on James's door.

"Come in," James's voice filtered through from the other side.

"I'll leave you to it." The secretary left me with a final squint and disappeared back up the corridor.

I walked into James's modern office. It was flanked on two sides by glass windows, giving it a great view, but it would become a sweaty suntrap in the summer. A leather sofa was arranged against one wall, with an identical one opposite it. Above the sofa on the wall were framed awards that their developments had won. In the center of the room was a large-scale model of a building.

James put his pen down and walked around his huge wooden desk, which was inlaid with a glass top. It was littered with papers and rolls of plans. I bet the cleaners had their work cut out every night trying to remove fingerprints from all that glass.

"Hello, Amber. Do you have any news about Chantal? Nicole and I are worried sick." He ran a hand through his immaculate hair.

"Not yet, but I've got some more questions for you."

He let out a soft sigh, and I couldn't tell if it was because he was relieved I had no news, or relieved that I didn't have bad news.

"Have a seat." James indicated the sofas opposite the model. "Would you like tea or coffee?"

"No, thanks." A vision of Marie's foul liquid sprang to mind. I'd had enough encounters of the tea kind to last for one day, thank you very much.

I nodded at the model building. "Is that the City Park Complex?"

"Yes." He smiled proudly, as if talking about his own child.

"I heard there were problems in getting the planning permission and site for it. You paid over the odds for the land, didn't you?"

"In this kind of business, you win some and you lose some. I wasn't going to lose out on this project, so I had to increase my offer for the site to stop Sage Developments obtaining it." He crossed his legs and wiped away an imaginary piece of fluff. "We'll still be able to make a significant amount of profit, even though we paid more than we anticipated." He waved a dismissive hand. "That's just business."

"But it was touch and go whether you'd get planning permission for it, wasn't it? After you'd sunk all your money into it, didn't that cause you a lot of worry?"

"We always consult the planning department before we invest in a plot of land. They gave us the initial go-ahead for our City Park project, but, of course, when people begin to complain, like Alfie Cross and his friends, the council has to do an in-depth enquiry and things take longer than anticipated. But I have a habit of getting what I want, Ms. Fox." He gave me an arrogant smile.

"Is that why you stole from Chantal's trust fund? Because you just wanted it?" I sat back and waited for his reaction. I didn't have to wait long. The smile dropped off his face quicker that you could say *busted!*

At least he had the good grace to look ashamed as his cheeks flushed and sweat broke out on his upper lip.

He took a deep breath before speaking. "That was only a temporary thing. We had some big backers pull out because of all the problems and delays surrounding the City Park Complex, so I did what I had to do to save the company. If I hadn't used Chantal's money, we'd be heading toward bankruptcy by now." He rubbed at his forehead. "Since we got the planning permission two weeks ago, we've managed to win back a lot of the investors. With their substantial cash injection, I would've been able to pay the money back into Chantal's trust fund before anyone found out." He leaned forward on his elbows, eyes pleading. "This has got nothing to do with Chantal's disappearance, I swear to you. You have to believe me. I love my daughter. I've never done anything to hurt her."

I took in his now slumped shoulders and watery eyes. He looked like he'd aged ten years in about two minutes. I thought about what he'd said. Did I believe this had nothing to do with Chantal going missing? If she hadn't disappeared no one would've been investigating James Langton and his company, so no one would've been any the wiser that he'd been dipping into the trust fund. No, it didn't make sense for him to be involved. In fact, it was very inconvenient for James that Chantal had gone missing and his little indiscretion with her trust fund had been discovered. He must've known when she disappeared that people would start looking into his finances and the theft would've been discovered. It was actually in his best interests that the whole matter stayed hidden, so any possible motive to get rid of Chantal had taken a nosedive straight out the nearest window. Plus, I was convinced the key to this case was more about the story Liza had been working on, and in turn, what Chantal had also discovered. I just didn't have a clue what that was yet.

"Actually, I do believe you," I said.

He closed his eyes for a moment and exhaled a deep sigh. "Thank you."

"What about Sage Developments? Do you think they could be holding a grudge against you because of the City Park Complex?"

He shook his head. "They weren't happy when I finally managed to acquire the City Park site, but they're not likely to do anything to Chantal. They're respectable businessmen, not the mafia."

"You've had to lay some people off recently. I heard that Philip Gates threatened you. Do you think he could've had something to do with Chantal's disappearance?"

"I think Philip was just distraught about losing his job. The pressure of having a new baby and no job got to him, and he just snapped and lost his temper. I didn't take his threats seriously. And, anyway, a few weeks ago he was offered a better job in Ireland and he moved his family out there. He left the country before Chantal went missing."

"How about Alfie Cross, who ran the campaign to try and get it stopped? Did you ever receive any personal threats from him?"

Another headshake. "No. And I understand he has an alibi for the time Chantal went missing."

While that was true, it didn't rule out Alfie getting a friend or associate to help him. "I think Chantal had a brief relationship with someone after she split up with Steven Shaw. Do you know who this man could be?"

"No. As I said before, I didn't know she was seeing anyone. The way she'd been acting lately, she wasn't in a fit state to have a relationship. She never spoke about a new boyfriend."

"Apparently she received a delivery of flowers here a few weeks ago. Do you know who sent them?"

He pursed his lips together, thinking. "No. I don't remember any flower deliveries—but, of course, I'm out of the office a lot of the time. She certainly didn't bring any flowers back to the house with her."

I pulled out the list Brad had found in Chantal's apartment. "Does this mean anything to you? I think they're initials and dates."

He studied the list, eyebrows knitted together. "I'm sorry, it doesn't mean a thing to me."

I gave him the list of phone numbers and names Liza and Chantal had called. "How about this? Do you recognize any of these names?"

More concentration before he finally shook his head. "No. I wish I could help. I just want to find her."

"Have you ever heard of the Second Chance Clinic or the Holbrook Clinic?"

"No. Do you think Chantal might've gone there?"

"That's what I have to find out. The Second Chance Clinic deals with family planning. It's a free clinic, providing contraception, checkups, and terminations. I'm not sure yet what the Holbrook Clinic does."

"She…" He paused. "Chantal was depressed, but she wasn't physically ill. And she couldn't have been pregnant." He stared off into the distance. "Could she?"

"It's possible. We found a pregnancy test in her bedroom."

James gasped. "And this could be why she went missing?"

"I don't know yet."

"God, if she'd just told us she was pregnant we would've given her the emotional support she needed. Why just run off without telling us? It's completely out of character."

"I don't think she did run off. She didn't take any real amount of money from her bank account, she left a lot of clothes both at your house and her apartment, and her passport wasn't missing. Liza was working on a big story at the time she disappeared. I think Chantal managed to find out what it was about, and because of that, she's gone missing, too. Somehow, I think it relates to these two clinics. And there's more."

He glanced up.

"Chantal was seen at Marie's house recently. And Marie's son, Andrew Scott, is a doctor who works at the Second Chance Clinic."

"Shit." He rubbed his hands over his face. "Marie is bad news. She's evil. Nicole will be devastated when she finds out Marie has seen Chantal. Nicole always wanted to protect Chantal from the bad side of voodoo. Nicole hasn't spoken to Marie since she found out she was using her powers for vicious things instead of helping people. I've never met Andrew. I didn't even know he was a doctor." A pained expression settled on his face. "Do you think they've done something to Chantal and Liza?"

"I'm pretty sure they're involved somehow, and I'm going to do everything I can to find out."

He nodded slowly, eyes barely registering what I'd said.

I stood up. "I need to ask the staff some questions. Is that okay?"

He regained his composure and stood. "Of course. Let me introduce you to my business partner, Elliot, first. And then you're welcome to question the rest of the staff."

I followed James out of the office and along the corridor. Farther down, another door opened and a man came out. "Ah, James, I was just coming to see you. I need a quick chat about one of the contractors on the City Park project."

"Elliot, I'd like you to meet Amber Fox. She's investigating Chantal's disappearance."

Elliot was in his early forties, and good looking—if you liked the polished, immaculate look. Perfectly gelled hair, manicured nails, eyebrows that were just too tidy to be natural. Wax or tweezers, I wondered? I was leaning more toward wax. The only thing detracting from his flawless appearance was the puffiness under his eyes. Allergies? A cold? Or tears?

Elliot shook my hand. "Please have a seat in my office." He motioned to the door behind him. "I'll be there in a moment."

James and Elliot walked toward James's office.

I entered Elliot's office, which was much the same as James's, including the model of City Park. Leaning over his desk, which was scattered with handwritten notes and plans, I perused the plans for City Park, then wandered over to the model of the complex in the center of the room and walked around it. It even had little model people in the communal garden of the site, sunbathing and walking their dogs. It was an impressive site, but one that had no place in a residential area of historical properties. The existing properties would lose their light and privacy—not to mention their road would be chock-a-block with cars and noise from City Park. This kind of development would be much more at home on the outskirts of town. No wonder Alfie and Co. weren't happy about it.

I was peering closer at the model when my brain suddenly registered something I'd seen on Elliot's desk.

I rushed back to check, grabbing a handwritten memo that was written to the office supplies department from Elliot, studying it intensely. I pulled out a copy of the love letter to Chantal from my rucksack and compared the writing. It was a match. I quickly replaced the memo where I'd found it.

One mystery solved. How many more to go?

Well, well, well. Elliot had slept with Chantal. Did he know she was pregnant? Was Elliot married? And, even more important, was there a reason he would want Chantal to disappear?

Elliot's return interrupted my thoughts. "We're all desperate to find Chantal," he said as he sat down. "I wish I knew something that might help you find her."

"Cut the crap." I verbally pounced on him. Chantal's life could be at stake here, and I was getting pissed off with people hiding stuff and lying to me. Plus, I was having severe chocolate withdrawal, which was about as much fun as a root-canal treatment. The things a girl has to go through to make sure she looks good on her wedding day! "You slept with Chantal. You were in love with her. You've obviously hidden that fact from James and Nicole. What else are you hiding?"

Elliot's jaw dropped open. "How…how did you know?"

I took the letter out again and read it out loud. "'Chantal, I am extremely sorry you won't return my calls. That night was never a mistake for me, you have to believe me. I've loved you for a long time, and I will continue to love you, no matter what. I promise I will not pressure you into anything. I am here for you when you need me. Lovingly yours. Big kiss.'" I looked up to see his reaction. "So, what happened, Elliot? You took advantage of her when she was vulnerable because of her depression about Liza's disappearance? Or wouldn't you take no for an answer when she didn't want to see you anymore? You were obsessed with her, weren't you? Did you think if you couldn't have her then you'd make sure no one else could, either? Where is she?" I bombarded him with questions, hoping to rattle him.

His skin had turned the color of a clammy piece of cod. He flopped forward, hands covering his face. "No, no, no. You've got it wrong. I'd never do anything to hurt her. I love her. And I…I think she was carrying my child."

"What do you mean, you *think*?"

"I followed her…to a clinic that carries out terminations."

"You mean you were stalking her?"

He dropped his hands and looked up at me, eyes strained with despair. "Look, I know how that sounds, but it wasn't like that at all. I just wanted to make sure she was okay."

"I think you'd better start at the beginning." I sat back and folded my arms.

"Chantal started working here a few years ago after she finished her architecture degree. We got on right away and we worked closely together, so we spent a lot of time in meetings, working long hours in close proximity, and grabbing late dinners at the office. The friendship grew and we became close, but I didn't want to make a move on her. She was twenty-five, twenty years younger than I was, and she was my partner's daughter. She was also seeing Steven Shaw." His voice cracked at the mention of Steven's name. "I fell in love with her but she didn't know. Not right away. When Liza disappeared, Chantal was distraught, obviously. She couldn't concentrate on work properly. She became withdrawn and sad. She was trying to get the planning permission sorted out for City Park Complex, as well, which was giving us a lot of problems, and everything seemed to be getting on top of her." He glanced down at a spot on the floor, as if remembering the details. "One night we were both working late and she came into my office to ask a question. She broke down, crying, saying she had to find out what happened to Liza. We had a long chat and I managed to get her in a more positive mood. She said she could do with a drink and we ended up sharing a couple of bottles of wine. Then in the heat of the moment, I kissed her. One thing let to another and..." He trailed off, embarrassed.

"Did James know about it?" I asked.

He shook his head. "I never told him. I was worried about how he would react to a forty-five-year-old man sleeping with his daughter."

Really? Ya think?

"And I know Chantal wouldn't have told him," he went on. "It seemed like she wanted to forget it had happened at all."

"Did you know James was dipping into Chantal's trust fund?"

"What?" His eyebrows pinched together in surprise. "Are you sure?"

"Absolutely."

"Well...I'm...shocked and surprised about that."

And he did look genuinely shocked and surprised, unless he was an Oscar-winning actor, and I didn't think so. He was definitely telling me the truth.

So Elliot had been lying to James about his feelings for Chantal and James had been lying to Elliot about where the money was coming from for their latest investment. It didn't seem to bode well for a future business arrangement.

"I mean, we'd been having a lot of financial problems lately and the company was only just keeping afloat. James was injecting cash into the business, but he told me it came from his private finances until we could get some investors back on board."

"When did you sleep with her?"

"It happened four weeks ago. I don't think I'll ever forget the date. She'd never looked more beautiful to me. I told her I was in love with her and we...we ended up making love." He glanced up at me. "I didn't mean to take advantage of her. It was something that just happened and...well, as you know from the letter, it was never a mistake for me."

"But it was for her?" I prodded gently.

"The next day she told me we couldn't get involved with each other. She said her head wasn't in a good place."

"Did you send her flowers to the office?"

"Yes. I was hoping I might get her to change her mind about us, but she didn't."

"So you started stalking her?"

Maybe there was a thin line between loving her and stalking her. Wasn't there a song about that? No, hang on a sec, that was "Thin Line Between Love and Hate." Still, both of them were probably true.

"No. I told you, it wasn't like that. I was worried about her. The police couldn't even find out what happened to Liza. I was worried that if Chantal started looking for her, something bad might happen. I only followed her a few times to make sure she was safe."

"Which clinic did you follow her to?"

"It's a place called the Second Chance Clinic. Just before she went missing, Chantal went there. I knew that they did abortions and I suspected she was carrying my child because whenever she was in the office in the mornings she kept throwing up, and one day I caught sight of a pregnancy test in her handbag. But before I got the chance to ask her about it, she disappeared." He looked up at the ceiling, shaking his head. "I need to find her."

"Where else did you follow her to?"

"The only other place she went out of the ordinary was Chequer Street."

"Chequer Street?" Chequer Street was a hangout for prostitutes. What would Chantal have been doing there?

"Yes. She talked to one of the street ladies for a few minutes and then went back to James and Nicole's house."

My brain went into shrieking mode. Chantal was tied into the Second Chance Clinic by the business card hidden in her teddy bear, although Hacker found no records of her being a patient. The Second Chance Clinic had a lot of prostitutes who were patients. Chantal was talking to a prostitute. Chantal and Liza had also phoned the clinic before they disappeared. Something was going on at that place and I needed to find out what.

CHAPTER NINE

The Second Chance Clinic was housed in an old Victorian building. With the help of government funding, it had been modernized about twenty years ago into a bright and airy clinic on the edge of town, but by now it was looking tired and dated again. With all the money that Chantal's family had, I found it hard to believe she would choose this facility to have a termination.

The entrance had an intercom system. I pressed the button and waited for someone to answer as I peeked through the windows.

"Second Chance Clinic, can I help you?" a female voice answered.

"I'm here to see Dr. Scott," I said.

"And your name is?"

"Amber Fox. I made an appointment."

The door made a buzzing sound.

"Okay, come in, please."

I pulled open the door and strode to the reception desk, where a middle-aged woman sat. Her hair was tied back in a ponytail so tight it was almost giving her a facelift, and her eyes had a constant look of surprise.

"Take a seat, please. Dr. Scott will be with you shortly." She nodded to a row of plastic chairs opposite the desk, where a young woman was sitting. From her short skirt, which was little more than a belt, heels so high she'd get a hip displacement if she wasn't careful, and makeup that would need an industrial paint scraper to get it off, it was pretty safe to say she was a prostitute.

I pulled out the picture of Chantal and showed it to Miss Facelift on reception. "I'm investigating the disappearance of Chantal Langton. Was she a patient here?"

She didn't glance at the picture, although maybe that was hard to do since her eyes were so tight from the ponytail that she couldn't move them anymore.

"Are you a police officer?" she asked.

"No, I work for Hi-Tec Insurance."

"Then I'm very sorry, but I can't discuss our patients with you," she said in a tone that indicated she wasn't in the slightest bit sorry.

"This could be a life-and-death situation. This poor woman has gone missing in suspicious circumstances. I need to find her before something bad happens to her." I pushed the photo under her nose so she couldn't avoid looking at it.

I studied her face for a reaction to the picture and saw a brief twitch of lips as she looked at it.

"I don't recognize her." Miss Facelift bent her head over her desk and started scribbling on some forms.

I'd seen all I needed to, though. That twitch was a dead giveaway that she was lying. So Chantal had been here, but why? Was it connected to her pregnancy or the story Liza was working on? If Liza covered a lot of human interest and women's rights issues, could her story have been about the prostitutes that came here? Before I could think about it more, a tall, slim nurse called my name.

I followed her past several consulting rooms to a door marked *Dr. Andrew Scott*. She opened the door and said, "Amber Fox to see you, doctor. I'll be in reception if you need me." Then she left me standing in front of one of the best-looking men I'd ever seen.

Like Chantal, Andrew Scott had mixed parentage. He obviously didn't get his features from Marie, so I was guessing his dad was a looker, too. He had huge, dark eyes framed by thick, long lashes that any woman would be jealous of, perfectly shaped lips, teeth so straight and white they had to be veneers, and skin the color of my favorite Galaxy chocolate bars. The whole stunning effect almost made me want to lick him.

Down, girl! You've got chocolate on the brain. And anyway, you're on a case. He could be a murderer for all you know!

I pushed all skin-licking thoughts out of my head. What the hell was wrong with me? I put it down to chocolate withdrawals again messing with my brain.

He stared back at me with amusement dancing in his eyes, as if this were the kind of impact he always made on women, and he wasn't surprised in the least.

He smiled, flashing his flawless set of gleaming white teeth. "Please, have a seat, Ms. Fox. What can I do for you?"

I wondered briefly how many members of the opposite sex he'd affected with that smile, and how many concocted weird gynecological problems just to make an appointment with him.

I sat down, pretty glad that he wasn't my gynecologist. There was something creepy and disarming about having a gorgeous doctor looking up your lady garden. "I'm trying to find out what's happened to your cousin, Chantal. Do you have any idea where she is?"

His eyes widened in surprise. "I take it you're not a patient, then?"

"No. I'm from Chantal's insurance company."

He reclined in his chair, stretching out his long, muscular legs. "Isn't it a bit early for an insurance investigation? I didn't hear on the news that her body had been found."

Stop looking at his legs! I tried hard not to picture him naked.

I flushed and tore my eyes back to his face, clearing my throat. "Her parents have also asked me to find her."

For a brief second he broke eye contact, glancing away and then back to me so quickly I was almost unsure if I'd imagined it. "I don't know how I can help you. I'm sure Nicole and James told you that their side of the family is estranged from ours. I've never met Chantal." He gave me a superior smile that didn't quite manage to reach his eyes.

Had I imagined it? Was his attractiveness blinding me to signs of lying that I would normally be certain of? "So why did she have your business card? And why did she phone the clinic on several occasions?"

"I have no idea." He waved a dismissive hand through the air and gave me a smile that was about as real as Jordan's boobs.

I waited in silence, an old cop interview technique I'd learned. Most of the time people were uncomfortable with silence. They'd do anything to fill it, babbling away, which often led to them giving out details that they didn't want to.

He shifted in his chair. "I'm sure hundreds of people ring the clinic each week, but I'm afraid I'm too busy being a doctor to filter all the calls. I can assure you that Chantal has never been a patient here." He scratched the side of his nose. "I don't know why you have this notion that I've seen her or even spoken to her, but I haven't had any contact with her at all."

I suspected that was a big, fat whopper, since Elliot had already told me he'd followed her to the clinic, and I already knew from her phone records that she'd called the clinic. Andrew must've seen and spoken to her.

"Even though I'm not close to her, I'm just as upset as everyone about her disappearance," he carried on. "Of course, I want her to be found safe and well."

"Well, maybe Chantal was a patient of the Holbrook Clinic. She also had their number. Do you know what they do?" I asked innocently.

"I'm afraid I can't help you. I've never heard of them." He scratched his nose and gave me that wide smile again.

The nose-scratching thing did it for me. He was definitely lying. Either that or he'd developed a sudden case of itchyitis.

"You say your side of the family is estranged from Chantal's, but there's a witness who saw Chantal going into your mum's house."

He shrugged. "I have no idea about that, I'm afraid."

"Are you involved in left-handed voodoo?" I changed the subject to try and disarm him.

He made a disbelieving sound at the back of his throat. "Pardon?" The smile melted quicker than a Popsicle in the desert.

"Apparently your mother is a bokor—someone who practices black magic."

He stood up, eyes flashing with anger. A muscle pulsed in his jaw and his face turned the color of a beetroot. Think "exploding beetroot" and that would be more accurate. "Firstly, voodoo is a religion, and not every person who believes in voodoo is involved in the darker side portrayed in Hollywood films. Secondly, our conversation is over." He pointed to the door.

Ooh, touchy!

At this rate, I'd be getting a complex about people not wanting to talk to me, although it didn't escape my notice that he'd completely avoided answering the question.

* * *

When I left the clinic, I was having an attack of the drooping eyelids. Either Andrew had put some kind of sleeping spell on me or I was suffering from the aftereffects of a late night tossing and turning. All this worrying about whether to give up my procrastinating and set a date for the wedding, or just carry on living together for a while and see what happened was really affecting my normally zonked-out sleep patterns. After everything we'd been through, getting married was the crunch time, and that was what was scaring me. If it didn't work out there would be no more second chances. This was it. Could I go through a marriage and then lose him forever if it didn't work out? Thinking about it made a cloud of worry form across my forehead, casting a shadow of doubts left, right, and center. I think deep down the problem was that the realization had finally hit home that our relationship *was* really right, and when something is so important, there's a lot more risk involved. If I stuffed it up somehow, I might never be able to get it back again.

I tried to blank my thoughts and fears from my mind. Coffee. That was what I needed—a hefty caffeine pick-me-up if I was going to make it through the day. Usually I'd hit Starbucks, but I wanted to have another chat with Steven Shaw, so I hit the Burger Land drive-through again.

"Can I take your order, please?" The crackly voice said at the microphone.

"I'll have a large white coffee, please."

"Would you like milk and sugar?"

"Just milk, please."

"Would you like it in a bag?"

"No, a cup will do fine, thanks."

"Would you like onions with that?"

"Not today, thanks. I find that the onions get a bit soggy in the coffee."

"Would you like fries with that?"

"No, thanks."

"Damn, I can't give them away today," the muffled voice said. "Please drive to the next window to collect your order."

Dad was serving at the pick-up window again. "Hey, Dad, how's the case going?"

He glanced behind him and back to me again. "Slowly. How about you?"

"Ditto. Is Steven in? I need to have another quick chat with him?"

Dad nodded. "He's in his office."

I paid for the coffee and Dad handed me a hot cup.

"I'll drink this in the car and go up."

"Good luck." Dad waved at me.

I pulled into the car park facing the building and took a sip of my caffeine fix, thinking about Chantal and everything I'd learned that morning. Was it possible that Steven had found out about Chantal being pregnant and killed her in a jilted lover's rage? It wouldn't be the first time it had happened. He'd also been lying to me about Chantal. But then what was Andrew and Marie's involvement in it? Had Chantal visited Marie for some kind of voodoo ritual to get rid of the baby? Had she, in turn, suggested Chantal visit Andrew for a termination? Or was something else going on that involved human sacrifices? Was the baby Elliot's, or had she been sleeping with Steven, too? Why was Chantal talking to a prostitute? Was it about the Second Chance Clinic? Was Elliot following her an innocent act of looking out for her welfare, or was he actually stalking her because he was a man obsessed? Was he also enraged at being jilted by Chantal after their night in the office? Who was this Emily Jacobs that Liza rang before she disappeared, and what did the list of initials and dates that Chantal made mean?

My phone rang as I was pondering the possibilities.

I glanced at the caller display. "Hey, Mum. How are you?"

"Hi, honey, I'm out shopping and they've still got that fabulous hat on special offer so I wanted to know if you'd set a date yet," she gushed down the phone.

I rolled my eyes. "Nope, I still haven't set the date."

"Well, can I buy it anyway?" she asked hopefully.

"No. Don't buy it yet."

"Why not?" She sighed. "You know it's perfectly normal to have wedding jitters. I did before I married your father."

"Did you?"

"Of course. I was worried about being with a man who had a career in the police force, and never seeing him, or, God forbid, if he got assaulted on duty."

"But I bet you're glad you made the right choice now—after all, Dad's worked his way up and is now on the checkout at the Burger Land drive-through."

Mum chuckled. "In the end, I loved him enough to put up with being a police widow and never seeing him. I think every woman goes through these worries before she gets married, but you and Brad are made for each other. You can't live without each other, so what's the point in wasting any more time? Life's too short for worrying about whether you're doing the right thing or not all the time."

I knew she was right, but...what if?

"So...can I buy it?"

"No!" It was my turn to sigh then. "Look, I promise you'll be the first to know as soon as I've set the date, okay?" Hopefully that would get her off my back until I'd made a decision.

She tutted. "Well, what about if—"

I made a static noise down the phone. "You're breaking up, Mum. I'll speak to you later." I hung up. Yes, I know, slightly cruel, but I wasn't in the mood for talking about the wedding every day. I had a missing woman to find. Well, that was my excuse, anyway.

I drained the dregs of my coffee, got out of the car, and dumped it in a nearby bin. Then I asked Pink Hair at the serving counter if Steven was free.

He came down and met me, looking haggard and pale.

"Have you found Chantal?" he asked as soon as he saw me.

His eyes darted around nervously, and it looked like he was actually worried about the possibility that she'd been found.

I studied him for a few moments, watching him squirm with obvious discomfort. "Why, do you know where she is?"

He stuffed his hands in his pockets and avoided my probing gaze. "No. Why would I know where she is?"

Liar, liar. Any minute now his pants would spontaneously combust. "You tell me." I cocked my head, waiting for an answer.

He swallowed and averted his gaze to the window. "I told you before, I don't know where she is."

"I need to ask you a few more questions."

"Oh." He shifted from one foot to the other. "Well, I suppose you'd better come up to the office."

I followed him upstairs.

"Did you know Chantal was pregnant?" I said as soon as we'd both sat down.

What color Steven had in his cheeks completely vanished at those words. His mouth gaped open for a few seconds then closed again. He shook his head, his lower lip trembling. "No. She couldn't have been."

"Why do you say that?"

"Well..." He glanced around the room as if searching for the right words. "We hadn't slept together in months and..." He trailed off as if a light bulb had suddenly pinged on in his brain. "You mean she was seeing someone else?"

"She'd been involved with someone else, yes." I hated to be the bearer of bad news but needs must—plus, this wasn't a game and I couldn't pussyfoot around people. I needed to find out what he was hiding.

He emitted a strangled cry. "No. No, no, no." He leaned forward, elbows on the desk, head in his hands in much the same display as Elliot.

"You know more about her disappearance than you're telling me. What is it, Steven? What happened to Chantal?"

"I don't know." He started rocking back and forth. "I don't know. I just knew that she was in trouble."

"What kind of trouble?"

"She wouldn't tell me. I swear!"

"So you're sure you don't know where she is?"

He hesitated for a beat, then said, "No." His voice was muffled behind the hands hiding his face.

I left my card on his desk "If you know something, something that could help me find Chantal and Liza, then you're not doing them any favors by hiding it." I left him with that thought and walked out the door, leaving him alone with his tears.

I got back in the Toyota and sat in the car park. If Steven did know something, and I was betting he did, maybe I'd spooked him enough to give me a clue. I figured I'd sit there for a while and see if he left, then I could follow him.

I sat on my hands to stop me eating the melted, out-of-date, heart-shaped chocolate blob in the glove box. What I wouldn't give for a chocolate muffin right about now. I clamped my lips together to stop drooling at the thought and watched the front door for signs of Steven as the day turned from dusk to darkness.

One hour and many fantasies about chocolate-covered donuts, chocolate ice cream, and chocolate-coated Brazil nuts later, Steven hurried out of the front of the building with his head down and a baseball cap pulled low over his forehead, quickening his pace as he reached the main road. He looked like a man on a mission to me, so I got out of the Toyota and followed on foot at a safe distance.

He walked through the town, pushing his way between the crowded streets and ignoring the busy market stalls hawking their wares before they packed up for the day and went home. As he neared the end of the town, he stopped outside the Catholic church. He stood for a few moments, glancing up at the building before striding up the concrete steps two at a time.

Was Steven coming here to confess to a priest about something that he'd done to Chantal? And if so, could I manage to eavesdrop? I'd never been in a Catholic church before. In fact, I'd only ever gone to Sunday school as a kid, and even then I'd been banned because of an unfortunate incident involving me, another kid called Julie Peterson, and a whoopee cushion. I swear it was just a joke to put it under her cushion before she sat down after reciting the Lord's Prayer to the whole Sunday congregation, but the vicar didn't seem to see the funny side of it.

As I climbed up the stairs, I saw a man in a purple priest's robe in the garden at the back of the church. He clutched a Bible in one hand and a set of rosary beads in the other, and was talking to an elderly woman holding a mountain bike against her legs and wearing a bike helmet. They had their heads together in deep discussion and every few seconds she'd nod her head thoughtfully. If Steven was waiting in the confessional box to blab about Chantal, somehow I needed to delay the priest so I could slip in there and pretend to be him, then listen to what Steven had to say. I wasn't entirely sure exactly how I'd be able to pull that off, but a girl's gotta try.

"Father!" I gave the priest a wave and rushed over to them.

He glanced up, his eyebrows scrunching together, trying to place me as someone he recognized.

The woman placed a hand on his arm and smiled at him. "Well, thank you, Father McGuire, it's been a fascinating conversation. Who'd have thought the Pope was into mountain-bike riding and other extreme sports?" She turned and smiled at me as I got closer to them.

He took her hands in his and smiled back. "Any time, Maude."

She disappeared through the garden and down the steps as he gave me his full attention.

"Hello." He beamed at me, his bushy eyebrows dancing as he spoke. "Can I help you?"

"I'm so glad I caught you," I said. "There's been a serious car accident in Ware Road, just by the bus stop, and there's this poor woman who's trapped in one of the vehicles in a bad way. The fire brigade is on its way to cut her free and there's an ambulance waiting, but they can't do much until she's out of the vehicle. She was asking for you, father."

The smile dropped from his face and his eyebrows scrunched together with concern. "Oh, my, that's terrible. Who is it?" He led me back toward the steps.

"Er…Sarah?" It came out more like a question than a statement.

He shook his head slightly. "Sarah? I don't recall a parishioner here called Sarah."

"Or maybe Sally?"

"Oh no. Not Sally Wilkinson?"

I nodded vigorously. "Yes, Sally Wilkinson." I clutched his arm. "You need to hurry. She may not have long left."

"Of course." He opened the door to a Ford Ka on the driveway next to the church and slid behind the wheel.

"Don't worry, if anyone comes in asking for you, I'll let them know you've been delayed."

"Thank you, my child." He slammed the door shut and shot out onto the main road.

Would I go to hell for that? I didn't have time to consider it as I yanked open the church door and poked my head inside, looking for Steven. There was no one on the pews or at the altar, so the only other place he could be was in the confessional box, waiting for Father McGuire.

I crept up between the pews and opened the intricately carved wooden door to the confessional box, shutting it carefully behind me. Sitting down inside, I slid open the hatch to reveal a latticed wooden window that separated the confessor from the confessee. On the other side, I could just about make out a figure in the gloom.

In the deepest voice I could muster, I said, "Do you have something to confess?" Okay, I sounded a teensy bit like the famous drag queen RuPaul, but maybe Steven wouldn't notice.

"Is that you, Father McGuire?" Steven asked.

"No, I'm afraid he's been called out on an emergency. I'm Father…" *Oh, crap, what's a fatherly kind of name? Damn, I swore in a church. Oh sh…sugar, I did it again!* "I'm Father Ted." *Oh, God, why did I say Father Ted? That was a comedy program on TV!*

"Oh, okay. Bless me, father, for I have sinned. It's been a year since my last confession."

Phew! He didn't seem to notice.

"What would you like to confess, my child?" I asked, trying to make my voice deeper.

"Well…" He paused for a moment.

"It's okay, my child, take your time." Although how long would it be before Father McGuire discovered there was no traffic accident and came back? "On second thought, it's actually better if you get it out in the open as soon as possible to avoid the wrath of the lord."

"Oh no. Will I get sent to hell?"

"No, my child. I'll give you the appropriate number of Hail Marys and then you'll be absolved. Unless you take too long, *then* you might go to hell."

"Er…okay. Well, the thing is…my girlfriend has gone missing. Actually, she's kind of not my girlfriend anymore. We were going out with each other and then she split up with me. It wasn't anything I did. I mean, I wasn't horrible or anything, it's just that, you know, she was going through a hard time, and her friend had disappeared and—"

Oh, for God's sake, spit it out! "Actually, this is a speed confessional box so you'll need to get to the actual confession in under a minute," I said.

"A speed confessional box?"

"Yes, it's like speed dating. We find that with people's busy lives these days they like to do speed confessions rather than the usual longer ones. So you need to confess quickly, I'm afraid, to be eligible for Hail Mary redemptions. Otherwise, the penalties could be very severe from the man upstairs. You're lucky I could fit you in; we've been taking phone bookings for the speed confessions and we're up to our eyeballs in appointments. So if you could hurry it along, please."

"Right. Okay. Well, my girlfriend—ex-girlfriend—has gone missing and I know something, but I don't know whether to tell the police."

"Well, you must tell them, my child."

"But if I tell them, then I'll get into trouble."

"Yes, but it's not all about you, is it? If you know what's happened to her, then you need to tell the police immediately. What *do* you know about her disappearance?"

"What if I did it for her own good, though?"

"What did you do, my child?" A bad, burny sensation rippled through my stomach. *What the fuck has he done to her? Agh! More sweary words coming out of my mouth. Why does being in a church make me want to swear? I'll definitely be going to hell for that. Oh, well, at least it's hot down there, not like the crappy British weather. Oh, fu…fudge, I've done it again!*

He ignored my question. "I was trying to help her but…maybe it's all my fault."

"What's your fault? What do you know? What did you do to her?" I pressed on. In my excitement, my voice rose to RuPaul level again.

"I…oh, God." I pictured him holding his head in his hands.

"Yes, he's listening. Carry on, my child." I forced my voice lower.

"I…"

Come on!

"If you did something you thought was good but it's not, is that bad? Will he punish me?"

"As long as you tell me about it, no, he won't punish you. Now get on with it!"

"Pardon?"

"Er…I mean, hurry up, my child. The lord wants to hear your confession now, and your time for speed confession is nearly up. You don't want to go to hell, do you?"

"I…I'm sorry. I was wrong. I can't do it. I thought I could but I can't."

I heard the confessional door open and close on the other side of the box and Steven's heavy footsteps hurrying to the entrance.

Bugger! Damn, I did it again!

I slipped out of the confessional box and walked slowly to the entrance, pondering his words. *I did it for her own good.* What the hell—oops, I mean, what the heck did that mean? Had he killed her? Had he done something to help her but it had ended up going badly wrong in some kind of accident?

As I was stepping out into the cold air, my pocket rang. Or, more accurately, my mobile in my pocket rang.

"Foxy," Brad said. "My guy watching Marie's house says he's followed her into town. At the moment, she's shopping. If we want to get in and have a nose around her house, we'd better be quick."

"Okay." I started the engine. "When I threw that tea out into the garden, I noticed the house backs onto some woods. We can get in from there and climb the fence at the end of her garden to avoid being seen by the neighbors." Yes, it was dark now, but I didn't want to take any chances. If Marie knew we'd been in her house, she might put a hex on us. Damn. It was too late to go back home and put my Wonder Woman knickers on.

"I'll meet you at the entrance to the woods." Brad hung up as I floored the Toyota, squealing up the road.

I parked near the woods, grabbed my stun gun from my rucksack, and put it in my pocket. I gripped it as I got out of the car and walked to the entrance of the woods. Brad was already waiting for me, thank God. Not that I was scared, you understand, just a teensy bit nervous about what to expect once we got inside. The night was starless and dark, magnifying the ominous feeling I had, and we were about to enter a house that could've been used for black magic rituals. Okay, I admit it, I *was* scared.

"Isn't Hacker coming?" I asked as I hustled forwards to where Brad was waiting. Don't get me wrong, I was more than capable of looking after myself, and Brad could protect himself blindfolded, but that was protecting ourselves from people and weapons we could see. What about creepy, things-that-go-bump-in-the-night invisible spirits and curses that we couldn't see?

"No. He said there's no way he's going in there."

Crappety crap. Hacker wasn't scared of anything. If he didn't want to go in there, it must be bad.

Brad handed me the chicken's foot Hacker wore around his neck. "He wanted you to wear this for protection."

I didn't know which was worse: wearing a poor, sacrificed chicken's bones, or not wearing it and being hexed. Either way, I quickly pulled it over my neck, just in case.

Brad nodded toward the woods and we silently crept through the trees to Marie's fence. Brad hauled himself over the fence first, closely followed by me. As I was swinging over the other side, my jeans caught on a nail and I heard a ripping sound.

Great! A pissy boot and now ripped jeans! Never mind a love curse, Marie's giving me a fashion curse.

I tugged my leg off the nail and with the momentum fell over the other side of the fence onto the hard, muddy ground right on my ass.

"Ouch!" I sat on the ground for a moment, waiting for the pain to subside from my coccyx.

"Are you okay?" Brad looked down at me, holding out a hand.

"I think I've broken my ass." I grabbed his hand and got to my feet, rubbing my bum. "Bloody voodoo!"

We walked toward the house and I saw a faint light glowing in one of the upstairs windows.

"You're sure she's not here?" I whispered.

Brad nodded. "My guy's going to phone when she's on her way back."

I gave an involuntary shudder and looked around the garden for any signs of Snowy. I didn't particularly fancy getting sprayed twice in one day. As we got closer to the French doors, the rhododendron bush shuddered in a sudden breeze that whipped up my hair around my cheeks. Maybe I'd watched too many bad horror films in the past, but I had a sudden thought about skeletons rising from the dead and leaping out of the bush to attack us. Scenes from *Night of the Living Dead* kept popping into my head, and it wasn't pretty.

Don't be a scaredy-Fox. Nothing like that is even remotely possible. My imagination seemed to be getting an ickle bit too overactive. I chuckled to myself and shook my head as the voice of reason took over again.

"What?" Brad threw me a questioning look.

I shook my head again. "Nothing. Just my crazy imagination."

He got his magic lock-picking tool out of his pocket and I watched him make light work of the French doors. In a couple of seconds they clicked and he pressed the handle down.

We were in.

Turning on his Maglite torch, he led the way into the kitchen, which was still as messy as earlier. If I were Marie, I'd magic up one of her zombie mates to do a spot of housework. I mean, I'm not the tidiest person in the world, but this place was a mess. The local rubbish tip looked positively spotless compared to Marie's house.

We poked around the worktops and in cupboards and drawers but didn't see anything connected to Chantal. As we searched, I filled him in on Steven's non-confession.

"So we still don't know what he knows?" Brad said.

"Nope. What do you think he meant when he said 'I did it for her own good'?"

Brad shrugged. "It could be anything."

"That's what scares me. What if he thought killing her was for her own good?"

We walked down the hallway lined with books. At the end of it, by the front door, sat Snowy, staring at us. In the darkness, with the torch reflecting on his eyes, he looked like a ghost cat.

An icy chill slammed through my veins and goose bumps broke out on my skin.

Snowy scowled at us then bared his teeth, hissing as we opened one of the doors that led to the lounge.

"Scary cat," I said.

"I thought you loved all cats."

"Yeah, but that's a voodoo cat. And it sprayed on me."

"The funny thing is, I used to hate cats until I met Marmalade."

I smiled. "Yes, but Marmalade's a cutie cat. Everyone loves him."

"I think Marmalade wants us to get married so he won't be illegitimate anymore." Brad tilted his head, a smile tugging at the corners of his mouth.

"Nice try!"

Inside was the same amount of clutter. Books, candles, various dolls, some made of plastic, some made of straw or cloth, bowls of stones, bits of bark, empty bottles, dice, flowers, money—you name it, Marie was hoarding it on every available bit of space.

"And I thought you were bad with clutter," Brad said. "Look at all this stuff."

So what if I had obsessive clutter disorder? I just felt comfortable with my stuff around me. And if you couldn't be comfortable in your own home, then you might as well live in a cardboard box somewhere. Although, strictly speaking, it wasn't actually my home, it was Brad's. Even though he'd been pretty good about ignoring all the knick-knacks I'd dotted around his house since I'd moved in, I was making an effort to curb my clutter fetish, and my stuff had nothing on this lot. I was positively a domestic goddess compared to Marie. It looked like she'd filled the place with a whole lifetime's supply of crap.

As we searched through the mountains of stuff, I came across a picture of a bride and groom with skulls for faces.

I showed it to Brad. "See, this might happen to us if I set the date. We might shrivel up and turn into a couple of skeletons after the wedding. This could be a sign." I waved the picture under his nose.

"A sign about what?"

"That we're not supposed to get married. That you might just disappear one day again, out of the blue. That we're not really right for each other. That it's all a mistake."

"We are definitely not a mistake. And there's no way I'm leaving you again. In fact, there's no way you're ever getting rid of me now." Brad grinned at my neuroticism. "And don't tell me you believe in all this voodoo now."

"Of course not!" I snapped.

"So what's the worst thing that can happen if you set the date?"

"Er…lots of things?" I said, but it came out more like a question than an answer.

He threw his arms up in the air and muttered something that sounded suspiciously like "Women!"

I pretended I hadn't heard him and rifled through a wooden cabinet that housed hundreds of empty bottles of alcohol. "Either Marie's a secret alkie, or these are used in some kind of ritual." Shame they were empty, I could've done with a stiff drink.

Upstairs there were four closed doors. Behind the first one was a small bathroom with a rusted bath, a mountain of hair products, a carved wooden mask on the wall that looked like a man in mid-scream, and a stuffed black crow on the windowsill. Ick.

One of the other rooms was a bedroom that had a single iron bed with a colorful hand-embroidered duvet cover. More candles and clutter. A picture of a Catholic saint.

The second bedroom had a double bed, a small metal dressing table covered with candles and dolls, and stuff that looked like it should've been thrown away about a hundred years ago. Yellowing bits of paper with weird writing, glass beads, bottles of foul-smelling stuff, a rusted machete. On the bed was a bright red duvet cover and matching pillow. Next to the bed on a small wooden table were a rickety old lamp and a couple of books. The lampshade had a red scarf draped over the top, giving the room an eerie glow. I was guessing this was Marie's room.

I walked toward the machete and stared at it. It was pretty blunt and didn't look like it had been used in a long time, but it would've been a pretty lethal weapon in its day. "Wonder what she used that for?"

Brad picked up the books on the night table, reading out the covers. "*Ancient Voodoo Black Magic Spells* and *Gray's Dissection Guide For Human Anatomy*." He glanced up. "A bit of light reading before bedtime?"

The blood drained from my face. "Omigod!" Images of the boy known as Adam and voodoo ritual killings crept into my brain again. A horrible picture of Chantal and Liza, held down in a darkened room, tied up, being sliced to death with a machete swam, before my eyes. "I'm getting a really bad feeling about what's happened to Chantal and Liza."

"You're not the only one."

The third bedroom was pretty much the same. Lots of macabre things and creepiness, but still no trace of Chantal or her friend.

We trudged back down the stairs and stood in the kitchen. That was when I spied a lump in the dirty carpet.

I kicked it and my boot connected with something hard.

I glanced up at Brad. "What do we have here?"

He pulled the edge of the carpet back, revealing a trap door.

"A basement," Brad said as he slowly pulled open the door.

I trained my Maglite down the dark stairs, but there was a small light source coming from somewhere below. Trudging down the creaky wooden staircase, we found ourselves in a whitewashed room with concrete walls.

I gave an involuntary gasp. This was Marie's voodoo altar room.

A table had been set up on one side of the room and was covered by a black cloth. My eyes swept the altar: candles galore, all lit up with shadows dancing around the room, making it feel like it was alive with ghostly spirits. Didn't anyone ever tell Marie not to leave lighted candles unattended? How irresponsible of her. Mountains of necklaces, several of which were made out of human teeth. I figured it was a pretty safe bet she hadn't bought them from the local Accessorize shop. Yet more bottles of spirits; two small wooden coffins, each with a skeleton doll wearing a top hat and tails lying inside; an alligator's head; two human skulls that were yellowed and looked ancient; three animal skulls that I was guessing were probably from a goat; wooden bowls filled with bones of smaller animals; plastic dolls that reminded me of Chucky, the killer doll from the film *Child's Play;* long wooden sticks; feathers, a bowl of fruit; a wooden cross that was crudely put together with bits of string.

"Creepsville," I said, my intestines suddenly turning into liquid goo. "I can smell zombies."

"What do zombies smell like?" Brad raised an eyebrow.

"Yucky and decaying, like the smell in this room, and the smell of Marie's tea. Urgh." I pinched my nose closed and breathed through my mouth. "Good job we didn't drink that tea. It's probably made from boiled-up zombies."

Brad's lips twitched in a smile. "It's amazing the things that go on in your head."

"Tell me about it. I have to put up with me all the time."

He inched closer to the human skulls. "They're not recent."

I eyed the skulls warily, wondering who they'd been when they were alive. Had they been sacrificed, or had they died of natural causes? I shuddered at the thought. "So this is where she does all her black magic rituals." I screwed up my face, half expecting Chucky to come to life and take a swing at us with an axe.

At the back of the altar, hundreds of photographs and pictures were taped to the wall.

"Hacker said in some of the voodoo rituals they use photos of the people they're trying to help or curse," Brad said.

"Can you see her?" My heartbeat clanged around in my chest as I wondered if I'd see Chantal or Liza's face staring back at me.

"No."

As I leaned forward over the altar, inspecting each one of them more closely, I heard a *shhhhhhhhhhhhhhhhh* noise and smelled something burning.

"You're hair's on fire!" Brad's eyes nearly pinged out of his head.

"Agh!" I glanced down at the left side of my hair and swatted it with my hand.

Ouch! Burny hands.

Probably not a good move, but at least it seemed to stop the flames before they engulfed the whole of my head.

Brad took his jacket off and swatted my head with it repeatedly to stop the residual flames.

I pulled my hair in front of my eyes to inspect the damage.

Great! Now one side of my hair was six inches shorter than the other. And it was at the front, so I couldn't exactly ignore it.

"Does it look really bad?" I asked Brad.

"Of course not, Foxy." He tried to suppress a chuckle and failed miserably.

I slapped him on the arm. "How bad is it?"

"It's not bad, it's just..." His eyes twinkled with amusement. "Different. Actually, it suits you."

I narrowed my eyes at him. "You're laughing at me, aren't you?"

He threw his hands up in mock surrender. "Of course not."

"Good. Because hair to a woman is as important as a willie is to a man. Just think how you'd feel if your willie caught on fire!"

"I hardly think it's the same thing. For starters, men don't have willies on their head."

"That's not entirely true, actually. I've met more than my fair share of dickheads in my time, but that's beside the point."

"What is the point?" Brad stared at me like he didn't have a clue what I was on about.

"Women think about their hair. A lot. If our hair looks crap, we feel crap. Men, on the other hand, think about their willies a lot. If they're not using them, they feel crap. Same thing, see?" I snapped.

"Right, I get it now." He gave me a look that said he didn't get it at all.

"Why is it always me?" I groaned, scrunching up my face.

He hugged me toward him. "Well, didn't you say you need to get a trim for the wedding anyway?"

"So you *do* think it looks bad, then?"

"Not at all," he protested. A bit too lamely for my liking

"Shit. I haven't got time to go to the hairdressers in the middle of this case. I'm going to have to walk round with even more scary hair now."

"Look on the bright side." Brad grinned.

"What's that?" I huffed.

"If you don't look in the mirror, you'll never even notice it. And at least you don't have a dick on your head."

"That doesn't exactly make me feel much better." I tutted, turning to the pictures again, making sure I was so far out of candle reach I was almost halfway across the floor.

Half an hour later, we'd looked at all of the pictures, but none of them were of Chantal. In fact, there was no trace of her or Liza in the house at all.

I couldn't help wondering if that was a good thing or a bad thing.

CHAPTER TEN

———

As soon as we got home, I poured us both a stiff brandy and resisted the urge to look in the mirror.

"Yuck. I never want to go back to that place again." I took a swig, feeling the burning sensation down the back of my throat. I swirled the amber liquid around in the tumbler, thinking. "I still don't know if the voodoo angle has got anything to do with Chantal and Liza going missing." I filled Brad in on my chats with James Langton, Elliot, Andrew Scott, and Steven Shaw. "I don't think James Langton stealing money from Chantal's trust fund has anything to do with it. If you think about it, Chantal's disappearance has only highlighted what he's been up to, and he wanted to keep it quiet. I spoke to all of the other staff at Langton Developments and none of them had anything to add that might be useful." I brought the glass to my lips but didn't drink, going over and over in my head a possible explanation for what had happened to Chantal. "Elliot followed Chantal to the Second Chance Clinic, although Andrew and the receptionist deny she was ever there—but they were definitely lying, I could tell. Hacker said there was no record of her ever being a patient, and even though it would be easy to get rid of her files, we know from Elliot that she was there."

"So do you think Chantal was there because of her termination or this story Liza was investigating?"

"It could be either, although I am convinced Liza's story is the key to this case. Elliot also saw Chantal on Chequer Street, talking to a prostitute, and prostitutes are some of the main clients at the clinic. Plus, Liza liked writing about women's issues. The idea she was doing a story about prostitutes is looking more and more likely."

"But Steven Shaw's also lying. Is he involved somehow in whatever's going on at the clinic?"

"I don't know. It's possible Steven, or even Elliot, could've killed Chantal in a jealous rage—a crime of passion, although somehow that doesn't feel right to me, either, because it can't be a coincidence that both girls have now disappeared."

Brad perched on the end of a breakfast stool. "The main question is, then, what is going on in that clinic?" He rubbed at his neck and moved it in a circular motion.

"You okay?"

He dropped his hand and said, "Yes, just a stiff neck. I must've slept funny last night." He waved a dismissive hand. "How's your ass?" He grinned.

"Better than my hair!" I ran a hand through my out-of-control curls and felt crispy bits crumbling off the ends. "I've been thinking about the clinic, and it could be any number of things going on there. It's a government-run clinic, so I doubt that the funds are enough to be worth embezzling. They could be doing experimental treatment on patients without them knowing, or they could be covering up patient deaths from botched terminations." I paused for a brandy hit, a horrible thought suddenly worming its way into my brain. "Did Hacker manage to find out who Emily Jacobs was?"

"No, he was still looking into it when I left the office."

"We know Liza called her number before she disappeared, and I'm betting it was to do with this story. On the list in Chantal's apartment were the initials EJ and a date. What if Emily Jacobs was a patient at the clinic who died from surgery that went wrong? Liza might've found out she was going to have treatment there and tried to warn her against it, but something happened. Or maybe Emily was one of her sources." I took a glug of brandy. "Both Chantal and Liza phoned the same number on the day they disappeared, and that number was written on Chantal's list next to a set of initials. Maybe the initials on the list are all women who are prostitutes who gave Liza information."

Brad narrowed his eyes, thinking. "The clinic could be doing some kind of medical experiments on the patients. Most of them are prostitutes, probably with no family looking out for them; they're basically considered throwaway members of society.

Who would notice if they disappeared because something was going wrong with the treatments?"

"And this Holbrook Clinic must be involved in it somehow, too. Their website definitely sounds iffy. I mean, if you're selling private medical treatments, why wouldn't you list exactly what you do on your website, instead of something vague like 'unique treatments, tailor made to suit qualified clientele'? What's that all about?"

"Sounds like: If you contact us, we'll tell you if you're a fit for our treatments, whatever they are," he said. "It could be something new and controversial like stem-cell treatments or designer babies, but what would that have to do with prostitutes?"

"I wish I knew." I sucked in a deep breath, feeling the coolness on my lips as Marmalade crept in through the cat flap and jumped on my lap. I kissed his head. "Hey, boy. What do you think about it, huh? Do you think Andrew Scott is doing weird scientific experiments on his patients? Meow once for 'yes' and twice for 'no.'"

Marmalade seemed a tad confused by that and just yawned, staring at me with huge green eyes. He nudged my hand with his head insistently, cat-speak for "feed me."

"I'll feed him." Brad slid off the stool and shook the box of kitty biscuits.

"I need to phone Hacker." I got my mobile out of my rucksack and dialed as Marmalade glanced back at me and meowed once. "See, I told you I could have conversations with him." I grinned at Brad.

Brad crouched down next to Marmalade "Should your mum just stop worrying and set the wedding date? Meow once for 'yes' and twice for 'no.'"

Marmalade burped.

I laughed as Hacker picked up. "Yo."

"Yo. How did it go at Marie's house?"

I told him about the altar we'd found.

"Glad I wasn't there. That black magic is powerful stuff."

"We didn't find any evidence of Chantal or Liza, though."

"Just because you didn't find it, doesn't mean Marie's not involved in it. And she'll know you've been in her house."

I rolled my eyes. "How will she know? We didn't leave any trace."

I imagined Hacker shrugging as he answered, "She can see things that can't be explained. She can do things that can't be explained."

"So, what, you think she'll put a curse on us because we were in her house?" I said.

"Yep."

"Great! I've got enough problems without being cursed, too. So what do you think she'll do to us?"

"Anything's possible. Make your teeth and hair fall out, give you a bad illness, destroy your relationship, even cause death."

Shit. I'm too young to die! No, I will not be cursed. I'm uncurseable. Yep, that's it. I'm totally uncurseable.

"The state of my hair at the moment, I think maybe she's cursed me already."

"Did you wear my chicken's foot for protection?"

"Yes. Will that stop a curse? You know, just in case she has done one," I asked, my voice coming out more anxious than I anticipated. "Not that I believe in them, of course," I added quickly.

"It should do."

See, of course I couldn't be cursed if I was wearing it. The only problem was, Brad hadn't been wearing one. What if something happened to him instead?

I pushed all thoughts of me as a toothless hag and Brad as a flesh-eating zombie wearing a top hat and tails out of my mind. "Have you found anything on Emily Jacobs?" I asked.

"Not yet. I'm still looking."

"Check out the records at the Second Chance Clinic to see if she was a patient there. I think she may also have been a prostitute."

"Will do."

I heard his fingers clacking over the keyboard.

"I'll phone you back when I know something."

"Yo." I hung up.

Brad walked toward me and stretched out his hand, tucking away a stray curl from the non-singed part of my hair. He ran a finger down my cheek, sending a hot shiver down my spine, not to mention other parts. "I'm not going to give up until I make you officially mine."

I knew that. Brad never gave up when he wanted something. And that something was me. So what was wrong with me? I loved him with all my heart. Why was I so afraid of getting married and making it all so official? Was the thought of losing him, or that something bad might happen, really enough for me not to take the chance? But what if Hacker was really right about those curses? What if Marie really put a hex on us to destroy our relationship? The way I was going, I'd probably do a good job of that on my own.

I tried to say something but my mouth had suddenly gone on strike, which was a miracle in itself.

His lips brushed mine, then he whispered in my ear, "Are you hungry?"

Oh yeah, I'm hungry all right! I wanted to ravish him on the spot. Thoughts of me licking chocolate sauce and whipped cream from all over his body pinged into my head. Food *and* sex, what a fab combo.

My phone rang.

Damn.

"It could be Hacker," I said.

He gave me a sexy, lopsided grin. "There's plenty of time later. The night's still young." He picked up my mobile from the breakfast bar and handed it to me.

"You were right," Hacker said. "Have you got the list of initials and dates in front of you?"

"Give me a sec." I pulled it out of my rucksack and stared at it:

MP - 28/01
DL - 15/02
CT - 01/03
EJ - 27/03
LS - 0787 5567893

"Emily Jacobs had an appointment at the Second Chance Clinic for a consultation about a termination on the twenty-sixth of March," Hacker said. "There's no record of any other treatment for her, but she suddenly disappeared on the twenty-seventh of March."

My breath caught in my throat. "Who reported her missing?"

"I hacked into the police report and one of her friends by the name of Cassie Knowles reported it. She's also a prostitute. Emily's never been seen since and the police have no leads."

"Shit."

"And that's not all. Based on that, I made an assumption that the other initials were a list of people who'd also gone missing. Mary Parker went missing on the twenty-eighth of January, Dana Little went missing on fifteenth of February, Claire Turner went missing on the first of March, Lucy Sawyer went missing on the twelfth of April. They all had initial consultations to have terminations at Second Chance Clinic, and they were all prostitutes."

My shoulders slumped. This case had just got even bigger. Now we had seven missing girls in total. Whatever experiments were going on at that clinic, it looked like people were dying as a result.

"Both Chantal and Liza phoned Lucy Sawyer's number on the day they disappeared. If Lucy went missing on twelfth of April, that was before Chantal and Liza disappeared, so why were they trying to phone her if they knew she was missing?"

"They probably didn't know she was missing. There was no date next to her initials like the others. Maybe Chantal and Liza heard from some of the other prostitutes that she hadn't been seen lately, or maybe they found out she'd also had an appointment at the clinic."

"Great work, Hacker. Did you manage to get into the Holbrook Clinic files yet?"

"I'm still working through their security firewalls. I'll let you know when I get in."

"Okay. Yo!"

"Yo." Hacker hung up.

I turned to Brad, eyes wide, trying to take in the enormity of what I'd just heard.

"What?" Brad said.

I told him about all the missing prostitutes.

He ran a hand over his cropped hair and paced the floor. "What the hell kind of experiments are they doing up there?"

"Something seriously bad. I need to get down to Chequer Street and try and talk to Cassie Knowles if she's around, seeing as she reported Emily Jacobs missing. Maybe she knows something that can help."

"Want me to come, too?

I shook my head. "Chequer Street is run by a pimp who goes by the name of Diamond Dozen. If he sees you talking to the girls he might think you're trying to take them over and things could get nasty."

"Diamond Dozen?" Brad tried not to laugh.

I shrugged. "What can I say? He's probably watched too much TV. If I blend in as one of the girls, he probably won't even notice me asking questions."

"You're going to dress up as a hooker?"

I nodded. "Yep."

He raised an eyebrow. "Nice."

I play-swatted his arm. "I mean, we don't know how far this thing goes. Diamond Dozen could be involved in it, too. What if he's sending his girls to the clinic when they get pregnant and taking some kind of payment for procuring new specimens so they can carry out their experiments?"

"Can I watch you get dressed?"

I rolled my eyes. "If you watch me, I'll never get out the door."

CHAPTER ELEVEN

———

At eleven thirty p.m. I was trotting down Chequer Street in my hookerish outfit. It was too cold for a skirt that masqueraded as a belt, so I had on a tight pair of black leggings, a glittery, low-cut top, a short faux leopard skin jacket, and the highest pair of stilettos I owned. I'd backcombed my hair so much it looked like my head had just exploded. Still, the good thing was you couldn't even tell now that one side was shorter than the other, unless you looked really hard.

Chequer Street was getting busy with working girls and seedy clientele. Prime time for finding Cassie Knowles. Some of the girls chatted in pairs at the side of the road, while some of them hung back, lounging against shop windows, ready to do business at the hint of a punter. Cars pulled to a stop now and then, the drivers haggling over prices or extras.

The first girl I met was in her mid-twenties: lots of makeup, a skirt so short you could see what she had for breakfast. She was looking up and down the road, hand on hip, and didn't notice me as I approached.

"Hi." I smiled at her. "I'm looking for Cassie Knowles. Do you know her?"

She looked me up and down, chewing gum loudly. "Are you Diamond's new girl?"

"Yeah, he said Cassie was going to show me the ropes."

She blew a bubble with her gum until it popped, then she jerked her head, gesturing farther down the street. "See the girl in the leather dress?"

I glanced past her and nodded.

"That's Cassie."

"Thanks."

"No problem." She turned her eyes back to the road.

Cassie was leaning on a lamppost, rummaging around in her bag, when I caught up to her. She had long blonde hair and tired eyes. The night was cold but her dress was strapless and short. She was all skin and bones, and there was nothing much holding up the dress except willpower.

"Hi, are you Cassie?"

She pulled out a packet of cigarettes, lit one, and regarded me warily. "Yeah, who wants to know?"

"My name's Amber Fox. I'm trying to find out what happened to your friend Emily Jacobs."

She took a long draw and turned her face away to blow out the smoke. "Why?" Suspicious.

"I've been investigating the disappearance of Chantal Langton, and I've discovered some information about the Second Chance Clinic. Several prostitutes who were using the clinic have disappeared. Emily's one of them. I think there's something going on over there and I need to find out what before even more people vanish mysteriously."

"You a cop?" She glanced around the street nervously.

"No, I'm an insurance investigator."

"Good. If Diamond catches me talking to a cop, he won't be happy."

"You reported Emily missing to the police, didn't you?"

"Hey," a middle-aged guy who'd pulled up at the curb shouted out the window. "How much for both of you?"

"Sorry, we're busy," I said, turning back to Cassie.

"You don't look very busy. How much?" he said. "You can be busy over here." He drew quote marks in the air as he said the word *busy*.

Ew, what a creep!

Cassie glanced up and down the street nervously, whispering to me. "I should take this guy."

I held up the palm of my hand to him. "I *said* we're busy." I made shooing motions to him. "Go on, run along." I turned back to Cassie and opened my mouth to speak.

"Okay, how about just one of you?" he butted in again.

I turned back to him and gave him the benefit of my sweetest smile. "Do you like sex and travel?"

He gave me a lecherous grin. "Yeah, who doesn't?" He was almost drooling at the thought.

"Well, fuck off!" I said.

"Suit yourself!" He finally got the message and wheel-spun up the road.

"So," I prompted Cassie again, "you reported her missing?"

Cassie glanced down at the cigarette, twirling it in between her fingers. "Yeah, I don't think the police were interested." She snorted with disapproval. "Why should they care about a hooker, right? To them we're just the lowest of the low."

I grabbed her arm and looked into her blue eyes. Eyes that had probably seen things I couldn't even imagine. "I care."

She regarded me for a while, trying to work out if I was genuine. Finally, she pulled me into a dark shop doorway. "I haven't seen Emily for about six months. We shared an apartment together, you see. She just went out one day and didn't come back. All her stuff's still there." She shook her head. "There's no way she'd leave all her clothes and personal stuff. No way."

"She had an appointment at the Second Chance Clinic to have a termination, didn't she?"

Cassie took another drag on the cigarette. "Yeah. She was pregnant. A broken condom one night with one of the punters. A lot of the girls use that clinic, so she went to see some doctor there."

"Do you know the doctor's name?"

She chewed on the corner of her lip, thinking. "Er…I think it was something that began with an S."

"Scott? Andrew Scott?"

"Yeah, that's it. So she went to see him and then when she came back he said that he was going to refer her to another clinic for the actual termination. He said this other clinic had better facilities or something and it still wouldn't cost her anything."

"What was the name of the clinic?" I asked, even though I knew what she was going to say before the words were out of her mouth.

"The Holbrook Clinic. She said this new clinic was going to ring her and make an appointment for the termination."

"And did they ring her?"

"I don't know. I went out one morning to get some milk and when I came back she was gone." Her eyes sparkled with tears. "What do you think happened to her? Did this clinic do something to her?"

I sighed, dreading to even think about the possibilities. "I don't know yet. Did you know Mary Parker, Dana Little, Claire Turner, or Lucy Sawyer?"

She smoked while she thought. "No. Who are they?"

"They were also prostitutes who used the clinic. They're all missing."

Her forehead crinkled with concern. "God. Maybe they use the patch over on King Street. I don't know a lot of the girls over there." She paused for a moment. "I didn't think this clinic had anything to do with Emily going missing. If I'd known, I would've told the police about it. Oh, God. I should've done more. I should've pressed the police to do something, but I knew from the way they acted they just weren't interested. But if a lot of girls have gone missing, they'll *have* to do something now, won't they?"

I nodded at her. "It's not your fault, Cassie. I'm going to find out what happened to her and the other girls if it kills me." I handed her my card. "If you think of anything else, or you want help to get off the streets, just give me a ring, okay?"

She took the card and tucked it into her bag. "You know, it's not as bad as you think." She waved a hand up the street. "I've got no qualifications. I ran away from home when I was fifteen. At least doing this I can earn more money than working in a supermarket checkout. And Diamond's okay most of the time, if you play by his rules. There are a lot worse pimps out there." She shrugged.

I stared into her eyes and her gaze slid away from mine. "If you keep telling yourself that, maybe one day you'll really believe it. My offer's there if you want it, Cassie. You can call anytime."

She gave me a sad smile. "Thanks. I'd better get back to work." She walked to the lamppost. "Let me know if you find anything out about Emily."

"I will."

I was just walking back down the street when I saw a big guy in a black puffer jacket and black baseball cap approach one of the girls farther along. He whispered something in her ear.

She shook her head, eyes wide with fear. "I've given you all the money I made last night, I swear."

He turned to look at me as I walked past.

"Hey!" he called out behind me.

I stopped walking and swung around to face him. The girl took the opportunity to scarper. This must be Diamond Dozen.

He walked toward me. In the light, I saw he had a round face, protruding eyes, a big, bulbous nose, and thick lips. Think Shrek, only not quite as green or cute.

"You must be Diamond Dozen." I tried not to laugh at the name but I couldn't help it, a tiny bit just slipped out. I caught a potent whiff of some very cheap and nasty eighties aftershave, like he'd just poured a whole bottle of Brut over his head. "Nice name. Very *Miami Vice*."

"Yeah, well, it's actually Sylvester." He shrugged. "My mum was a big fan of the Rocky films, but 'Diamond' sounds more cool."

That was debatable. "I don't think I've ever heard the name Actually Sylvester before. It suits you, though. Say hi to Tweety Pie for me." I started to walk away.

"Huh?" He looked confused. "Who are you, anyway?" Diamond said, taking in my outfit, his eyes lingering on my boobs.

Yuck!

"You're not one of my girls. What are you doing on my piece of material?"

I frowned. "What?"

"My piece of material. My patch." His gaze flickered to my boobs again.

Ew. Totally gross. "Oh! Right, your patch. Well, I got lost."

He walked around me, looking me up and down. "Nice ass."

I cringed inwardly. "Yeah, my ass is actually a stunt ass for Jennifer Lopez." I gave him my sweetest smile.

His eyes narrowed. "Are you mockering me?"

"Huh?"

"Are you mockering me?" he repeated.

"You mean mocking you?"

He glared at me. "That's what I said."

"Of course I'm not mocking you. I'm pretty sure you don't need me for that." I grinned.

"Don't pastasize me."

"Is that even a word?"

"Of course it's a word." He snorted in disbelief.

"What does it mean, then?" I challenged him with my eyes.

"Speaking to me like I'm stupid." He puffed his chest out, or maybe it was his jacket, it was hard to tell.

"Oh, you mean, patronize?" Hey, this was fun.

"Yeah." He lifted his chin up, gazing at me down the end of his nose. "Are you pastasizing me?"

"Er…no. I'm definitely not pastasizing you. Next question?" I tilted my head.

"Who's your pimple?"

I bit my lip to stop myself bursting into laughter. "My pimp?"

He huffed out a loud breath as if he were talking to a stupid child. "That's what I *said*!"

"Oh, that's weird, because I could've sworn you asked who my pimple was."

"No, I didn't." His face inched closer to mine.

He could definitely do with a nasal hair trimmer. I thought about suggesting it to him, but he probably wouldn't have a clue what I was on about. Instead, I thought I'd keep it simple. "You did."

"Didn't."

"Yes, you did."

"No, I didn't."

"Did."

"Did NOT."

My eyes glazed over and I felt myself going into a coma. I could see this conversation going on all night. "Whatever." I shrugged and did an exaggerated yawn.

"So who is he?" he asked.

"Who is who?" I said.

"Your pimple!" His voice rose a few octaves with impatience.

"I don't have a pimple. Clearasil works wonders for acne." I peered closer to his face, examining a few blackheads on his chin. "You should try it sometime." Was that cruel of me? Oh, what the hell, he was a halfwit who preyed on vulnerable women so he totally deserved it. Actually, maybe *fuckwit* was a better description.

He drew his face back from mine, rubbing his chin. "Are you trying to insulate me?"

I glanced at his puffer jacket. "Nah, that's what the jacket's for."

"What are you talking about?" He frowned.

"That depends. What are you talking about? Did you swallow a dictionary backwards, or something?"

"Look, I'm not some kind of oxymoron you can talk to with no respect, you know."

Okay, that time I did let out a small chuckle. I couldn't help myself. "No, you're definitely not an oxymoron. A moron, yes, but an oxymoron, no."

He stared at me, trying to work out in his plankton-sized brain whether I was taking the piss. "Good, because I don't let anyone call me an oxymoron."

"I'm so glad. Anyway, now we've cleared up that little misunderstanding, I'll be off."

"Well, don't come back on my piece of material unless you want to elbow grease for me."

"Pardon?"

"Elbow grease for me. Work for me." He threw his arms around in the air for emphasis like I was an idiot.

"Didn't Emily Jacobs *elbow grease* for you? Now she's disappeared. You wouldn't happen to know what happened to her, would you?"

He actually looked upset. His shoulders slouched and the corners of his mouth turned downwards. "I don't know what happened to her. I try and project all my girls."

"You mean protect them?"

"That's what I SAID!" he shouted. "What's wrong with you? Don't you understand English?"

"That depends on who's speaking it."

He ignored my comment. "If you find Emily, tell her it isn't good ettycott not to let me know where she is."

"Will do. Anyway, it's been great fun talking to you. Maybe next time we can sit down and do a crossword together." I gave him a beaming smile and walked back to my car.

One thing was for sure, Diamond was telling the truth. I was certain he didn't have a clue what happened to Emily. Come to think of it, he probably didn't have a clue about a lot of things.

When I got back to my car, there was something resting on the windscreen. A small package wrapped in newspaper and tied with a piece of string.

I unwrapped the paper and immediately wished I hadn't.

CHAPTER TWELVE

Inside the paper were two voodoo dolls dressed as a bride and groom. The dolls had been made by putting two wooden sticks together to form a cross that made a body and arms. Straw had been wrapped around the cross, and what looked like doll's clothes had been placed over the makeshift couple. They had black buttons for eyes and a circular black piece of material sewn where the mouths should be, which made it look like they were frozen in a scream. The bride had crazy, curly hair that shot out at all angles, with one side of it shorter than the other. The groom had a black pin sticking through his head. The bride had a pin sticking through her heart.

Yikes!

I wrapped the dolls back in the paper and threw them on the rear seat so I wouldn't have to look at them on the drive home. Even though I wasn't looking (okay, I did peek in the rearview mirror a couple of times to make sure they weren't coming to life to axe me to death like Chucky), I couldn't stop thinking about them.

Why was it always me that got the crap presents? Why couldn't people send me nice things like Belgian chocolates? Damn, I wasn't supposed to be thinking about chocolate either. Okay, why couldn't I get a Molten Brown luxury gift set, or a new bottle of Light Blue Perfume by Dolce & Gabbana, or a new pair of UGGs that didn't smell like cat's wee?

Okay, so it didn't take an expert to realize that a pin sticking out of the groom's head wasn't a good thing. But what did it mean exactly? If we got married, would Brad drink too much on our wedding night and wake up with a hangover? Somehow, I doubted it meant something as simple as that. And what about a pin through the bride's heart? Did that mean I'd have a heart attack from eating too much junk food, or would my heart be broken by Brad?

I turned on the radio to try and take my mind off the dolls. A rapper was singing about lying dead in the arms of his enemy.

No, no, no! I don't want to hear about death and dying!

I turned the radio off so hard the button nearly popped out.

* * *

"The hair on the bride is a pretty good likeness of yours," Brad said as he examined the dolls when I got home.

I glanced at the wild hair that looked like Medusa on a windy day. "Look at how one side of her hair is shorter than the other. How did she know that? She wasn't even at the house."

"Hacker said she'd know we'd been there."

"Yes, but logically, that's just not possible, is it?"

"Who said life was logical?"

Brad was right. If Marie knew about my hair, she must have some seriously freaky powers. "Omigod, what do you think the pins mean?" I glanced up sharply. "What if you've been cursed so you get a brain tumor or something? What if I have a heart attack or she's cursed our relationship?"

Brad enveloped me in his muscular arms, gently stroking my back. "Nothing's going to happen. And anyway, I thought you didn't believe in it."

"I don't, although I can't get over the fact she knew about my hair, which means that she's got some kind of all-seeing eye, and maybe this black magic voodoo curse stuff really does work. And, just in case something horrible does happen, maybe we shouldn't get married after all. What if getting married triggers off some kind of hex she's put on us?" I nodded at the dolls again. "I mean, she's made the dolls to look like a bride and groom."

"Nice try." He pulled back, gazing into my eyes. "There is no hex. They're just dolls made by a crazy woman. And I'm never going to leave you again. I learned my lesson the last time, and that wasn't even strictly my fault."

I opened my mouth, biting back the urge to disagree. Strictly speaking, that *was* true. It wasn't his fault he'd been sent on an

SAS mission to protect innocent people. It was, however, his fault that he hadn't contacted me for months and I didn't have a clue whether he was alive or dead, or whether he just left because he didn't love me anymore. And that hurt. It hurt big time. I could still remember my heart cracking into a million pieces as I waited for news about what had happened to him, and I just didn't know if I could go through all that pain again.

He pressed a finger to my lips. "You can't put it off forever, so stop making excuses. I love you more than anything. You feel the same way. My SAS days are behind me now so I'm definitely not going anywhere. Let's just make it official." He gave me a penetrating stare, like he could read my mind and knew I was about to make excuses again.

And before I could say anything else, he smothered my mouth in a pretty sexy kiss with a nice bit of tongue acrobatics.

When we resurfaced for air, he said forcefully, "Okay, that's it."

A sudden panic made my heart clench. What did he mean? Was he going to finish with me because I wouldn't commit to getting married? "What's it?"

"I'm not going to say another thing about the wedding. I'm here when you want to go ahead with it, but I'm not mentioning it again. Ever."

I gave him a questioning look. When Brad wanted something, he never let it go. For him to just give up on getting married was weird. Unless...unless he was having second thoughts, too.

"Are you having second thoughts?" I asked, biting the inside of my cheek as I waited with trepidation for an answer.

He grinned. "Nope."

Well, something was up. "Ah, I know." I nodded. "You're trying a bit of reverse psychology on me, aren't you? Trying to act like you're not bothered when really you are, so I'll definitely set the date." I grinned back at him.

He gave me a noncommittal shrug.

"Sneaky!" I wagged a finger at him. And, strangely, it started having the desired effect. Woman logic again!

Before I could question him further, he changed the subject in another sneaky maneuver to make it seem like he wasn't bothered. "According to Cassie, Andrew Scott referred Emily to the Holbrook Clinic for a termination. He probably did the same with all the other missing girls who went for a consultation, but judging by what it said on their website, it doesn't seem like the kind of treatment they'd offer to non-paying prostitutes. I hope Hacker manages to find out something soon. God knows how many more women who were sent there have disappeared." He paused for a minute and I imagined the cogs in his brain turning. "Do you think Diamond Dozen's got anything to do with it?"

"No, not unless he was going to confuse someone to death. He's too much of an idiot to be involved in something this big."

* * *

That night I dreamed Brad and I were on our honeymoon. It started off great. We'd just boarded the plane and we were staring in each other's eyes, all loved up. The air stewardess wheeled her trolley down the aisle to serve us champagne, and as she approached I saw it was Chantal. I called out to her as loud as I could, but no words would come out of my mouth. Then the plane started bouncing through the air as we hit a patch of turbulence, and things started falling out of the overhead lockers. A laptop fell down and banged me on the arm. A sticker on the front of it read *Liza's Laptop*. I was just about to get out of my seat and grab it when the plane nosedived, crash landing on a beach in Haiti. Then I was being dragged from the plane by Marie and Andrew. Marie was wearing a gorgeous Umberto Fandango wedding dress and had white makeup smeared all over her face, with black circles around her eyes and mouth, making her look like a skull (note to self: Don't attempt that kind of makeup on my wedding day. It wasn't very flattering). Andrew wore a red cloak and a goat's skull over his face. They tied me up to some palm trees on the beach and Andrew had his foot pressed onto my head so I couldn't move at all. Marie slid a machete from underneath her wedding dress. It glinted at me as the sunlight hit the shiny metal surface. She swung it above her head, and as the machete was just about to slice through me, I woke up, gasping for breath and bathed in sweat.

I glanced at the clock in the darkness. Five a.m. I'd obviously been grinding my teeth in my shattered sleep, as my jaw was aching (either that or I'd been talking too much, which was entirely possible). My eyes were itchy and tired, and I felt like a woman just back from the dead. Marmalade was curled up asleep on my head. No wonder my hair was always wild and uncontrollable. I dislodged him and he let out a satisfied snore. Silently pulling the duvet back, I got out of bed as stealthily as I could. From all his years in the SAS, Brad was awake and alert at the slightest sound or movement, and I could never manage to get up before him without him waking up.

I grabbed a pair of skinny jeans, a black jumper, my standby pair of UGGs—since the others still smelt of cat wee—and my Wonder Woman knickers, just in case. I headed silently for the shower, taking a last look over my shoulder to admire Brad's sleeping form. Boy, he must've been really tired if he hadn't even stirred yet.

I shrieked when I caught sight of my hair in the bathroom mirror. A combination of half a ton of hairspray in aid of backcombing, being singed by Marie's stupid candle, and a cat on my head made me look like something out of *The Rocky Horror Picture Show*. There was no denying it—my hair was downright scary.

I dived in the shower, shampooed and conditioned as if my life depended on it, and scrunched my hair dry with the hairdryer. I peered closer to the mirror to survey the finished look. Better. Much better. Unless you counted the fact that one side was still very much shorter than the rest. I teased it around, trying to make it less conspicuous.

Damn. Nothing worked. The only way to hide it was to get some layers put in, but the luxury of a hairdresser was something I didn't have time for. I had some missing girls to find. I settled for stuffing it under a flat cap instead.

Despite the steamy shower and coiffeuring overdose, I still hadn't woken up properly by the time I came out of the bathroom, and Brad hadn't even stirred. I drove through slitty eyes to Hi-Tec's office in zombie mode. *Agh! Don't mention the Z word!* Okay, scratch that. I drove to the office in half-asleep mode. I needed a monster-sized Starbucks latte with extra caffeine to wake me up, but it was too early for them to be open. *Agh! Don't mention the monster word either!*

Hacker was already at his desk, engrossed in something on one of his computer screens with the remains of last night's dinner scattered around him.

"Have you been here all night?" I dumped my rucksack on the desk and unzipped it.

"Pretty much. In a few minutes I think I'll have cracked the Holbrook Clinic's system." He grinned.

"Someone left me a present last night."

"Another one?"

I nodded grimly, handing him to the two dolls.

He stared at them but didn't take them. He shook his head, his plaits quivering, eyes wide. "No way am I touching those."

"What do you think the pins mean?" I gnawed on my lip, waiting for his answer.

"Well, sometimes a pin in the head represents gaining knowledge about something, but in this case..." He tore his eyes away from the dolls and back to me. "Probably not. It can't mean anything good, that's for sure. A pin in the heart can mean death or a broken heart or some sort of love curse."

"Shit. That's what I thought you'd say." I quickly wrapped them back up and threw them in the bin by the side of my desk. There. If I couldn't see them, I could just be in denial about them, and nothing would happen. "Emily Jacobs might've had a phone call from the Holbrook Clinic the day she disappeared, telling her to go to the clinic for an appointment. Can you check Emily's phone records for the twenty-seventh of March?"

"Sure. Give me a sec." He swiveled in his chair to a keyboard and monitor on the opposite side of his desk.

Since Starbucks wasn't open at this ungodly hour, I made an instant coffee for me with three heaped spoonfuls, and a peppermint tea for Hacker while I waited for him to come up with some info. I sniffed his tea. Blah! It wasn't quite as bad as Marie's, but it was close. I'd bet it would taste a hell of a lot better with half a tin of hot chocolate thrown in.

Ten minutes later, he took a printout of his screen and highlighted a number in yellow marker pen. He handed it to me.

"That number phoned Emily at twelve thirty p.m. on the twenty-seventh. The number's registered to the Holbrook Clinic."

So my theory was right. They must've called Emily shortly after Cassie had gone out for milk. Maybe they told her there was a cancellation and wanted to see her as soon as possible. Whatever they said, I was pretty certain the call had lured her to her death.

One of the monitors on Hacker's desk beeped and he turned his attention to it. He looked up, a huge grin on his face. "I'm into the Holbrook Clinic's records."

I sat on the edge of his desk as he scrolled through pages and pages of information. Doing weird computer commands that looked like gobbledygook, we moved through patient and staff records and financial spreadsheets.

Two hours later, I knew exactly what was going on, and it was even scarier than anything I could've imagined.

CHAPTER THIRTEEN

———

I struggled to get my words out for a moment, which was pretty amazing for me. The last time I stopped talking was when I was asleep.

I glanced at Hacker, a shiver of horror working its way up my spine.

His eyebrows shot up to his plaits in shock, his eyes as wide as dinner plates.

"Omigod!" I finally said. "They're murdering people for their organs." I'd seen a lot of horrible things in my seventeen years as a police officer, but this was just pure evil.

The Holbrook Clinic had been performing organ transplant operations for the past year. If you wanted a kidney, no problem—a transplant would cost you a cool £150,000. A heart transplant went for three hundred thousand. A cornea, fifty thousand. A new set of lungs was £250,000. But they didn't limit their operations to the major organs. Skin, tendons, intestines, veins, limbs—anything was possible for a fee. If it could be transplanted, the Holbrook Clinic would oblige. The clinic offered "Transplant Tourism" with an "All-inclusive Package" that included the operation, drugs, any medical tests required, and a two-week convalescent stay at their five-star facilities. Their recipient patients came from all over the world: Israel, the Middle East, Russia, America, UK, Iran, Europe. The list of donors was huge, and I was betting a lot of them weren't willing participants. Emily Jacobs, Mary Parker, Dana Little, Claire Turner, Lucy Sawyer, and Liza Bennet were all listed amongst the donor files.

I shook my head sadly. "They've got the ideal setup. Andrew Scott refers these girls to the clinic. And the beauty of it for them is they're picking people that no one will miss. Society doesn't care about missing prostitutes. Except Liza Bennet, of course. I suspect she was intending to blow this story sky high, and now she's dead, too. These women think they're going in for a termination, but the reality is they're never going to wake up from the operation." I paused, letting it all sink in. I shook my head. "Chantal's name isn't on their list. Does that mean they're keeping her alive somewhere until they need her organs harvested?"

Hacker's forehead crinkled in a frown of disgust. "That is some nasty shit."

I couldn't have put it better myself.

"But why kill them for their organs? Aren't there plenty of willing donors available?" he said.

"I don't know." I turned to my laptop and Googled organ donations. It didn't make for pleasant reading.

"There's a global shortage of available organs for transplants," I said. "Each country has a never-ending list of patients awaiting organ donors. Allocations for the organs are usually based on a points system—time on the transplant waiting list, patient's age, health status, and compatibility of the organ. Some patients would never make it on the list for health or other reasons, meaning they have no chance of receiving a donor organ legitimately. It's basically an organ lottery. Those who can afford it are taking advantage of the big boom in transplant tourism and going to private centers like the Holbrook Clinic."

"I guess that makes sense. Patients waiting for a donor or those who've been refused are going to do all they possibly can to stay alive."

"A natural survival instinct, I guess. In most countries, it's illegal to sell organs, so with no incentive to donate them, demand is outweighing supply in the majority of the world. Other countries put further obstacles in the way for patients by requiring that the donor and recipient are related. There are basically not enough donors to go round." I glanced up at Hacker. "Which is why organ trafficking seems to be such a big business."

Hacker let out a slow whistle.

I clicked on another site and read. "In China they legally take organs from dead prisoners. It's estimated that ninety percent of organs come from this source, and yet there's still a shortage. In India six private transplant centers have opened up in the last decade that offer transplant tourism because the market for it is booming. In Pakistan there were two thousand renal transplants in 2005 and two-thirds of them were estimated to be for foreign recipients. In South Africa between 2001 and 2002, more than a hundred thousand illegal transplants were done in hospitals. An investigation revealed the existence of a massive organ-trafficking syndicate. The donors were mainly from Brazil, Russia, Moldova, and Romania, and were paid around ten thousand dollars for their kidneys. The recipients were from America, Israel, and Iran, and paid $120,000. In the Philippines there are whole slums of people who specialize in selling their body parts. It's even estimated that thirty to fifty percent of UK patients are going abroad for commercial kidney transplants because they can't get one here."

"So Andrew Scott and the Holbrook Clinic open up a niche market just at the right time."

"Exactly, but it's not just them." I leaned closer to the screen, clicking on different sites. "An NGO human rights group called Organ Watch did a study that uncovered an astonishing worldwide system of organ and tissue trafficking. And get this, a lot of people from poorer areas in Iraq, Turkey, Eastern Europe, Brazil, and Peru, are selling their organs for just a thousand dollars, which is a small fortune for them."

"You don't need to be a mathematician to realize the profits involved by the organ traffickers and illegal clinics performing the operations, then."

"Yep." I nodded. "But some of the donors aren't even willing participants. Some are tricked into thinking they're going abroad for a job, and when they arrive, they're held against their will and operated on. Some people are just being abducted from slums and having their organs harvested. It seems like organ thefts and abductions are rife."

Hacker let out a disbelieving snort. "Why pay a donor when you don't have to? No wonder they're killing these women."

"It also says here that some religions prohibit organ harvesting from cadavers, so recipient patients want live donors to harvest. Also, the success rate of transplants is higher with live donors rather than cadavers." I swiveled in my chair, taking it all in. "This has been going on for years and yet I've never even heard about it in the media." I shook my head. "So the Holbrook Clinic is probably keeping these women alive until they operate, then harvesting all viable organs, which kills them anyway. Plus, they don't have to pay them and no one will notice they're missing." I reached for the phone. "I need to call Brad and tell him." I glanced at my watch: ten a.m. "Where is he, anyway? He's normally in way before this."

I punched in his mobile number but it went to voicemail. I left a breathless, excited message and hung up, then I tried the landline at home. Ditto.

"Did he tell you he had a meeting?" I asked Hacker.

"No," he said as my mobile rang.

I glanced at the caller display, expecting it to be Brad. Instead, it was Dad.

"Hey, Dad. How's the case going?"

"Slowly." He let out a loud sigh. "I'm sick of being here. I come home stinking of burgers, and the smell is making your mum feel ill."

"What, more ill than when you were disguised as a tramp?"

"I thought we'd come to an agreement about me doing part-time neighborhood watch jobs. Now she's insisting that I give it all up again." Another big sigh. "I can't just sit around and do nothing all day. What am I going to do if I can't catch criminals?"

Bless him. When he'd retired from the police force, he'd been bored out of his skull. It was only my suggestion about volunteering for the neighborhood watch that got him out of his mini-depression. Although, yes, sometimes I had to admit he took things a teensy bit too far, but he always got a result.

"Why don't you set the wedding date and that will take the heat off me for a while?" he said.

"Dad! I can't just set the date to get Mum off your back."

"Go on," he pleaded. "Please, love."

I glanced up at the ceiling and did a sigh of my own. "Is that why you phoned up? To badger me into getting married?"

"No. I've been going through the CCTV cameras at Burger Land to see if there are any clues as to who's stealing the money, and I've found something you definitely want to see."

"Ooh, intriguing." I glanced at my watch. Ten past ten. "And great timing, since I haven't even had breakfast yet. Are you still doing bacon and egg breakfast burgers?"

"No, they finish at ten."

"Bummer. I'll be there in twenty."

"Okay."

When I put the phone down, I stretched and rolled my shoulders that were knotted up from too many hours leaning over a computer screen. My ass was in snooze-land, too. I stood slowly to wake it up and grabbed my rucksack. "Do you want me to get you a veggie burger or something?" I had a sudden thought. "Actually, maybe I'll get one, too. Veggie burgers are healthy, aren't they?" I'd never actually tried one, but how gross could they be?

Hacker scrunched up his face in disgust. "Do you know what they've got in them?"

"Er…vegetables?"

"They're not real vegetables. They're only pretend vegetables."

"Right. How can you tell the difference?" What did I know? I hardly ever ate them, so I wouldn't recognize a pretend one if it poked me in the eye. Well, apart from asparagus. I think I'd definitely recognize those freaky little stick things again.

"The vegetables you get in the burgers are processed to oblivion and pumped full of preservatives. They've got no nutritional value left in them at all." He shook his head at me.

"Okay, great. So I'd actually be better off eating a big, fat, juicy cheeseburger, then?" I asked hopefully.

"There's no hope for you, is there?"

I grinned. "If you see Brad, can you get him to call me?"

"Sure."

Tia breezed into the office wearing a brown miniskirt, a lime-green polo neck, and a brown scarf. Lime-green boots and hooped earrings finished off her Dayglo look. Actually, in today's getup she kind of looked like a mint chocolate truffle. Damn. I had chocolate on the brain again. Giving it up was so bad for my mental health.

"Morning!" She kissed Hacker on the cheek. "I missed you last night. Have you been here all the time?"

"Yep." He grinned back at her with a dopey look on his face. Young love.

"You're very perky today," I said. "How's the cold?"

"It's completely gone!" She threw her arms in the air in a dramatic fashion as if she were just about to do a star jump in the middle of the office. "Hacker did some reiki on me and it vamoosed! How cool is that?" She draped an arm around his shoulder with pride. "I'll never have to go to a doctor again."

I grinned at her enthusiasm, especially the use of the word "vamoosed," which tickled me for some reason. Maybe it was an Americanism. "Well, I'm glad you're better."

"Any news on the case?" Tia asked.

"Yep, and it's pretty unbelievable, but I've gotta run. I'll let Hacker fill you in. You want anything from Burger Land?"

"No, I'm good, thanks."

I glanced between them, watching their crackling chemistry. At this rate, they'd be getting married sooner than me.

"Okay." And, like Tia's cold, I vamoosed.

* * *

I pulled up at the drive-through window of Burger Land, perusing the menu. Maybe I should try something different. Chicken was probably a healthier option.

"Can I help you, please?" the familiar voice echoed through the microphone.

"Can I have half a dozen chicken nuggets, please?" Oh, wait. Did nuggets mean the chicken wasn't real chicken? I glanced at the menu again. Damn Hacker for getting me all worked up about it. All this wedding diet business was messing with my head. "Actually, I'll have half a dozen chicken premium breast strips instead, please." Breast strips sounded much more like real chicken.

"Sorry, we don't have half a dozen. We only have six, nine, or twelve."

Hmmm. I shook my head. "So I can't have half a dozen but I can have six?"

"Yes."

"Okay, I'll have six, then. And large fries."

"Would you like fries with that?"

"Do you mean extra fries or the ones I just ordered?"

"Pardon, madam?"

"Do you mean do I want two large fries or one?"

"Yes, do you want fries with that?"

"I don't want fries with the fries, but I want fries with the chicken."

"Okay, anything to drink?"

"A chocolate thickshake, please."

"Do you want fries with that?"

"No, thanks. Just fries with the chicken."

"Thank you. Please drive to the pickup window."

I drove up, wondering what the hell I was going to actually get. Dad's eyes lit up when I got there.

"I'll meet you in the car park in a minute," he whispered to me as he handed me my bag of food. "Amber, don't you think three portions of fries is a bit much, even for you? Think of the wedding dress!"

I undid the bag and peered inside. Bloody people. How difficult was it to order a meal these days? If I got fat, it would be all their fault. "I only ordered one portion!" I rolled my eyes at him. "You need some new staff. They haven't got a clue."

He leaned on his elbow, sighing. "Tell me about it."

"Do they get commission on the amount of fries they sell, or something?" I asked.

He nodded. "There's an all-out chip war going on between the staff at the moment."

Any other time, extra fries would be welcome, but now I was on a diet—well, sort of a diet (hey, it was a start!)—I didn't appreciate any fries wars going on when I was at the drive-through. If they were there, you just had to eat them, didn't you? I mean, it would be a complete waste of food otherwise.

I handed him the money. "See you in a minute."

He nodded and I drove round to the car park. I pulled apart a steaming piece of chicken breast, inspecting it for signs of pretend breastiness. I took a sniff. Nope, it looked pretty real to me. I popped one in my mouth. Yum. I was halfway through them when Dad opened the passenger door and slid in, glancing around to make sure no one was around.

"Here." He handed me a CD. "I was going through the CCTV tapes and I saw Steven meeting Chantal in the car park. I recognized her right away from the newspaper report about her disappearance."

I swallowed a chunk of chicken and grinned. "When did this happen?"

"The day she disappeared. It was seven p.m. and pretty dark, but you can still make it out clearly on the copy I burned for you. They met in the corner of the car park and had a heated chat about something, and then she got into Steven's car and drove out."

"Well, well, well. Sneaky Steven. I knew he was hiding something." I wondered whether him meeting Chantal was a good thing or bad thing. Chantal wasn't on the list of donors for the Holbrook Clinic. Did that mean she was still alive for the time being? Hadn't they found a suitable recipient yet for her organs? Or did it mean that she wasn't being held by them at all? Had she disappeared for another reason entirely? If so, what was it? And what was the extent of Steven's involvement in all of this? "Is Steven here?"

Dad shook his head. "He's on duty in a couple of hours."

"I'll be back to have a word with him later, then, after I've checked it out." I took a slurp of shake. "Thanks, Dad."

"You owe me one." He pointed a finger at me. "Tell your mother she can buy that hat and it will get her off my back."

I offered him the packet of fries. "Fries?"

"Not likely. They're only pretend potatoes."

"What's wrong with everyone around here? Don't you appreciate good junk food when you see it?"

Pink Hair came out of the restaurant and went round the back of the building for a smoke.

"I've got to go." Dad climbed out of the car. "I'm pretty sure she's the one nicking the money." He leaned back inside. "Think about what I said."

I chewed on my fries and nodded. Dad would move on to another case soon and Mum wouldn't have to deal with burger smells anymore, then they'd both forget about harassing me. I hoped.

I finished off my breakfast and checked my mobile phone battery and reception. They were both working fine, so why hadn't Brad called? I phoned his mobile again.

Voicemail.

I phoned the house.

No answer.

I phoned Hacker. "Yo, has Brad come in yet?"

"No. He hasn't rung in, either."

"Where the hell is he, then?" A picture of the voodoo doll flashed in my head with the pin through its head.

I was starting to get that horrible doomsday feeling again.

CHAPTER FOURTEEN

I floored the Toyota through town, breaking a few speed limits on the way home. I yanked the handbrake on, flung open the door, and was out of the car before it had even come to a complete stop.

"Brad?" I called out in the lounge.

No answer.

I rushed into the kitchen.

No sign of him. No breakfast dishes, either, and he always ate breakfast.

Marmalade ran down the stairs, meowing at me.

I scooped him up. "Where is he?"

Marmalade blinked and meowed again. He jumped out of my arms and ran back up the stairs.

I followed, taking them two at a time to our bedroom.

My breath caught in my throat.

Brad lay in bed, the sheets tangled around him. His eyes were shut, his breathing slow and labored, and he was shivering.

For a moment I just stood there, rooted to the spot with fear and surprise. Then a tsunami of adrenaline took over and I ran to the bed. "Brad?"

No response.

I shook him gently. "Brad? What's wrong?"

He moaned but didn't open his eyes or speak.

That was when I noticed the rash on his chest.

Shit. I knew what that meant. My heart seemed to stop pumping for a few seconds.

Tears sprang into my eyes. "Brad? Can you hear me?" My voice came out croaky and high-pitched.

No response.

I think I let out a scream at that point, but it sounded like it was far off in the distance, as if the sound were coming from someone else.

I punched in 999 on my mobile and called an ambulance.

I went into full-scale panic mode as I waited for them to arrive. I stroked his head, which felt burning hot, and yet he was still shivering.

Rushing to the bathroom, I soaked a flannel with cold water. I pressed it to his head and he made a gargling sound in the back of his throat.

"It's okay, babe. I'm here." I choked back the tears. "The ambulance is on its way."

His eyelids fluttered open and he stared at me with glassy eyes.

"My...head...hurts," he croaked before falling unconscious again.

My heart twisted inside. A guttural sob worked its way from my stomach up to my throat.

This couldn't be happening. Brad never got ill. He was the fittest person I'd ever met—a roughty toughty, kick-ass ex-SAS guy. He'd done the toughest missions and always came out on top.

I gripped his hand tight until I heard the ambulance pull up outside.

Rushing down the stairs, I slipped, sliding down the last one, nearly falling on my ass.

I ran to the door and let them in. "He's upstairs. Hurry!"

Two paramedics followed me with bags of equipment.

"I think he's got meningitis." I didn't want to say it out loud, but I had to. Saying it would make it true, and I couldn't bear to let it sink in. It was the voodoo curse. That fucking voodoo doll had done this. That was the only answer.

I stood around helplessly, flapping my hands as they took his vital signs and asked me questions. They hooked him up to an IV drip and maneuvered him onto a stretcher.

"Do you want to ride in the ambulance with us?" they asked as they loaded him into the back of it.

"Yes," I cried, jumping on board.

I reached out for his hand as the paramedic monitored him. "You'll be okay, Brad. I'm here."

His eyelids fluttered but didn't open.

My stomach lurched. I let out a whimper that sounded like an animal in pain. I was so scared that even the roots of my hair felt like they were trembling.

You'll be fine, Brad. You're strong. You'll be better in no time. You have to be okay, we're getting married. I love you. I repeated that over and over in my head until we reached the hospital.

As the paramedics wheeled him into the emergency room, my heart flip-flopped around.

"Suspected meningitis," one of the paramedics said to a young male doctor who had rushed to meet us.

"Take him to exam room one," the doctor said.

Before I could worry about how young the doctor was and whether he could possibly be any good, since he looked about twelve, he said to me, "What symptoms did he have?"

"Last night he was complaining about a sore neck. He was unconscious when I got back home this morning, although he woke up briefly and complained about his head hurting. And he's got a rash on his stomach," I said in a garbled rush as we all hurried along the corridor to an isolated examination room.

It was all my fault. I should've known something was wrong when he didn't wake up as I got out of bed this morning. What if I'd got there too late? What if he d…d…no, I couldn't even think the D word. God, I'd been such an idiot wasting all this time. Sod all the messing around I'd been doing. Life was too short to spend worrying about whether I'd be happy with the person I loved. Life was for living the happiness right here and now. I was so going to marry him as soon as he got better.

I wiped away tears with the heel of my hand as the paramedics transferred him from the stretcher to a bed.

"Does he have any illnesses or allergies?" the doctor asked.

"No." I shook my head, unable to tear my eyes away from Brad's pale face.

Nurses rushed into the room, hooking Brad up to all kinds of monitors.

"We need to do some tests," the doctor said to me, opening Brad's eyelids and shining a light in his eyes.

"If you can have a seat in the waiting room, we'll take it from here," a matronly nurse said. "We'll let you know as soon as we have some news for you."

I nodded blankly, letting out a huge gush of air that I hadn't even realized I'd been holding as she steered me carefully out the door.

In the corridor, I leaned against the wall, fighting the urge to throw up. I needed air.

It wasn't until I got outside and took huge gulps of it that I realized my heart was beating so hard my whole body was shaking. I paced the entrance, trying to get a grip as I attempted to phone Hacker with fumbling fingers. Three times I punched in the wrong number before I finally managed to get my fingers to cooperate with my brain.

"Brad's in hospital," I said breathlessly as soon as he picked up. "I think he's got meningitis."

"Shit. I'll be right there."

I hung up and dialed Mum.

"Amber, honey! How are you? Suzy's here at the—"

"Mum," I wailed down the phone. "Brad's in hospital." I told her what had happened.

"Okay, honey, don't worry," Mum, ever calm in a crisis, reassured me. "Brad's as fit as they come. I'm sure he'll pull through just fine. I'm coming down there now."

"No, it's okay. There's nothing much you can do at the moment, and Hacker's on his way."

"Are you sure?"

My stomach did a weird swirly thing and I tried again not to throw up. I took a deep breath, steadying myself against the outside wall of the hospital. "I'm sure."

"Well, is there anything else I can do?"

"Yes. Go out and buy the damned hat." I knew it was a ridiculous thought, but I figured if mum bought the hat, then Brad would be okay.

Ridiculous or not, that was the thought I was clinging to.

CHAPTER FIFTEEN

I sat next to Hacker in the waiting room, jiggling my leg up and down. The clock ticked away on the wall at what felt like a snail's pace.

"I've been trying to get hold of Tia to tell her, but she's on her lunch break and not answering her phone," Hacker said.

"It's okay. If you get hold of her, tell her not to come. There's nothing she can do and it's no fun sitting around hospitals, waiting for news."

"Do you want some coffee?" Hacker asked, his panicked face mirroring how I felt.

I shook my head. "What's taking them so long?" I looked at the clock again for the gazillionth time. Only an hour had passed, but it felt like a hundred.

Hacker threw his arm around my shoulder. "He'll be okay. Brad's the toughest guy I know."

I rested my head on him. "Of course. Of course he's going to be okay," I said with more confidence than I actually felt. "I think it was that bloody voodoo doll that cursed him."

I felt Hacker stiffen at the mention of voodoo. "I told you this stuff wasn't to be messed with."

"I was trying to find Chantal. Who knew it would all lead to this?" I sniffed.

"I'm not blaming you. This isn't your fault."

I pulled away, looking him straight in the eyes. "Hacker, can't you do some good voodoo to counteract the curse?"

"A healing spell?"

I nodded, biting my lip. "Why not? You can do healing reiki, so you're the perfect person, and you know how to do voodoo spells, don't you?" So what if I was always taking the piss out of Tia and her spells? So what if I didn't believe in all the hocus-pocus, heebie-jeebie shit? If ever there was a time to try it, it was now.

"Yes, I know how to do it." Hacker nodded. "But if Marie really has cursed him, then my spells probably won't be strong enough to counteract hers."

I gripped his arm tightly. "Please. Just do it. We have to at least try."

"I'll need some of his hair, and I need to go home to make a voodoo doll to transfer the healing power to in a specific ritual."

I rummaged around in my pocket. "Here's my key. You can get some hair from his comb."

"Don't you want me to stay with you?"

"No." I pulled him to his feet. "This is more important. Go." I pushed him toward the door.

"I'll be back as soon as I've done it."

I nodded and slumped down on the chair again, gnawing on my thumbnail and watching the hands of the clock tick around with intolerable slowness.

Two hours later, the young doctor came into the waiting room.

I leaped up. "How is he? What's happening?"

A frown crinkled his brow.

Uh-oh. That can't be a good sign.

"We've performed some tests and they've confirmed he has got bacterial meningitis. We're administering high doses of antibiotics and fluids." He paused, looking uncomfortable.

"What? Just tell me."

"He has a lot of swelling in his brain tissue so we're also administering some steroids and other drugs to counteract the inflammation. At the moment he's still unconscious and his blood pressure is quite low. We're monitoring him constantly."

"But he will recover, won't he?"

Another pause.

Stop fucking pausing and spit it out!

"Meningitis can cause complications such as hearing loss, brain damage, paralysis, blindness, and...even death."

I gasped. My hands flew to my mouth.

No, no, no. This can't be happening. My mind jumped around all over the place, imagining the worst.

"It's too early to tell if he will have any long-term effects from it, but you got him here in time. You may just have saved his life." He patted my arm. "We're doing everything we can."

"Can I see him?"

He nodded. "He's in the intensive-care unit on the second floor."

I didn't have time to wait for the lifts, so I ignored them and ran up the stairs. Through a glass window I saw him in one of the rooms, hooked up to all sorts of equipment, drips going into his arms.

I stifled a sob in the back of my throat and raised my hand to the glass.

A nurse came up behind me. "It's okay, love, you can go in. He's only allowed two visitors at a time, though."

I nodded dumbly and opened the door.

Sitting on the bed next to him, I gripped his hand. It felt lifeless and cold. "You're going to be fine, Brad." If I kept repeating it, maybe I'd believe it. And maybe he would, too, in the depths of his unconsciousness.

I stroked his face as the tears snaked down my cheeks, and listened to the *beep, beep, beep* of the monitors echoing in the room.

Hours passed with nurses coming and going, taking his temperature and recording his blood pressure, adjusting his drips, adding more medication, but he didn't wake up. I kept my vigil on the bed. Somehow, I knew he could feel me there.

A tapping on the glass window caught my attention. I turned to see Mum and Dad waiting outside. Kissing Brad's hand, I said. "I'll be back in a minute."

Mum enveloped me in a hug as Dad stroked my hair.

"How is he, honey?" Mum asked.

"It's too soon to tell. Oh, God, what if he doesn't get better?" I clutched her arm.

"Ssshhhh," she whispered into my neck. "He's got a fighting spirit."

"Of course he'll get better," Dad said softly. "I'm not missing out on the wedding, not now your mother's finally bought the damned hat she's been raving on about for months."

I managed a slight smile at that. I had to think positively.

"But the doctor said there might be some complications." I turned to look back at Brad, dread seeping through my veins.

"Do you want us to stay?" Dad asked.

I shook my head. "No. I'd rather be alone with him. And there's no point in you both sitting here doing nothing. I'll phone you if anything changes."

Mum gave me a quick squeeze. "Everything will be okay. I'm sure of it."

"If you need anything, just call us," Dad said.

I waved them goodbye and went back in the room.

At some point, I must've fallen asleep. I woke with a start when Hacker entered the room.

I rubbed my swollen eyes and leaned forward, hoping that his spell had miraculously worked and Brad would be awake and talking.

No such luck.

"Did you do the spell?" I asked Hacker.

He slumped down in a chair on the opposite side of Brad's bed, nodding. "I fed Marmalade while I was at your house, too."

"Thanks. So how long do they take to work?"

Hacker shook his head, staring at his best friend. "Impossible to tell. Sometimes they work straight away, sometimes it takes a few days."

What if Brad didn't have a few days?

"If the black magic is too strong, sometimes they won't work at all." He gave me a solemn look.

I choked on a new wave of panic.

A nurse came into the room and hooked up another packet of drugs to the IV. "You may as well go home and get some rest. We'll phone you the minute he wakes up."

I shook my head. "I'm not leaving."

She gave me a smile. "Of course. It's your choice." And she slipped out the door.

I glanced at Hacker. "You don't have to stay."

"I'm not leaving either."

A few hours later, I stood up and stretched, pacing the tiny room like a caged lion, gnawing on my thumbnail again so much I made it bleed.

"You're making me dizzy," Hacker said after a while.

"I need something to concentrate on to stop me worrying. Can you get your laptop?"

"Sure."

"Dad gave me a CD of some CCTV footage that shows Steven meeting Chantal on the day she disappeared. It's in my rucksack at home. Can you bring them both here so we can check them out?"

He stood up and hugged me. "If there's any news, call me."

"Will do."

"Want me to get you something to eat?"

"No. I'm not hungry."

He pulled back. "But bad news always makes you hungry."

"I know. Maybe it's just other people's bad news that makes me hungry. Right now my throat's so tight I couldn't even swallow a wafer-thin mint."

"Okay. I'll be back soon."

After he'd left I thought about the case, not taking my eyes off Brad for a second in case he stirred. I had a hunch about where Chantal was, but I needed to see the CD first.

An hour later, my hunch was confirmed.

CHAPTER SIXTEEN

———

Hacker and I watched the CD on his laptop as Brad's monitors continued to beep around us. It showed Chantal arriving on foot at the Burger Land car park at seven p.m. on the day she disappeared. She hastily made her way to the rear where the bins were stored and where Pink Hair had gone for her smoke break. Chantal was nervous, her eyes constantly darting around. Ten minutes after she arrived, Steven exited the building from the rear entrance and met her. They had an animated conversation, Chantal's arms flying around, Steven trying to calm her down. Then he handed her something and she kissed him on the cheek. Steven stood watching her with worry as she got into a Ford Focus parked in the spot reserved for the manager and drove off.

I thought back to Steven's words in the confessional box: *What if I did it for her own good?* He was doing something he thought would protect her—providing her with a vehicle to run away with.

"Chantal's car was parked in the train station car park in a blind spot from the CCTV cameras," I said. "I think she did that deliberately. She knew where those cameras were, and she wanted it to look like her car had been abandoned there."

"So then she walks to meet Steven and borrows his car."

"She wanted to disappear without a trace. She knew that Andrew Scott and his cronies at Holbrook would be after her because she'd worked out what was going on with the transplants. She panicked and took off. That's what Steven was lying about when I spoke to him. He was involved in her disappearance by helping to protect her, not by doing something to hurt her."

"So where is she?" Hacker asked.

I had a mental eureka moment. "I've got a good idea." I glanced at Brad, who was still unconscious, and chewed on my bottom lip to give my thumb a rest.

"Go." Hacker rubbed my arm. "I'll be here. If he wakes up, I'll phone you."

"But I want to be the first person he sees when he wakes up."

"But you also need to find Chantal and make sure she's okay."

I was torn. Hacker was right—I couldn't do anything for Brad at that moment. I'd been trying really hard to hold it together, but if I stayed there, I might end up falling apart, and that wouldn't be any good for anyone. Someone needed to find Chantal before Andrew worked out where she was and caught up with her, and I needed to channel my energy into not thinking about the possibility that Brad might never regain consciousness.

I stood up. "Okay, but promise me you'll call the minute there's any change."

"Guaranteed."

I hugged Hacker and rushed out of the hospital, dialing Steven's number.

"Hello?" he answered.

"Steven, it's Amber Fox."

"Look, I've told you everything I know. I haven't got—"

"She's in danger," I said. "I know she took your car to try and disappear to a safe place."

He paused for a second. "How did you know?"

"I saw the CCTV camera recording from Burger Land car park."

"I was just trying to help her," he wailed down the phone. "She said if anyone found out where she was they'd kill her."

"She's at Liza's parents' house in Dorset, isn't she?"

"How did you know?"

"It's somewhere she feels safe. A place probably not many people know about."

"Yes," he said. "Please bring her back safe and well."

"That's my plan." I hung up and dialed Romeo as I walked to the Toyota.

The phone rang for a while and then his sleepy voice picked up. "Amber?"

"Sorry, did I wake you up?" I glanced at my watch. Eleven forty-five p.m.

"Who is it?" a female voice said in the background.

I wanted to feel jealous but I didn't. Romeo was getting on with his life just like he needed to. I was happy for him. My future was in a hospital bed, fighting for his life.

"It's nearly midnight," he said to me.

"I think I know where Chantal is and I need your help." I filled him in on everything I'd discovered about the Holbrook Clinic. "Chantal's hiding out at Liza's parents' house in Dorset. Can you get in touch with the local police and get them to check out the address?" I gave him Steven's vehicle details, praying that they'd find her alive and out of harm's reach. The other more chilling possibility was that Andrew and his gang had found her before she'd managed to get away. "And you need to get a warrant and do a raid on the Holbrook clinic. There could still be women there that they're keeping alive for these transplants. Hacker printed off the evidence from their patient and financial records."

I heard rustling and his voice was now alert. "Organ trafficking? That's unbelievable."

"Isn't it just? It's a massive business."

"I'll meet you at Hi-Tec in half an hour. Give me the address of Liza's parents."

I told him and hung up, then beeped my key fob to unlock the Toyota door.

That was when I had a cramping pain in my back and the whole world turned black.

CHAPTER SEVENTEEN

My brain was alert before the rest of my body. When I woke up, I knew I was lying on something cold and hard, like concrete or brick, but my eyes felt heavy, struggling to open. My throat was parched, and my whole body was weak and achy, like I'd just come down with a bumper flu bug.

When I managed to get my eyes open, a feeling of pure dread turned my stomach over.

I was lying on the floor of Marie's altar room, and I had only one thought in my head: However this was going to end, it wouldn't be pretty. Either they'd hack me up for some freakishly scary voodoo ritual like poor Adam, or they'd hack me up to harvest my organs. Both scenarios included far too much hacking for my liking.

The last thing I remembered was unlocking the car door. I suspected I'd been stun-gunned and then injected with some sort of sedative and brought here.

I lifted my head and glanced down at my spread-eagled body, which seemed to have jolted back to life at the hacking possibilities. My hands and feet were tied with thick rope to heavy metal rings embedded in the concrete floor that I hadn't noticed when Brad and I broke in.

I wiggled my fingers and toes to make sure they were still working.

Yep, there was movement.

I tried to circle my hands and feet to get the circulation going again, but the rope dug in tightly, preventing me from moving them.

I glanced around. The room was pretty much the same as when we'd been there before. Candles were burning, creating eerie shadows dancing off the walls. The door was closed, and I suspected it would be locked.

Steel door, me tied to metal rings in the floor = not much chance of escaping. I was in human-sacrificing, zombie-inducing territory now.

Oh, fuckerama!

I listened for sounds of Marie or Andrew upstairs, but the only thing I could hear was the banging of my pulse in my ears and a hissing sound.

What was that noise? A gas leak? I took a giant sniff. No, I couldn't smell gas.

That was when a humongous snake poked his head from around the back of the altar and stuck his tongue out at me, closely followed by another hiss.

Okay, now the stakes had got even higher. Steel door, me tied to metal rings in the floor, and a massive angry snake who looked like he'd overdone it on the steroids = no fucking possible chance of escaping.

I know I said I didn't mind snakes, but that was before I was stuck in a room with one that was looking at me like I was dinner.

It slithered toward me in a horrible, slithery, snakey way, tongue doing that disconcerting flicking thing in my direction.

My breath caught in a big lump in my throat.

"Nice snake," I croaked out. I know, I know, it couldn't understand me, but I figured if I spoke to it soothing tones it might not want to take a huge bite out of me, poison me slowly with its venom, and then swallow me whole (or crush me to death and swallow me whole. I wasn't really sure whether it was a constrictor or not, and I didn't particularly want to get close enough to find out). So talking to it in soothing tones was the best thing I could come up with under the circumstances. "Please tell me you've already had dinner," I cooed softly as it got closer.

If it had, the snake wasn't telling. When it was an inch from my stomach, I squeezed my eyes shut, my heartbeat doing an out-of-time tap dance.

I felt it sliding on my stomach and tensed my muscles involuntarily. Maybe that was a bad move. I was sure I'd watched a TV program once about snakes that said if they detected movement, it meant they were more likely to strike. Uh-oh, too late, I'd already moved. I was probably going to wet myself in a minute, too. What did that do to a snake?

I opened my eyes, pressing my back harder into the concrete floor, as if somehow I could get away from it. Highly unlikely since it was now slithering all over me, its head veering dangerously close to my head.

"Er...nice snakey-wakey."

The snake looked up at me, moving its head from side to side as it studied me with those beady black eyes.

While I seemed to have its attention, I thought I'd carry on. At least if it was listening to me, it wouldn't be taking a chunk out of me or squeezing me to death. "You don't want to eat me. I'm not very tasty, at all. I'd taste yuck. Definitely *not* anything like chicken. Chicken's much better for snakes. I read that in the *Snake Owner's Manual*. Have you tried a nice, juicy, plump chicken lately? I'm sure your mum sacrifices them all the time. Why not wait for one of those instead? There's not much meat on me. I'd only be a quick mouthful and then you'd be hungry again. Nice snake."

It carried on staring at me, but at least the head bobbing had stopped. Was that good or bad?

"You'd actually get indigestion and irritable bowel for weeks if you ate me." Did snakes even have bowels? Oh well, no time to think about that now. "On National Geographic channel once there was a snake that actually died from eating an antelope because it was too big." I nodded at the snake for emphasis. "Oh, yes. It actually died. Plus, I eat far too much junk food. Just think of all those preservatives and E numbers. You'd pickle your insides in seconds. So think about that before you get any ideas about scoffing me. I'd get stuck and then you'd be pickled and die. Definitely not a win-win situation for either of us, is it?"

Its tongue flicked in and out.

I was just about to carry on in more detail about why I was bad for the snake's intestinal health when I heard the heavy trap door unlock and creak open.

Andrew made his way down the stairs, a mocking smile on his face.

Okay, I take back what I said before about him being good looking. Now he just looked evil and, well, a bit manic, actually. Especially since he was wearing a top hat and a black cloak, and had paint all over his face. The white paint covered most of his face, and the black paint had been put on in circles around his eyes and on his nose and lips, just like in my dream. The whole effect made his face look like a skull. A chillingly scary skull.

He walked down the stairs and stood over me, grinning. At least, I think he was grinning. It was a bit hard to tell since he'd also painted black lines curling upwards from the corner of his lips, like the Joker in *Batman*.

"I see you've met Monty," he said.

"Monty?" I glared at him.

"Monty Python." He threw back his head and cackled.

Yeah. Hilarious. "I wouldn't try out for an audition at the Comedy Club if I were you."

He stopped laughing abruptly and narrowed his eyes. "What do you think of our ritual altar?" He swept an arm around, proudly displaying his sick little room.

"Well, the ambiance leaves something to be desired. Have you thought about getting *Changing Rooms* in to do a makeover? And, I have to ask, don't you ever watch Fashion TV? Top hats and cloaks are so un-trendy and out this season. A very bad fashion faux pas." I eyed his hat as Monty slithered off me and disappeared back toward the altar."

"You've got a big mouth, Ms. Fox, and a lot of attitude."

Like I hadn't heard that one before! "Did you ever hear the joke about the wide-mouth frog? It had a much bigger mouth than me."

He ignored me. "Your big mouth has got in the way of my business *and* my pleasure."

"Does that mean I'm off your Christmas card list? Shame," I said.

I wasn't sure which part he considered business and which was pleasure. Murdering people for voodoo rituals or murdering them for their organs. Either way, he was pretty sick in the head. And if I could put my so-called big mouth to use, maybe I could keep him talking long enough to come up with some sort of plan to get out of there.

"So, anyway," I carried on, "this wide-mouth frog is in the zoo and he goes round asking all the animals what they like to eat." I babbled away, not pausing for a breath in case he tried to shut me up. Or kill me. "He goes up to this lion and says, 'Hello, lion, I'm a wide-mouth frog and I eat flies, what do you eat?' and the lion says, 'I eat buffalo.' And then he hops off to a zebra, hoppety, hoppety hop, and—"

"Shut up!" He scowled at me.

"But I haven't got to the punch line yet. You're going to miss the good bit."

He walked toward the altar, picking candles up and placing them all around me.

"I'm allergic to candle wax. It brings me out in hives," I said. "Plus, leaving candles unattended is such a hazard, you know. Didn't you see that advert on TV by the fire department where that—"

"It won't matter if you're allergic to them. You'll be dead soon," he said, and let out a throaty chuckle.

"What are you going to do? Sacrifice me or rip out my organs?" I asked, even though I didn't really want to hear the answer.

"Both."

I took a hard swallow. Gee, lucky old me. I was going to die twice.

"So whose idea was it to start the transplant tourism business and kill those poor girls?" I asked. If I was going to die, at least I'd die knowing some answers. "Yours or one of your other cronies at the Holbrook Clinic?"

"Mine." He did the Joker grin at me as he mixed up some red, gloopy concoction in a pestle and mortar. "And it was incredibly easy, too. Those girls were so stupid. They never suspected a thing when I sent them to the clinic for their abortions. Anyway, it was their own fault. If they hadn't got themselves into trouble, they wouldn't have needed my assistance." He rubbed the paste all over my face and down my arms and legs.

I arched my body away from him as best I could, but it was no use. I wasn't going anywhere. "Yes, but your *assistance* wasn't supposed to mean killing them," I spat.

He ignored that and carried on. "And it was all going so well, too, until that reporter started asking questions."

"Liza. She has a name, you know."

"Yes, her. Of course, I had to shut her up. And then, of course, Chantal started."

"And you killed her, too?"

He stood back to admire his body paint handiwork. "Let's just say Chantal is in limbo at the moment." He gave me a smile. A big, fat, creepy smile. Think Hannibal Lecter's smile and you'd be near the mark.

Limbo? What did that mean? Had he or Marie turned her into a zombie until they were ready to use her organs? "Where is she?"

"What does it matter?" He waved a dismissive hand. "She'll be gone soon, too, just like the others." He narrowed his eyes again. "Just like you. If you hadn't started looking for them, none of this would've happened."

"Oops, so sorry about the inconvenience for you."

Marie came down the stairs then, dressed pretty much like Andrew. Same black cloak, same painty face that did nothing to hide her wrinkles, minus the top hat.

She crossed her arms and stared at me. "Did you like the doll?"

"Yeah, it was fab. I think you got the hair a bit wrong, though," I said.

She glanced at my hair. "I think not."

"Well, probably being stun-gunned doesn't do much for my curls. Has it gone frizzy?" I asked, trying to delay the inevitable.

"Shut up about your hair," Andrew said, his nostrils flaring with anger.

"But I only washed it this morning," I protested.

Marie reached into her cloak and pulled out a knife. A big, serrated, and very sharp-looking knife. Had my dream really been some kind of premonition? Even if it had, there was no way I was going to wake up and be saved this time. No one knew where I was.

I fought the urge to throw up.

"Are you ready?" she said to Andrew.

He nodded.

They both bent down either side of me. Andrew closed his eyes and threw his head back. Marie did her weird-gurgling-in-the-depths-of-her-throat thing, and her eyes rolled back into their sockets. Then she started chanting some weird gobbledygook.

Omigod! This was it. I was going to die. I heard my breathing get faster and faster. I stifled a scream, not wanting to give them the benefit of knowing I was shitting myself.

They say when you're about to die your life flashes before your eyes but that wasn't what happened. Instead, I saw my obituary, like I was reading it in the newspaper:

Amber Fox. Died much too young. Never quite managed to get in her five a day. Never flossed. Had crazy hair. Talked too much. Loved lie-ins but rarely got the chance because she was too busy catching bad guys. Worried too much about taking the plunge in her love life and never got married. Still had an overdue library book. She had no children but was survived by her faithful cat, Marmalade.

Marie raised the knife in the air above my chest, looking too similar to the Grim Reaper for my liking.

I clenched my eyes shut. I definitely didn't want to see it coming.

Holding my breath, I waited for a stabbing pain to rip into my heart.

In my mind I saw Brad lying in the hospital bed. There was no chance of us getting married and living happily ever after now. No chance of making little Amber-Brad babies. No chance of holding him again. No chance of seeing Mum and Dad and Suzy. And what about Marmalade? Would Brad still be alive to feed him? How would Marmalade cope without me? How would Brad cope? Would they miss me?

Then I heard the door burst open and I opened my eyes.

Romeo and a bunch of police officers came storming down the stairs, guns drawn. Dad brought up the rear.

I let out a gasping breath of relief.

"Put the knife down." Romeo aimed his gun at Marie.

She glanced at Andrew, then back to Romeo again, weighing up what to do.

Andrew shook his head.

"Put it down," Romeo repeated.

She scowled and threw the knife on the floor. "I never get to have any fun."

One police officer cuffed her hands behind her back and another one did the same to Andrew.

"Well, that was fun. We must do that again some time," I shouted to Marie and Andrew as the officers led them up the stairs.

Romeo and Dad rushed toward me, untying my hands and legs.

"Are you okay?" Dad's face wrinkled with concern.

"I am now."

"Did they hurt you?" Romeo asked, looking equally concerned.

"No. You got here just in time," I gasped. "How did you know where I was, anyway?"

"When we left, your mum was worried about you not eating anything so she went home to make a sandwich for you," Dad said. "I was just bringing it to the hospital when I saw something weird going on in the car park. I was driving around, trying to get a car-parking space, and I saw what I thought was a domestic going on at the other side. But by the time I finally got round there, I saw it was Andrew bundling you into his car. Then another car pulled out in front of me and slowed me down, so I lost Andrew's car when I tried to follow you. I drove around, seeing if I could spot it, and phoned Romeo to try and find out possible addresses where you could be."

"Sorry it took so long," Romeo said. "We checked out Andrew's house and the clinics, looking for the car, before we came here."

"Well, you just got here in time." I sat up and rubbed at my wrists and ankles. "There's a big snake in here somewhere." I glanced around, waiting for Monty to rear his slithery head.

Romeo nodded to one of the officers. "See if you can find the snake."

"Can you stand up?" Dad asked.

I nodded. "I think so."

I tried to stand but my legs were wobbly, so Dad and Romeo helped me to my feet.

The room swirled a little as I leaned against them for support. "If you hadn't turned up when you did, I'd be—"

"Shush." Romeo pulled my head toward him, resting it on his shoulder.

He felt warm and strong and I rested my weight on him, waiting for the room to stay still.

"I got the local police to check Liza's parents' address. There was no sign of Steven's car or Chantal."

I closed my eyes briefly, rubbing at my wrists, which were red and grazed from the tight ropes. "I think she must be at Holbrook Clinic, then. Andrew said she was in limbo, whatever that means. He must've managed to get hold of her before she made it to Dorset. We need to get a move on before they kill her."

Dad helped me up the stairs and out into the dark night toward Romeo's car.

I slid in the back seat and started shaking in an adrenaline anticlimax. "Have you got a mobile phone I can use?" I asked Dad and Romeo, pressing my hands on my legs to stop the shakes. "Andrew must've taken mine when he grabbed me."

Dad rummaged in his pocket and handed it to me in the backseat.

I dialed Hacker to find out how Brad was. What if he'd woken up and Hacker hadn't been able to get hold of me?

After a few rings, Hacker answered. There was no change. Brad still hadn't woken up.

I leaned back on the seat and rubbed my hands across my face. This would probably rank right up there as the shittiest day of my life, and it wasn't even over yet.

"Sorry to hear about Brad." Romeo's eyes caught mine in the reflection of the rearview mirror. "I hope he makes a full recovery soon."

"Thanks." I gave him a half-smile. "Did you get the warrant?"

He nodded.

I turned to the window, watching the world speed by as we raced to the Holbrook Clinic.

Would Chantal be there, and would she still be alive?

CHAPTER EIGHTEEN

———

We screeched to a stop on the paved driveway of the Holbrook Clinic. Six police cars brought up the rear, their blue flashing lights illuminating the dark sky.

We all rushed to the entrance.

The building was set on the edge of a wood. It was an impressive, ultra-modern glass building with tinted windows and doors, and looked more like a weird research facility in a sci-fi movie rather than a hospital.

It was impossible to see if anyone was inside.

Romeo tried the doors.

Locked.

He banged on them. "Police. Open up! We've got a warrant."

The other police officers stood behind us. Two of them had battering rams in their hands, ready and waiting to force the doors. Although, looking at all the toughened glass, I suspected it was going to be pretty hard to get inside. I glanced up at the security cameras over the door and gave whoever was watching a finger wave.

No one answered the door.

He banged again.

This time a security guard came rushing toward the door. "Okay, okay," I heard him shout as he fumbled with his keys. He unlocked the doors and they slid open.

"You four stay outside and make sure no one leaves the building." Romeo pointed to some of the officers, then rushed inside. "Who's in charge?" he asked the guard.

"Dr....Van Pelt," the security guard spluttered.

"Get him down here," Romeo said.

The guard hesitated.

"Now!" Romeo said, then nodded to the other officers. "Do your thing and search the premises."

The security guard got on the phone, muttered into it, then hung up, looking like he was about to have a coronary on the spot. "He's coming down."

"I'm going to see if I can find Chantal," I said to Romeo, and left him standing there, waiting for Van Pelt.

I rushed up the corridor to my right, my boots squeaking on the pristine lino floor. It was filled with rooms of ultrasound machines, X-ray equipment, MRI and CT scanners. Plenty of diagnostic equipment, but no patient beds and no sign of Chantal. What if we were too late?

I retraced my steps to the entrance. Romeo was having a heated discussion with a tall guy with white hair that stuck up on end, making him look like he could be part of the cast of a Hammer Horror movie. I ignored them and hurried down the opposite corridor.

This area had private patient beds on either side and a nurses' station in the middle.

A woman dressed in a navy-blue sister's uniform came around the station and tried to block my entrance.

"You can't come in here."

"Oops, too late, I already am." I left her standing there, agog, as I searched in all the rooms.

Some of the beds were empty. Some had male and female patients of all age ranges. Those who were awake looked pretty surprised to see me.

Still no Chantal.

We searched all the floors but there was still no trace of her, and Van Pelt had clamped his mouth tighter than the Bank of England vault.

"Where is she?" I said to Romeo when we'd finished searching the top floor.

"Maybe she's not here after all. Maybe she really did escape."

I shook my head. "No, Andrew said she was 'in limbo.' She must be here."

We rode the lift back downstairs to the reception area, my stomach sinking to my feet. She had to be here somewhere.

I glanced down at the CCTV camera screens hidden behind the reception desk. One of them was monitoring a large darkened room packed with women lying on trolleys, covered by a simple sheet. All the women had their eyes closed.

I pointed at the screen. "I didn't see that room and we've searched the whole building." I peered closer. "That's Chantal!"

I looked at Romeo. He looked at me.

"There must be a basement here that we haven't found," I said.

Romeo shook his head. "The officers have searched every inch of this building and there isn't one."

"What about an outbuilding?" I asked.

Romeo got on the radio and rounded up some officers to search the grounds.

Five minutes later, we found what we were looking for.

A locked concrete bunker-style building underground. The entrance was only barely visible because it had been covered by delivery crates.

Inside the bunker it was cool and smelled musty and damp. Chantal lay on one of the trolleys, unresponsive, doped up to the eyeballs.

I called an ambulance to take her to the emergency room. It was the first of many ambulances that night.

CHAPTER NINETEEN

―――――

When I finally got back to the hospital, Brad still hadn't woken up. What if his soul had already left his body and he was just an empty shell lying in the bed?

An unbearable ache permeated every inch of my body.

Hacker was asleep on the chair next to Brad's bed. Even if his voodoo wasn't powerful enough to heal Brad, maybe Nicole's was.

I kissed Brad's cheek and went downstairs to find out where Chantal and her parents were.

Nicole and James Langton were in Chantal's room. Nicole held on to her daughter's hand, her face crumpled. James paced the floor, much like I'd been doing hours earlier.

They looked up when I entered.

"How is she?" I asked.

"They've given her something as an antidote to all the drugs those animals have been pumping her with," Nicole said. "The doctors said she's going to be okay. It will take a little while to get out of her system, but she's going to be fine." She smiled at me. "Plus, I've done my own healing ritual on her." She pressed one hand against her chest. "I know she's going to be all right." Tears of joy filled her eyes.

James Langton pumped my hand with his. "Thank you so much for finding her. I don't know what we would've done if…" He paused. "If anything had happened to her. These people are monsters. And to think that our own nephew was involved in this." He shook his head. "It's just sick."

I nodded. "That's an understatement."

Nicole stood and embraced me. "I don't know how to thank you for bringing my baby home safe. Is there anything I can do for you in return?"

I patted her back. "Actually, there is. My fiancé is in the ICU upstairs. He's got meningitis, although I think he was actually cursed by your sister." I told her about the voodoo doll. "My friend did a voodoo healing spell for him but it doesn't seem to be working. Do you think…?"

She pulled back. "Marie is evil like the rest of them. Of course I'll help." She picked up her handbag and tilted her hand toward the door. "Show me the way."

We got into the elevator.

"Does this voodoo stuff really work?" I asked her. "Do you have to actually believe in it for it to work?"

"Voodoo is powerful magic. Sometimes there's no explanation as to why it works; it just does. It can bring you health and happiness, wealth and fortune, but"—she tapped her heart—"unless you are a good person in here, it won't help you be happy. You don't have to believe in it for it to work, although I think that you do, anyway." She smiled at me.

If ever there was a time I had to believe in it, it was now.

We walked down the ICU corridor in silence. Hacker was awake and yawning when we entered Brad's room. He sprang out of the chair, smiled at Nicole, and said something in French.

They shook hands.

"I'm honored to meet you," she said to him.

Hacker looked like a schoolboy with a crush. "You're one of the most famous voodoo priestesses of all time. It's me who's honored."

"Now, let's get started. There's no time to waste." Nicole unzipped her bag, taking out various items and placing them on the bed.

She placed two amethyst crystals either side of his head and some small stones over his heart, and emptied several drops of sweet-smelling oil into his hair. She put a bag of herbs in his hand. I could smell garlic, rosemary, and sage permeating the air.

"Tia will be so pissed off she missed Nicole doing this spell," Hacker whispered to me. "She's her new hero."

"Don't tell Tia I'm doing this. Otherwise she'll be trying to get me to do more of her spells again," I whispered back.

"Yeah, and you don't believe in all this stuff, do you?" Hacker grinned.

I elbowed him in the ribs.

Nicole sat on the bed next to Brad and took a deep breath. Her eyes rolled back in her head and she made some croaking sounds in her throat, much like Marie had done. When she opened her eyes she ran her hands above the length of Brad's body and said, "I call upon the loa and ancient spirits to restore health to this man. I empower this spell three times three. As I do will, so mote it be." She pressed her hand against his forehead to end the spell.

"How long will it take to work?" I asked as she gathered everything up and put it back in her bag.

"It shouldn't be long," Nicole said, taking my hands in hers. "Now, if you'll excuse me, I must get back to my daughter." She paused at the doorway and turned back to me. "I'll be sending your bonus check in the mail first thing."

"There's no need, Nicole. Honestly. I was just doing my job. I really can't accept your bonus check."

"I'll be deeply offended if you don't take it. Nothing can make up for you giving Chantal her life back. I'm mailing that check, whether you like it or not." She smiled and made her way back down the corridor.

I sat on the edge of the bed, taking Brad's hand in mine. I squeezed it gently.

This will work. You're going to be okay, babe.

His hand squeezed mine back.

I gasped. "He just squeezed my hand," I said to Hacker.

"Told you this stuff worked."

"Omigod!" I stared at Brad's face in disbelief as his eyelids fluttered open. My hand instinctively flew to my heart.

He glanced slowly around the room, swallowed, then focused on me.

I flung my arms around his neck and smothered his face in kisses. "How are you feeling?"

"Like I've got a million hangovers at once."

I grinned.

"What the hell happened?" he asked.
So I told him.

CHAPTER TWENTY

"Transplant tourism? Organ trafficking?" Brad repeated back to me. "I'd heard it goes on, but I had no idea how rife it was."

"Me neither. Marie, Andrew Scott, and all the staff at the Holbrook Clinic have been arrested. They won't be seeing the light of day for a long time. We rescued five girls from that place tonight, including Chantal. The police are finding evidence of hundreds of girls they've killed since the clinic opened. Andrew was handpicking girls who had no relatives to kick up a fuss and report them missing, and since the Second Chance Clinic was the only free clinic in the whole county, Andrew seemed to have an endless supply of girls to murder for their organs." I plumped Brad's pillows again. "Are you sure you're comfortable?"

He laced his fingers through mine. "I'm fine."

"I'll get a coffee and leave you two alone," Hacker said, grinning at us both. He patted Brad on the shoulder. "Glad to have you back, man. You freaked us all out there."

Brad grinned back. "Glad to be back."

Hacker slipped from the room.

"It's a good job you got to all those girls in time," Brad said. "It sounds like they had a lucky escape."

I nodded. "I can't say the same for all the other girls they murdered."

"You got to me in time, too. Who knows what might've happened if you hadn't come home when you did." Brad squeezed my hand.

"What can I say?" I grinned. "I'm an impeccable-timing kind of girl."

"You saved my life." His voice took on a more serious tone.

I rolled my eyes. "Don't be such a drama queen. It'd take more than an infection to finish you off. And now it makes us even in the lifesaving stakes."

He traced his finger down my cheek, sending an explosion of shivers shooting in all directions. "I can't wait to get you home."

Down, girl! You're in a hospital!

The young doctor entered the room, blowing a nice fantasy I was having about jumping into bed with Brad.

"How are you feeling, Mr. Beckett?" The doctor picked up Brad's chart, leafing through it and giving a pleased nod.

"I feel great," Brad said. "Better than I did before, actually."

"You've made a very sudden and remarkable recovery," the doctor said. "It's amazing, considering how ill you were when you were admitted. Normally we don't see such a massive improvement this quickly. I've never seen anything quite like it. Quite extraordinary, really."

"When can he get out of here?" I asked. "It's just that we've got a wedding to go to very soon."

A look of confusion passed over Brad's face. "Whose wedding?"

"Ours!" I said, beaming back at him.

Brad broke out into a humongous grin. "Really?" he said to me.

I nodded. "Really."

Which reminded me, I needed to get a dress, and shoes, and get my hair trimmed, and a leg wax, and—

"Congratulations," the doctor chimed in. "But we need to do some more tests to confirm the meningitis has definitely gone. If it has, I'd still like to keep you in for another few days for observation." He nodded at us. "Let me go and arrange those tests." And he disappeared out the door.

"Why wait?" Brad interlaced his fingers through mine.

"Huh?"

"The doctor said I'm going to be in here for observation for at least another few days, but I don't want to risk you changing your mind again."

I waved a dismissive hand. "I won't change my mind."

"I want to do it as soon as possible. I'm not losing you again." He pulled me onto his chest. "So what kind of wedding did you have in mind?"

I kissed his warm neck. What kind of wedding did I want? I didn't have a clue. I'd been so busy worrying about whether to actually get married I hadn't really thought about the wedding enough to have a proper idea of what I actually did want. I wasn't a floating-down-the-aisle-in-a-meringue-dress kind of girl. I didn't fancy a big all-eyes-on-me occasion. I wanted something with just my closest friends and family. And after everything that had happened in the last few days, I didn't want to wait a second longer, either.

I ran a hand through my unruly and crispy curls, thinking about it. Yep, I definitely needed to get my hair sorted. There was no way I was having lopsided hair in my wedding piccies.

"I've got a good idea," I said. "Let's fly out somewhere exotic and do it on a tropical beach!"

Brad raised his eyebrows. "I'm game. Where did you have in mind?"

"I don't know yet. Jamaica? Thailand? Somewhere hot with sandy beaches and palm trees and cocktails. Lots of cocktails."

"But what about your family? Don't you want them at the wedding?"

"Yes, we can all go. I've got a million-pound bonus check coming." I winked at him. "We can fly everyone out to see us get married. Hacker and Tia, too."

Unfortunately, Brad had no family left, but there was no way I could get married without mine being there.

"Sounds like a good plan," Brad said, and leaned forward to kiss me on the lips. "So what are you waiting for? Go home and book it now. How about next week?"

"Where am I going to get a dress from at such short notice?" I said, going into panic mode.

"Umberto Fandango?" he said.

I laughed. "Are we crazy?"

"Yes, but who cares?"

CHAPTER TWENTY-ONE

———

I had one more thing to do before I left the hospital.

Chantal was awake when I got to her room. Hell, who could sleep in a place like this with people snoring and nurses coming in every five minutes to check you were still alive? She had the color back in her cheeks and she was staring into space, fiddling with the corner of the sheet with one hand. Nicole held her other hand.

"Hi." I smiled at them.

"Hello," Nicole said and turned to Chantal. "This is Amber, the investigator I told you about."

I motioned to the edge of the bed. "Is it okay if I sit?"

"Of course." Chantal smiled a halfhearted smile back.

"How're you feeling?" I asked her.

She turned red-rimmed eyes on me. "I'm okay. Thanks to you. I don't really know how to thank you for getting me out of that place."

I felt bad for her. She'd been through a lot and it was going to take some time to get over the fact that her friend had been murdered and she'd nearly ended up inhabiting several different people's bodies. How long would it take to get over a trauma so horrific?

"How did you find out about the clinic and what Andrew was up to?" I asked.

She glanced down at the bed, a faraway look in her eyes. "Liza was my best friend. The police didn't seem to be getting anywhere with their investigation, but I just had to find out what had happened to her. One day I had the idea of trying to get into her email account to see if there was some sort of clue there. It didn't take me long to work out her password." She glanced up at me, anguish plastered all over her face, as if she'd done something wrong.

I nodded for her to continue.

"Mum, could you get me something to eat from the cafeteria, please? I'm suddenly really hungry."

Nicole stood up and retrieved her purse from her bag. "Of course, darling." She pushed away a few curls from Chantal's face. "What would you like?"

"Any kind of sandwich they have. And anything with chocolate."

"See you in a few minutes." Nicole disappeared out of the room.

"Sorry about that. I just didn't want Mum to hear some of the things. I'll tell her in my own time." Chantal paused. "Anyway, I found out Liza had sent an email to the Holbrook Clinic enquiring about their treatments and they'd sent her one back that detailed the different transplants they carried out. At first I thought maybe she was sick and needed treatment, then I realized it must've been for this big story she was working on." She took a deep breath before continuing. "So I watched the clinic for a few days and saw my cousin Andrew coming and going."

"Nicole said you'd never met him before. How did you know who he was?"

She looked embarrassed for a moment. "Just because Mum and Dad didn't get along with my aunt, didn't mean I wasn't curious about her and Andrew. They're my family, after all—part of my heritage. So I went to Marie's house once on the pretext of having a reading, just so I could see what she was really like. Mum always said she practiced bad voodoo and I wanted to see for myself. To be honest, Marie gave me the creeps, and I got a really bad feeling about her. As soon as the reading was over, I just wanted to get out of there and never come back. As I was leaving Marie's, Andrew turned up, so I recognized him as soon as I saw him at the clinic." She took a sip of water from a cup by her bed and swallowed slowly. "I thought that seeing as he was my cousin it might be easier for me to try and find out what was going on, rather than the police."

A thought popped into my head. "I forgot to ask, how's your baby?"

"What baby?"

"I found a pregnancy test in your room."

"It was a false alarm. Thank God. Everything was so complicated, what with Liza and Steven and Elliot, I couldn't have handled being pregnant as well."

"So you didn't use the pregnancy as a way to see Andrew at the Second Chance Clinic?"

She smiled for the first time. "Actually, I did. I knew they did terminations there, and even though I'd done the home pregnancy test and it was negative, I thought I'd use it as a way to get to talk to him—you know, pretending that I wanted a proper pregnancy test done to confirm it." She tucked her matted hair behind her ear. "When I was there, I noticed that there were a lot of prostitutes using the clinic. One was the same woman I'd seen coming out of the Holbrook Clinic before, and it got me thinking. Why would she be using this Holbrook Clinic when the Second Chance Clinic could've performed the termination? How could she even afford the Holbrook Clinic if she was a prostitute?"

"So you went to talk to some of the working girls at Chequer Street?

She nodded. "I found out several of them had gone missing and kind of put two and two together. I started researching transplants and found out about organ trafficking and transplant tourism, and I realized they must be luring these women to the Holbrook Clinic to have their organs harvested."

"So you wanted to make it look like you'd disappeared so you could hide out at Liza's parents' house in Dorset?"

She bit her lip. "But Andrew must've been suspicious and followed me. As soon as I got to Liza's parents' house, he managed to grab me and drug me. The next thing I knew I woke up in here." She reached out her hand and held mine. "And I have you to thank for saving my life."

"No thanks needed. I'm just glad you're safe." I smiled at her.

"Unlike Liza and all the others." She shook her head.

"I'm really sorry about Liza." I gave her hand a squeeze.

"Me too. But at least Jeff and Val will finally know what happened to her."

I nodded. "Where's Steven's car?"

"I don't know. Maybe Andrew got someone to move it so no one would find it."

"You know, if Steven had just told me what was going on from the beginning, I could've helped you sooner."

"I made him promise not to tell anyone where I'd gone or something bad would happen to me."

"He's still in love with you."

She glanced away. "I know. It's just…well, I'm not in love with him anymore."

"And what about Elliot? He's pretty loved up, too."

She shrugged. "I need to get myself back together again before I think about having a relationship."

I grinned. "Wise move. And speaking of relationships, I've got a wedding to sort out." I stood up and hugged her. "You take care now."

CHAPTER TWENTY-TWO

At six a.m. I was knocking on the door of the number one fashion designer in the world. A while ago I'd got the mob off Umberto Fandango's back and stopped them from giving him some very unflattering concrete boots, so he owed me a favor. If he couldn't sort out a gorgeous wedding dress for me, then who could?

I knocked on his door and waited, tapping my foot. His two cars were outside, so I guessed he was in. Any normal person would be snuggled up safely in bed at this ridiculous time in the morning.

Umberto answered the door with a steaming cup of coffee in hand. He wore his usual smoking jacket and I've-just-been-Tangoed spray tan. Yep, I know. Who wears smoking jackets in the twenty-first century? Still, he knew a lot more about fashion than me; maybe they were making a comeback.

"Amber, honey! Whaddaya doing here at"—he glanced at his watch—"some God-awful time in the morning." His American accent echoed in the stillness of the morning air. "Are you okay?" He pulled me toward him in a big bear hug.

"I'm fine. I need a favor, actually." I grinned.

He spread his arms wide. "Anything for you, you know that. Whaddaya need?"

"A wedding dress. And I've seen just the right one in your new collection."

"You're getting married? Congratulations! Who's the groom? Brad?" He tilted his head in question.

"Yep. We're finally going to do it."

"Well, it's about time! So, let me guess…" He stood back, examining me. "You want something subtle and understated, right?"

"Yep."

"When do you need it by?" He pulled me into the house.

"Next week."

He threw his head back and laughed. "I like a challenge!"

* * *

Three hours later, after I'd been pinned, primped, adjusted, and admired to death by Umberto, I let myself into Mum and Dad's house with my spare key.

"Amber!" Mum looked up from reading a magazine at the kitchen island. She slid off the breakfast stool. "How's Brad? We've all been waiting for news." She hugged me.

"He's great! He's made an amazing recovery and should be out in a few days. I'm pretty sure that's thanks to Nicole."

She hugged me tighter. "Oh, that's wonderful news. Do you want some breakfast? I bet you haven't eaten since yesterday, have you?" She popped some bread in the toaster without waiting for an answer and switched the kettle on.

As if on cue, my stomach gave a protest rumble. "That sounds great, thanks. Have you got the number of a decent hairdresser? I wasn't impressed with the last one I used."

"What have you done now? Have you got paint in your hair again?" She glanced back at me, narrowing her eyes at my hair.

"Nope."

"Set a building on fire? You know heat is not good for your hair."

"Nope. I did kind of set my hair on fire, though."

"Agh!" She gasped and walked over to me, examining my hair. "I thought there was something different about you. It's shorter on one side."

"Yes, that was an accident. Oh, and by the way, I'm getting married!" I squawked, which sounded a lot like a budgie on speed.

"Agh!" More gasping. She clutched her chest. "When? I need to get mine done, too."

"Next week. We're going to go somewhere romantic and exotic. We haven't decided where yet. I need to have a look at some travel companies on the internet."

"Oh." Her voice deflated and her eyebrows crinkled in a hurt expression. "So…we won't be there for your wedding?"

"Of course you will! You're coming, too. We're going to fly everyone out there. I hope your passports are in date."

Her eyebrows shot up to her hairline. "How fantastic! We renewed them last year so they're fine. Oh, this is so exciting." She delved in one of the kitchen drawers. "Suzy uses a hairdresser called Amanda who comes to the house. Where did I put Amanda's number?" She found an address book and pulled it out, dropping it on the floor in her excitement. "Butter fingers!" She picked it up and flicked through it, scrawling out a number on a piece of paper.

I took it and sniffed the air. "The toast's burning."

"Oh!" She flicked the switch on the toaster to eject the very black-looking toast. "The excitement's too much for me."

Suzy waltzed into the kitchen dressed in an immaculate black pencil skirt and fitted white blouse. "Something's burning." She wiggled her nose like Samantha from *Bewitched*.

"Amber's getting married!" Mum said to her, bursting with excitement.

"Really?" She raised a perfectly plucked eyebrow. "When?"

"Next week," I said. "We're going to go abroad and do it. And we'd like you to come, as well. We're going to fly everyone out."

"Why so soon?" She tilted her head, waiting for an opportunity to analyze me again.

"We're sick of waiting."

"You're the world's worst procrastinator and biggest commitment-phobe I've ever met, and now all of a sudden you're rushing to get married," Suzy said.

"Well, you're always moaning at me for being a commitment-phobe, so now you should be happy."

"It's because you might change your mind, isn't it?" Suzy raised a knowing eyebrow. "If you wait, you think you might change your mind."

"Stop trying your psychoanalyzing rubbish on me," I said. "Even I can't work out what's going on in my head, so there's no way you'll be able to."

"I'm just trying to help." Suzy stuck her nose in the air. "I don't want you to do something you'll regret."

"You're the one who keeps telling me to face my fears and make a decision, and now I've made one! And the only thing I'll regret is if I don't marry him as soon as I can." I resisted the urge to stick my tongue out and say, *So there!* Nothing was going to aggravate me when I was planning my wedding. I was too happy that we were both alive to be doing it. "Oh, and I'll also regret it if I have to give up chocolate forever, so as of now I'm officially a chocoholic again."

"What about a wedding dress?" Suzy asked. "Where are you going to get one so quickly?"

"I've got one from Umberto Fandango."

"I can't believe you got a Fandango dress. He's got a waiting list a mile long!" Suzy frowned. That was her normal face. I couldn't remember the last time she'd actually cracked a smile. Oh, wait, there was that one time when she was little and she pulled the legs off a cricket with a manic grin. See, I told you psychiatrists were as nutty as their patients!

Mum hugged me. "You will look beautiful." She clapped her hands together. "This is so exciting."

"Where are we all going, then, for the wedding?" Suzy asked. "I need to know what to pack."

"Somewhere hot, where you can thaw out a bit." I grinned at her and stood up to leave. "Don't worry about the breakfast, Mum. I need to go home and trawl through the internet for some travel websites. I'll give you a ring as soon as I know the details." I kissed Mum on the cheek and bumped shoulders with Suzy.

"Of course, honey. Oh, I'm so happy for you. I need to sort your dad's tux out now," she gushed.

* * *

I let myself into Brad's house, where almost twenty-four hours before I'd been so close to losing him.

Marmalade glanced up from his snoozing on the sofa, then closed his eyes again. He obviously had the hump because I'd left him alone for so long. I sat down next to him and kissed the top of his head. He stretched, his eyes half open.

"So, where should we go and get married?" I asked him, switching on my laptop to Google wedding packages abroad.

Marmalade yawned.

"You're no help."

As I waited for the laptop to connect to the internet, I thought about Brad in a tux. I'd never actually seen him wearing one, but he would look pretty damn hot. A few different role-playing scenarios sprang into my head. A James Bond scene with me as a sexy spy was coming up trumps so far. Definitely not one that had any voodoo in it, though. Or, I know, maybe I was a jewel thief with a priceless diamond concealed somewhere and Brad had to find it. With his tongue! Ooh, hold that thought!

The Google search engine sprang up on the screen.

Last chance. I could spend countless hours worrying if it was all going to work out with the man I loved, the man I'd nearly lost, or I could take a chance on love and hang on to him forever. No contest. I wasn't wasting any more time.

Let the wedding begin! Muwahahahaha!

ABOUT THE AUTHOR

Sibel Hodge is the author of bestselling romantic comedy *Fourteen Days Later*. She has eight cats and one husband. In her spare time, she's Wonder Woman! When she's not out saving the world from dastardly demons, she writes books for adults and children.

Her work has been shortlisted for the Harry Bowling Prize 2008, Highly Commended by the Yeovil Literary Prize 2009, Runner-up in the Chapter One Promotions Novel Comp 2009, and nominated Best Novel with Romantic Elements in 2010 by The Romance Reviews. Her novella Trafficked: The Diary of a Sex Slave has been listed as one of the Top 40 Books About Human Rights by Accredited Online Colleges.

To learn more about Sibel, visit her online at
www.sibelhodge.com

Enjoyed this book? Check out these other romantic mysteries
available in print now from
Gemma Halliday Publishing:

CPSIA information can be obtained at www.ICGtesting.com
Printed in the USA
LVOW08s1552111213

364878LV00001B/118/P

1989

BEFORE FRANCE
AND GERMANY

BEFORE FRANCE AND GERMANY

The Creation and Transformation
of the Merovingian World

PATRICK J. GEARY

New York   Oxford

OXFORD UNIVERSITY PRESS

1988

Oxford University Press

Oxford   New York   Toronto
Delhi   Bombay   Calcutta   Madras   Karachi
Petaling Jaya   Singapore   Hong Kong   Tokyo
Nairobi   Dar es Salaam   Cape Town
Melbourne   Auckland

and associated companies in
Beirut   Berlin   Ibadan   Nicosia

Published by Oxford University Press, Inc.,
200 Madison Avenue, New York, New York 10016

Oxford is a registered trademark of Oxford University Press

Library of Congress Cataloging-in-Publication Data
Geary, Patrick J., 1948–
Before France and Germany.
Bibliography: p.
Includes index.
1. Merovingians—History.   2. France—History—To 987.
3. Germany—History—To 843.   I. Title.
DC65.G43   1988   943'.01   87-7927
ISBN 0–19–504457–6
ISBN 0–19–504458–4 (pbk.)

2 4 6 8 10 9 7 5 3 1

Printed in the United States of America

To My Father
Walter Thomas Geary, Sr.

Preface

The Germanic world was perhaps the greatest and most enduring creation of Roman political and military genius. That this offspring came in time to replace its creator should not obscure the fact that it owed its very existence to Roman initiative, to the patient efforts of centuries of Roman emperors, generals, soldiers, landlords, slave traders, and simple merchants to mold the (to Roman eyes) chaos of barbarian reality into forms of political, social, and economic activity which they could understand and, perhaps, control. The barbarians themselves were for the most part particularly eager to participate in this process, to become "authentic" peoples, that is, to achieve structures which made sense within the seductive orbit of classical civilization. So successful was this effort that already from late antiquity it was impossible for the Goths, Burgundians, Franks, and other "peoples" who had become masters in the Western Roman Empire to understand themselves and their past apart from Roman categories of ethnography, politics, and custom, just as it was impossible for them to prosper apart from Roman traditions of agriculture and commerce or to exercise power apart from Roman traditions of politics and law. Thus did such classical ethnographers as Pliny and Tacitus present the history of the barbarian peoples in terms of Greco-Roman categories of tribes, peoples, and nations and describe their religious and social customs either as assimilable to or in contrast with values and vices of Roman society. When, in the sixth century, authors such as Cassiodorus and Gregory of Tours wrote the histories of now victorious barbarian peoples, both they and their Romanized barbarian informants used these same categories to render intelligible their past and present.

Since both the historical and ethnographic or sociological disciplines which now dominate scholarship were the direct descendants of these very traditions, it has been quite difficult for modern historians to step back and view the origins of European society apart from these same categories and structures. Only in recent decades have anthropologists and ethnographers, by focusing on the internal structures of non-Western traditional societies, begun to show how scholars can break out of the perceptual categories of the Western experience not only to understand other societies but, to some extent, the distant origins of our own. Assisting this process is the work of archaeologists, whose evidence is the only source for understanding the non-literate world of barbarian society not filtered through the language, and thus the categories, of Greco-Roman culture. As a result, our understanding of how to interpret the sparse evidence of the barbarian world of late antiquity is in a process of transformation.

However, even as one begins to reinterpret this world in light of modern ethnography and archaeology, one is constantly reminded of the deep penetration of Roman culture into this world long before Roman conquests or barbarian migrations. The Roman creation of the barbarian world was not simply a perceptual one in which the Romans processed the data of contact with barbarians through the grid of Roman values. Roman perceptions and influences, both active and passive, transformed and structured this world even while trying to understand it to an extent only recently beginning to be recognized. This process is particularly evident in the case of the Franks, whose origins and early history form the subject of this book. Their very existence as well as every phase of their history makes sense only within the context of Roman presence in northern Europe, for their genesis as a people and gradual transformation into the conquerors of much of Europe were from the start part of the Roman experience. However, this Roman experience is a far cry from the vision most people have of classical Rome. It was part of the provincial Roman world, especially that of late antiquity, a world in some ways even more alien to modern sensibilities than that of the barbarians.

The history of the barbarian kingdoms and especially that of the Franks is thus a history of the transformation of the Roman provincial world, a process which, while occasionally marked by violent episodes that continue to have reverberations through the Western consciousness, such as the sack of Rome in 410 or the defeat of the last Roman commander of Gaul in 486, is actually much more the history of a gradual and at times imperceptible amalgamation of complex traditions. Its developments are by no means always unidirectional, and the principals, Romans and barbarians, are usually indistinguishable. Rather than marked by great events, this transformation is best followed in incidental details and examples. Where we begin is in a sense arbitrary, just as where we end. We shall start with the first century and the early phase of the Roman invention of the barbarian world, and end by looking forward to 800, when at last the barbarian world feels compelled to reinvent the Roman.

Presenting Merovingian Europe

I am reminded of a particularly vicious academic dispute in the early ninth century, in the course of which Florus of Lyon accused his opponent, Bishop Amalarius of Metz, of the cardinal sin of medieval intellectual activity: originality. In a description of a synod at which the bishop was condemned he explains:

> They asked him where he had read these things. Then he, quite clearly restrained in his speech, responded that he had neither taken them from scripture nor from the teachings handed down from the universal Fathers, or even from heretics, but rather he had read them in his own heart.

The assembled fathers replied: "Here in truth is the spirit of error!"[1]

This author would certainly stand acquitted by Florus and the synod. The unfortunate constraints imposed on this book, which is intended as a first introduction to Merovingian history, are such that it contains few notes and only a brief bibliographical orientation. Those familiar with the literature on Merovingian Europe will find little here that is novel: at every point I have drawn on an enormous body of literature, largely by Continental scholars. The justification for writing is not to launch some new theory about the origins of European civilization, but to make available the vast literature on late antiquity and the early Middle Ages which has, for a variety of reasons, seldom been presented in a manner accessible to a broader audience, particularly to an English-reading one.

Merovingian specialists tend even more than other medievalists to eschew writing for anyone but themselves. Moreover, until quite recently, virtually all of this specialist writing was being done in German and, to a lesser extent, French. Thus the dominant understanding of this crucial period continues to be that formulated over fifty years ago under the twin influences of nostalgia for the high cultural tradition of antiquity and of modern nationalistic fervor fanned by the fires of French–German hostilities. To the French, the Merovingian period has too often been seen as the first time (of many) when crude and faithless Germanic hordes would invade and occupy Gaul, plunging this civilized and urbane world into three centuries of darkness. For some German scholars of the past, the Merovingians represented the triumph of new and vigorous peoples over the decadent successors of Rome. The elements of these viewpoints have been eroded bit by bit, and little now remains. However word of this demise has not reached much beyond academic circles, much less word of the new understanding of this crucial period which has taken its place. I hope to present the results of these important reappraisals and evaluations to a wider audience with little or no previous familiarity with this period of Continental history.

While I have been extremely dependent on the great scholars—Eugen Ewig, Friedrich Prinz, Karl Ferdinand Werner, Michael Wallace-Hadrill, among others—I have exercised selective judgment in interpreting, arbitrating, and selecting elements of these scholars' work. No area of Merovingian history is free of controversy, and every topic treated in this book should be accompanied by a historiographical essay and could be replaced by a series of arguments contradicting its conclusions. In some places, opposing positions have been mentioned, in other places they have been passed over because of limited space. Thus, while the individual details are overwhelmingly derivative, the synthesis itself may prove somewhat novel and certainly controversial. The best one can hope is that other specialists will be so enraged by the errors, omissions, and distortions they find herein that they will be inspired to write their own, better accounts of Europe before France and Germany.

Professor Peter Brown first urged me to write this book, and I am grateful to him for his encouragement and advice. Professors Maria Cesa, Friedrich Prinz, and Falko Daim have read portions of the manuscript and are responsible for much of value in it. My students at the University of Florida, among whom an early draft of the manuscript circulated, also provided valuable criticism. Professors Barbara Rosenwein and Edward Peters read the completed manuscript and corrected numerous errors and inconsistencies. Those that remain are the fault of no one but myself.

Gainesville, Florida   P. J. G.
August 1987

Contents

BEFORE FRANCE
AND GERMANY

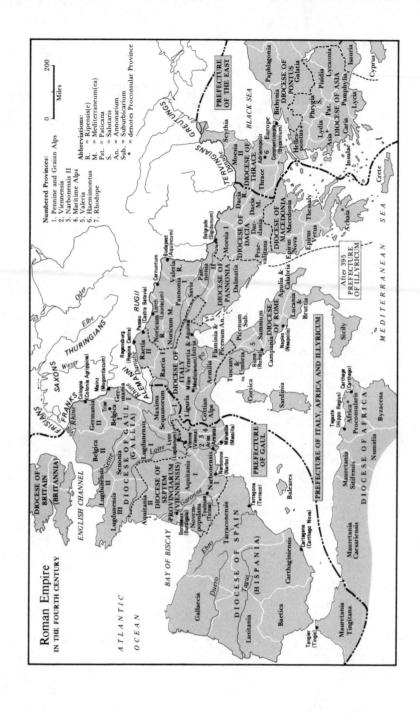

Roman Empire
IN THE FOURTH CENTURY

Numbered Provinces:
1. Pennine and Graian Alps
2. Viennensis
3. Narbonensis II
4. Maritime Alps
5. Valeria
6. Haemimontus
7. Rhodope

Abbreviations:
R. = Ripensis(e)
M. = Mediterraneum(ea)
Pat. = Paticana
S. = Salutaris
An. = Ammonarium
Sub. = Suburbicarium
* = denotes Proconsular Province

0   200
Miles

PREFECTURE OF THE EAST

DIOCESE OF PONTUS

DIOCESE OF ASIA

DIOCESE OF THRACE

DIOCESE OF MACEDONIA

After 395
PREFECTURE OF ILLYRICUM

DIOCESE OF PANNONIA

DIOCESE OF ITALY

DIOCESE OF ROME

PREFECTURE OF ITALY, AFRICA AND ILLYRICUM

DIOCESE OF AFRICA

PREFECTURE OF GAUL

DIOCESE OF GAUL (GALLIA)

DIOCESE OF BRITAIN (BRITANNIA)

DIOCESE OF SEPTEM PROVINCIARUM (VIENNENSIS)

DIOCESE OF SPAIN (HISPANIA)

MEDITERRANEAN SEA

BLACK SEA

ATLANTIC OCEAN

BAY OF BISCAY

ENGLISH CHANNEL

CHAPTER I

The Roman West at the End of the Fifth Century

Around A.D. 30, a Roman merchant named Gargilius Secundus purchased a cow from Stelus, a barbarian who lived near the present-day Dutch town of Franeker. The village lies across the Rhine, which then formed the border between the Roman province of Lower Germany and what was known by the Romans as Free Germany. Secundus was probably in the business of supplying the local military garrison, which depended on such petty merchants for fresh meat as well as leather. Roman soldiers ate well, and beef was their favorite food. Moreover, archaeological finds from other points along the Roman fortifications in northern Europe indicate that tanneries erected in the shadow of the Roman frontier fortifications were essential (if not particularly high quality) sources of shoes, tents, harness, and the like not only for the soldiers but also for the civilians who together constituted the avatar of Rome on this furthermost edge of the civilized world. The transaction, which cost the Roman 115 silver *nummi* or cents, was witnessed by two centurions from the First and Fifth Roman Legions and guaranteed by two Roman veterans, Lilus and Duerretus, who had settled after their military service near their former units.[1] The purchase of a single animal was a minor and banal commercial exchange no doubt repeated all along the Roman frontier, or *limes,* which began at the Firth of Clyde in what is now Scotland, crossed Great Britain and the Channel, and then began anew a few miles west of Franeker at the mouth of the Rhine, following that river across northern Europe through what is today Holland and Germany, then into the

Swiss Alps. There it turned east and followed the Danube along the great Pannonian plain across present-day Austria, Hungary, and Rumania to the Black Sea—a distance of over 3,000 miles.

At another Roman frontier post, more than 400 years and 1,000 miles distant from this transaction, another group of Roman merchants sought to trade with the barbarians. In the late fifth century, around the same time that the penultimate emperor in the West, Romulus Augustulus, was being forced into retirement by the Roman military commander Odoacer, merchants at Passau-Innstadt approached Severinus, a holy man with a reputation for serving both as protector of the Romans and friend of the barbarians, and asked him to request Feletheus, the king of the neighboring barbarian tribe of Rugii, to establish a market at which the Romans could trade with them. The saint's far-sighted and blunt reply must have sent a chill through the community: "The time is approaching when this city will lie abandoned just as the other fortifications further up the river already are. What need therefore is there to provide a place for trade, where there will no longer be any traders?"[2] By the end of the fifth century, the legions were gone or would soon be recalled from the old frontiers, the centuries-old commercial links that had followed them were rapidly dissolving, and the political and military power of the Empire had disappeared from all but a fraction of the West.

The contrast between these two frontier negotiations might be seen as representative of the decline and fall of the classical world. The civilized Romans of Passau were about to be overrun by Feletheus's barbarian hordes, two alien worlds on the brink of a confrontation that would end civilization in the West for almost a millennium. In fact, the realities behind this contrast were quite different. By the end of the fifth century, twenty-five generations of barbarians and Romans had so deeply affected each other that the world of Severinus of Noricum would have been incomprehensible to Gargilius Secundus, just as that of Feletheus would have bewildered Stelus. The two worlds had largely merged into one, as barbarization within the Empire transformed the Roman world while a concomitant Romanization transformed the barbarians even before they set foot inside the Roman *limes*. One need only consider that the father of Emperor Romulus Augustulus (and quite probably Severinus) had served in the entourage of Attila the Hun and that when the Rugii finally tried to attack the Roman kingdom of Italy, it was at the instigation of the Roman emperor Zeno, to realize that, in the world of late antiquity, earlier categories of civilization and barbarity no longer applied. In this final confrontation, the "barbarian" Rugii were the agents of the central, imperial power while the threat to imperial stability was posed by the "Romans" of the Italian kingdom headed by the patrician Odoacer.

To understand how this transformation took place, the first two chapters of this book will follow the principals involved in these commercial transactions, first the Roman merchants and soldiers and then the barbarian herdsmen, and examine the worlds they and their successors inhabited from the first until the end of the fifth centuries. Because two different perspectives are presented, the accounts will at times overlap and even contradict each other, since the "realities" of the time depend on the perceptions of its inhabitants. Our purpose is to sketch the general outlines of the dynamic social and cultural processes transforming Europe during these centuries. Only with this background can we begin to understand the Franks and their neighbors in the new world of the sixth through eighth centuries.

The Western Provinces

Banal as it was, the exchange near the mouth of the Rhine was nevertheless a microcosm of the relationship between Romans and barbarians all along this vast border, which served not so much to separate two worlds as to provide the structure for their interaction. Hostilities between them, not only in the first century but even in the turbulent fourth and fifth centuries, were never the most frequent form of this interaction. Much more significant than the years of war were the decades and even centuries of peace, during which time the two societies came to resemble each other more than either resembled its own past.

On the Roman side of this frontier a process of civilizing— Romanizing—had been under way for over a century and would continue for another three. Here on the fringes of the world, where, as Romans were wont to complain, the inhabitants were so primitive that they didn't even drink wine, civilizing had little to do with high culture. Instead, its agents were ordinary people like our cattle merchant and the soldiers he supplied. For such people, mostly peasants from the more settled areas of the West who hoped, after their retirement, to become prosperous farmers in the area of their military service, Roman civilization meant a sort of rough-and-ready literacy good enough for military work but only distantly related to the language taught in the schools of rhetoric; it meant the establishment of creature comforts to ease the gray northern winters, such as baths, arenas, and the like; and it meant the enjoyment of the perquisites of power, available here not only to the wealthy but even to simple soldiers, merchants, and veterans settled around the camps of their old legions.

Still, beyond these material aspects of Roman life, provincial elites in their villas, rhetoricians in the schools of Bordeaux, Lyon, Trier, and other cities, and the cadres of Roman administrators continued to cultivate much of traditional Roman values. These values included first and foremost Roman justice and law. They included a strong adherence to traditional Roman *pietas,* or subordination and dedication to family, religion, and duty. And they included a love of Latin (if not Greek) letters, which were cultivated and supported by the leisured elites of the provinces both as a way of participating in the essence of Roman civilization and, increasingly, as a way of convincing themselves that the essence of this civilization would never slip away. None of these values would ever be entirely abandoned in the western provinces of the Empire.

The conquest of this vast territory had been haphazard and the boundaries the result of Roman reversals rather than intentions. Within Gaul, divided administratively into the provinces of Gallia Narbonensis, under the control of the Roman senate, and Gallia Lugdunensis, Aquitania, and Belgica, all under the control of the emperor, Romanization spread out from administrative cities into the surrounding Celtic countryside. These cities, with their baths, monuments, and theaters, as well as their schools and temples, provided Roman administrative personnel the essential amenities of civilized life while luring the indigenous Celtic population into the Roman orbit. As elsewhere in the Roman world, these cities had their own local public life centering on the local senate or *curia,* composed of the leading men of the municipality from whose ranks magistrates, called *decurions,* were elected to fill public offices. The municipal government was directly responsible for little other than maintenance of roads and bridges, while individual curials shouldered a variety of other public services (*munera* such as the collection of taxes and fees, maintenance of post animals for the imperial post service, and the entertainment of visiting Roman magistrates).

In spite of the presence throughout Gaul of Celtic workshops producing traditional fine metalwork and textiles, as well as more recently established pottery and glass production modeled on that of Italy and the eastern areas of the Empire, the Gallic and Germanic provinces were overwhelmingly agricultural. Roman surveys and field divisions, whose marks are still visible from the air across much of southern France, formed the basis of the organization of the countryside. Cereals were the main produce in most of Gaul, although viniculture, introduced by the Romans, developed to such a point that the Emperor Domitian (reigned A.D. 81–96) attempted to limit its growth in order to protect Italian wine production. Essentially, however, Gaul posed little threat of economic competition to the rest of the Empire. Fortunes could be made here, but this was possible by production for local consumption and, increasingly, by supplying the Roman armies situated on the Germanic frontier who, from the North Sea to the Danube, looked to Gaul for men and materiel.

Each city was intimately tied to the surrounding countryside, where the leading citizens owned estates or villas. These estates, worked by slaves imported from border areas as well as by free Celtic peasants, could cover thousands of acres and formed the economic basis for the wealthy senatorial families who dominated provincial life. The local aristocracy was composed of those who had gained wealth and prominence through imperial service as well as some local Celts who had risen through civil service and the military and managed to marry into the Roman local elite. Such social mobility required the adoption of Roman religion and the acquisition of a classical education. Thus Celtic society was drawn at both ends of the spectrum into the Roman orbit—at the lower end peasants in the villages and hamlets were integrated into Roman systems of agriculture, and at the top Celtic elites sought to adopt Roman culture for their sons as a means of participating in the good life offered in the Roman world.

Throughout this Romanizing world, the Roman military presence was everywhere. After the suppression of the uprising under Vercingétorix in 52 B.C., the Gallic provinces had largely accepted and even embraced their incorporation into the Empire. However as one moved north and east toward the Rhine and Danube, the influence of the military forts, or *castra,* increased relative to that of the civilian city and villa. The provinces of Upper and Lower Germany, unlike those of Gaul, were administered directly by the military commanders stationed there, evidence of the continued threat to *Romanitas* (a broad concept that covers everything that refers to Rome) posed by the peoples across the Rhine. Here, the military was omnipresent—it was no accident that the two witnesses to the cattle purchase mentioned earlier were centurions—and this presence depended on the more settled regions of Gaul for supplies, for manufactured goods such as clothing and weapons which could not be produced locally, and for troops. The legions and settlements of veterans along the Rhine, like those along the Danube, protected Roman merchants (such as Stelus) who traded with the barbarians and secured the nascent Roman agricultural structure in the borderlands from local anti-Roman uprisings as well as from lightning raids carried out by young barbarians eager to acquire booty and glory. More significantly, the presence of the legions served to discourage the more ominous threat of large-scale, organized border violations that might threaten the settled areas of Gaul and the Danubian provinces.

During the more than five centuries of Roman presence in the West, the regions of Britain, Gaul, and Germany were marginal to Roman interests. The Empire was essentially Mediterranean and remained so throughout its existence; thus Italy, Spain, and North Africa were the Western areas most vital to it. However, the Empire's cultural, economic, and population centers were the great cities of the East: Alexandria, Antioch, Ephesus, and later Constantinople. The West boasted only one true city, although admittedly the greatest of them all—Rome. In the first centuries of its Empire, Rome could afford the luxury of maintaining the *Romanitas* of the West. Still, these regions, while supplying the legions of the *limes,* or borders, with men and arms and supporting the local senators with the *otium,* or leisured existence, necessary to lead a civilized life of letters, contributed little to either the cultural or economic life of the Empire.

In the West, the critical frontier was the northern border that followed the Danube. While only three legions were permanently stationed in Britain, and four kept watch on the Rhine, eleven were stationed along the Danube, and for good reason. The great Pannonian plain that runs from the steppes of central Asia to the Alps is one of the great invasion routes of Europe, and the Danube, which it follows, offers not a frontier so much as a water bridge to the Balkans and Italy. Thus the provinces stretching from the Alps to the Black Sea—Rhaetia, Noricum, Pannonia Superior and Inferior, Dacia, and Moesia Superior and Inferior—stood as a vital defense line across the northern half of the Empire. Well into the second half of the second century, the presence of Roman troops along the Rhône–Danube border had discouraged any such movements on the part of the tribes of "Free Germany," although sporadic attempts to test the borders in Upper Germany and Rhaetia, while easily suppressed, would bode ill should the Roman presence be reduced.

Just such a reduction occurred in the 160s, when the attention of the philosopher-emperor Marcus Aurelius (reigned A.D. 161-180) was drawn to military problems in the eastern part of the Empire. In order to pursue his war against the Parthians, the emperor moved troops from the Rhône and Danube eastward. He did not take many—probably only three legions and those from widely separated regions—but it was enough. During the Parthian war, various barbarian tribes across the Danube, under the name of the Marcomanni, began a process of consolidation and military preparation that would soon challenge the Empire.

In the next chapter we shall examine this process from the perspective of the barbarians. From the Roman perspective, the rapid change in the barbarian world was significant essentially because it produced the Marcomannian wars, which began in 166 when over 6,000 barbarians crossed the Danube and began to devastate the rich Pannonian hinterlands. This first attack was repelled, but not without difficulty, both because of the barbarians' strength and because of a plague, probably a form of smallpox, which the legions returning from the Parthian war had brought back and which was ravaging the Roman provinces. Following the restoration of order, Marcus Aurelius planned a major offensive to drive the barbarians back from the river and establish a more easily protected frontier in the mountains to the north, but the Germanic tribes moved too quickly. In 170 an enormous force of Marcomanni and Quadi crossed the Danube and fought their way across Pannonia, penetrated into Noricum, and finally reached Italy itself, raiding the cities of Aquileia and Oderzo, just north of modern Venice. The barbarians had arrived in Italy, and although Marcus Aurelius and, after him, his son Commodus eventually defeated and subdued them, the Empire would never again be the same.

The Empire from the Third to the Sixth Centuries

The political history of the late Empire is well-known and need only be briefly sketched here so that it might be referred to later in our more systematic examination of Western society during this period. The pressures of the barbarians along the Danube and the Parthians in the East accentuated the inherent instability within the Empire and ushered in a period of political and economic unrest lasting roughly ninety years (from the assassination of Commodus in 192 to the ascension of Diocletian in 284) that was referred to as the "time of troubles" or the "crisis of the third century." During this period, the military made and destroyed emperor after emperor in an attempt to find a leader capable of both enriching the army and leading it to victory against the renewed pressures from the Germanic tribes and Persians. This period of violent conflict between imperial pretenders and their armies, enormous inflation, and general insecurity, ended with the reforms of Diocletian, a soldier from Dalmatia who rose through the ranks to command the imperial bodyguard and ultimately to wear the purple.

Diocletian (reigned 284–305) was able to check the external and internal threats through successful military expeditions as well as by astute diplomacy. In order to deal more effectively with the vast Empire, he made his lieutenant, Maximian, his coruler in the West, giving him the title of Augustus. Around 292 he added two younger associates, Galerius and Constantius, to this joint rulership, giving them the title of Caesar and designating them as their successors. This division of the Empire into East and West and the establishment of the tetrarchy did not become permanent, but in the long run it pointed the way toward a division that was increasingly accentuated in politics, society, and culture over the next centuries.

Diocletian needed more than ten years to reestablish military control over the entire Empire. He also sought to reorganize its administrative and economic structures. He accomplished this by reorganizing the Empire into several prefectures for the East and the West and then further subdividing the Empire into approximately 100 provinces (roughly double the previous number), by separating the military and civil bureaucracies, and by enlarging the latter to handle the increasing load of judicial and financial affairs. We will look at the bureaucracy in more detail later.

Diocletian's efforts to reform the economy through price and wage controls and currency reform met with much less success than his administrative and military measures. The peace during his reign increased prosperity, particularly in the cities, but the accompanying increase in taxes required to finance his expanded bureaucracy and his military severely strained the resources of of the Empire.

The least successful but most notorious program undertaken by Diocletian was his persecution of the Christians. Probably at the instigation of Caesar Galerius, one of the corulers, he published edicts in 303 that ordered all copies of Scriptures to be surrendered and burnt and places of worship destroyed, forbade assemblies of Christians, depriving them of citizenship, and ordered the arrest of all bishops and clergy. The Great Persecution, pursued with more vigor in the East than the West, ultimately proved ineffectual, although its effects were long felt within the Christian community.

This Christian sect, which had originated as a reform movement within Judaism, had spread to urban centers throughout the Empire by the end of the third century. Its members, united under their bishops, followed a wide variety of occupations and lifestyles, but were united by their private and quasisecret religious rites and beliefs which stood in sharp contrast with those of their neighbors. Their radical and exclusive monotheism, their belief in an eternal afterlife of bliss for the few elect and of eternal torture for the rest of humankind, and their insistence that only those of their cult could achieve this salvation were all likely to build resentment in the rest of society. However, the firmness of their belief in their God, the effectiveness of the tales of miracles worked by Christians, and the convincing manner in which their preachers related such manifestations of power to the content of Christian beliefs helped spread Christianity throughout the urban world and attracted the interest of those most in need of power, the new elites rising during the turmoil of the third century and hoping to rise still further.

In 305 Diocletian and Maximian abdicated and were succeeded by caesars Galerius and Constantius. However, the principle of constitutional succession was disputed by the armies throughout the Empire, who viewed succession as a hereditary right. Following Constantius's death in 306, new wars broke out that lasted until 312 when, at the battle near the Melvian Bridge in the northern suburbs of Rome, Constantine defeated and killed Maxentius, the son of Maximian and his rival in the West. Later, Constantine attributed his victory to the Christian God and within a year he and his Eastern counterpart, Licinius, had granted full toleration to Christianity as well as to all other religions.

Constantine was not the sort to be content with only half an empire; by 324 he had invaded the East and at Chrysopolis he defeated Licinius and his caesar, both of whom he had executed. Shortly after this, he determined to rebuild the city of Byzantium, which lay on the Bosporus and thus commanded the strategic straits between the Mediterranean and Black seas. He gave the magnificently restored and enriched city his own name and established it as a memorial of the final victory of the Christian God. Although initially only an imperial residence such as Trier and Milan in the West and Sardica and Nicomedia in the East, it soon became the "new Rome"—the capital city of the Christian empire.

The dynasty founded by Constantine was plagued by internecine rivalry, and, after the death of Julian in 363, the dynasty founded by Valentinian, a Pannonian soldier, faced the same problems. Valentinian focused on the western half of the Empire then threatened by the Alemanni and Franks, giving the East to his brother Valens. The arrival in the Black Sea area of the Huns in 373 brought renewed pressure on Rome, and the Eastern and Western emperors came increasingly under the control of their military commanders, usually barbarians who had risen in the service of the Empire. Moreover, following Valens's defeat and death in the battle of Adrianopolis in 378 at the hands of the Goths, a decisive event which we shall consider below, his successor, Theodosius, concluded a treaty with the Goths that allowed them to settle within the Empire—an ominous precedent. Although in the East the tendency to rely on barbarian commanders and their followers was checked by a reaction against barbarian commanders around 400, the long-term military crisis and the poverty of the public treasury in the West brought about a continuous increase of the influence of these individuals and their armies. By the time that the Scirian officer and king Odoacer deposed the emperor Romulus Augustulus in 476 and ceased to recognize the pretender Nepos four years later, the office of emperor had long lost its meaning in the West, as it was almost entirely commanded by barbarian kings whose de facto positions were enhanced by Roman titles granted by the Eastern emperors. Such barbarian leaders were, in the eyes of the emperors in Constantinople, more legitimate than such "Romans" as Syagrius, who was overthrown by the Franks in 486, or his contemporary, the semimythical Ambrosius Aurelianus, whose resistance to the Saxons in Britain would give rise to the legend of King Arthur.

The Transformation of Western Society

The barbarization of the West had not begun with the Germanic settlements of the late fourth and fifth centuries or with the crises of the third century or even with the Marcomannian wars. Nor was it exclusively a process of implantation of barbarian peoples and their customs within the Empire. The West was always primarily Celtic and Germanic, and from the third through fifth centuries these indigenous traditions increasingly reasserted themselves as the Italian monopoly on politics and culture began to decline. Nor was this process unique to the West. In fact it was much more marked in the East, where Latin culture was an equally alien implant. But while in the East the renaissance of "sub-Roman" traditions meant the growth of ancient forms of high culture, the most notable being Greek, in the West it meant the reassertion of Celtic and Germanic tradition.

Barbarization was but part of the rapid changes in Roman society, culture, and government that took place during the third and fourth centuries. Partially spurred by such internal problems as plague, a falling birthrate, constitutional instability, and the failure of the Roman world to develop from a labor-intensive system based largely on slavery to a more efficient mercantile or protoindustrial system, and partially by the increased external pressures on its overextended frontiers, the Empire had to seek a new equilibrium. The result, which emerged at the end of the third and beginning of the fourth centuries, was a very different but vital world.

Just as the army had been the primary agent of Romanization throughout the Empire, from the third century it became the primary agent of barbarization. This internal transformation of the army was closely allied to the militarization of Roman society and government generally, so that at the very time that the army was increasingly a barbarian element in the Empire, it was the all-pervasive agent and model of imperial organization.

MILITARIZATION

The Roman legions protecting the frontiers had been an effective means of Romanization for a number of reasons. First, they were relatively permanent—legions often remained in specific sites for generations and even centuries. Second, since actual military activities were extremely rare even along the frontier, soldiers, largely recruited in the first centuries of empire from among the Italian peasantry, had abundant time and capital to become involved in local agriculture and manufacture. Finally, because of the usual process of granting veterans land in the area and the high rate of intermarriage of veterans and legionaries with the women of the local population, the active and retired military came to dominate local life.

Thus the presence of Roman soldiers resulted in a fundamental transformation of a region's economy and society. The needs of supplying the army and providing land to veterans was the primary agent in the organization of the countryside. Each legion owned a vast amount of land, which could be worked by soldier-farmers, granted to veterans, or sold or leased to civilians. Near the camps sprang up the inevitable civilian settlements that appear around any military post. They were called *canabae*, technically "cabarets" or wineshops, a clear indication of their main role. These rough settlements provided soldiers with drink, women, and increasingly, with workshops, hostels, and other services and diversions.

As long as the legions received regular recruits from the Romanized provincial peasantry, the reaffirmation of the Romanness of this military presence, albeit of a modest sort, was assured. However, since the time of Hadrian (reigned A.D. 117–138) recruits were assigned to legions in their native provinces. While this may have had the desired effects of increasing the number of recruits and improving their efficiency, since native recruits were defending their own homes, it also encouraged the growth of localism and particularism in religion, art, language, and increasingly, in political identity. By the fourth century, service in the military had become, like other occupations, a hereditary obligation. Thus legions and auxiliary units were largely self-perpetuating entities. The wives of veterans and soldiers (who, although theoretically prevented from marrying while on active duty prior to 197 had been establishing families for decades) were drawn largely from the local populations. Thus generations of soldier-farmers and local notables among the *limes* became increasingly tied to local, non-classical customs and traditions. Prior to the third century, however, the impact of this transformation had not been felt widely outside the frontier regions because such people had a relatively minor role in the internal life of the Empire.

Political power within the Empire had long been a juggling act in which participated the senate, the army, and of course the emperor, but all three institutions up to the death of Commodus in 192 had been largely Italian. Over half of the senators were from Italy, and the remainder were, with few exceptions, drawn from the most strongly Latinized provinces—Spain, Africa, and Gallia Narbonensis. Moreover, since they had to invest a considerable amount of their wealth in Italian land, were required to attend meetings regularly in Rome, needed permission to travel outside of Italy, and tended to intermarry extensively, senatorial families of provincial origin rapidly became Italian, just as at a lower level of society, military families were becoming provincial. This senate owed its importance to constitutional, economic, and social factors. First, the constitutional tradition obliged an emperor to select senators to command all of his legions except the one in Egypt, to govern major frontier provinces, and to command the armies. Second, while the senate possessed a strong hereditary nucleus, it was in every generation open to a certain number of candidates who, along with the old established senatorial families, controlled enormous wealth, principally in land. This was especially true in the West, where even in times of crisis the poverty of the imperial treasury often contrasted with the private wealth of individual senators. Finally, through their networks based on political dependents and landholding throughout the Roman world, the influence of senators reached into every corner of the Empire. When provoked, the senate could be a formidable opponent to even the most ambitious emperor.

Prior to the third century, the military power on which rested imperial control was still primarily found in the Praetorian Guard, that elite body of approximately 10,000 soldiers who served (and sometimes selected or eliminated) the emperor and his household. They were required to be Roman citizens, and, like the senators, were, until the end of the second century, largely drawn from Italy. Thus they too maintained the centrist Latin character of the Empire.

Not surprisingly, therefore, the emperors had all come from Italian families of senatorial rank. Whatever the differences between emperor, senate, and army—bitter, bloody, and brutal as they often were—these conflicts had been among parties that shared major cultural, social, and political values.

With the reign of Septimus Severus (193–211), the commander of the Danube army who was proclaimed emperor by his troops, began an important new phase of Roman history. The defenders of the provinces, and particularly those of the West, now came into their own as control of the Empire passed into the hands of those who had saved it—the frontier armies and their commanders. From the perspective of the old Italian senatorial aristocracy and the inhabitants of more settled and civilized areas, this was a period of disaster and crisis. A succession of provincial military commanders, often openly scornful of the senate, were raised to the purple by their armies, fought each other for hegemony, and were usually assassinated for their efforts when they proved incapable either of bringing victory against internal and external foes or of sufficiently enriching their supporters. The senate's attempts to control the selection of the emperor was constantly thwarted by the tendency of the provincial armies to view succession as hereditary, particularly when the new emperor had come from the military. However, from the perspective of those in the frontier and particularly from Pannonia, it was a golden age. The Western legions had demonstrated their strength and their vitality, and as the Severans sought to consolidate their position they looked to the personnel and the models of their border armies for support.

Initially Severus himself was willing to work with the senate of which he had been a member, but senatorial opposition led him to rely on the provincial army, which he and his successors rewarded with considerable pay increases, donatives or special bonuses, and the right to marry. The added expenses of this military largesse were financed through the liquidation of the vast wealth he confiscated from the senatorial opposition. His son, known to posterity by his military nickname Caracalla, expanded his father's promilitary policy, raising soldiers' pay by 50 percent. To finance this he resorted to two measures. First, as his father had done earlier, he debased the denarius, the silver coin used to pay the troops; within a few decades, this led to the total collapse of imperial coinage. Second, he doubled the traditional 5 percent inheritance tax paid by all Roman citizens, and, to expand the base of this tax, made all free inhabitants of the Empire Roman citizens. This latter measure acknowledged a largely de facto situation, since the distinction between citizen and foreigner no longer had much real significance. However it did strengthen the relative position of provincials in the Empire who, henceforth, from Britain to Arabia, looked upon themselves as Romans with the same rights and possibilities as Italians. These measures, like the increase of military pay, tended to strengthen the position of those peoples on the periphery of the Empire at the expense of those at the center, and those in a position to benefit most from these changes were soldiers and veterans.

This led to increasing militarization of the Empire and particularly the provinces, where civil administration had long been a pastiche of overlapping positions and jurisdictions. For the first time, not only officers but even common soldiers had considerable disposable income to enrich the *canabae* and local civilian communities along the *limes*. Areas such as Pannonia, which had hardly begun to recover from the Marcomannian wars, suddenly experienced a tremendous burst of new construction. At Aquincum, for example, the old *canabae* was given the status of *colonia,* or colonial town, and, befitting its new dignity, its old wood and mud shanties were replaced with stone houses neatly arranged along a gridwork of paved streets. These new houses boasted hypocaustic (hot air) heating systems, running water provided by an extensive city waterworks, and elegant frescoes. The city was provided with a wall and a new forum, used more for display than for business since the old one was entirely adequate. In Carnuntum, likewise elevated to a *colonia,* a similar transformation took place, including the construction of a magnificent public bath with a public columned hall of 143 x 103 m and a wall approximately eight feet high.

This construction, both public and private, was matched by a growth in the production of luxury goods and even locally made crafts, indicating that for the first time the region was sufficiently prosperous to support local artisans, even if the quality of their work seldom matched the Gallic, Rhaetian, Syrian, and Italian products they copied. All these signs of prosperity were directly related to the increased status and wealth of the military.

By improving the economic status of the frontier provinces, the military came to play a central role in even the civilian aspects of daily life. Locally, the provincial curia were increasingly dominated by officers and veterans who were able to qualify for local senates on the basis of their retirement bonuses. The physical separation of military camps and civilian settlements disappeared as the two merged, both as a result of a laxity of discipline and the necessity of protecting these settlements. Increasingly, as the free-spending days of the Severans degenerated into the anarchy of the barracks, peasants, driven by ever increasing taxation, resorted to armed robbery and even organized resistance. The only way to deal with these "brigands" was to use soldiers who kept the peace within the provinces by putting down these outlaw bands that, by the third century, had seemed to spring up everywhere. The use of soldiers as police became increasingly the norm as military commanders took on important roles in tax collection and in the administration of justice in an increasingly hostile society.

These crises, which led to an even more expanded role for the military, had ironically been caused by it. Because the Severans could never trust the senate to support them, they were forced to find ways to circumvent the role of the senate in commanding the military and to constantly augment the army salary to maintain its good will. This was financed by still more confiscations of senatorial property for real or imagined plots and by drastic devaluation of the silver coinage. This naturally further alienated the senate and brought about enormous problems in the financial stability of the Empire. Exacerbating all this was the fact that the provincial armies, having gotten a taste of their power as emperor-makers, set about it with tremendous vigor, assassinating emperors and raising others at a great rate. Between the death of Severus Alexander (235) and the ascension of Diocletian (284), there were at least twenty more or less legitimate emperors and innumerable pretenders, usurpers, and coregents. The longest reign during this period was that of a pretender, Postumus, who established himself as ruler of Gaul, Britain, Spain, and at times parts of northern Italy for nine years.

The restoration of order by Diocletian solidified the increasing role of the military. Although credited with having separated civil and military administrations, under him and his successors the civil service was reorganized along military lines, hardly a surprising development given that during the third and fourth centuries the route to high office normally meant military service. Thus many ambitious civil servants either rose primarily through the military or spent some time in it. By the beginning of the fourth century, military organization and structure, along with the soldier's cultural and political values, had become the primary model along which Roman society was ordered. But these soldiers were no longer the Italian peasants of an earlier age—increasingly they were the very barbarians they were enlisted to oppose.

BARBARIZATION

Already Marcus Aurelius had found it necessary to use slaves and barbarians to fight other barbarians and had incorporated Germanic warrior groups along the *limes* into the Roman army.

Of course, while the extent to which he did this was extraordinary, the use of barbarians in the military was not novel. While only citizens could serve in the legions and praetorian cohorts, foreigners had long been used in auxiliary units. However, in the third and fourth centuries A.D., as the increasing pressure on the frontiers from east and north and the frequent internal strife placed greater demands on military manpower than the internal resources of the Empire, reduced by plague and a falling birthrate, could meet, the ranks were increasingly filled with barbarians.

The first barbarian elements in the Roman army were recruited from neighboring tribes. Roman foreign policy sought constantly to bring the leadership of tribes along the frontiers under Roman influence by bribing them with Roman citizenship, gifts, and military and economic support in order to use them to keep their own peoples pacific and as buffers against more hostile tribes. Treaties were established with these leaders, usually providing them primarily with gold for the chiefs and grain for the masses. In return, Rome was guaranteed troops from these tribes. In the latter half of the third century this practice grew enormously, and Roman units recruited from throughout the frontiers of the Empire carried the names of barbarian peoples. In the East alone we find units of Franks, Saxons, Vandals, Goths, Sarmatians, Quadi, Chamavi, Iberians, Assyrians, and others. Normally, these barbarians were recruited, served for a period of time, and then returned to their own peoples, becoming the migrant labor force of the ancient world. For these people, the military experience was an opportunity to gain riches and learn firsthand of the Roman world. But this use of foreign troops often caused tension and strife; not infrequently pressure for recruits resulted in resistance and revolt against the Romans and their puppet leaders in the barbarian world. Partly to avoid such resistance, which was perceived to arise from the contamination of likely sources of recruits by contact with hostile tribes living in "Free Germany," some time in the third century Romans began settling groups of barbarians within the Empire.

The first barbarians to be settled in the Empire, called *laeti,* were small groups of either refugees or prisoners of war, assigned either to Roman prefects or individual landowners. They were settled with their families in depopulated regions of Gaul and Italy. These people served a twofold purpose: first, they cultivated areas that had been abandoned due to the plague, general population decline, and the flight of the free population from tax collection. Second, since they and their children were obligated to serve in the military, their communities served to produce and raise recruits for the army under the watchful eye of Rome.

A world of difference existed between these *laeti* and the free barbarian units, or *foederati,* who, from the end of the fourth century began to dominate the military, and in particular the elite mobile units, called *comitatenses,* which, beginning with Constantine around 300, were stationed not on the frontiers but within or near the major provincial cities. These units could be rapidly deployed to meet invaders at any point along the frontier or to impede their advance in case they had already broken through and thus were an important strategic innovation. However, their close proximity to Roman communities charged with feeding and equipping them accelerated the assimilation of barbarian soldier and Roman civilian.

These units of *foederati* were under the command of their own chiefs who, while often members of families that had served Rome for generations, nevertheless owed their power to their barbarian followers. Archaeological evidence from the different sorts of barbarian settlements in the Empire suggests that, while *laeti* settlements were intentionally isolated from indigenous Roman population areas and still more from Free Germans, *foederati* in the Empire not only found themselves in intimate contact with the local population, whom they tended to dominate through their military roles, but also remained in close and constant contact with the tribes across the Rhine or the Danube.

The leaders of these groups, called "imperial Germans" by scholars, rose in the fourth and fifth centuries to the highest ranks of the Roman military. This is hardly surprising when one considers the overall importance of Germanic troops and the well-established tradition of advancement through military service. As early as the reign of Constantine we hear of a certain Bonitus, a Frank who became a Roman general, and as the fourth century progressed Frankish commanders provided much of the leadership of the army in the West, becoming virtual rulers who could make and break emperors at will: Arbogast, Bauto, and Richomer were military commanders (*magistri militum*) under Gratian and Valentinian II; the latter two even served as consuls. The official oration praising Bauto, a pagan Frank from across the Rhine, on the occasion of his consulship in 385 was written by no less than the future St. Augustine, then a young rhetorician in the imperial capital of Milan.

Such Germanic-Roman commanders were anything but illiterate and uncultured barbarians. They moved in the highest and most civilized circles of the Empire, some even comfortable with such people as Bishop Ambrose of Milan and corresponding with rhetoricians such as Libanius. They were pagans, it is true, but their paganism was that of the senatorial aristocracy, as exemplified by Richomer's acquaintance with the man of letters Symmachus, rather than the religion of Free Germany. After forcing Valentinian II to commit suicide in 392, Arbogast had a rhetorician, one Eugenius, proclaimed emperor, in part because the two men shared the common values of Roman pagan culture. Arbogast and his pagan Roman puppet were defeated two years later by the Orthodox emperor Theodosius, but the Orthodox victory was due largely to the efforts of yet another group of barbarians, the Arian Visigoths, and their leader, Alaric, who, unhappy with the reward he received from Theodosius for his assistance, sacked Rome some sixteen years later. By the late fourth century, categories such as barbarian and Roman, pagan and Christian, were much more complex than is often imagined.

The last, most decisive, and most misunderstood phase of barbarian presence in the Empire was the entry of entire peoples, *gentes*, into the Empire, a process that had begun with the people whom Alaric led. The precipitating factor was the arrival in 376 of the Huns, who destroyed the relatively stable confederation of barbarian peoples living under Gothic domination around the Black Sea. These Goths, about whom we will learn more in the next chapter, had been living in close symbiotic relationship with the Empire for over a century, alternately serving in or fighting against the imperial army. The kingdom of the Greuthungi (or, later, Ostrogoths) was destroyed and their king, Ermanaric, sacrificed himself to his god in a ritual suicide. His heterogeneous people were then largely absorbed into the Hunnic confederation. The Tervingians (later called Visigoths), faced with the collapse of their kingdom and imminent starvation, abandoned their king Athanaric and under the leadership of the pro-Roman generals Fritigern and Alavivus, petitioned Emperor Valens to receive them into the Empire in return for military service. Valens, thinking to solve his military manpower problems, agreed, promising to settle them in depopulated parts of Thrace.

The effects of the incorporation of an entire people into the Empire were disastrous in both the short and the long term. Initially the Goths were divided, some being sent immediately to reinforce the eastern frontier and others being camped at Adrianopolis for the winter, while the majority were settled in Thrace, where the local Roman authorities proceeded to make a fortune by exploiting their desperate condition, forcing them to sell their own people in return for dog flesh (the going rate was one dog for one Goth). The conflicts which naturally erupted were exacerbated by the arrival of Ostrogoths, disgruntled Goths from Adrianopolis, and others who had been sold into slavery. The conflict developed into general rebellion and, when Valens attempted to crush them on 9 August 378, to everyone's surprise (including, apparently, the Goths), his army was destroyed and he and many of his high command were killed.

The Goths, joined by various other bands of barbarians, moved on toward Constantinople, but their real goal was food rather than booty, and in any case they were in no position to take a strongly fortified city. The various groups fell to fighting among themselves, and in 382 Theodosius made a formal treaty with the Visigoths, settling them along the Danube in Thrace, where they were allowed to be governed by their own chiefs and to fight under their command as *foederati*. This settlement did not last long and shortly after the defeat of Arbogast, the Visigoths, under their king Alaric, were on the move again, sacking Rome in 410 before finally being settled in southwest Gaul in 418.

This settlement of an entire people—some estimates put their number at over 20,000—provided a model for the future absorption of barbarian peoples who had either fled across the Danube and Rhine or had invaded and been checked, if not defeated. These would include the Ostrogoths, Vandals, Burgundians, Sueves (Suebi), and, later, the Lombards (Langobardi). Traditionally, resettlement has been thought to have meant directly assigning either empty land or confiscated property to the barbarians. The process by which Visigoths, Burgundians, and Ostrogoths were settled has usually been seen as an extension of *hospitalitas,* or the system by which soldiers were billeted on the civilian population and given one-third of the estates on which they were placed. Such a procedure suggests large-scale disruption of the economic and social fabric of those regions in which barbarians were settled. More recently, it has been suggested that rather than assigning real property to the barbarians, they were granted shares of the tax income from the land, thus leaving proprietors in undisturbed possession of their land.[3] The reality was probably somewhere between the two extremes and varied widely from region to region. Contemporary authors speak unambiguously about the allotment of land to the Goths and others, and systematic attempts to read all of these references as hyperbole or rhetorical license are forced. On the other hand, to judge from archaeological evidence, it appears that barbarian warriors settled in inhabited lands such as Gaul and Italy and did not usually physically occupy the lands to which they were assigned. They tended to remain in cities or at strategic points along the borders of their regions, collecting the rents or taxes from their allotted properties just as did many Roman aristocrats. Roman officers, eager to preserve at least the illusion of the imperial system, may at times have seen such arrangements in terms of taxes; the tax third traditionally collected for the central administration may have been turned over to the federated barbarians. That the barbarians receiving or the Romans paying made such a distinction between taxes and rents is not at all clear. However, it is clear that in the fourth and fifth centuries the taxation system in the Empire underwent enormous changes, which directly affected its ability to provide for public defense and maintain the social structure.

TAXATION

The maintenance of the army required enormous expenditures, which could only be met through a transformation of the means by which the state collected its income. The Roman Empire, for all of its wealth, never developed a system of borrowing against future revenues through anything resembling bonds—this would be a medieval invention. Instead, emperors sought to meet their enormously increased financial demands through a radical overhaul of the tax system—a transformation that had far-reaching implications not only on the economic but on social and political structures as well.

Traditionally, the annual income the imperial government collected from the provinces were the various sorts of *tributum,* apparently forms of direct assessments or "contributions" that the central administration authorized local *curia* to impose in order to meet their communal obligations. Just how these assessments were collected seems to have been left largely to the individual community, only the total amounts being fixed by province. Because of the prestige to be gained through the demonstration of local civic virtue, in good times these assessments were often paid almost entirely by the wealthy as part of their role as leading citizens, *curiales* or decurions, who were members of the local *curia.* Likewise, many of the public services of the Empire were based on the voluntary contributions of the rich in public offices and the labor of the poor working on roads and the like. This system was advantageous to local magnates since it placed the center of public attention on the local community in which they played the leading role. It also benefited the imperial government since it saved money and manpower by utilizing the services and wealth of local magistrates. However it was flawed by the possibility that these individuals, by their prominence, could exert influence on the imperial government to lower temporarily the assessments demanded. When this occurred, as during the reign of Marcus Aurelius, since the emperor could not borrow against future revenue, he was forced to debase the currency to meet shortfalls. However, these fixed assessments, in a period of expanding need and runaway inflation, did not begin to meet the requirements of the imperial army. Although by the fourth century, the real salary of the military and civil servants had been reduced by debasement to one-half of what they had received at the end of the second century, the increased numbers of military and civil service personnel, inequalities in collection, loss of population, and destruction caused by plundering and war left imperial finances in a serious crisis.

During the crisis of the third century, the collapse of the currency and the tremendous demands on the treasury to cover the needs of the military forced changes in this tax system. The first, instituted, under Diocletian, was the introduction of a tax, the *annona,* essentially agricultural produce which, like the assessment tax, was collected through the local government. In order to assure proper apportionment of this tax, a new system was devised in the fourth century, one based on personal rather than communal assessment. All citizens had a tax liability indicating their ability to contribute to the *annona.* This liability was calculated in a measure called the *iugum,* which was based on the amount of arable land, and the *capitatio,* which some scholars believe was a head tax while others interpret it more generally as the "tax liability" of an individual or of a piece of property. Although initially this assessment was based on the personal wealth of individual citizens, by the end of the fourth century the entire system was based on shares of land values.[4] Ultimately, the focus of Roman taxation efforts was on extracting these payments from the wealthy in the form of gold. Free tenant farmers, called *coloni* since they owned no land themselves, were obligated to cultivate specific land in order to meet their tax obligations. Gradually, their landlord was placed in the position of their tax collector and thus was granted considerable power over their persons to ensure that they generated the necessary income from the land.

Initially, this assessment was periodically updated and collection, as before, was made by the local curial magistrates. However, as population and agricultural productivity declined, as individuals secured exemptions from their personal shares of the assessment, and as the Empire's need for military financing grew ever greater, serious and extremely burdensome inequalities appeared in the system. At the same time, the assessment came to be seen as abstract units of potential tax proceeds that could be transferred from one tax roll to another.

The effects of this taxation system in the fourth and fifth centuries led to a transformation in the role of local elites in imperial government. Individual *curiales,* responsible for paying the annual assessment even when it could not be collected locally, were faced with economic ruin. Thus the prestige and importance of traditional voluntary public service declined. While some wealthy individuals, through a variety of legal and illegal tax shelters, could lessen their personal burden, the burden on those responsible for the community grew without cease. The natural effect was the destruction of the importance of the local *curia* as the center of public life and of the tradition of civic service as a mark of prestige. The burdens of *curiales* were such that it was necessary to force individuals to take these offices and to forbid them from escaping their duties by fleeing the cities. Those individuals willing or even eager to participate in tax collecting (and there were always some) clearly hoped to use their power to extort money from the population for their personal profit. As this vital local community declined in importance, the provincial administration became more directly involved in the collection of the *annona,* and the long arm of imperial revenue agents reached for the first time to individual citizens too weak to obtain the sorts of special privileges that protected the powerful. The decline of voluntary civic service, the direct result of the tax burden, led to a growth in imperial bureaucracy, which in turn increased the demand for still more tax revenue.

The Winners: An Aristocracy of Landowners

The primary beneficiaries of this transformation were the great senatorial landowners of the West, who, by virtue of their imperial connections and private military means, were virtually immune to the increasing burden of taxation. Thus the West was faced with the paradox of immensely wealthy individuals and an extremely poor treasury. It has been estimated that by the middle of the fifth century, the total annual revenues of the eastern half of the Empire were around 270,000 gold pounds, of which 45,000 pounds were for the military. At the same time, in the West the entire annual budget was approximately 20,000 gold pounds—an almost insignificant figure when one considers that a single wealthy Italian senator could easily have an annual income of 12,500 pounds. For such individuals, their devotion to *Romanitas* meant primarily fidelity to an elite cultural tradition and the preservation of the immunities and privileges of their class. Such concerns had long taken precedence over the preservation of imperial control, which was, if anything, a threat to their autonomy. To the extent that barbarians might be the means employed by Constantinople to return the wealthy few to accountability, they were to be resisted; to the extent that the barbarians and their kings might preserve the privileges of the senatorial aristocracy, they were to be welcomed. It is no wonder that by the mid-fifth century an aristocratic Gallo-Roman landowner at the court of the Burgundian king could taunt a Christian holy man who had long predicted the ruin of the Roman Empire by asking him why his predictions had not come true. The Empire as a political reality was indeed gone in Burgundy, but since his own position had not been adversely affected, he had not noticed its demise![5]

The Roman who did not know that he was no longer living in the Roman Empire was representative of a relatively new aristocracy whose origins went back at the most no further than the time of Constantine. The fourth century had been particularly prosperous for those in the West who enjoyed imperial favor. Initially, this meant the Roman and barbarian aristocrats in the court at Trier. Trier, which served as the imperial residence and place of the prefect of the Gauls until the 390s, could be described allegorically in mid-century as the equal of Rome and Constantinople. This city, celebrated by Ausonius and other Latin poets, served as a vital center for the interaction and assimilation of Roman and Germanic elites. Here many Frankish and Alemannic chieftains first entered Roman service, and from here "imperial Germans" could be returned to rule their peoples in order to assure their cooperation with Rome.

For all of its wealth and importance, Trier's significance was based almost entirely on its role as an administrative center. The city began to decline after Emperor Honorius moved his residence to Milan and then finally to Ravenna in the last years of the fourth century. The military commander Stilicho decided around 395 to move the prefecture to Arles. The families whose favor at court had brought them to power followed the emperor and the prefect south and east. The decline was further accelerated by the sacking (but not, apparently, the destruction) of the city by barbarians no less than four times between 410 and 435.

The families whose power in the West was based not only on imperial favor but also on their local resources were to be found further away from the *limes*. Particularly in the regions of the Rhône valley, Aquitaine, and along the Mediterranean coast, the great families such as the Syagrii, Pontii, Aviti, Apollinares, Magni, and others expanded their networks of intermarriage, patronage, and landholding. Here Roman civilization had put down its deepest and strongest roots, and members of these great families continued the traditions of Roman culture well beyond the demise of imperial power in the West.

The processes of local power transformation discussed above had long contributed to a growing sense of regionalism within the Empire. Already during the third century, the aristocracy in Gaul had shown its willingness to see political control pass to regional pretenders, with the result that the armies had been able to raise up a series of Gallic emperors. In fact, it was the threat of usurpers arising in these regions rather than that of barbarians from across the Rhine that had led Stilicho to move the prefecture to the lower Rhône.

The culture that most clearly defined this aristocracy was increasingly different from that of the Eastern Empire. In the East, the resurgence of Greek culture through the patina of Latin resulted in the growing importance of philosophy and, among the Christianizing elite, led to doctrinal factionalism and dispute. In the European West, the fourth and fifth centuries saw the progressive abandonment of serious Greek studies, and with them, the deemphasis of philosophy in favor of rhetoric. Education, which remained exclusively the domain of the secular schools of grammar and rhetoric, was designed to prepare young members of the elite with the common cultural background and oratorical skills necessary to direct the work of the imperial bureaucracy. This education, conducted by rhetors hired and paid by the state, was exclusively literary, that is, pagan. The Church took no role in the formal education of its members—no schools of theology existed in the West as they did, for example, in Alexandria and Antioch. Thus young aristocrats, Christian or pagan, continued to be bound together by a common cultural heritage which was the essential prerequisite to advancement in imperial service and, in a society increasingly stratified into hereditary occupations, one of the few means of social mobility outside of the military, which was, as we have seen, increasingly barbarian.

This training in the literary and rhetorical tradition of Rome was the great unifier of Roman aristocratic society. The values of Christian and pagan Romans of the fourth and early fifth centuries were virtually indistinguishable. The real gulf was between the educated elite and everyone else. It was on a basis of education, not religion or political organization, that the Roman elite separated itself form the barbarians increasingly present in their midst.

Some of the most notable aristocrats withdrew entirely into a world of almost unbelievable luxury and pleasure, with little or no role in the public domain, while others devoted their lives to literature. Symmachus, best known as a man of letters and defender of the old pagan traditions of Rome, for example, spent no more than three years of his life in public affairs. The tradition of public service had not entirely died out, however, and with the erosion in the West of central political power as well as local curial power, some members of the senatorial aristocracy moved to fill the comparable positions in the two spheres which replaced them: the barbarian courts within the Empire and the Church. The Roman at the Burgundian royal court described above was typical of those Romans who provided the necessary administrative skills for barbarian kings facing the complex tasks of settling their peoples into the world of Rome. Such advisors were an established presence in barbarian courts even before they had entered the Empire. Some of these individuals, such as Cassiodorus and Boethius, in the court of the Ostrogothic king of Italy or the Roman patricians of Burgundy, are known by name. Many other Romans, who must have run the fiscal and administrative offices of barbarian kings, were anonymous, leaving their traces in the elaboration of barbarian law codes dependent for their form and often even their content on late Roman law, and in the types of royal administraive documents and procedures derived from late Roman provincial administrative systems.

At the local level, the aristocracy also filled the power vacuum left by the disintegration of civic government through the church office of bishop. During the fourth and fifth centuries, this was much more prevalent in Gaul, where the bishops came from the highest aristocracy, than in Italy and Spain, where bishops came from important but not truly outstanding families, perhaps indicating the relative vigor of other local forms of authority in these regions compared with those north of the Pyrenees and the Alps.

By the end of the third century, the basic organization of the Church had been long established and with it the undisputed priority of the *episcopus,* or bishop. Although appointed with the consultation of the local community and consecrated by another neighboring bishop, once in place a bishop held office for life and could be deposed only by a council of neighboring bishops. He thus effectively enjoyed autocratic powers, ordaining his priests, deacons, and deaconesses, admitting new members to the community, excommunicating those whose beliefs or morals he disapproved of, and completely controlling diocesan finances. Normally his jurisdiction corresponded to the territorial jurisdiction of the secular administration. It was essentially urban, and normally each city possessed its own bishop. The bishop's authority extended in theory into the countryside, but since Christianization of rural Europe was an extremely gradual process, not complete in a formal sense before the tenth century, his focus was the city.

Of course, the actual power of the bishop prior to Constantine varied greatly, particularly in the West where the bishop commanded little respect outside of the Christian community. Imperial favor from Constantine and his successors changed this situation radically. For the first time, the position of bishop became sufficiently powerful to be part of the aristocracy's means of preserving and extending its power. Bishops were granted imperial subsidies and exemptions and were even given powers of Roman magistrates that had traditionally been reserved for provincial governors. The wealth of bishops had also been greatly increased by donations from the pious, largely from aristocratic women who, in the fourth and fifth centuries, played an enormously important but until recently little appreciated role in the growth of western Christianity. This new religion provided a rare means by which women could move out of their normally subordinate and private world and participate in the public sphere. As benefactors, pilgrims, and, increasingly, by remaining virgins dedicated to God, women could obtain a status otherwise unknown to them in the thoroughly male-dominated world of antiquity.

Still, in the fourth century the election of aristocrats to church office was exceptional. It caused a scandal when a wealthy Gallic senator, Paulinus, abandoned his career and estates to enter religious life and eventually became a bishop. It was also highly unusual for Ambrose, the son of a praetorian prefect, to allow himself to be elected bishop of even so important a see as Milan.

But in the fifth century, particularly in Gaul, aristocrats in church office became rather the rule. Bishops tended to come from the senatorial class and were selected, not from among the clergy, but usually from the ranks of those with proven records of leadership and administration. Election to episcopal office became the culmination of a career pattern or *cursus honorum* which had nothing to do with the Church. Not surprisingly, the values of these bishops reflected the values of their class and of the secular society in which they had spent their long careers. Those virtues for which these bishops are most remembered in their epitaphs and funerary orations were the worldly fame and glory that had been the traditional values of pagan Roman soci-

ety rather than religious virtues. Completely lacking in religious
or clerical backgrounds, most bishops in the West were little involved in issues of theology or spirituality.

However, the selection of such figures probably accurately reflected the needs of their communities. As local curial offices lost
their ability to deal effectively with ever more demanding imperial fiscal agents, with barbarian commanders assigned to provinces by distant Constantinople, and with local magnates often
richer and more powerful in their own right than civil authorities, local communities needed new power brokers who could offer them protection. In the East, different religious and political
values led to the rise in the social and political importance of
ascetic holy men who, living outside the secular human community, could by their very neutrality serve as patrons and arbitra-
tors. Their position as men of God gave them prestige and power
in worldly affairs. In the West, one looked rather to those who
had achieved prestige and power in this world and made them
leaders of the Church. Although holy men did appear from time
to time in the West, the Gallo-Roman episcopacy was largely
successful in ensuring that the prestige and authority of these as-
cetics was strictly subordinated to the bishop. The safest way to
do this was to develop the cult of dead holy men rather than re-
vere living ones. From at least the fifth century, the cult of martyrs and holy men in the West, firmly under episcopal control,
became the focus of popular religious enthusiasm, and episcopal
propagandists sought, in the literary productions on the lives and
miracles of the saints, to emphasize their submission to the hierarchy. Thus, without rejecting the importance of the "friends of
God," Gallo-Roman bishops were able to annex their power in
order to strengthen their own social and religious hegemony.

To such Western bishops, the most important virtue did not
come from Christian spiritual or ascetic tradition but was *pietas,*
the central virtue identified from antiquity with the patriarchial
role of the emperor, the *pater patriae,* and since Constantine
with high office in general. This essentially conservative tendency
further strengthened the power of the senatorial aristocracy, which
alone could provide such figures and from which therefore came
virtually all Gallic bishops. Sees of Gallic cities tended to be

filled for generations by individuals from certain powerful senatorial families, who used these offices to further promote family interests. Even before the last vestiges of secular Roman authority had disappeared in the West, it is proper to speak of "episcopal lordships" as one of the most enduring characteristics of the Western political landscape.[6]

Gradually, however, under the influence of such exceptional figures as Hilarius of Arles and of Eastern monastic traditions introduced into Gaul at the island monastery of Lérins off the Provençal coast, ascetic values common to Eastern Christianity began to penetrate the episcopal tradition, at least in theory if not always in practice. So closely did the office of bishop come to be identified with the Gallo-Roman aristocracy that in the fifth century, as these new values altered the Western concept of episcopal office, so too did they permeate the idea the aristocracy held of itself. Thus the aristocracy increasingly focused on the episcopacy as its central institution, and in so doing began slowly to redefine itself and its *Romanitas* in terms of Christian values.

The Losers: Everyone Else

It is no wonder, in such a context, that the position of the Gallo-Roman aristocrat at the Burgundian court had changed so little that he had not noticed the disappearance of the Roman Empire. It is also no wonder that the cause that had brought the holy man he was confronting into court was the plight of the poor. They had been the victims of imperial taxation and continued to be the victims of the senatorial aristocracy. They too may not have noticed the demise of Rome, if only because whether called tax collectors or estate managers, the agents collecting their rents varied little from regime to regime or indeed century to century. As we shall see, the sorts of taxes introduced in the fourth century continued to be collected in only slightly altered forms in the eighth.

The economy of the Empire was of course overwhelmingly based on agriculture, especially in the West. Traditionally, most of the agricultural work outside of Italy and Spain was not done by slaves but rather by free tenant farmers called *coloni*. This may have been due in part to the cost of slaves and their relative inefficiency as agricultural workers; it was certainly also because free *coloni,* unlike slaves, were liable for military service and thus it was in the Empire's interest to maintain a large pool of potential recruits.

Even when used in agricultural work, slaves were normally settled on plots of land which they worked and for which they paid rent. Often they could not be sold apart from the land. They could acquire property of their own which they could transmit to their children and often married into the lower levels of free society.

In the course of the third century, the status of free tenant farmers, or *coloni,* grew increasingly indistinguishable from that of *servi,* or serf-slaves. Under Diocletian, peasants who owned no land were registered under their landlord's name on the farms that they cultivated and were thus tied to the place where they paid their *capitatio* and *annona* taxes. Such an arrangement benefited landlords, who were thereby assured labor supplies, and the Empire, which could use landlords to enforce tax collection. By the end of the fourth century, in many regions of the Empire *coloni* were distinguishable from slaves only in that they continued to have a juridical personality, and even this was severely limited: they were bound to the land on which they were born, had no right to leave it, and had to look to the landowner as master and patron.

Free farmers who owned land did not cease to exist in the late Empire, but they became increasingly rare. Without the protection of powerful patrons or imperial favor, they were the most frequent victims of the tax collector, and literary evidence suggests that their lot was often indistinguishable from that of *coloni.*

Individuals unable to escape these taxes had few alternatives for survival. In Gaul, from the late third century one hears of periodic revolts of the Bagaudae, heterogeneous groups of provincials pushed into revolt by taxation. They posed a threat sufficiently grave to require prolonged military operations. They appear again in 417, 435–37, 442, 443, and 454. These uprisings were often massive, requiring full-scale military operations to suppress them, and in some cases they were not simply inchoate peasant violence but real separatist movements in which the leaders expelled Roman officers and landowners and set up both an army and a judicial system. In every case, however, these uprisings were doomed, they were ruthlessly suppressed by the full force of the imperial army or, as in the case of the Bagaudae in Aquitaine in the 440s, the Visigoths were sent to destroy them.

More successful than the Bagaudae were the bishops who, because of their social and political background, were able to represent and protect local communities. The late fourth-century Germanus of Auxerre, who rose to the rank of general before becoming a bishop, typified the best of these aristocratic bishop-protectors. Twice, for example, when Gaul faced an unusually high tax assessment, while some took up arms as Bagaudae, he traveled to Arles to appeal for relief. Ultimately the rebels were crushed and their leader killed; by contrast, Germanus succeeded in obtaining relief. Small wonder that he was called upon to secure tax relief by groups from as far away as Armorica (modern Brittany) and even Britain, and he willingly undertook journeys to the praetorian prefect in Arles and even the imperial court at Ravenna. Such bishops as Germanus in time inherited the role of the Bagaudae, whose memory they Christianized, making them into something akin to Christian martyrs.[7]

Another way for oppressed freemen to obtain tax relief was to place themselves under the protection (*patrocinium*) of wealthy, powerful senators or other notables who, through their military power or wealth, could exert more leverage in dealing with local curials and even imperial tax agents. This option, however, left the individual at the mercy of his patron, seldom a desirable situation.

The last and perhaps most frequent option was simply flight. Throughout late antiquity the phenomenon of abandoned lands (*agri deserti*) became common as peasants, free or not, simply fled the pressures of landlords and tax collectors, usually to become the *coloni* of other landlords under more favorable circumstances. Landlords, burdened by the tax liabilities on unworked land, abandoned it in turn. At its height, this may have included as much as 20 percent of all the arable land of the Empire. Although some of this abandonment may have resulted from the exhaustion of the soil, most was caused by the impossibility of meeting tax obligations and rents. The results of abandonment were catastrophic, since empty lands meant that tax revenues had to be made up elsewhere and increased the burden on areas still worked. Moreover, the attempts to bring such areas back into cultivation resulted in the large-scale settlement of barbarians within the Empire.

Flight from overtaxed land and submission to landlords powerful enough to protect peasants and craftsmen from public taxes resulted in increasing the privatization of the West. By the end of the fifth century, society was well on the way to becoming a two-tiered world, composed on the one hand of wealthy, autonomous aristocrats, themselves virtually public institutions, and on the other of their dependents, bound to the land and dependent economically and politically on their patrons. Within this world, neither the elite, who had managed to separate themselves culturally, socially, and politically from the institutions of the Empire, nor the masses, who had sought protection from the Empire in subordination to this elite, had anything to mourn in substituting Romanized barbarian kingdoms for a barbarized Roman Empire.

CHAPTER II

The Barbarian World to the Sixth Century

Wax tablets, such as the one on which was recorded our Germanic herdsman Stelus's transaction with the Roman merchant Gargilius Secundus, were quite likely the only written documents with which he and his barbarian contemporaries ever came into contact. Aside from the occasional use of runes, enigmatic letters carved into bits of wood or stone, usually for ritual purposes, it would be centuries before descendants of such people would use writing, and even longer before they would record their thoughts and lives in their own languages. Thus, when historians attempt to understand the barbarian world of late antiquity they must invariably turn to the written sources of their civilized neighbors, the Greeks and Romans with whom they came into contact. To do so, however, is as dangerous as it is essential, because in describing the barbarian world, ancient ethnographers and historians had their own purposes and followed their own conventions that had little to do with what might today be called descriptive ethnography. Faced with a tribal world organized along radically different principles, the classical authors sought to impose an order on what appeared to them as chaos, and the order which they chose was the received Greek ethnographic tradition within which writers since at least Herodotus had described "barbarians."

Thus, while not usually introducing intentional distortions or blatant falsehoods into the details of their descriptions, classical observers of barbarians attempted to make these alien peoples comprehensible by means of an *interpretatio romana*, that is, by placing them within their received cultural and social categories. Perhaps because of curiosity, fear, moralizing, or missionizing, authors placed their data into preconceived structures and described their subjects with an inherited vocabulary and images that responded to their needs.

This tendency to understand the barbarians not in their own terms but in those of "civilization" was particularly marked among Roman scholars who, beginning with Pliny (62–114) and Tacitus (55–116/20), drew on their own experience and that of their Greek predecessors to describe the wider world beyond the Roman *limes*. Romans were not primarily creators; they were organizers. Their greatest contributions lay in providing structure, form, and regularity to the rich chaos they inherited from the peoples they conquered. In architecture, this meant the expansion and repetition of simple forms of vaulting and arcading to enclose and organize vast amounts of space; in government they accomplished their supreme achievement, the organization and regulation of a vast multiethnic empire. When Romans turned their attention to the barbarian world, here too they undertook a task of organization, first intellectual, through a description of barbarians that imposed Roman order and values on this otherwise incomprehensible world, and then political, as their active diplomatic and military efforts as well as the lure of their culture brought the barbarians progressively into the Roman orbit.

For the civilized Roman, the further one moved from the city and its cultural and political forms, the further one moved from the world of men toward that of beasts. Man was, after all, a political animal, that is, an animal particularly suited to life in the *polis,* or city. In such authors as Tacitus this tendency is particularly marked; even while moralizing about the extent to which certain Germanic tribes had been corrupted by Roman civilization, as he gets further from the Roman world the wilder and more bestial the peoples he describes become. At the extreme are the Fenni, who have no horses and no arms; they eat grass, dress in skins, and sleep on the ground. Labor is not divided on the basis of sex, and they are even devoid of religion. They are truly on the edge of what it meant for a Roman to be human. Beyond them, Tacitus adds, "is the stuff of fables—Hellusii and Oxiones with faces and features of men, but the bodies and limbs of animals."[1]

Not surprisingly then, barbarians could, in Roman ethnography, be described with almost monotonous similarity: all barbarians resembled each other and animals more than Romans in both their virtues and in their vices. They were generally tall, blond, and foul-smelling; they lived not according to fixed, written laws but according to senseless and unpredictable customs. They were fierce and dangerous in war, but slothful, easily distracted, and quarrelsome in peace. Their faithlessness to those outside their tribe was proverbial; their love of drinking and fighting with each other the cause of their own destruction. Their language was more like animal cries than true human speech, their music and poetry rough and unmeasured. Their religion, when pagan, was a confused image of Roman religion perverted by superstition, when Christian, a crude, heretical version of the true faith.

These peoples poured out of the North, the "womb of peoples," in a seemingly inexhaustible supply, impelled by a constantly expanding population to search for new lands. In a sense, so similar were the barbarians that one could assume that all barbarians were one; there were never new peoples but rather a constant replacement of those destroyed or dispersed.

Nevertheless, Roman historians and ethnographers still struggled valiantly to classify, describe, and assign these chaotic hordes to specific places and groups—a Herculean task but exactly the sort most appealing to a Roman. Thus one finds among Roman writings extremely detailed descriptions of the various Germanic and Scythian peoples organized according to origin, language, custom, and religion. Once more, order was being brought to chaos in the best Roman tradition.

One need hardly wonder at the Roman approach to barbarians—the methods, classificatory categories, stereotypes, and purposes of this literature were intimately tied to classical culture. What is perhaps more amazing is that few Roman constructs have endured as long as their image of the barbarians in general and the Germanic peoples in particular. The heritage of classical

ethnography is twofold. First, and for our purposes most important, it continues to dominate most historical descriptions of the
Germanic tribes of late antiquity and the early Middle Ages.
Maps, based on Tacitus' *Germania* and Caesar's description of
the Germanic tribes in his *Commentaries*, are often placed at the
beginning of medieval textbooks, and valiant efforts are made to
attach the barbarian peoples of the migration period to one or
another tribe of Tacitus's day. More significantly, scholars tend
to take Tacitus's first-century description of Germanic customs as
directly applicable to the societies of Goths, Franks, Burgundians,
and others who entered the Empire in the fourth and fifth centuries, and they attempt to explain the development of social and
political institutions in the barbarian kingdoms in terms of these
earlier tribal practices, an effort analogous to taking a description of seventeenth-century New England and using it as a description of twentieth-century America. Likewise, they tend to
accept classical characterizations of barbarian mores, character,
and general "barbarism" as explanations for the process of conquest and settlement in the early Middle Ages.

Second, and more pernicious, these classical descriptions have
deeply influenced the way that modern Germany is viewed by
much of Europe and America. In the nineteenth century, fantasies of primitive communistic societies and quasireligious devotion to freedom among the early Germanic peoples influenced
much early social science speculation. In the 1930s National So-
cialist ideologues attempted to connect the establishment of the
Third Reich with the tribes of Tacitus's *Germania,* seeing the
history of the migration period as an integral part of the history
of the "German nation and people." While this attempt to ex-
ploit a mythic German past for modern propaganda purposes
has been overwhelmingly rejected in the aftermath of World
War II, those with whom the European wars of the past century
have left a residue of suspicion and hostility toward Germany
and Germans still often see in the ancient negative judgments on
Germanic fierceness, sloth, quarrelsomeness, drinking, and faithlessness, explanations for much of recent German history.

Both of these regrettable tendencies must be rejected. Classical
sources must be interpreted with great care in light of the pre-

occupations and traditions of classical ethnography and viewed keeping in mind the data collected by archaeologists. Scholars should be very careful to use the precious information provided by these authors while aware of the system within which Roman and Greek observers attempted to structure it. Moreover, for better or worse, the history of the barbarian world must be seen, not in context of "German history" in any modern sense but rather in terms of the history of late antiquity. As such, it belongs no more to the history of modern Germany than it does to that of France, Italy, or, for that matter, the United States.

Premigration Barbarian Society

If we attempt to reconstruct the world of our Germanic cattleman Stelus from the perspective of the material, physical evidence of archaeology rather than from Roman authors, we find ourselves on very unfamiliar and disorienting terrain. First, not only do we find no physical evidence of the myriad tribal divisions within the Germanic peoples, but we even have great difficulty talking about sharp divisions separating them from Celts and Slavs. The peoples referred to collectively as the "Germani" by classical authors included a complex mixture of peoples, some of whom no doubt spoke languages that belonged to the general Indo-European language group known as Germanic, but others were Slavs, Celts, and Finns constantly absorbed and reconstituted into new social groups. Since linguistic data does not exist from the earliest period of "Germanic" civilization, it is safer to talk from an archaeological perspective. According to this, Germanic society originated with Iron Age peoples who arose in the northern parts of central Europe and the southern regions of Scandinavia from the sixth century B.C. The earliest phases of this society, known as "Jastorfkultur," is contemporary with and often indistinguishable from the early Iron Age Hallstatt and Latène cultures further south and west. Its primary distinguishing characteristics, for our purposes, are its emphasis on cattle raising and its mastery of iron, the former uniting it with and the latter in some ways separating it from neighboring Celtic and Slavic societies.

GERMANIC CULTURE

Because Germanic settlements varied in size and form depending on the climate and topography of the region, generalizing
about them is difficult. Usually, except along the sea coast, they
were established on the edges of extensively cultivated natural
clearings. The Germanic tribesmen settled along the coast of the
North Sea between the Rhine and the Oder rivers inhabited
fairly large timber houses supported by four rows of posts that
divided the dwelling into three parallel rooms. These rooms were
used not only for the family but also housed its precious cattle,
whose body heat helped warm the family in winter. In this most
typical form of Germanic building, humans occupied a large
room separated from the remainder of the building by an inte-
rior wall with a doorway. Beyond this door lay a double row of
animal stalls separated by a central corridor. The number of
animals that could be accommodated varied considerably—some
houses could hold no more than twelve while others could contain thirty or more.[2]

More inland, in the area of modern Westphalia and in the
area between the Elbe and Saale rivers, Germanic peoples inhabited a different sort of house. Here, as for example in a village
excavated at Harth bei Zwenkau (near modern Leipzig), the traditional dwelling was a sort of small, rectangular building already well known in the Bronze Age. These dwellings were also
supported by upright posts but did not have internal support
posts and were usually between five and seven meters long and
only three to four meters wide. Alongside these houses were constructed a variety of buildings, including large houses with two
rooms that might be as much as sixty square meters in area, long
narrow houses with twenty-five square meters of floor space,
and smaller, almost square buildings of about twelve square meters in area that apparently served for storage and as stalls for
animals. Finally, some Germanic communities in the Elbe-Oder
region, as, for example, at Zedau near Osterburg, constructed
small "dug-outs," buildings partially underground and usually
about twelve meters square, which probably served chiefly for
storage.

Whatever the form of the dwellings, they tended to be grouped in small villages that supported themselves from a combination of farming and animal husbandry, supplemented where possible by fishing. At one site near modern Leipzig, for example, a village consisted of two of the larger houses described above and six smaller houses and their outbuildings.

The most important crop was barley, followed by wheat and oats. Beans and peas were also cultivated fairly extensively. Flax, raised more for oil than for linen, which was not widely used for clothing, was grown in coastal regions. The fields in which these crops were raised were organized into series of individual plots of roughly rectangular shape which varied greatly in size. Their organization and arrangement suggests that crop rotation was practiced to allow the soil to recover from intense cultivation. Fields were also improved by adding limestone and sometimes manure to the soil in long-farmed areas, although depleted soil was occasionally abandoned for new land brought into cultivation through slash-and-burn techniques.

Tilling these fields was performed in two manners, both apparently dating from the Bronze Age. Most fields were cultivated by using a fairly simple scratch plow. This simple wooden implement consisted essentially of a plowshare or coulter which cut into the ground and a handle to guide it as it was pulled by oxen. It had no moldboard to turn and thus aerate the soil and therefore had to be drawn across the field twice at right angles to prepare the soil properly.

In addition to these fairly light plows, some fields were cultivated with a heavier plow which was capable of turning and thus aerating the dense clay soil of northern Europe. Although such implements have not survived (hardly surprising since they were made of wood with only a bit of iron for the coulter), careful examination of the layers of topsoil and undersoil in some Celtic and Germanic fields indicates that the soil was in fact turned over in a way that strongly suggests the use of such an implement.

Grain was harvested with a sickle, in some sense a step backward from the use of both sickles and scythes in the Celtic world, although the iron sickles of the Germanic cultivators may have been more effective than the bronze and flint tools of the Celts. The grain, left attached to the hay, was often roasted slightly to preserve it from spoilage and then stored in raised granaries made of wood and sealed with earth. When the grain was needed, it was separated from the hay and threshed. The kernels were ground using a simple hand grindstone of the sort in use for millennia. Progressively, around the time of Stelus, under the influence of neighboring Celts and Romans, some Germanic tribes between the Elbe and Rhine began to use more sophisticated and efficient turning grindstones. Once ground, the flour was mixed into a sort of porridge or made into dough that was baked on clay trays into flat cakes. A significant portion of the grain was also fermented into a strong, thick beer which was both an important source of nourishment and a major element in social interaction.

Cereal cultivation was essential for Germanic society, and Pliny in his *Natural History* correctly described the product thus obtained as the basic element of Germanic diet.[3] But farming had no social prestige, and the preservation, grinding, and preparing of cereals was left to women—a clear indication of the low status accorded it in this male-dominated society. The agricultural occupation that most interested Germanic males, especially in the relatively open coastal areas, was animal husbandry, in particular cattle raising. Julius Caesar had noted that "the Germans place no importance on cultivation, their nourishment comes for the most part from milk, cheese, and meat."[4] Undoubtedly he was incorrect in terms of nutritional reality, but he accurately reflected the cultural self-perception of the Germanic peoples. The number of cattle that one possessed determined social prestige and was the most significant material mark of wealth and status. Cattle were so much the quintessential indicator of wealth in traditional society that the modern English term "fee," which developed from the medieval term "fief," had its origin in the Germanic term *fihu* (modern German: *Vieh*), meaning cattle, chattels, and hence, in general, wealth. (The Latinate terms cattle, chattel, and capital underwent a similar and related development in late antiquity from the late Latin *captale*, meaning property in general or, more specifically, livestock.)

In addition to cattle raising, Stelus's contemporaries also raised, in descending order of importance, domestic pigs, sheep, goats, and horses as well as recently introduced chickens and geese. In spite of the image of Germanic society as constantly engaged in hunting, domestic animals accounted for virtually all of the meat in their diet. In no archaeological site that has been investigated do wild animal bones account for more than 8 percent of all animal remains found, while the average percentage of domesticated animal traces is closer to 97 percent. The most significant game animals were deer and wild boar. Wild cattle, the European bison, and the auroch were probably hunted for hides and horn as well as for meat. However, the almost insignificant percentage of bones from such animals found in village sites could be attributed to hunting for sport (actually practice for war) or the elimination of nuisance animals that competed with livestock for food instead of hunting specifically intended to supplement diet.

Given the importance of cattle raising, it should come as no surprise that the early Germanic peoples were quite systematic in the management of their herds. Like others, Stelus probably slaughtered, traded, or sold approximately 50 percent of his cattle before they reached the age of three-and-a-half years. These formed the expendable increase in the herd, which thus remained relatively constant in size. He kept the remainder of the herd for about ten years, during which time they served as breeding stock and provided milk. After that age, since they were less productive, they would be slaughtered, traded, or sold to the Romans.

Because they were foraging animals, hogs were particularly suited to more forested areas of Europe, and as one moves away from the coastal plains, the percentage of hogs raised increases while that of cattle decreases. They too were the object of systematic triage and management. About 22 percent were slaughtered in their first year, 28 percent in their second, and 35 percent in their third, when they had reached an average weight of 110 pounds.

Every portion of the animals was used either for food or for the production of clothing, shelter, and utensils. Meat was eaten raw, roasted, baked, or boiled. It could be preserved by smoking, drying, or, when supplies of salt were available, by salting. Milk

was consumed fresh or curded for storage. Butter was both consumed and, in rancid form, used as seasoning, medicine, and as
a hair dressing—a practice noted with disgust by Romans (who
preferred to grease themselves with olive oil).

Crafts

In contrast to the Celts, Germanic peoples of the first centuries
produced fairly crude ceramic bowls and utensils. Clay, almost
universally available, was worked by hand, without the assistance of a wheel, to make such simple objects as pots, vessels of
various kinds, ladles, and spinning weights. Such objects were
ornamented with fairly simple geometric designs either incised
or pressed on the objects with a rolling stamp that repeated a
pattern as it was moved across the damp clay. Although kilns
had long been known to the Celts, Germanic ceramic ware was
apparently fired in open wood fires. Such utensils, practical rather
than ornamental or status-signifying, were apparently, like cereal
production, the work of women.

Women too were responsible for weaving, spinning, and the
production of textiles, about which a great deal is known due to
the excellent state of preservation of clothing on bodies found
remarkably preserved in the anaerobic environments of the bogs
of the Weser-Ems region, Schleswig-Holstein, Jütland, and the
Danish islands. Some of these so-called "bog corpses" had simple
burials, but others were often apparently the victims of execu-
tions or ritual sacrifices. The bodies wore clothing made of hand-
spun wool woven on small looms. The wide variety of patterns
and styles of clothing apparently differentiated social status and
possibly communities. The people near the mouth of the Rhine
were particularly known for their fine woolens, which were even
popular within the Roman Empire.

In general, women wore long, sleeveless garments fastened at
the shoulders by *fibulae,* or brooches. The lower portion of the
dress was often pleated and rather full and was secured by a belt.
In addition, they wore blouses, undergarments, and a necker-
chief. Young girls often wore a sort of short woolen skirt and
possibly a short fur wrap.

Men wore woolen trousers, smocks, and cloaks as well as fur

wraps. Some trousers were full length and even had feet; others reached only to the knee and were followed by leg bindings. A smock was worn over the trousers and held fast by a belt. The cloak was a large rectangular piece of wool, decorated and fastened at the shoulder by a fibula. Leather shoes and caps, and, in winter, a fur cloak, completed the costume.

Clothing, along with hair and beard styles, was an important indicator of social identity. However its production did not enjoy high status in the society. The most important and sophisticated craft of the Germanic peoples of antiquity was iron-working. In the last century B.C. and the first century A.D., the production of iron increased dramatically in the Germanic world. The essential raw materials were near at hand: low-grade iron ore lay on or near the surface of the earth across much of northern Europe, and the great forests provided wood for charcoal production. Virtually every village or settlement had its own production center and specialists capable of producing iron implements and decorations. These men (for, like cattle raising, iron production was a male activity) built small, crude, but effective furnaces of earth in which they melted the ore on charcoal fires which, with the help of a bellows, could reach the necessary temperatures of 1,300 to 1,600° Celsius. The ovens could contain only about one liter of ore and were capable of producing, from the best available ore, at the most 150 to 250 grams of iron at a time. The entire process was time-consuming and required considerable resources and skill. It involved no less than eight separate steps, three demanding different, carefully controlled temperatures. Nevertheless, in spite of the small amount of iron produced when compared with the more massive techniques known in the civilized world at the time, the quality of iron was extremely high. In the hands of an experienced and skillful smith, this iron could be hammered, folded, reworked, and made into exceptionally high-quality steel. The finest products of these smiths, sword blades with cores of softer steel for flexibility and harder exteriors to hold their edge, were magnificent examples of the armorers' craft, far superior to the equipment of Roman troops.

However, while excellent objects could be produced, the overall amount of such objects was highly limited; the Germanic world remained iron-poor well into the Middle Ages, especially in weapons. Objects requiring large amounts of steel, such as long swords, were extremely rare, as were the long broad-headed lances that later were characteristic Germanic weapons. More common were iron arrow points and shorter, one-edged swords. Iron was also used as a central boss on their shields. The most frequent use of iron was in making tools for working wood, which remained the primary material for the tools of daily life, and for making small iron decorative objects. Quality depended on individual smiths, and most of what was produced was probably mediocre.

The agricultural and craft occupations of the Germanic peoples were primarily directed at a subsistence-level economy, not for trade purposes. Goods circulated within the Germanic world and between the Germanic world and beyond, but this circulation was not primarily through commerce. Among individuals and groups, pacific exchanges took the form primarily of gifts which, although they may have appeared voluntary, were in fact obligatory and normative. Gift-giving was a means of acquiring prestige and power—the real gain in an exchange accrued not to the receiver but to the giver, who thereby showed his superiority and placed the receiver in his debt.

An even greater source of prestige was the circulation of goods and chattel through raiding and warfare. This, more than anything else, characterized Germanic society and defined an individual's status. Raiding was carried on between tribes and between feuding clans within tribes, and booty consisted primarily of cattle and slaves. Germanic society found its purpose, its value, its identity in warfare, and both its economy and its society were structured to this end.

Society

The various groups we have just described never thought of themselves as one "people" who could be assigned a collective name. The term "German" was imposed by the Greeks; the modern *Deutsch* means simply "the people" and developed in the late ninth century. Nevertheless, scholars have long at-

tempted to describe "the Germans" as a whole as well as to sub-
divide them according to some objective criteria. The first such
modern attempts, based exclusively on linguistic evidence from
a later, postmigration period, divided the Germanic world into
North Germanic peoples, including the inhabitants of Scandinavia; East Germanic peoples, including the Goths, Burgundians, Vandals; and West Germanic peoples, including, among
others, the Franks, Saxons, Bavarians, and Alemanni. Whatever
the merits of such a division for linguists of postmigration Germanic languages (and in fact even here there is considerable
dispute), this schema does little to help us understand the differences among the Germanic peoples of the first and second
centuries. More useful distinctions have been made on the sorts
of material differences described above and compared with later
linguistic evidence. These suggest that a more useful way of distinguishing significant differences is to divide the Germanic peoples into the Elbe Germanic tribes, that is, those peoples who
lived between the Elbe and Oder rivers; the Rhine-Weser Germanic tribes, those living along these two rivers closer to the
Roman *limes*; and the North Sea Germanic tribes, who lived
along the coast. These groupings seem to reflect certain cultural
and religious affiliations that occasionally manifested themselves
in the formation of fairly wide confederations of peoples within
these groups for specific purposes. However, these groups should
not be thought of as social, ethnic, or political entities. The actual structure of Germanic society was far too fluid and complex
for that.

The physical remains of Germanic settlements provide important evidence concerning the social structure of these peoples. As we have seen, they tended to live in small villages. In
spite of attempts to see theirs as a primitive form of communism
and equality, already in the first century B.C., Germanic communities display a wide variation in wealth and status, as well
as important indications of what might be called a remarkably
homogeneous aristocracy.

The largest class in Germanic communities was that of free
men whose social status was largely determined by the number
of cattle they possessed and whose freedom was confirmed in

their participation in warfare. Within a village, the number of cattle an individual owned could vary greatly, indicating considerable differentiation in wealth. In one village excavated near Wesermünde, West Germany, for example, one finds some houses with stalls for only twelve cows while others could have accommodated as many as thirty-two. In other villages, the arrangement of small buildings around quite large, substantial ones suggests that at least some individuals in the society probably had dependents who were housed in outbuildings around the leader's home.

Slaves, usually prisoners of war, also formed a part of Germanic society. They were normally settled in individual households and were required to provide certain amounts of foodstuff, cattle, and textiles to their masters, although they might also be used as herdsmen or house slaves.

Germanic society was unambiguously patriarchial, and individual kindreds were organized under a male leader. The individual household was dominated by the father, who held authority over all members—his wife or occasionally wives, children, and slaves. Germanic peoples practiced resource polygyny, that is, those wealthy enough to do so might have two or more wives; others had only one.

The household was integrated into the larger kindred known as the Sip (German: *Sippe*), or clan. This wider circle of kin, whose size and composition is extremely difficult for historians to determine, probably did not extend beyond fifty households and seems to have included not only agnatic (paternally related) but cognatic (based on bilateral descent) groups. The primary unifying principles of the clan seem to have been, internally, the shared perception of relationships reinforced by a special "peace" that made violent conflict within the clan a crime for which no compensation or atonement could be made, an incest taboo, and possibly some rights to property. Externally, the most powerful uniting principle was the obligation to participate in interkindred feuds on behalf of one's kin and thus to be liable for the actions of one's kindred. Such feuds seem more than anything else to have constituted and defined the extent of kinship.

The kindred, although fundamental, was also essentially unstable and was in a constant process of division and transformation. Largely defined by the obligation of peace within and war without, every breach of the peace could lead to the foundation of a new clan, as could every failure to accept the obligation of mutual help. Likewise, since these groups were bilateral, important marriages might well result in the absorption of smaller, less successful clans into larger ones. This same instability was present to an even greater degree in the larger social unit, the tribe.

The Germanic tribe, more than any other Germanic institution, has been the victim of an uncritical acceptance of Greco-Roman ideas concerning tribes inherited from both the Romans' own early traditions of tribal origins and from Greek ethnography. The tribe was a constantly changing grouping of people bound together by shared perceptions, traditions, and institutions. As these commonalities changed, tribes changed; they expanded to absorb other groups, they split apart to form new tribes, they disappeared into more powerful tribes. Thus, throughout the tribal history of the Germanic peoples, these groups were more processes than stable structures, and ethnogenesis, or tribal formation, was constant, although certain historical moments saw this process accelerated.

According to Tacitus, the Germanic peoples believed that they were descended from the god Tuisto, whose son Mannus was the ancestor of them all. This belief in common ancestry is shown in the names for the tribe: *Stamm* in modern German, *Theoda* in Old High German, *ethne* in Greek, and *gens* in Latin, all terms derived from words implying kinship and thus emphasizing the fiction of a shared biological, genealogical origin from some common ancestor. The belief in this common mythical ancestor and hence in the equally mythic purity of blood was an important constituent of tribal identity and the foundation of other important characteristics of the tribe. In this sense, the tribe was but a large clan or family, sharing common values and a common "peace" which made cooperation appropriate.

In addition to being unified in their belief in a common ori-

gin, tribes shared cultural traditions. Although traditionally
scholars have emphasized common language as first among these
cultural traditions, it is not at all clear that language was so
important to early tribes. The central cultural characteristics
seemed to have been clothing, styles of hair, ornamentation,
types of weapons, material culture, religious cult, and a shared
oral history. All of these served not only to distinguish one tribe
from another, but also to clarify the social distinctions within
a tribe.

Shared common ancestry myths and cultural traditions formed
the basis for a community of law and particularly of peace. Essential to the survival of the tribe was a shared peace or sense
of nonaggression that made cooperative efforts possible. This
peace was preserved and embodied in tribal "law," that is, the
customary way by which clans interacted with each other and
handled disputes. Our word "friend" is closely related to the
German word *Frieden,* peace. Tribal members were friends;
they shared a peace or pact of traditional "law." However, unlike the peace within the clan, this peace was not deemed to
have been destroyed by violent dispute; in fact revenge and
feuding were the normal means by which clans within a tribe
handled their conflicts. The tribal "law" did not so much forbid or discourage interclan violence as it set the rules according
to which these feuds were to be carried on and set certain limits
to the times and places of these feuds. In particular, violence
was forbidden during religious festivals, at the assemblies of the
free men of the tribe, and during military expeditions. Failure
to observe the peace at these times might result in the trial of
the offender by the tribe itself and either his execution or banishment. By declaring him an outlaw—literally one who was no
longer protected by the customary peace of the tribe—the offender might be killed by anyone without risking revenge.

Finally, the tribe was a political community. Although primarily organized according to clans, the necessities of united action, particularly of a military nature, called for larger political
units. These could be larger or smaller than the groups that
shared the other cultural, mythic, and legal customs. For example, various tribes might share a common cult tradition with-

out having common political institutions; on the other hand, different groups might unite temporarily for military purposes.

The supreme political unit of the tribe was the assembly of its free male warriors. This assembly, called the "Thing," served as the court of highest instance for dealing with individuals who had broken fundamental elements of the tribal pact, an occasion to meet and to reinforce ties among members, and, often, an assembly which preceded a military campaign. The organization and leadership of this assembly, and indeed of the tribal units, varied widely among tribes and within the same tribe across time. Within some tribes, the free men from particular areas (gaus) were under the leadership of "princes," who may have been selected by the warriors or who may have come from leading families, or both. These princes led them in battle and at other times served as leaders of roughly the territorial units of the tribe.

At the top of some tribes stood a figure whose title is only poorly translated by our English word "king." Apparently Germanic peoples before the migration period had two sorts of kings, one essentially religious, the other military, although not all tribes possessed both. The first was what sources call the *thiudans*. This king was apparently chosen from a royal family, that is the family with which the ethnic, historical, and cultural traditions of the tribe were most closely identified. He was the king described by Tacitus as having been selected "ex nobiliate," that is, because of his noble family origins. Presumably this king was closely tied to the traditional, relatively stable "established" tribe living in perhaps violent relationship with its neighbors, but at least in a state of rough equilibrium within this violence. The *thiudans* was closely associated to the Germanic (in fact, Indo-European) god Tiwaz, who was the protector of a stable social order and guarantor of laws, fertility, and peace.

The role of this king varied among the Germanic peoples. With some, he served largely a religious role, with others he presided at assemblies; elsewhere he might also exercise military command. But some tribes did not have this position at all. In still others, military authority was entrusted to a nonroyal leader, called by Tacitus a general (*dux*). Chosen for his military prowess, he rather than the "king" assumed command of the tribe in warfare. This military leader will be discussed later in detail.

The Comitatus

As we have seen, the tribe was built of family or familylike units united through common beliefs and social bonds. In contrast to this unity-enforcing structure stood another social group that cut across kindreds and even tribal units and could be at once a source of tribal strength and of enormous instability. This was the warrior band, termed *comitatus* by Tacitus and *Gefolgschaft* by modern German scholars. Warfare, as we have seen, was the primary activity of Germanic men—it largely determined their prestige and their wealth. Within the society, therefore, some (but by no means all) young free men eager for glory associated themselves with important leaders well known for their ability and formed elite groups of mounted warriors. The youths entered into close, personal bonds with their leader, who was responsible for providing for them, equipping them, and leading them to victory and booty. For their part, they were totally devoted to him, and in the case that he should fall it was considered shameful if they should not also fight to the death.

These *comitatus* were not the fundamental military unit of the tribe. They were instead individual warrior societies organized for constant plunder and fighting. Moreover, while they might participate in tribal wars, their own expeditions were not tribal wars. Instead, they were individual raids which could endanger the peace within the tribe or the armed truce that might exist among tribes. Thus these warrior bands were destabilizing groups within an already fragile tribal structure. However, they were also potential nuclei around which might form new tribes. Successful warrior leaders acquired great prestige and power through the size of their following, and in time tensions within the tribe might lead to the splintering off of the warrior band and its dependents to form a new tribe.

Obviously the nature of Germanic society, with its military structure, loose kindreds, and weak central organization all contributed to constant instability. Infratribal conflict was the norm, and unity could only be maintained through joint hostility against other tribes, which occupied the warriors and maintained the prestige of princes, and through religious and social rituals that sought to reinforce the solidarity of the people. Chief among the latter were exchanges of daughters in marriage, an attempt to unite kindreds, thereby preventing or ending feuds. Other social rituals for eliminating conflict were the expressions of solidarity made at banquets and drinking bouts. These occasions were extremely important in village tribal society—sharing food and especially drink were vital in maintaining fragile social bonds. Of course, banqueting and drinking could also become all too easily destructive contests, and drunken arguments could awaken old grievances and lead to new violence.

Small wonder then that tribes seem to appear and disappear with great frequency. Inherently unstable, these units constantly underwent transformation as kindreds feuded and split apart, warrior bands struck out to establish themselves as new tribes, and as tribes weakened by internal divisions were conquered and absorbed into other tribes. Still, so long as this process took place among Germanic, Celtic, and Slavic peoples all at rightly the same level of material and social organization, this instability remained in a state of equilibrium. But this equilibrium would be destroyed by contact with Rome.

ROMAN INFLUENCE ON THE GERMANIC PEOPLES

Although the Germanic peoples were intimately tied to and often indistinguishable from their Celtic and Slavic neighbors, even in the first century Germanic society did not exist in isolation from the Roman world. Rome made its presence felt throughout the Germanic world in a variety of extremely significant ways. First, in the narrow zone of approximately 100 kilometers wide along the *limes,* fairly intensive commercial interaction between Romans and barbarians brought Roman products to the Germanic world. In this zone, one finds that a great variety of Roman goods were in use, and as transactions such as that between Stelus and the Roman merchant indicate,

Germanic herdsmen were rapidly becoming involved in the monetized economy of the Roman world.

While everyday products of Roman provincial manufacture did not extend much into the hinterland of "Free Germany," Roman luxury products apparently attracted the attention of Germanic elites everywhere. Throughout northern Europe, from the Rhine to beyond the Oder, archaeologists have found remarkably similar graves containing weapons, jewelry, and Roman luxury exports. These so-called Lübsow-type graves indicate the importance to the Germanic elite of Roman products and Roman lifestyles, as well as the similarities and possibly interconnections among elites throughout the region. We do not know whether these Roman luxury goods were acquired through trade or, more likely, through gift exchange. However, by the first century, well before the Germanic migrations, a Germanic aristocracy which defined itself by its military role was beginning to come under the spell of Rome.

The effects of the penetration of Roman commercial and material culture on Germanic society were profound. First, the introduction of money and the expansion of markets for Germanic cattle, hides, and probably other products such as furs, amber, and slaves, widened the extremes of social differentiation within this society. Not that before this time the Germanic peoples had lived in some forest utopia of primitive communism; we have seen that differences in sizes of cattle herds indicated a hierarchical structure of society. However, while differences in cattle herds might mean a twofold or threefold difference in wealth, the possibility of accumulating specie and luxury goods from the Empire could greatly accentuate the differences among individuals and families. By extending the distance between members of Germanic tribes, the power and prestige of traditional leaders was thus greatly increased.

Second, the desire for Roman articles, which could be acquired only by trade or by warfare, transformed the range of activity and extent of interaction among Germanic peoples. As tribes were drawn into the Roman commercial network, their leaders were necessarily drawn into political relationships with Romans, a result specifically desired by Roman imperial officials.

From the Roman perspective, it was highly desirable to have Germanic tribes ruled by authoritarian leaders who could negotiate on behalf of their tribes binding treaties with Rome and whose personal loyalty to Rome could be maintained by gifts. Also, it was desirable to make such tribes dependent on Roman sources of iron, grain, and other exports. Thus Roman policy aimed at the stabilization, in Roman terms, of barbarian political structures and the development of barbarian economies in order to secure markets for Roman exports.

However, the net result of this Roman policy was to destabilize German society still further, to accentuate social and economic differentiation within Germanic tribes, and to form within these peoples pro- and anti-Roman factions that often led to the splintering of tribal units. This destabilization spread like a chain reaction across the Germanic world and set into motion a tumultuous process of rapid ethnogenesis and social transformation that led to the conflict which had no name in the Germanic world but which we have already encountered from the other side of the *limes* as the Marcomannian war. Whole new peoples and confederations were created in its aftermath, among these the people with whom we are most concerned—the Franks.

The Romans viewed the Marcomannian war primarily as a confrontation along the Danubian border between Romans and barbarians. However, even they were well aware that they faced many more barbarian tribes in addition to the Marcomanni and Quadi, two tribal confederations closest to the Roman *limes*. These two groups had long belonged to the belt of Roman client states which lay along the frontier, and their relationship with Rome had been intimate and largely pacific. Ambiguous archaeological evidence even suggests that the chieftains of these groups were well on the way to becoming Roman in their style of life and in their military fortifications. They may have occupied rustic villas and camps constructed for them by the Romans or at least made of building materials supplied by the Roman legions. However, during the war, the Marcomanni and Quadi were joined by elements of numerous other groups. During the negotiations with the Romans after the first invasion in A.D. 167, the Marcomannian king Ballomarius spoke for at least eleven tribes.

Probably even more groups were involved. Archaeological excavations have found materials of northern Germanic origin dating from this period in the regions of modern Bohemia and Austria, the regions from whence came the Marcomanni and the Quadi. Moreover, Roman arms that had probably been taken as booty by Germanic warriors and later buried with them have been discovered as far north as Schleswig-Holstein, Jütland, and the island of Fyn in modern Denmark. Taken together, this evidence suggests that tribes from as far away as southern Scandinavia took part in the confrontation. This evidence also suggests that, as the Romans suspected, the pressure on the Danubian frontier was caused by the movement of peoples from the north. It appears thus that the whole of Free Germany was in a period of disequilibrium and stress.[5]

Nor were the Marcomannian wars the only effects of internal Germanic changes felt by Rome. Everywhere on the Rhine-Danube frontier, the effects of the inner barbarian upheavals were experienced: in 166/67 the Langobards (Lombards) and Obierii were pressing on the Danube; in 170 the Chatti were raiding across the Rhine while the Sarmats and Costobocii were active on the lower Danube; in 172 the Chauci from southern Scandinavia were raiding the coast of modern France; and in 174 various groups of "Germans" were pressing Rhaetia. Thus the Germanic world was apparently convulsed from one end to the other, and the pressures on the Roman world were but the distant echoes of this internal upheaval. What was taking place was a radical restructuring of the Germanic world, a process in which formerly powerful tribal confederations like the Marcomanni were splintered, old tribes disappeared or were radically reorganized, and new "peoples" and confederations, such as the Franks and Alemanni, took their place. In the course of these transformations, many groups, such as the Goths, who had previously been subordinate to larger groups, suddenly expanded into major confederations and chiefs led their followers into new areas, generally to the south and east, while others sought protection through the amalgamation of smaller groups into new peoples. In all, the last decades of the second century were the most vital period of ethnogenesis in Germanic history.

THE NEW GERMANIC SOCIETIES

The unrest of the latter part of the second century radically changed the structure of Germanic tribes, both those closest to the Roman *limes* and those so far away that the Romans had only a vague knowledge of their existence.

In this period of constant sustained warfare, the already important role of tribal military activity became even more essential. In order to survive, the tribe had to become thoroughly militarized—it became an army. The transformation increased the significance of the role of nonroyal war leaders within Germanic tribes. These commanders had traditionally been entrusted with the conduct of warfare. However, their attempts to turn their limited military role into a broader and more permanent command, attempts often made with the encouragement of the Romans, had met with determined opposition from their tribes. Now, when organized tribal warfare became a constant, all-consuming aspect of existence, their status increased greatly. As successful military leaders, these commanders, designated by the Celtic loanword *reiks,* although originally not necessarily of royal lineage in the sense of the *thiudans,* could claim that victory was a sign of the gods' favor and thus add a religious aura to their position.

Under the command of the *reiks,* or, as called by modern German scholars, *Heerkönig* (literally: "army-king"), the identity and composition of the tribe, always an essentially unstable group at best, underwent further transformation. The dislocation of traditional areas of settlement led to a deemphasis on the agrarian traditions of the community and, along with it, on the cult of fertility gods such as Tiwaz. In their place many Germanic tribes turned to Woden or Oden, the god of war and the particular deity of the military kings, who looked to them as givers of victory and, through victory, a new sort of religious justification for their position. The new cult was more appropriate for the highly mobile and rapidly changing nature of the tribe.

The victories created new traditions, and participation in them centered on the warrior king as the agent (and often descendant) of Woden. This in turn transformed the community identity. Although the old tribal names might continue to be used, the identity of the tribe was now related to the identity of these warrior leaders. Anyone who fought with them was a member of their tribe, regardless of previous ethnic, linguistic, political, or cultic origins. Anyone else was either enemy or slave.

But military leadership, however brilliant, could not alone transform the charismatic power of a war leader into an enduring institutional kingship. A *reiks* who hoped to raise himself and his family above the other aristocratic clans of his polyethnic tribe needed greater wealth, honors, and support than he could garner alone. For this, barbarian leaders needed Rome and the emperor, who, even for the inhabitants of "Free Germany," was alone the great king whose support they eagerly courted.

Along the northern borders of the Eastern and Western Empire, these military leaders sought the financial and political support of alliances with Rome. They needed Roman titles and office to legitimize their positions vis-à-vis not only their own peoples but in their relationships with other tribes as well; they needed Roman grain and iron to feed and equip their warriors; and they needed Roman gold and silver to "represent" their high position through conspicuous and dazzling displays of precious metals. All of this Rome was, as we have seen in Chapter One, eager to provide, but at a price. Rome needed most the one thing that the barbarians could provide—military manpower. Together, barbarian warlords and Roman emperors cooperated in the creation of the new barbarian world.

The Eastern Empire and the Goths

The course of this process in the East can be best illustrated by examining the gradual creation of the Goths, the barbarian tribe most respected and feared by other barbarians and Romans alike in late antiquity. Thus, instead of providing a comprehensive view of the various barbarians who entered the Empire, we will examine in some detail the successive stages of Gothic ethnogenesis. Although their legends, formed after their astounding victories within the Empire and their territorialization in Italy and Spain, speak as though the whole people had migrated from Scandinavia to the east before settling around the Black Sea, their real history, as recently illuminated by Austrian historian Herwig Wolfram, indicates quite a different past. Instead, one sees a people with widely differing ethnic, cultural, and geographical backgrounds become Goths, and in the process transform the meaning of what it was to be a Goth.[6]

In the first century A.D. the people who called themselves the Goths, or *Gutonen* (the name probably simply means "the people," as do many early names of tribes), inhabited an area between the Oder and the Vistula rivers and were closely allied, and often dominated, by three other Germanic-Celtic groups, the Vandals, the Lugii, and the Rugii. In their cultic and material existence they hardly differed from other closely related barbarian groups, although, if one can believe Tacitus, already in the first century their king was unusually powerful—he seems to have combined the power of the *reiks* and the religious prestige of the *thiudans*. These kings, with their central kernel of warriors, were the bearers of a tradition and an efficient military organization that could attract non-Goth warriors to fight alongside them. In little more than five generations this small, dependent tribe grew into a major power in the barbarian world. It was in large part the shock waves of their consolidation along the right bank of the Vistula River that set in motion the violent changes which the Romans experienced as the Marcomannian war.

In the later second and third century some of the bearers of this "Gothic" tradition began gradually to infiltrate to the south and east, ultimately traveling to the banks of the Dnieper, near present-day Kiev. Not that the entire "Gothic" people migrated as one to this region, but rather that the various Pontic, Sarmatic, Slavic, and Germanic peoples already in the Dnieper region were organized by the Gothic leadership into a powerful confederation under the Gothic military kingship. From here, the continuous expansion of the reconstituted Gothic people came into direct and violent conflict with Rome in 238 as these Goths, to which the Romans gave the name of the ancient inhabitants of the region, Scythians, began raiding and plundering the eastern provinces of the Empire around the Black Sea under the command of their king, Cniva. The resulting wars were far more devastating to the Empire than those against the Marcomanni. The Goths penetrated far into the Empire and in 251 even managed to kill Emperor Dacius and his son when they attempted to prevent the Goths from returning home with their booty. Only with enormous difficulty were the emperors Claudius II (who died in 269) and Aurelian able to stem the onslaught of the "Scythians" and finally defeat them in 271.

The defeat was carried out with typical Roman thoroughness and the unified Gothic kingdom was virtually destroyed. But just as victory could be the decisive event in the creation of a people, so, too, could defeat. Out of the ruins of the Gothic confederation developed two "new" Gothic peoples—east of the Dnester the royal family of the Amals reorganized as a smaller Gothic kingdom, while along the lower Danube arose a decentralized but vital territorialized Gothic society under the leadership of aristocratic families, particularly the Balts, who carried on part of the old Gothic tradition. In 332 Ariarich, the Balt leader of this polyethnic confederation known as the Tervingi, who eschewed the title of king in favor of judge, concluded the first of a series of treaties, or *foeda,* with the emperor Constantine and thus acquired the necessary peace and support to consolidate a territorial state within the sphere of influence of the Empire.

BALTS AND TERVINGIANS

Tervingian society and culture were complex mixtures of the various groups composing it. The Gothic formula of political organization built around powerful war leaders could be quickly and effectively expanded, so that a small group of aristocrats could organize any large population of warrior peoples into a "Gothic" confederation. The "Gothic people" were thus hardly a tribe in the sense of a group of common origin but rather the political constellation of smaller groups, or *Kuni,* with various cultural, linguistic, and geographical origins led by their individual *reiks* and sharing a common cult. Different *reiks* ruled from strongholds in the countryside rather than from villages or towns, although the former certainly existed in this ancient region. The *reiks* governed his region with the assistance of his military following, his *comitatus,* while even free villagers were largely excluded from the political process. This is a long way from the participatory political organization described by Tacitus, and for one main reason. The Tervingian Goths were not "Germans" in Tacitus's sense, but were a Near Eastern society. The unifying elements of the Gothic confederation were the army, which was largely composed of infantry except for a small elite cavalry, and the traditions carried on by the Balt family.

Following the conclusion of the treaty with Rome, the Tervingian Goths served as generally faithful federates. Not only did they undertake expeditions against their barbarian neighbors on behalf of the Romans, but many of them served individually or in groups for varying amounts of time within the Roman army. In fact, until around 400 Gothic military commanders were among the most important *magistri militum* in the eastern half of the Empire. Exquisite jewelry, vessels, and decorative objects produced in the Tervingian state during this period indicate the extent to which Roman, Greek, and other craft and artistic traditions were valued and imitated by the Gothic elites. So deeply did Roman imperial values and structures penetrate this society that even the trappings of Roman constitutional structures were admired and imitated in this border state, although submitted to what might be called an *interpretatio barbaria,* in contrast with the better known *interpretatio Romana* of which I have spoken earlier. The most striking example of this is a copy of a Roman commemorative medallion found in a treasure hoard at Szilágysomlyó (in modern Romania) on which are the images of emperors Valentinian I and Valens (ruled jointly 364–375) with the legend "Regis Romanorum" (Kings of the Romans). This is probably a Latin translation of the term *thiudans.* To the Goths, the emperor was the great king, an essential if sometimes ambivalent element in their own political framework.

Admiration for and cooperation with the Empire was not unqualified within the Tervingian confederation. One can speak of pro- and anti-Roman factions within the aristocracy since various Gothic leaders attempted to consolidate or improve their positions within the confederation by either looking to Constantinople for support or by attempting to unite the Tervingians against the Romans. On the other side of the Danube various factions within the Empire attempted to win Gothic cooperation in order to advance their own political ambitions. Under the great Balt leader Athanaric (reigned 365–371) the Tervingi relationship with the Empire was particularly tense. His father had lived as a Gothic hostage in Constantinople, and although the emperor had had a statue of him erected in the New Rome, he had had his son swear never to set foot within the Roman Empire. The Balt judges apparently saw Roman political maneuvers as a potential threat to their control of the confederation, and Athanaric fought a series of engagements against Emperor Valens, which ended in 369 with a treaty allowing the Goths to deal virtually as equals rather than as federates of the Romans.

Athanaric's difficult relations with the Romans were closely tied to his internal problems with competitors for control of the Gothic confederation and in particular with the strongly pro-Roman group led by the Tervingians Fritigern and Alaviv. The internal rivalry between the conservative Athanaric, who sought to strengthen the unity of the confederation around the ancient Gothic tradition, and the *reiks* Fritigern was largely played out in terms of religious opposition and persecution. Among the various groups within the confederation were numbers of Christians of various sorts who had been captured in war or whose communities had been absorbed by the Goths. The most important of these individuals was Wulfila (c. 311–383), who was probably the son of a Gothic father of important social status and a Cappadocian mother whose parents or grandparents had most likely been captured by a Gothic raiding party in 257. In the 330s he visited Constantinople as part of a Gothic mission and apparently acquired a good education in Latin and Greek. In 341 at Antioch he was consecrated "Bishop of the Christians in the Getic [Gothic] land" and returned to spread his faith, which had previously been introduced by both Latin and Greek missionaries. His high status, his official commission, and his excellent education that enabled him to translate the Bible into the Gothic language, all contributed to his success in proselytizing the Goths.

Wulfila's own position on the major theological issue of the fourth century, the divinity of Christ, was a compromise between the position of those who came to be called the orthodox, who maintained that Christ was one in substance with the Father, and that of the Arians, who denied His divinity altogether. Instead of completely accepting one of these positions, Wulfila chose not to speak of the substance of the divine at all. For this, he and his later Gothic followers have been incorrectly classified as Arians.

Although Wulfila was the most important and successful Christian missionary, others were also active. The orthodox church was represented by Bishop Vetranio of Tomi and found support within the Tervingian aristocracy. The rival Arians were particularly supported by the opposition group led by the Tervingian Fritigern, who hoped to please the Arian emperor Valens. Athanaric saw all varieties of Christianity as a threat to the Gothic cultic tradition, which had been one of the major constitutional elements of its political success, and began a number of prosecutions, the most important of which started in 369 and was aimed indiscriminately at all varieties of Christians. During these internal conflicts the issue was determined from without—in 376 the military confederation under Athanaric was destroyed by the sudden arrival from Asia of the Huns in the area of the Black Sea, and the infrastructure of the Gothic state was replaced by an equally polyethnic Hunnic confederation. The majority of the Tervingian elite abandoned Athanaric and followed Fritigern and Alaviv across the Danube into the Empire. Athanaric himself had to break the vow he had made to his father and seek protection in Constantinople, where he was received with honor in

381 only to die two weeks after his arrival. This crisis was the
prelude to a new phase of Gothic ethnogenesis. Henceforth the
followers of Fritigern entered history as the Visigoths.

While the Balts were organizing the disparate peoples along the
lower Danube and Black Sea into a Tervingian confederation,
the remains of the royal family of Amals was organizing in southern Russia a new Gothic kingdom. The first king of this group
was Ostrogotha, who lived in the first generation after the Roman victory of 271, and can in a sense be seen as the founder of
the Gothic kingdom in its new, reduced form. Because this kingdom lay so far from the Roman frontier, we know little of its
history, except that it, too, must have been a polyethnic confederation organized according to the "Gothic" pattern of central
military kingship and a thoroughly militarized aristocracy. This
steppe confederation was known to the Romans as the Greuthungs, or Scythians, the former being a new ethnic label, the
latter a designation of steppe peoples inherited from Greek antiquity. Just as the more western confederation continued the
cultural and military traditions of the region under the political
control of the Balt aristocracy, the Greuthung kingdom, although
identifying itself with Gothic tradition, was thoroughly a steppe
people in its customs and ethnic groups, particularly in the military tradition of mounted steppe warriors.

The Greuthung king who emerges from legend into history
was Ermanaric, "The most noble of the Amals" according to
later Gothic history and the king of a wide variety of conquered
peoples of the Russian steppes. His kingdom commanded the
traditional trade routes connecting the Black Sea and the Slavic
world. His control of this confederation was by no means undisputed, and he was engaged in a deadly struggle for control with
other groups when the Huns' arrival in 376 shattered his kingdom. Ermanaric killed himself in what was possibly a self-sacrifice
to the gods, and the majority of his people were absorbed into
the Hunnic confederation. A minority continued to resist for
about one year before they, too, were subjugated or fled like

their Tervingian counterparts into the Roman Empire. Only after the disintegration of the Hunnic confederation would those under the Amal tradition reemerge as the Ostrogoths.

FROM TERVINGIAN TO VISIGOTH

After their settlement in southern Gaul, the Visigoths looked back on the forty-year period between 376 and 416, during which they concluded a treaty with Emperor Constantius, as analogous to the forty years the Hebrew people wandered in the Sinai. The analogy, which carried the Gothic theological and political interpretation of themselves as the new chosen people, was also appropriate in that just as the Sinai period created the Hebrew people from the disparate group of refugees who left Egypt, the forty years of uncertainty and wandering within the Empire transformed the Tervingian refugees under Fritigern into what history knows as the Visigoths. This final process of the creation of a territorial kingdom within the Empire was possible because the Gothic people, traditionally organized as a Gothic army, could become a Roman army and its leaders could acquire legitimacy and support as duly appointed Roman officers. The formation of a Visigothic state, rather than the introduction of a barbarian, much less a "Germanic" society into the West, was the adaptation of the "Gothic system" within the context of a Roman administrative and military system.

We have seen in the previous chapter the reception of the Goths under Fritigern by the Romans and the desperation which led them to risk a confrontation with the emperor himself at Adrianopolis—a confrontation from which they emerged victorious. However the victory at Adrianopolis was short-lived. The Goths needed food and in the long run could obtain this only through cooperation with the Roman Empire. Thus after a short and futile period of rampage, in 382 Fritigern concluded a treaty with Emperor Theodosius, according to whose terms the Goths were settled in Dacia and Thrace as a federated people who were to retain their command structure intact and to serve the Empire when needed.

The settlement did not last long, but it did provide time for the emergence of a new and powerful Gothic leader, Alaric, whose position was much more that of a true monarch than had been the Tervingian judges such as Fritigern and even Athanaric. Although frequently betrayed by the imperial government, Alaric's entire career was dominated by his futile quest for recognition and legitimacy as the supreme military commander in the Empire. Alaric led his people, who were again threatened by the Huns, out of Thrace into the Balkans, Greece, and the Illyrica. In 397 the emperor, who had previously viewed Alaric not as a king but as a tyrant or usurper, was forced to name him the military commander of the eastern Illyrican prefecture—a move that provided the model for future dealings with the commanders of barbarian *gentes* within the Empire. This new treaty lasted even less time than the first, and in 401 Alaric once more led his army across the Empire. This final expedition culminated in the sack of Rome in 410. Roman booty was not, however, his primary need—it was food. Alaric had really sought to lead his people to North Africa, a goal ultimately reached by another barbarian people, the Vandals.

Alaric died the same year he captured Rome, and his successor, Athaulf, ultimately concluded a treaty with the emperor Honorius to rid Gaul of the usurper Iovinus. In 413 he led his Goths as a Roman army into Aquitaine. Only when the emperor broke his part of the bargain to supply the Goths did Athaulf seize the major cities of the region. Athaulf, like Alaric, sought imperial recognition and approval, and in 414 concluded a Roman marriage with Galla Placidia, daughter of Emperor Theodosius, to connect his family with that of the Theodosian dynasty and thus repair his relationship with Constantinople. He also worked with the Aquitainian aristocracy to establish a territorial lordship not just over Goths but over all the region's population. His assassination in 415 ended the hopes of this program. His successor, Walia, led the Goths into Spain hoping to resume Alaric's move toward North Africa, but was unable to reach his desired destination and was ultimately enrolled in Roman service. He returned to Aquitaine, where he and his Goths, at once a barbarian people and a Roman army, were settled, creating the Visigothic kingdom of Toulouse. This marked the end of the forty years of wandering and the culmination of the long process of Visigothic ethnogenesis.

FROM GREUTHUNG TO OSTROGOTH

After Ermanaric's death, the majority of the Greuthungs were integrated into the Hunnic confederation, but a small group fled to the Empire and were settled among the various federates in Pannonia. Although the Goths felt a strong ambivalence toward the Hunnic conquerors, those who remained with the Huns served Attila faithfully, even following him into Gaul under three Gothic royal brothers—Valamir, Thiudimir, and Vidimi. They also absorbed many of the Hunnic traditions, adopting their clothing, weapons, and even the practice of skull deformation of children. Further evidence of the close relationship between the Huns and the Goths is shown in their sharing of names: Attila itself and many other names of Huns are actually Gothic, while many Goths bore Hunnic names. However, even while serving the Huns, the Goths retained their own organization and even consolidated their sense of identity around the traditions of their early kings. However, between 378 and 453, when the Hunnic confederation collapsed with Attila's death, a new identity and a new name emerged for this group: the Ostrogoths.

After the disintegration of the Hunnic confederation, some of the newly independent and reconstituted Ostrogoths, like many other former members of the confederation, such as the Gepids and Rugii, entered into a treaty with the Empire and were settled as federates in Pannonia. A militarized tribe such as the Ostrogoths could only prosper in a region in which the Roman agricultural infrastructure was intact, something Pannonia had long lost through the clashes with barbarians. Thus whenever the usual payments from the Empire were not forthcoming, the Ostrogoths were tempted to break their treaty and conduct raids into the Empire. At the conclusion of one such revolt in 459, the young son of Thiudimir, Theodoric, was sent as hostage to Constantinople. He lived there from about the age of eight to eighteen, during which time he gained an intimate knowledge of the Empire and in particular of the imperial system of government.

Shortly after his return home, Theodoric took over the kingdom along with his father upon the death of his uncle Valamir, and shortly thereafter led the Goths into Illyricum, as had the Visigoth Alaric in the previous century. There he was much more successful in playing the political games within the Empire, and by 485 his cooperation with the emperor Zeno had won for him the position of *magister militum,* the consulate, and even adoption into the imperial Flavian house. Nevertheless, he was equally willing to use his army against the emperor to further his own position.

Hoping to rid himself of both Theodoric and the Germanic king Odoacer, in 488 Zeno sent Theodoric to eliminate the latter. To do this, Theodoric gathered an extremely heterogeneous army of barbarians and Romans and began his ultimately victorious war against Odoacer, which left him, by the end of 493, the undisputed commander of Italy. The treaty that had legitimized his invasion of Italy had granted him supreme power in the peninsula until Zeno would personally appear to take command. But by then Zeno had died, and his successor was too occupied with other matters to appear in the West. Thus Theodoric was free to establish his own political system.

He sought to consolidate his control through a dual system, both of which ultimately rested on Roman rather than barbarian traditions. He even took as his official title *Flavius Theodericus rex.* He made no attempt to eliminate or replace the system of Roman government under which the Roman population of Italy continued to be governed. Instead, as Flavius Theodericus, a member of the imperial family, he represented the emperor, heading the government at the emperor's desire.

The barbarians to whom he owed his victory were not part of this civilian Roman system. Although he had risen as king of the Ostrogoths and had expressly affiliated himself with the ancient Amal tradition, he made no attempt to rule as king of the Goths. He ruled his barbarian followers, whether Ostrogoths or members of other tribes that had followed him into Italy, as part of a thoroughly military organization, the *exercitus Gothorum,* an officially recognized Roman army that incorporated all men, regardless of their origins, who participated in the army.

Within this dual system, both elements of which culminated in this thoroughly Roman Goth who became a barbarian member of the imperial family, the process of Ostrogothic ethnogenesis was complete. Theodoric's importance was not limited to the barbarians of Italy. As the most successful of the barbarian commanders, he dominated the peoples of the West in a loose confederation which included the Burgundians, Visigoths, and, to the north, the Alemanni and the Franks.

The Western Empire and the Franks

The ethnogenesis of the western barbarian peoples is less dramatic than that of the eastern but ultimately proved to be of more enduring importance. These peoples too were created in the great pan-Germanic turmoil of the Marcomannian wars, when the threat posed by neighboring warrior tribes forced the constitution of new confederations among the peoples along the Rhine. However, unlike the Goths, Burgundians, Lombards, and others who, although formed in the fourth century, carried names and traditions linking them with ancient peoples living in southern Scandinavia, the Franks, Alemanni, and Bavarii did not for the most part preserve ancient tribal traditions. Although the Alemanni generally called themselves Suebi (Sueves), these tribal confederations were not organized into stable *regna,* or kingdoms, prior to their entry into the Empire, nor did their internal affairs or even arrival within the *limes* impress their Roman contemporaries sufficiently to take much note of them. They arrived not as an invading army nor as federates. Instead, slowly and almost imperceptibly, small groups of their warrior-peasants crossed the Rhine to serve in the Roman military or to settle in the western provinces of the Empire.

Given the silence of contemporary writers on these peoples, our best source of information on the changes taking place within these Rhine-Weser Germanic communities is the ambiguous evidence of their burial practices. Sometime around the end of the third century, under circumstances related to the military transformations of which we have spoken above, first appeared new cultural attitudes toward the disposal of the dead. For example, at the fourth-century cemetery of Lampertheim, east of Worms, archaeologists have found fifty-six burials that indicate the beginning of a transition from earlier Germanic practices. Here one finds a profusion of burial types: cremation, burials in urns, and uncremated burials. Twenty-nine of the burials were without any grave articles; all but three of the remainder contained personal ornamentation and objects but no weapons. Three tombs, however, were burials of armed men.[7]

In the course of the fourth century, the exception begins to be the rule, both outside and within the *limes*—the dead are found increasingly buried in cemeteries arranged in rows and oriented east-west or north-south. While earlier Germanic burials within the Empire had contained no weapons—Roman soldiers used government-issue arms, not personal property—increasingly the weapons and jewelry within these tombs resembled that found in Free Germany. Likewise, tombs in Free Germany began to contain more provincial Roman products, such as belt decorations which had probably been brought home by soldiers completing their military service in the Empire. Such row-type burials even began to appear in Roman provincial cemeteries and in close proximity to Roman settlements. In fact, these new cemeteries apparently began to appear first within or near the Roman *limes* and spread out toward Free Germany. To judge from the archaeological evidence, one might almost conclude that this new barbarian custom began within the Empire itself. In sum, the militarization of the Roman Empire created a society of increasingly wealthy Germanic warriors in northern and eastern Gaul who kept in close contact with their relatives and friends outside the Empire and in intimate social contact with the Gallo-Roman population.

So characteristic is this form of burial across most of northern central Europe that it has given rise among modern German scholars to a descriptive name for the entire barbarian West: *Reihengräberzivilisation* ("row-grave civilization"). Although at one time historians, who thought of the barbarian migrations as actual movements of whole tribes, saw this burial transformation as evidence of the arrival of "new" peoples from Scandinavia or elsewhere, today scholars recognize this change as a reflection of those occurring in the social, political, and cultural structures of the peoples already living in western and central Europe. These changes were similar to those that had earlier transformed the Goths into a powerful and successful military machine.

The same pressures that created the Marcomannian wars also led to the formation, among the western Germanic peoples, of new, militarily organized confederations and peoples. As in the East, the demands of constant warfare resulted in the increasingly prominent role of military leaders (*duces* or *reiks*) and an increasing militarization of society. The new forms of burial indicate this progressive militarization, as warriors were buried with their weapons. Whether it was expected that these arms would be needed in a military afterlife or simply that as personal property the deceased retained rights to them after their deaths is unclear. What is clear is that, judging by the wealth of ornaments and magnificent weapons in these burials, the rewards for the groups which made a successful transformation to this new form of organization were great.

The "West Germanic Revolution" was so thorough that, unlike the Goths, Burgundians, and other eastern barbarians who transmitted an ancient name and thus a sense of identity across successive social formations, most of the West Germanic tribes appear not to have even had a clearly defined myth or origin; thus they later adopted those of other peoples. The Alemanni, for example, had no great historical tradition. Their name probably means simply "the people" (manni—"the people"; ala—an intensive prefix). Although they sometimes referred to themselves as Suebi, they were probably a confederation of small tribes that had long settled in the region east of the Rhine and south of the Main. A few sporadic raids across the Rhine and Danube in the late second through mid-fifth centuries, whose significance and force have probably been greatly exaggerated by modern historians, bore witness to the process of ethnogenesis taking place across the border.

Cautious archaeologists avoid giving ethnic names to their finds—bones carry no passports—but certainly the varieties of archaeological material are evidence of the genesis of several new peoples, including those who perhaps even then sometimes referred to themselves as the Franks.

CHAPTER III

Romans and Franks in the Kingdom of Clovis

> Many say that the Franks originally came from Pannonia and first inhabited the banks of the Rhine. Then they crossed the river, marched through Thuringia, and set up in each county district and each city long-haired kings chosen from their foremost and most noble family.[1]

> Blessed Jerome has written about the ancient kings of the Franks, whose story was first told by the poet Virgil: their first king was Priam and, after Troy was captured by trickery, they departed. Afterwards they had as king Friga, then they split into two parts, the first going into Macedonia, the second group, which left Asia with Friga were called the Frigii, settled on the banks of the Danube and the Ocean Sea. Again splitting into two groups, half of them entered Europe with their king Francio. After crossing Europe with their wives and children they occupied the banks of the Rhine and not far from the Rhine began to build the city of "Troy" (Colonia Triana-Xanten).[2]

These two versions of Frankish origins, the first written in the late sixth century by Gregory of Tours, the second in the seventh century by the Frankish chronicler Fredegar, are alike in betraying both the fact that the Franks knew little about their background and that they may have felt some inferiority in comparison with other peoples of antiquity who possessed an ancient name and glorious tradition. The first legend connects the Franks with the great Pannonian plain, which was both the homeland of the man who would become the chief religious patron of the Franks, Martin of Tours, and the proximate place of origin of the Goths—the great barbarian success story of the migration period. The legend thus implies that the Franks are the equals of the Goths in their origins and by implication in honor. The second, later legend combines the origins of the Franks with that of the Romans—equally ancient and from the same heroic city, the Franks and Romans of Gaul could claim common ancestry as a basis for the creation of a common society.

Frankish Ethnogenesis

Both legends are of course equally fabulous for, even more than most barbarian peoples, the Franks possessed no common history, ancestry, or tradition of a heroic age of migration. Like their Alemannic neighbors, they were by the sixth century a fairly recent creation, a coalition of Rhenish tribal groups who long maintained separate identities and institutions. The name Frank first appears in Roman sources of the mid-third century. It designated a variety of so-called Iistwaeoni tribes so loosely connected that some scholars have denied altogether that they formed a confederation, while others, although not wishing to deny categorically their unity, have referred to them as a "tribal swarm." These groups included the Chamavi, Chattuari, Bructeri, Amsivarii, and Salii, and probably others such as the Usipii, Tubanti, Hasi, and Chasuari. (The name Ripuarian is much later—it does not appear before the eighth century. The name Sigambri, used by Gregory of Tours and others, is probably just a classical reminiscence of the Sigambri of classical authors.) While maintaining their separate identities, these small groups occasionally banded together for common defensive or offensive operations and then identified themselves by the name Frank, which meant "the hardy," "the brave," and, only later, by extension, the meaning favored by the Franks themselves, "the free."

In reality, the early Franks were anything but free. Living in close proximity to the Empire, relatively insignificant and divided, these people prior to the sixth century were either subjugated as Roman client states or, within the *limes,* served as largely faithful sources of military manpower and leadership. Beginning in the later third century we hear of sporadic "Frankish" raids and uprisings and even of "Frankish" pirates penetrating into the Mediterranean and raiding North Africa and the coast of Spain near Taragonna. However, in the reigns of Constantius Chlorus and Constantine they were brutally crushed, their leaders were thrown to wild beasts in the arena, and a great number of their warriors were incorporated into the imperial troops. Eventually, those known as the Salians were settled as *laeti* in the area known as Toxandria (Tiesterbant near modern Campine in the Netherlands) in order to return the area to cultivation, to provide a buffer zone between the more civilized regions of the Empire and other, as yet imperfectly subdued barbarian peoples, and finally to serve as a secure source of Frankish recruits for the imperial army.

This brutal treatment of the Franks was largely effective. Henceforth, although sporadic attempts might be made by anti-Roman factions to raid the Empire, the Franks provided loyal troops and leadership in the West for over a century. As we have seen, Franks such as Arbogast and Mallobaudes proved faithful officers of the Empire even against fellow Franks, and when in 406 the West faced the invasions of Vandals, Alans, and Sueves, the Franks proved faithful allies in attempting to repulse them.

During the long period of service to Rome, punctuated by short-lived rebellions or skirmishes, the Frankish identity and their political and military structure could not but be greatly influenced by contact with imperial traditions. Service in the military was long the primary means of Romanization, and the Frankish tribes of the middle and lower Rhine were more affected by this process than most. This deep penetration and transformation is clearly seen in such evidence as the third-century funerary inscription erected for a soldier in Pannonia: *Francus ego cives, miles romanus in armis* ("I am a Frank by nationality, but a Roman soldier under arms").[3] That a barbarian would employ the Roman term *civis* to describe his identity, a term incomprehensible without some sense of the tradition of Roman statecraft and law, indicates forcefully how much Frankish society was being molded into an integral part of the Empire. The second half of the inscription is equally indicative: a "Frankish citizen" was indeed a Roman soldier, for increasingly one found one's Frankish (as opposed to more narrow Chamavian,

Chattuarian, Bructerian, Amsivarian, or Salian) identity by serving in the Roman army.

Their service was well rewarded, and gradually in the fifth
century the Salians were able to spread out from their Toxandrian "reservation" into the more Romanized areas of what is
today Belgium and northern France as well as along the lower
Rhine, encroaching on the traditional territory of the Thuringians. Most of this expansion was peaceful, although in 428 and
again in the 450s the Roman general Aetius had to crush Frankish uprisings led by the Salic chieftain Chlodio. Such violent in-
terludes did not prevent close cooperation at other times, however, as in the Frankish support given Aetius in his defeat of the
Huns near Orléans in 451.

In the course of the fifth century the Salians came to dominate
the "tribal swarm" of Franks under the leadership of Chlodio's
kindred, which included Merovich (who was possibly but not
necessarily his son) and the latter's successor (and again possibly
his son) Childeric. However these Salic chieftains were related,
they were certainly part of the leading family of the Salians and
were distinguished, like other Germanic aristocratic families, by
the fashion of allowing their hair to grow long—the origin of the
later characterization of the family as "reges criniti" or long-
haired kings.

Childeric, one of several tribal leaders of the kindred of Chlodio,
began to lead the Franks prior to 463 and was the last Frankish
commander to continue the tradition of service as an "imperial
German." We know that he fought under the command of the
Gallic military commander Aegidius against the Visigoths at Orléans in 463 and again under the Roman commander or *comes*
Paul at Angers in 469. Although some sort of falling out resulted
in his departure from northern Gaul into exile in "Thuringia"
(it is uncertain whether this meant trans-Rhinian Thuringia or
simply Tournai), he remained intimately involved in the world
of late Roman civilization. Historians have even suggested, with
cause, that after his "exile" by the Roman commander of Gaul
he may have received direct subsidies from Constantinople. The
magnificent objects found in 1653 in his tomb in Tournai, the
center of his power, indicate the wealth and international hori-

zons of a successful federate in the late fifth century. The weapons, jewelry, and coins with which he had been buried at his death in 482 came from Byzantine, Hun, Germanic, and Gallo-Roman workshops. Service to Rome was still the surest means of achieving and expanding wealth and power.

However, the Roman world which he served was increasingly indistinguishable from his own. Aegidius himself had ended relations with Rome after the murder of the emperor Mariorian in 461 and was an opponent of the powerful Richomer. Geographically isolated by the territories of the Burgundians and Goths from the regions directly controlled by imperial armies, Aegidius commanded allegiance from his stronghold in Soissons less through any Roman office than through the power of his barbarian *bucellarii,* or personal army. Following his death in 464, his son Syagrius assumed his position, and the later report of Gregory of Tours that he had been elected *rex Romanorum,* "king of the Romans," a thoroughly barbarian title, probably accurately reflected his position. Whether or not Syagrius held some imperial title, possibly that of *patricius,* the real basis of his authority was that he had been raised to the position of *rex,* or military chieftain, of his barbarian army. Indeed, following the conclusion of peace between the emperor Julius Nepos and the Visigoths in 475, in which the former surrendered virtually all of Gaul to the latter, Syagrius may have been viewed as a renegade by the Empire. But he was not the only chief of a barbarian people north of the Loire. The tomb of Childeric contained a signet ring with the inscription *Childerici regis.*

The greatest power in the West was the Visigothic kingdom, and Childeric was too wise a commander to maintain an unambiguously hostile attitude toward it. That his sister was married to a Visigothic king is evidence that he had established positive relations with the heterodox but legitimate kingdom of Toulouse. However, like barbarian commanders in Roman service before him, Childeric maintained good relations with the Gallo-Roman society both in the kingdom of Soissons and, apparently, in the territories over which he ruled directly. Although a pagan (perhaps more in the Roman than in the Germanic tradition), he was seen as a protector of *Romanitas* and thus of the Ortho-

dox Christian church. In his frequent cooperation with Aegidius
and Syagrius and his friendly relationship with Gallo-Roman
bishops, he was clearly establishing his position not only with his
Frankish warrior following but with indigenous Roman power
structures as well. In all of this he lay the groundwork for the
rise of his son Clovis (Chlodovic), who succeeded him in 482.

Clovis

Upon the death of Childeric the leadership of the Salian Franks
passed to his son Clovis, who followed the policies of his father.
A letter from the Gallo-Roman bishop Remigius of Reims written immediately after Childeric's death indicates that the young
Frank was recognized by the Gallo-Roman leadership as the administrator of Belgica Secunda and that although a pagan, he
was expected to serve the Christian Roman community:

> A great rumor has reached us that you have undertaken the com-
> mand of Belgica Secunda. It is no surprise that you have begun just
> as your forefathers had always done . . . the bestowal of your favor
> must be pure and honest, you must honor your bishops and must
> always incline yourself to their advice. As soon as you are in agree-
> ment with them your territory [provincia] will prosper.[4]

This advice to a pagan chieftain to administer fairly and to
seek out the advice of the bishops did not reflect any new state
of affairs but described the tradition of imperial Germanic commanders in the service of the now Christian *Romanitas*. This
Clovis apparently did for a few years, but the tendency of military leaders to expand their command combined with the death
of the powerful Visigothic king Euric, which left a power vacuum
in the West, led him to turn his attention to the kingdom of
Syagrius, which probably included the Lyon provinces and portions of Belgica Secunda. In 486, with the cooperation of other
Frankish chieftains, Clovis began a campaign against Syagrius,
which was decided in one battle near Soissons. Syagrius was defeated and although he escaped, fleeing to the Visigothic king
Alaric II, he was turned over to Clovis, who had him secretly
killed.

Clovis's absorption of the kingdom of Soissons was, from one perspective, a coup d'état: the replacement of a barbarized Roman *rex* by a Romanized barbarian one. Clovis acquired intact what remained of Syagrius's *bucellarii,* Roman provincial administration, the notaries and agents of provincial government, as well as the fiscal lands previously controlled by Aegidius and Syagrius. Likewise, according to our principal source, Gregory of Tours, who wrote over two generations later, his position was recognized in some formal sense by the Gallo-Roman aristocracy. But Clovis's conquest had more far-reaching effects. Some Frankish groups had already been established within the kingdom of Soissons, possibly having remained after Childeric's exile. Indeed, Clovis's move against Syagrius may have been precipitated in part by the desire to reestablish control over these Franks. The conquest accelerated the movement of Frankish groups from north to south, and the heartland of Syagrius's kingdom rapidly became the center of Frankish power. This is most clearly seen in the disposition of Clovis's body upon his death. While his father had made his center of power the area of Tournai, where he was buried, in 511 Clovis was interred in Paris.

Clovis, an ambitious barbarian king consolidating his power in the early sixth century, had to come to terms with other power blocs in the West. First, he had to deal with the other Celtic, Germanic, and Frankish peoples on both sides of the Rhine, including the Armoricans, Thuringi, Alemanni, and Burgundians. Further afield was the Roman Empire, now limited to the East and a portion of central Italy, the Visigoths of Toulouse and Spain, and the Ostrogoths of Italy.

The chronology of Clovis's reign is hopelessly obscure; even the identity of the various peoples he is said to have defeated and absorbed into his kingdom is debatable. Apparently, he first fought the Armorican Celts to a stalemate, obtaining at best a very limited recognition of Frankish supremacy from that region later known as Brittany. According to Gregory, around 491 he conquered the Thuringi, presumably not those beyond the right bank of the Rhine, but a small group that, like the Franks, had drifted across the lower Rhine. In all likelihood, the conquest was a much more prolonged affair than Gregory would have one believe, and warfare continued until at least 502 if not later. Clovis's third and most significant barbarian victory was over the Alemanni. The decisive victory against the Alemanni occurred at Tolbac (modern Zülpich, north of Trier), apparently around 497. However, a significant number of the Alemanni escaped into the region of Rhaetia south of Lake Constance and the upper Rhine, where Theodoric the Ostrogoth took them under his protection. Having dealt with the Thuringi and Alemanni, Clovis then became involved in an indecisive campaign against the Burgundians around 500, a campaign ended through the intercession of Theodoric.

Clovis, like his father before him, cemented relationships with the Gothic kingdoms through marriage alliances. Clovis may even have adopted their religious beliefs. In spite of the claims of Gregory of Tours to the contrary (Gregory, writing two generations after the chieftain's death, created an image of Clovis that can hardly be reconciled with the fragmentary evidence we have of the historical Clovis), the British historian Ian Wood and the German Friedrich Prinz have suggested that Clovis flirted with or even converted to the Arianism (or quasi-Arianism) of his Gothic and Burgundian neighbors.[5] Such a suggestion makes abundant sense, particularly given the place of the Frankish ruler in the loose Ostrogothic confederation. Throughout his reign, Clovis maintained a respectful if not always accommodating attitude toward the great Ostrogothic king Theodoric, after whom his eldest son was named, and who not only protected Clovis's enemies such as the Alemanni, but also established a temporary truce between Clovis and the Visigothic king Alaric II.

Ultimately, however, Clovis determined to risk a decisive contest with the Goths, particularly in the region south of the Loire. Certainly this decision was related to his much discussed (and hopelessly obscure) conversion to Christianity, which took place at Reims on Christmas day in 496, 498, or possibly even as late as 506. From what Clovis was converted is not certain. To Gregory of Tours, it was from polytheism, specifically the Roman gods Saturn, Jupiter, Mars, and Mercury. This is not necessarily a case of *interpretatio Romana*. As we have seen, barbarian Roman commanders had a long tradition of involvement in Roman state religion. Alternatively, or additionally, the conversion may have been from a syncretistic Frankish polytheism that probably included Celtic gods; a sea god that was part sea beast, part man, and part bull, which seems to have been a particular family deity for the Merovingians (as Clovis's descendants would be called after the name of his *Sippe* legendary ancestor Merovich), Woden; and Ingvi-Frey, after whom was named the second of Clovis's sons. Finally (additionally?), if the hypothesis of Wood and Prinz is correct, the conversion may have been from a politically expedient Arianism.

To what he was converted is equally problematic. Given the syncretistic nature of late antique religion, one need not suppose that his conversion to Christianity was a conversion to radical monotheism—Clovis may have viewed Christ as a powerful, victory-giving ally to enlist on his behalf. The account of his conversion as presented by Gregory certainly does not contradict this. According to Gregory, it was Clovis's orthodox Burgundian wife Clotild who first urged Clovis to embrace her religion. However, the decisive moment came, as it had two centuries earlier for another ambitious pagan commander, Constantine, in battle. Pressed by the Alemanni at Tolbac, he vowed baptism in return for victory. The parallel with Constantine, explicitly developed by Gregory, was unmistakable.

Whatever its nature, the conversion was hardly an individual affair. The religion of the Frankish king was an integral component of the identity and military success of a whole people, who drew their identity and cohesion from him. The conversion of the king necessarily meant the conversion of his followers. Small wonder, then, that Gregory tells that before his baptism Clovis consulted with his "people"—presumably his most important supporters. And small wonder that not only was he baptized but at the same time were baptized "more than three thousand of his army." However many Franks followed their king into the font, the conversion was clearly a military affair— the adoption by the commander and his army of a new and powerful victory-giver.

The conversion of Clovis to orthodox Christianity had extremely important internal and external consequences. The victorious Franks were, like other Germanic peoples, primarily an army which, though monopolizing military power, represented a minority of the total population and largely lacked experience in civil governance or other activities essential to the maintenance of a society. Now no cult barrier separated the army from the indigenous inhabitants of Gaul—the peasants, artisans, and most importantly the Gallo-Roman aristocracy and its leaders, the bishops, for whom religion was as essential an element of their identity as it was for the Franks. Christianization made possible not only the close cooperation between Gallo-Romans and Franks, such as had long been the norm in the Gothic and Burgundian kingdoms, but a real amalgamation of the two peoples, a process well under way at all levels in the sixth century.

Externally, the conversion was a repudiation of the religious traditions of the Franks' neighbors, the Burgundians and the Goths, and presented an immediate threat to both kingdoms. This was not so much because, as Gregory suggests, the orthodox convert Clovis "found it hard to go on seeing these Arians occupying a part of Gaul."[6] Instead, as a ruler bent on expansion, his orthodoxy increased the likelihood that the Gallo-Roman aristocracies within these neighboring kingdoms would be inclined to collaborate with him. Thus the king's conversion was a threat to the internal stability of his neighbors, and whatever the actual chronology of the conversion, it must be understood as part of the Frankish challenge to Gothic dominance and Burgundian presence in the West.

The relative weakness of the Visigothic kingdom of Toulouse following Euric's death no doubt encouraged Clovis to expand to the south. In addition, as Syagrius's successor, Clovis now shared an uncertain frontier with the Visigoths, a frontier that in 498 he and his Franks had already crossed in a drive toward Bordeaux. After this, his campaigns against the Alemanni and Burgundians occupied him, but by 507 he was free to turn his attention again to the Visigothic kingdom south of the Loire. The campaign was well-coordinated; participating were both some Burgundians and contingents led by his Rhenish kinsman

Chloderic, son of King Sigibert of Cologne. Clovis had made an alliance with Emperor Anastasius; the expedition was coordinated with Byzantine fleet movements off the Italian coast, which effectively prevented Theodoric the Ostrogoth from coming to the aid of the Visigoths. At Vouillé, northwest of Poitiers, the Goths were soundly defeated, Alaric II killed, and during the next year the Gothic capital of Toulouse was taken and the Gothic presence north of the Pyrenees reduced to a narrow stretch of coastline as far east as Narbonne.

On his victorious journey homewards, Clovis was met in Tours by emissaries from Emperor Anastasius who presented him with an official document recognizing him as an honorary consul. Clovis used this honor, which apparently included imperial recognition of Clovis's kingdom or at least the symbolic adoption of Clovis into the imperial family, to strengthen his authority over the newly-won Gallo-Romans. He appeared in the basilica of St. Martin of Tours dressed in a purple tunic and a chlamys, or military mantle, and placed a diadem on his head. None of this was part of consular tradition, but he probably wished to enhance his kingship by associating with the Roman imperial tradition. In a famous but ambiguous passage, Gregory says that "from this time forward he was acclaimed 'consul or augustus.' "[7]

Whatever the meaning of this ritual, Clovis soon turned to the practical affair of strengthening his position among the Franks. He had risen as the most successful chieftain of this decentralized confederation to a position of power unheard-of for a barbarian north of the Alps. Now he began eliminating other Frankish chieftains, his own kinsmen for the most part, in order to consolidate his power over the Franks as he had done over the Gallo-Romans. This he did with efficiency and brutality. Among others, he liquidated the family of King Sigibert, who ruled the Franks living along the Rhine near Cologne, he had the rival Salic chieftain Chararic executed along with his son, and he orchestrated the destruction of Ragnachar, a Frankish king at Cambrai. By the time of Gregory, Clovis's ruthless but clever maneuvers had become legend, and orally transmitted poems or songs about him were no doubt among Gregory's sources. Even through these legendary accounts transmitted by a Gallo-Roman bishop, however, one can catch a glimpse of both the personality and the political acumen of Clovis. In each case he was careful to absorb not only his victim's treasure, but his *leudes,* or closest followers, as well. By the end of his reign, Gregory tells us, he was wont to complain "How sad a thing it is that I live among strangers like some solitary traveller, and that I have none of my own relations left to help me when disaster threatens!"[8] This comment was made, Gregory assures us, not because he grieved for them, but in the hope of finding some relative still alive whom he could kill.

Governing Francia: Legacies of Administration

The image most commonly held of Clovis's control over his vast conquests is a lordship established and maintained by personal charisma and fear. Gregory's descriptions of Clovis's elimination of his kinsmen and of his brutal retaliation for an affront made by a Frankish warrior who dared dispute his share of booty captured at Soissons reinforce this image of the barbarian conqueror, quick to lie and quicker to kill. Such qualities he may well have possessed, although they were not particularly barbarian—they can also characterize late Roman emperors. However these traits alone would hardly have made possible not only his conquests but the creation of a kingdom which, although weakened and divided upon his death, was visible enough to be passed on to his successors. The very heterogeneity of the lands and peoples he conquered provided multiple, complementary systems of political, social, and religious control on which to establish continuity and stability. Unlike most barbarian conquerors, including Attila and even Theodoric, Clovis's kingdom and his family endured for centuries.

The failure of Attila to establish a dynasty was hardly surprising. The rise and fall of such charismatic rulers was common enough in antiquity. The fate of Theodoric's Gothic kingdom deserves more consideration. His brilliant achievement suffered from two fatal weaknesses. First, he never attempted a synthesis of Roman and Gothic societies, thus bequeathing an unstable situation to his successors. Second and more fundamentally, Italy was simply too close to Constantinople and the center of Roman interests to be allowed to go its own way.

Theodoric had attempted to preserve virtually intact two traditions, that of his orthodox Christian Roman population and that of the Arian Gothic army settled largely around Ravenna, Verona, and Pavia. The attraction of Roman tradition and culture was, however, too seductive for members of his own family, and after his death in 526 the next generation of Amals found themselves alienated from the more traditional Gothic aristocracy and bitterly divided among themselves. Ultimately Amalasuntha, the widow of Theodoric's son and regent for her minor son Athalaric (516–534), was driven to plan to secretly deliver Italy to Emperor Justinian. Her murder in 535 gave Justinian the opportunity to declare war on the Goths, and the ensuing twenty years of bloody conflict annihilated the Ostrogoths and left Italy prostrate.

In contrast to Theodoric's brilliant and doomed political structure in Italy, Clovis's kingdom from the beginning experienced a much more thorough mixture of Frankish and Roman traditions. Moreover, Gaul and Germany were simply too peripheral to Byzantine concerns to attract more than the cursory interest of Justinian and his successors. Thus the Franks were left to work out the implications of their successes in relative peace.

The charisma conveyed by the long hair and mythic origins of Clovis's ancestors, and his ability in convincing others that he was the only channel through which this charisma might be transmitted to future generations, may no doubt be credited with some of his success. Too much can be made of this, however. More important for the establishment of continuity and effectiveness in rule was the dual Roman heritage of both conquerors and conquered.

The indigenous population both of the north and especially of Aquitaine, the region south of the Loire that had been part of the Visigothic kingdom, had preserved the late Roman infrastructure virtually intact. Not only did Latin letters and language continue to be cultivated and vulgar Roman law continue to order people's lives, but Roman fiscal and agricultural structures, the network of Roman roads, towns, and commercial systems, although greatly privatized, had nevertheless survived without serious interruption. All of this was inherited by the Franks, along with the remains of the Roman bureaucracy that continued to operate them. After their victory, Clovis's Franks, accustomed to working closely with Romans, were in an ideal position to absorb them into the administration.

The Franks themselves were likewise deeply Romanized. Even prior to the victory at Soissons, Clovis and the Franks had been accustomed to the discipline of Rome. Generations of Roman service had taught the Franks much about Roman organization and control. This heritage is even visible in that supposedly most Frankish tradition, the Salic Law. Sometime between 508 and 511 Clovis issued what is known as the *Pactus Legis Salicae,* a capital and controversial text which we shall be mentioning often in our discussion of Frankish society. The *Pactus,* in its oldest extant form, consists of sixty-five chapters and is, after the Visigothic Law, the oldest example of a written code for a barbarian kingdom. Written law was certainly not a barbarian tradition; the very act of codifying traditional custom, in whatever haphazard manner, could only originate under the influence of Roman law and could have been done only by persons trained in that tradition. The text is in Latin, and scholars have long abandoned the hypothesis that the Latin was a translation of a now-lost Frankish version. Concepts of Roman law and Roman legal organization appear in the very form of the text. In issuing the text, Clovis was acting not as a barbarian king but as the legitimate ruler of a section of the Romanized world. Moreover, the *Pactus* applies not simply to Franks. It is intended for all the *barbari* in his realm.

The bulk of the *Pactus* does not represent "new" legislation. Probably much of it was already antiquated at the time of its issue. With only minor exceptions, it is free of any Christian elements; it describes a society of simple peasants and herdsmen, not the victorious conquerors of Gaul; and some sections are less in the form of precepts than simple lists of fines and penalties and even traditional advice. The overwhelming thrust of the *Pactus* is to limit feuds or revenge on the part of family groups by establishing fines and penalties for offenses, an ancient concern in Germanic society, according to Tacitus. Thus, while the codification itself as well as some parts of the *Pactus* are the result of Clovis's initiative, much of the text harks back to a much earlier period.

This does not mean, however, that one sees in this law pure Germanic custom. On the contrary, the older traditions may themselves be quite Roman. The primary evidence for this is the placenames mentioned in the *Pactus* and the earliest prologue attached to it. The prologue tells that because there were interminable quarrels among the Franks, four leading men who were commanders (*rectores*) came together and decreed the Salic Law.[9] This has usually been seen as a mythic origin account or perhaps a reference to otherwise unknown subkings from the time of Clovis. In a subsequent passage of the *Pactus,* it appears that the normal area of Frankish occupation is between the *Ligeris* river and the *Carbonaria* forest, although already the Franks had spread out beyond these boundaries. The majority of scholars today identify these landmarks as the Loire River and the Charbonnière forest between the Sambre and Dyle rivers in modern Belgium. They formed roughly the northern and southern boundaries of Clovis's kingdom, although some still argue that the *Ligeris* is the Lys, which would have formed the northern boundary of Toxandria. Recently the French historian Jean-Pierre Poly has proposed as the meeting places of the four *rectores* the villages of Bodegem, Zelhem, and Videm between the Lys and the Charbonnière, which is still roughly within the old Toxandrian area. Further, he believes the four *rectores* represented four high-ranking "imperial German" officers of the fourth century, who, not by any Frankish right but by their Roman military authority over their troops, had the power to preserve the peace, quell violence, and negotiate blood payments from family elders to end feuds. Thus he would conclude that long before Clovis's conquest the Franks had incorporated notions of Roman authority into their legal and political structure. Clovis's legislative activity then drew upon this older tradition for his codification.[10]

The Franks of Clovis's time were accustomed to Roman traditions of law. They were equally accustomed, or soon made themselves so, to the use of Roman administration. As we have seen, even before his defeat of Syagrius, Clovis had been recognized by Bishop Remigius as a legitimate Roman governor, and after his victories over internal and external rivals, Roman and barbarian alike, his legitimacy had been acknowledged by the emperor. Thus the court of Clovis and his successors included not only the traditional officers of a Frankish aristocrat's household, here elevated to royal prominence—the king's *antrustiones*, or personal following, which enjoyed particular royal favor, headed by his *maior domus* or mayor of the palace, the constable, chamberlain, and the like—but Roman officers as well. Although no royal documents from Merovingian kings prior to 528 have survived, the form of later diplomas indicates that the kings had absorbed the secretaries (*scrinarii*) and chancellors (*referendarii*) of late Roman administration. Moreover, as in late Roman and Gothic administrations, this personnel was secular; the tradition of using clerics in the royal chancellery would be a Carolingian innovation.

The written word was vital in the administration of the Merovingian realm because the late Roman tax system, a fundamental aspect of royal power, continued to function, and accurate control of taxation meant reliance on paperwork. If little of it survives in contrast with later medieval administrative sources, the reasons are that it was written on fragile papyrus rather than on durable parchment, and being abundant and commonplace, less care was taken to preserve it beyond the time of its immediate usefulness. Nevertheless, we find references to a wider variety of written administrative instruments produced by the Frankish kings and their agents than would appear again before the twelfth century.

However we must not suppose that, because both Franks and Gallo-Romans were heirs of Roman traditions they were heirs of the same tradition. As we saw in the previous chapters, *Romanitas* had, for provincial Romans, virtually ceased to have anything to do with governance and certainly nothing with the military. By starving it financially, the Gallo-Roman aristocracy had long before managed to reduce provincial administration to a shadow and had privatized much of revenue collection, police protection, and even justice. If the central administration of the early Frankish kings was primitive, it was no more or less than the administration Clovis inherited from Syagrius. For all of their love of Rome, the Gallo-Romans had long considered a strong central government a threat to their familial hegemony.

As long as provincial governors or barbarian kings allowed the Gallo-Roman elite autonomy, with control over their local dependents, these aristocrats were accustomed to providing assistance to the state. We have seen that Remigius had recognized Clovis's political legitimacy prior to his victory at Soissons and his conversion; similarly at the Synod of Agde in 506 Archbishop Caesarius of Arles had prayed on bended knee for the success, prosperity, and long life of the Arian Visigothic king Alaric. Rather than claiming the right to central government, this aristocracy was much more comfortable allowing the bishop, chosen by and of themselves, to direct what remained of the public sphere, the *res publicae,* at the local level of the *civitas,* which included the city and its immediate territory. Thus Remigius's plea to Clovis to follow his bishops' advice is no more than a plea for him to follow the advice of the Roman aristocracy. Power over the people was held by the great landowners, who were the real authority. Thus their sense of belonging to a wider world of Rome was much more a function of classical culture, particularly rhetoric, and of orthodox religion than of imperial administration.

If the cultural legacy of Rome was claimed as a monopoly by the aristocracy, it was the military that belonged to the Franks, as it had to generations of imperial Germans before them. As deeply Romanized as Franks were in terms of military discipline and participation in the power politics of the Western Empire, they were, except for a small elite, as untouched by Roman social and cultural traditions as the Gallo-Roman aristocracy was by Roman military tradition. The unique achievement of Clovis and his successors was that, through his conquest and conversion, he was able to begin to reunite these two splintered halves of the Roman heritage. The process was a long one and not without difficulty, but in time it created a new world.

In the early sixth century, the duality of the heritage was most clearly in evidence in local administration. Our sources are extraordinarily meager, but apparently Gallo-Roman bishops continued to represent their communities, and the remains of local judicial and fiscal administration were left intact. The primary change was that a *comes* or count, personally connected to the king and thus in some sense Frankish, was assigned along with perhaps a small garrison to major towns. His responsibilities were largely military and judicial. He raised the levy from the area and enforced royal law as it applied to Franks when he could. Without the cooperation of the bishop and other Gallo-Romans he could accomplish little, but this cooperation was usually forthcoming provided he did not attempt to increase the burden of taxation or interfere in the sphere of influence created by the local elites. In fact, he often seems to have married into these elites, particularly in remote areas of the kingdom where Franks were few. We shall see more of this process in subsequent chapters.

At the top of the political spectrum, the dual heritage was seen in a decision that had far-reaching implications for Francia: the division of Clovis's kingdom upon his death in 511.[11] No one really knows why it was divided among his four sons, although there is no lack of hypotheses: perhaps it was part of a wider tradition of Germanic societies, which can be found among the Burgundians, Goths, Vandals, and Anglo-Saxons, all of whom knew multiple kings without necessarily multiple kingdoms; perhaps this was demanded by Salic Law; perhaps it was because of the almost magical force of Merovingian blood. More likely, the division was the result of the peculiar dual nature of Clovis's kingship. He had managed to make himself the sole commander of the Franks and, while he was probably not as successful in exterminating his relatives as Gregory suggests, there were no close claimants for succession other than his sons by two wives. To judge by other Germanic traditions this might have been dealt with in a variety of ways. The elder son Theuderic could have inherited his father's kingdom in its entirety. Alternatively, his half brothers by Queen Chrodechildis could have each obtained a position as subking while Theuderic became king of a united Francia. As Ian Wood has suggested however, given the age disparity separating him from the others, there would have been a great possibility that the younger sons would have in time lost their positions and their lives to him. In any event, this possibility seems to have been exactly what Clovis, through his systematic elimination of kinsmen, was attempting to end.

The solution of dividing the kingdom among his four sons seems less a Frankish than a Roman one. Clovis's territories were divided along roughly Roman political boundaries, and each brother was established with his own court and (no doubt Roman) advisors centered in a major city. The divisions reflect less the Roman imperial tradition than the particularist traditions of the Gallo-Roman aristocracy; they did not respect the integrity of Roman provinces but rather that of the smaller Roman *civitates,* which had become the focal points of Gallo-Roman interest. Thus Theuderic, whose court was in Reims, received in addition the areas centered on Trier, Mainz, Cologne, Basel, and Châlons, as well as the recently subdued lands on the right bank of the Rhine. Chlothar received the old Salic heartlands between the Charbonnière forest and the Somme River along with Noyon, Soissons, his capital, and Laon. Childebert's portion included the coastal regions from the Somme to Brittany, probably including, along with Paris, his capital, Amiens, Beauvais, Rouen, Meaux, Le Mans, and Rennes. The last brother, Chlodomer, reigned from Orléans over Tours, Sens, and probably Troyes, Auxerre, Chartres, Angers, and Nantes.

Just how these portions were determined is unknown. Certainly they must have been devised by Romans with a knowledge of fiscal receipts from each region as well as an eye to maintaining the integrity of their own power bases. Even in this most central question of the fate of the Frankish kingdom, it is most likely that decisions were made by Franks and Romans working in close harmony.

The Peoples of Francia

The population of Clovis's kingdom was complex and heterogeneous in its social, cultural, and economic traditions. Not only were the Franks and Gallo-Romans different from each other culturally, but neither of these populations was itself homogeneous.

THE ECONOMY OF COUNTRYSIDE AND CITY

The Roman society had continued to develop into the regionally fragmented and socially stratified world that we examined in Chapter I. This society was deeply rooted in the nature of its economic system, which was characterized by the monopoly of landowning in the hands of a small, extraordinarily wealthy elite, with the vast majority of the population, slave and free alike, destitute and often in desperate straits. The result was an agriculture woefully inadequate to the support of the population and a commercial and artisanal infrastructure catering almost exclusively to the elite.

This agricultural system, which characterized the early medieval economy for centuries, resulted in little surplus production in good years and frequent and often catastrophic famines in bad. Occasionally the fragility of this economic base has been blamed on the arrival of the barbarians, who in fact had little effect on either landholding or agricultural techniques. The continuity with late Roman field division, agricultural techniques, and manorial organization, when they had survived to the sixth century, was enormous. This was less the case in the Rhenish regions but was common elsewhere, both in the north of the Frankish kingdom and especially in the south. More disruptive than barbarians had been the general decline in population and flight from marginal or overtaxed lands beginning in the third century. The lack of sufficient agricultural labor continued to be a major problem, and the steps that had been taken since Diocletian had, if anything, probably exacerbated the situation. In 517 the council of Yenne forbad abbots to enfranchise slaves from the estates received from laymen because "It is unjust that slaves should enjoy liberty while monks work the land day and night."[12] Well into the ninth century, kings, aristocrats, and churchmen were engaged in bringing abandoned and uninhabited lands into production.

The cultivation of the land relied on the techniques of provincial Rome, but they were, if anything, even more labor-intensive than previously. Machinery such as the mechanical harvester used in Gaul in the time of Pliny had disappeared; water mills, although in use along the Rhône and Ruiver, as well as in a few other areas, were rare; and the other tools, ploughs, scythes, hoes, etc., were largely or even entirely of wood. Iron was a rare and precious commodity. So important was it that appeals were commonly made to local saints to find lost iron objects, and when they did so, the fortunate event was likely to be recorded among the saint's miracles. Carefully guarded, sparingly used, iron tools were employed primarily to make wooden ones.

Cereal production, which within the Roman world had consisted primarily of wheat, came to be dominated increasingly by darker grains such as barley, known to the Germanic peoples. This change reflected in part a change of taste from the traditional Mediterranean to a more northern one, but was also due to practical survival and efficiency. Dark grains were not only more hardy, but because they could be readily converted into a strong and nourishing beer, they could be conserved longer than the more delicate wheat.

One area of agriculture that actually expanded in the early Merovingian period was viniculture. Rome had introduced vines wherever it had come, but they were cultivated in the more northern areas of Europe only with the expansion of ecclesiastical institutions in these areas. Wine was not only essential for eucharistic liturgy, it was the drink of the elite. The increasing investment in wine cultivation at the expense of traditional subsistence-type agriculture probably indicates the growing dominance of agricultural decisions by the aristocracy.

The prehistoric concern of the Germanic peoples with cattle herding continued and expanded with the Frankish kingdom. Throughout the Salic Law and other early law codes, cattle figure prominently, and the detail with which cattle raising is treated reinforces the overall impression that these animals continued, as in the age of Stelus, to form the foundation of barbarian wealth and prestige.

Although the vast majority of the population still lived on the land, the cities of Francia played an important role in the kingdom, both as residences of bishops, counts, and kings and as centers of economic activity. The actual population of these cities is extremely difficult to determine. The only evidence comes from archaeology, and since it is largely based on the area included within the third-century city walls, there is abundant room for speculation about the size of the population residing in suburban quarters. Thus some historians have speculated that in the sixth century Paris might have had a population of 20,000 inhabitants and Bordeaux 15,000, while others have argued that these estimates should be reduced by almost 50 percent. What is certain is that the social, cultural, and political significance of these cities was far greater than what one might expect from their small populations.

Most of the Roman aristocracy had long before abandoned the cities for the security and autonomy of their vast country estates, but some had returned, and in the poetry of Sidonius Apollinarius and the lives of early saints we read of the presence of rich and powerful Romans living not only in the cities of Aquitaine and Gaul, but even in Trier, Metz, and Cologne. The most important Gallo-Roman residents were, however, the bishops. They and their clergy maintained much of the public life of the cities, undertaking the traditional civic obligations of poor relief and the maintenance of walls, aqueducts, and the like. So important were they that ancient cities which did not become the sees of bishops tended by and large to disappear in the early Middle Ages. The presence of an episcopal court made the difference between life and death for an urban center.

Although one hears much less about them than about the bishop and clergy in our sources, another important resident of the cities was the Frankish king or his representative, the count, and his military garrison. Frankish elites, like their Gothic and Burgundian counterparts, were attracted to Roman cities where they could both enjoy the good life they and their ancestors had long desired and find the safety in numbers that their political position and social rank demanded. Unlike the later Merovingians and certainly unlike the Carolingians, the early Merovingians and their representatives resided in cities, where they received and spent the revenues of estates they had acquired, thus contributing to a continuing mercantile and craft economy which flourished through the seventh century. While it is certainly true that the bishops and their clerics formed the central nucleus of urban continuity and that their building programs gradually came to dominate the physical space of the city with their cathedral groups, baptisteries, hospices, and, outside the walls, basilicas and cemeteries, one must not forget the effects on city life of a Theudebert, who had games held once more in the amphitheater of Arles, or of a Chilperic I, who built circuses in both Paris and Soissons.

The sixth-century city was more than the residence of the bishop and the Frankish count or king. It continued to play a vital commercial role as well. In spite of barbarian pillage and Gallo-Roman internal strife, in spite of depopulation and the archaization of Western society, the network of Roman roads and, more importantly, of commercial waterways continued to function. The nature of this circulation was, however, quite different from what had been the norm in previous centuries or was seen in the later Middle Ages when urban growth was accompanied by a resurgence of commercial activity. In order to understand the peculiar nature of commerce in the Merovingian world we must first understand the circulation of goods in general in sixth-century Francia.

Much ink has been spilled in the debate over the relative vitality of the Western economy in the sixth, seventh, and eighth centuries. On the one hand, numismatic evidence indicates the continued importance of gold coinage into the seventh century, and both archival and narrative sources mention merchants, import goods, and a functioning customs and tariff collection well into the eighth century. On the other hand, it often appears that precious metal was more important for display than for use as an exchange medium and that the primary means of circulation of goods and prestige objects was not commerce but military expeditions and local plundering, or else the exchange of gifts. Thus from one perspective the commercial world of late antiquity appears intact and perhaps even expanding in the north; Syrian, Greek, and Jewish merchants travel the length and breadth of Francia, sometimes in camel caravans, selling their wares, and local grain merchants buy and sell in flourishing markets. From the other, one sees an archaic society in which warfare and gift exchange characterize the modalities of circulation and in which gold is more prized for jewelry, for church ornamentation, or for horse trappings than for its exchange value. The confusion is the result of the complex nature of the Merovingian economy in which circulation mechanisms were intimately connected to social relationships. With different people, at different times, all of these mechanisms operated, and each played a vital role in the distribution of local, regional, and international goods and services.

The overwhelming majority of foodstuff were made available for local consumption either by the peasants who produced it or by their lords. The small surplus not consumed or lost to spoilage circulated by sale, gift, or theft, depending on the social and political relationships between the exchange partners. The second two were more significant than the first. Great aristocrats, whether Frankish or Roman, supported their followers and the members of their households by supplying them with food, clothing, arms, and other necessities of their livelihood and social rank. Bishops distributed alms to the poor inscribed in the municipal poor rolls as a continuation of the traditional obligation of imperial largesse and in order to maintain the support of the populace. Friendship was sealed by the exchange of gifts. This network of gifts and countergifts probably accounted for much of the equalization and distribution of agricultural surplus.

Between enemies, that is, any persons not bound by a mutual relationship of friendship, goods circulated by plunder and theft. This could mean warfare or simply periodic raids on enemies' goods and chattels as part of continuing feuds. Also, kings and their representatives received, in addition to taxes, gifts of livestock, wine, wax, and other products, which were essentially tribute.

Both of these sorts of transactions could and did take place within the city as well as the countryside. However, it was in the city that the less normal but still significant form of goods exchange between neutral parties took place—sale. One hears of the sale of foodstuffs primarily during times of crisis when those who had stockpiled them could realize enormous profits, although regular markets certainly existed. The more important types of commercial transactions were in commodities not everywhere available, relatively easy to carry, and in great demand. The most basic of these was salt, which was produced in low-lying coastal regions by evaporation and then transported inland. Also important were wine, oil, fish, and grain.

Products of artisanal workshops also circulated regionally and even over great distances, although the mechanisms of this circulation is uncertain. In the south, traditional Mediterranean pottery of late classical design continued to be produced into the eighth century; glass produced in the Ardennes and around Cologne found its way as far north as Frisia and even Sweden; Frankish weapons, which enjoyed a great reputation across Europe, have been found throughout Francia and in Frisia and Scandinavia. Textiles also circulated between regions: Provence was particularly known for its inexpensive cloth as far away as Rome, Monte Cassino, and Spain.

As reduced in size as the population of Frankish cities was, a diverse population of merchants continued to exist. Gregory of Tours mentions that the bishop of Verdun, Desideratus, obtained a loan from King Theudebert of 7,000 gold pieces guaranteed by the merchants of his city, who presumably specialized in foodstuffs. However, the story told by Gregory demonstrates the parallel existence of a gift-based circulation of wealth and commerce: Theudebert granted the loan as a favor to Desideratus to show his generosity. According to Gregory the loan enriched "those practicing commerce,"[13] and the bishop was able to attempt to repay the loan with interest. The king refused repayment, saying that he had no need of it. That enough merchants existed in the city to repay such a loan indicates that commerce was not insignificant; that their repayment was later dismissed by the king out of generosity indicates that the system of commercial credit was alien to him—he preferred to have the city in his political debt. For a Merovingian king, gold was not primarily a form of money with which to make more money by clever investment; it was a means of manifesting his generosity and of cementing the bonds with his people.

In addition to urban merchants, the owners of great estates, both lay and ecclesiastic, had their own agents, sometimes Jews, in other instances members of their own households, either serf or freedmen, who were responsible for the sale of their surplus and the purchase of necessities not produced locally. Again, however, these agents operated not only in a commercial mode; the same individuals might be charged with the delivery of gifts to other magnates and with the reception of reciprocated gifts. One can suppose that much of the circulation in which they were involved was neither sale nor, strictly speaking, barter, but the delivery of goods that cemented relationships among the elite.

Finally, in every important city was a community of foreigners engaged in supplying luxury goods to the aristocracy. This long-distance commerce was largely in the hands of Greeks, Syrians, and Jews, who are found in Arles, Marseille, Narbonne, Lyon, Orléans, Bordeaux, Bourges, Paris, and elsewhere. They provided a supply of jewelry, precious cloths, ornaments, as well as papyrus, spices, and the like. These merchants could form considerable communities in Frankish cities with their own judicial officers or "consuls" and perhaps even took an active role in the wider community. Gregory of Tours mentions that a Syrian merchant, Eusebius, bribed his way into the position of bishop of Paris and, dismissing the household of his predecessor, replaced them with other Syrians.[14] Clearly international merchants wielded considerable power.

They acquired this power because they could provide the aristocracy with the magnificent luxury goods they needed to make manifest their social positions. The merchants were also important because import duties and tariffs collected from them were a major source of liquid revenue for the Merovingians. Particularly in Provence, where the bulk of Mediterranean imports arrived, royal customs officers collected considerable sums which went to the royal coffers. The division of Provence among the subkingdoms of Francia probably involved as much a division of important customs dues as a division of land.

In return, the West had little to offer these international merchants but gold. This was nothing new. Gaul had never been a major exporter of anything but timber and, occasionally, of slaves. To this the Franks could add weapons. However the exportation of slaves was, in theory at least, forbidden—labor was scarce and the Franks themselves imported slaves from the Slavic regions— although it certainly did go on via the Rhône. Likewise, Frankish arms were a dangerous export item since they could be turned against them by other purchasers. Thus the East–West commerce was largely one-way. Gold that had been acquired as booty or subsidies from the Eastern Empire flowed back again in payment for luxury goods. As the amount of booty decreased in the later sixth, seventh, and early eighth centuries, commerce decreased with it. This gold drain, which temporarily ended only with renewed Frankish conquests under the Carolingians, ultimately reduced international trade to a trickle. And, as trade disappeared, so did the international communities of merchants which added color, sophistication, and excitement to the cities of Francia.

FRANKISH SOCIETY

Franks had been settling heavily in Gaul long before Clovis, probably in fact before they were Franks. As we have seen, the conquest of Syagrius's kingdom may have been as much a response to this situation as a precipitator of it. Some Franks gradually moved, a few families at a time and a few kilometers at a time, into the Roman world. But some peoples living in the Roman world, whether *laeti* or federates, gradually turned into Franks. Given the paucity of written evidence, it is extremely difficult to determine just how those regions of northern Europe became "Frankish." Our best evidence lies in the cemeteries arranged in rows about which we spoke in Chapter Two. In the late fifth century these cemeteries show an important change. Prior to that time row cemeteries within the Empire had been generally poor in grave goods. Now, increasingly one began to bury the dead with more weapons or jewelry, indicating the great wealth that came with military service and increased raiding. Moreover, to judge from the great differences in the quality and variety of grave goods found in these late fifth-century tombs, military service, either to Childeric and Clovis or to the various competing Gallo-Roman commanders, or even independent raiding could result in real wealth for leaders of warrior bands.

A significant example of the archaeological evidence left by

these late fifth-century migrants and their successors is the cemetery at Lavoye (Meuse), excavated at the beginning of this century. The findings, analyzed scientifically, were published by René
Joffroy a little over a decade ago.[15] The cemetery, established on
an early Gallo-Roman site (probably a rustic *villa*) contains 362
tombs, of which 192 can be dated from the late fifth or early
sixth century until the second half of the seventh century, after
which time the disappearance of grave goods makes dating impossible. The tombs are arranged in rows and oriented north-
south. The cemetery seems to have grown up around a group of
nine tombs that probably form the family burial group of an
important Frankish chieftain. The central tomb (number 319),
that of the chief himself, is the oldest, largest, deepest, and richest of the group and contains the remains of a man between fifty
and sixty years old. Buried with him are weapons and objects of
extraordinary value and beauty, including a golden cloisonné
belt buckle decorated with garnets; a purse with a similarly decorated clasp; a dagger with a handle of gold; a magnificent long
sword almost a meter in length decorated with gold, silver, and
garnets; three javelin heads; a shield; and, at his feet, a glass
bowl and a Christian liturgical pitcher covered in bronze and
decorated with scenes from the life of Christ, which was probably
pillaged from a Christian church. These objects are similar to
others found across a wide region of northern France and Germany both within and beyond the former Roman *limes* and
show not only the martial character of his identity and wealth,
but also the wide cultural zone to which the chieftain belonged.

The nearby tombs that also date from the early sixth century
were probably for members of his family. Of the five closest to
the chieftain's, three are of women, also richly furnished with
jewelry, vessels, and spinning weights. These may have been his
wives; like the Germans of Tacitus's day the Franks of the sixth
century practiced resource polygyny, and certainly this chief could
have afforded several wives. The two remaining tombs are of
small children, evidence of the infant mortality that plagued European society well into the nineteenth century.

North, east, and west of this burial group spread the other
tombs of the Frankish community. Some have similar but poorer

grave articles; most are without any furnishings at all. This community, living on the site of a previous Roman villa and possibly incorporating into it the descendants of the local Gallo-Roman inhabitants, will be our base as we examine the structure and organization of Frankish society in the sixth century.

HOUSEHOLDS

The burials at Lavoye tend, like those surrounding the chieftain, to be grouped together, probably indicating kin groupings. What exactly these were in the sixth century is difficult to determine. Frankish society continued the organization of the migration period, and although the large kindred groups or *Sippe* continued to be important to the aristocracy, they were probably less important to ordinary Franks than individual households and villages.

Roman and Germanic traditions of patriarchal family structure differed little, and the two fused rapidly and easily in terms of control over the household. The father was the head of the household and exercised his authority, *munduburdium,* over all of its members—wives, children, and slaves. The wealthier the man, the larger the household. Merovingian kings before and after Clovis's conversion frequently had several wives, and important chieftains such as the one buried at Lavoye no doubt did also. Well into the ninth century, Frankish and other Germanic societies had a variety of marriages. The most formal type involved transfer of property and of *munduburdium* over the woman. Women were highly valued in Frankish society, primarily because of their value in bearing children. According to Salic Law the wergeld of a woman of childbearing age was three times that of an ordinary man or a woman under twelve or over forty.

Thus the transfer of a woman from one man to another demanded compensation. This was originally in the form of a bride-price, but by the sixth century it was becoming a ritual payment. The more important gift was the reverse dowry the groom gave to the bride, which in Frankish custom amounted to one-third of the groom's property. After the marriage had

been consummated, the husband traditionally gave his wife another gift, the *Morgangabe*. Finally, it was normal for the father
of the bride to give the couple a gift after the marriage.

The negotiations leading to marriage were carried out between the heads of the households and, in important families,
sealed with a formal written contract. The wedding itself was
publicly celebrated and marked the formation or reaffirmation
of an alliance between the two households.

A second, less formal kind of marriage, which required no
transfer of authority or dowry, was also common. This was the
Friedelehe, a union effected privately between husband and wife.
Such unions were a threat to the authority of the heads of households and to the Church, which was increasingly concerned
about the legitimacy of children and the enforceability of marriage contracts. However, such unions were publicly recognized,
even if frowned upon by many. Often the marriage was arranged
as a kind of bride theft; the man would abduct the woman, frequently with her consent and agreement. After the marriage had
been consummated, the family of the woman had to choose
among seeking vengeance, reparation for the rape of their daughter, or accepting her abductor as her husband.

In addition, Franks often had concubines, either between or
along with marriages. Such arrangements were considered normal well into the eighth century, although from time to time
churchmen raised objections to them, and their children posed
a potential threat to the claims of the legitimate children for
their inheritance.

Like kinship, inheritance was bilateral in Frankish society,
although daughters were excluded from some forms of real property inheritance. This is stated in the famous chapter of the
Pactus Legis Salicae, resurrected in the fourteenth century by
French jurists eager to avoid seeing the French crown pass to
the king of England, which excluded women from inheritance
of "Salic" land. However, no one is quite sure what Salic land
was, and by the second half of the sixth century Chilperic II
specifically allowed daughters to inherit Salic land in the absence
of brothers. Women certainly did participate in inheritance of
movables, and upon the death of a husband a wife might well

inherit all of his property, which she could then control without male authority.

Besides one's wife or wives, the household included the underage children, legitimate and illegitimate. Scholars have suggested that the practice of polygyny and concubinage probably concentrated the number of women in the households of the magnates, leaving fewer for marriage with the rest of the population and, as a result, fewer children. This may be so, but it is also clear that when resources were scarce, Franks, like other peasant societies before and after them, occasionally practiced infanticide or child selling. Entirely too much has been made of this in recent literature, however. There is no evidence that infanticide was a normal practice or that female infanticide in particular was deeply ingrained in the popular culture of Francia.

In addition to one's kin, the household also included a wide variety of servants, slaves, and retainers. In fact, to judge from later peasant communities, the position of householder was an elite one, requiring a sufficient economic base in land and chattels to establish a house and thus to marry. Many, if not most, people probably lived as members of other households, whether they were of kings, wealthy magnates, or simply more prosperous peasants. These included household slaves (unlike Romans, Franks did not normally employ gangs of slave laborers unless they were wealthy and had been thoroughly Romanized), unmarried relatives, abandoned children of less prosperous neighbors absorbed and raised as servants, and hired hands lacking the wherewithal to establish their own households. The size of such households could thus vary enormously from just the nuclear family to dozens of retainers in the service of great men or women.

THE VILLAGE

The normal form of agricultural exploitation established by Romans in Gaul, as elsewhere in the Empire, was the villa, that is, the isolated estate of varying size (80 to 180 square meters for small ones to over 300 square meters for large ones). Within the walls of the villa were found the house of the owner and the habitations of his slaves, who provided the labor on the estate. In the course of the third and fourth centuries most of the isolated northern villas were abandoned in favor of more concentrated areas of habitation, often near forests or waterways. This was done possibly as a security measure in uncertain times. These new communities were distinguished from the older *villae* not only by the relative concentration of population but also by the insubstantiality of their buildings, which were lightly constructed wooden dwellings irregularly grouped. In the course of the fifth and sixth centuries, these new concentrated centers began to develop into the villages of the Middle Ages.

In western Germany the same period saw equally important changes. Much of Germany experienced a drop in inhabited sites in late antiquity. Then, beginning in the early fifth century, the Romanized areas of Germany began to experience considerable growth of new habitations. Around Trier, twenty new sites appeared between 450 and 525, twenty-eight between 525 and 600, and sixty-seven between 600 and 700. Around Cologne, a similar growth took place; the number of inhabited sites grew from around twenty-eight in the sixth century to sixty-seven in the seventh. At the same time, the more northern and eastern regions were undergoing a decline of populated sites that did not end until the eighth century.[16]

The communities thus created during the fourth through sixth centuries formed the physical space within which northern Europe's population would live for three centuries, until the great changes of the Carolingian period. Through the Merovingian centuries, they played important social and cultural roles in the society of Francia.

While peasants and herdsmen might travel a considerable distance to their fields, the village itself was the center of religious and social life. The original impetus for the establishment of concentrated villages in particular places was often the presence of a cult center. In pagan times this meant perhaps a rural temple; later it could be a chapel or hermitage. Merovingian religion was intensely individual and local, focusing on reverence for individuals who had, during their lifetimes, been defenders and patrons of their commmunities and who, after death, could continue, as the favored companions of God, to look after their communities. This intimate tie between the living and dead also extended to the local cemetery. At Flonheim in Germany, for example, the central tombs (corresponding to the chieftain's tomb in Lavoye) dating from the pre-Christian period subsequently had a chapel built over them, which then formed the center of this growing Christian necropolis. Far from forgetting their pagan ancestors, the local population had Christianized them ex post facto.[17] The physical continuity of the community with the habitation of the dead gave permanence and stability to the village.

The village was also the level above the household at which the social and political life of the people was organized. The most immediate rung of justice was provided at the village level. The Roman judge or Frankish count might appear there or send his representative to deal with local disputes involving free men of the area. More frequently, the heads of households and *Sippe* met to resolve conflicts and settle scores without recourse to public justice.

Finally, once established the village became an important fiscal unit in the Roman and then Frankish administration. Fixed dues to landlords and taxes owed the fisc established a continuity. Villages became units of income and sources of manpower for aristocrats and kings.

SOCIAL STRUCTURE

Was the man buried in tomb 319 at Lavoye a noble? This question has been at the center of an unending debate in European history for over a century. As traditionally posed, the issue is whether the Franks of the sixth century had a nobility independent of the king, or whether Clovis eliminated any original Frankish nobility in the same manner that he did his kinsmen. At the heart of this debate is the question of the origins of European nobility and its relationship to the monarchy. Did European nobility, as it emerged in the later Middle Ages, derive from control of landed wealth and the nonfree persons who worked the land (German: *Grunderrschaft*), or did it derive from military and political power over free men (German: *Volksherrschaft*), and if from the latter, did the nobility achieve this power through usurpation of royal authority or from earlier inherited right? The whole issue is perhaps the classic example of asking the wrong question and then being unable to find the right answer, but the issues raised, when clarified, do illuminate important characteristics of Frankish society.

Clearly, the Gallo-Roman aristocracy comprised an independent, self-perpetuating elite whose social status and political power was based on their ancestry, inherited wealth, and special status under law *(viri inlustri)*. While they often did cooperate with kings, they were not created by them. An earlier generation of scholars, accustomed to modern European nobility with its legally protected status, sought in vain to discover a similar group among the Franks. In contrast to other barbarian peoples, such as the Alemanni and Bavarians, one finds no mention of nobles in the *Pactus Legis Salicae*. Instead one finds the major distinction to be between *ingenui,* free men, also called simply *Franci,* and various types of nonfree. A special group of *ingenui* were the *domini,* lords, who controlled various groups of nonfree and thus probably possessed important amounts of land. However these *domini,* while part of an "upper stratum" of Frankish society, do not have a special legal position, as would have been recognized by a higher wergeld.

A higher wergeld for men came only with proximity to the king. The members of the royal household and bodyguard, termed *ludes, trustis dominica, convivae regis,* or *antrustiones,* were the individuals whose special status was protected by a higher value. Legal historians such as Heike Grahn-Hoek have thus concluded that, if such a group of nobility had existed among the Franks before Clovis, he had effectively exterminated them, and he and his successors created a service nobility that only gradually separated itself from the king through intermarriage with the Roman nobility and by profiting from the internecine wars of the Merovingian family.[18]

Social historians such as Franz Irsigler, on the other hand, are not as concerned about the existence of legal definitions of noble status as they are with the de facto status and power of social groups.[19] In fact, evidence from other regions, Scandinavia for example, suggests that the failure of the *Pactus* to mention the nobility may simply indicate how little conrol even a king like Clovis could exercise over the Frankish nobles. The *Pactus* attempts to limit the blood feud by establishing a tariff of compensations that all parties are forced to accept. A free noble could not be forced to accept compensation, which would offend the honor of his family, and thus could not be listed alongside simple freemen and royal agents. In the other barbarian laws, such as those of the Alemanni and Bavarians, the fact that these tariffs had been imposed from without by the Frankish kings may explain why the aristocracy there is under the law.

If, instead of looking for a legally defined stratum one looks for an aristocracy characterized by inherited status, wealth, and political power, then a Frankish aristocracy is clearly in evidence from the fifth and sixth centuries. In fact, the Frankish aristocracy was similar in many essential respects to that of the Gallo-Romans, a similarity which greatly assisted the rapid amalgamation of the two, particularly north of the Loire where Franks were numerous. Frankish magnates such as the Lavoye chieftain enjoyed considerable landed wealth, land which had been distributed *secundum dignatationem,* according to rank, and which was allodial, that is, not rewarded for years of royal service but instead inherited and alienable. That aristocratic position could be passed on to the next generation is clear from the excavation of children's tombs. These often contain weapons and jewelry similar to those found in the tombs of adults, their status as indicated in their burial furnishings certainly came not from their own merits but from that of their parents.

Thus a Frankish aristocracy of inherited wealth preceded or developed along with Merovingian kingship. In fact, while the Merovingians did occasionally make use of men of humble origin, most of the holders of offices, such as duke or count, were selected from among these aristocrats. Gregory of Tours makes frequent allusion to the private property held by such men, who could in turn use their offices both legally and illegally to extend their wealth in estates and villas.

Along with landed wealth, Frankish aristocrats also had their own followings, the equivalent to the royal *trustis,* in addition to servile followers, the *pueri* or "boys" recruited from their estates. These followers too belonged in some sense to the aristocrat's household, which was also composed of kin and of allies, or *amici,* with whom they were sworn to mutual assistance. These followings were particularly important in the conduct of feuds, the normal means by which Frankish aristocrats maintained their relative status and prerogatives vis-à-vis each other.

In addition to land and followers, a Frankish aristocrat enjoyed an immaterial but essential quality that separated him from others—the inherited charisma (German: *Heil*) attached to families that were renowned for their successful leadership, or in other words "noble." Intimately bound up with this quality was the importance of the family's fame. A noble family was one that was known to produce men of military ability and suitability for great deeds.

The aristocratic charisma had to be made manifest to the rest of society, and this was done in the sixth century through the aristocratic lifestyle. Frankish magnates, unlike their Roman senatorial counterparts, did not depend on fortified strongholds for their protection, but practiced a life of fighting, hunting, and perhaps most important, of banqueting, at which solidarity with their potential enemies could be created and their largesse could be demonstrated to their followers through the distribution of gifts.

We have already seen that this openhanded gift giving was one of the most important means by which goods circulated hierarchically in Frankish society. It established and reinforced relationships between giver and recipient in which the latter, by accepting, placed himself in the debt of the former. A leader showed his nobility in his generosity just as he did in his ability to lead his followers against his enemies in acquiring the wealth, largely cattle and movables, which he then distributed. Thus plunder and generosity formed the two parts of the system of exchange and circulation of goods, existing alongside the commercial economy still flourishing in Frankish cities and the agrarian economy on which all else depended.

The majority of the other equipped burials at Lavoye were presumably free men and women, the *ingenui* of the *Pactus,* who formed the majority of the Frankish people and the backbone of its military. Exactly what freedom meant for these people is unclear; freedom is always relative, and particularly in traditional societies in which dependency is a given, the real issue is the nature of the dependency—political, economic, juridical— rather than whether it existed.

The free Franks at Lavoye and elsewhere in Francia were free in that they were obligated to military service under the king and as warriors had the right to participate in public justice. The ability to fulfill military duties was the essential line separating them from the nonfree, not their relationship to the local landholding aristocracy, who might well own the land they worked, command them in times of war, and pressure them into dependency. They were what historian Karl Bosl terms the "king's free," those born free whom the king could, in theory, command through his dukes and counts.[20]

In addition to these "unfree free," Frankish society had various kinds of more deeply and personally dependent persons, the *servi casati,* or slave tenant farmers, and *coloni* of the late Empire, as well as household slaves and, rarely, field slaves on large estates. Traditionally, slaves in Germanic societies were prisoners of war and individuals who lost their freedom as a result of crimes. However, as Germanic tribes moved into the Empire and established themselves alongside and in place of Gallo-Roman landlords, they absorbed the tradition of Roman slavery. Moreover, the increasingly academic distinction between *coloni* and slave tenant farmers largely disappeared. Neither group served under arms, the primary distinction for Frankish freedom, and thus they tended to merge. Both groups were considered part of the land, and juridically belonged to the family of the landlord, be he simple *ingenuus* or aristocrat. To this group might also be added in time those descendants of free Franks who, for economic reasons, could no longer afford to do military service. Gradually they too sank to the level of the nonfree, losing the right to judicial identity and becoming dependents in the strictest sense of the lords on whose lands they lived and worked.

Thus at both ends of the social spectrum an amalgamation of traditional Gallo-Roman and barbarian societies was under way. The primary factor affecting the extent of amalgamation was the relative density of Franks (and other barbarians) relative to the indigenous population.

The extent of the physical settlement of Franks as opposed to the political control by Franks varied enormously across the kingdom. In the east and the north along the lower and middle Rhine the settlement was extremely dense. In these regions the Roman presence, in the form of clerics, merchants, and the remains of the bureaucracy, continued only within the walls of cities such as Cologne, Bonn, and Remagen. In the countryside, the remaining Roman peasants were absorbed into the nonfree dependents of the Franks, whose system of farms and estates replaced the previous Roman organization of the countryside.

There were, however, exceptions. In the area of Trier, for example, which around 480 became part of *Francia Rinensis* even in the eyes of the Eastern Empire, while the fiscal lands entered the royal domain, ecclesiastical land and even small Roman estates and farms continued to exist alongside new Frankish settlements. This pattern is more typical of the settlements further south in the Burgundian kingdom and in the areas of the West acquired by the Goths.

The Ardennes forest formed a natural southeastern boundary for the area of densest Frankish settlement, although as far south as the Seine the generations of slow Germanic migration and settlement before Clovis, which greatly increased after his victory over Syagrius, introduced an important Frankish presence in the region. Between the Seine and the Loire, the Frankish presence was even less significant; archaeological and linguistic evidence suggests scattered islands of Frankish settlement in an overwhelmingly Gallo-Roman countryside.

South of the Loire, the Frankish presence was even less in evidence. Prior to 507, the region had been largely unaffected by its Visigothic lords, who mostly resided in towns from which they controlled the countryside with the assistance of the Aquitainian aristocracy. Little changed with the Frankish conquest in terms of actual population. Certainly some Franks were sent south as counts and others no doubt settled in the rich cities of Aquitaine, but these scatterings of Franks had little effect on the population, its language, or customs.

While population estimates are impossible to make with any accuracy, one guess puts the number of Franks in the entire kingdom at a maximum of about 150,000 to 200,000 spread out within a population of six or seven million Gallo-Romans. While these figures are almost certainly exaggerated, it is reasonable to think that an estimate of a bit more than two percent Franks is not entirely unreasonable.

This two percent, concentrated above the Loire and dominating the rest of the population, had an effect far beyond its numbers. While in the south, the rare Franks seem to have quickly adopted Roman customs and probably language and identity, the opposite is true in the north. There, Frankish identity came to replace Roman within a few generations. Germanic names predominate, and one rarely hears of a native of the region referred to as a Roman; *Romani* are those who live south of the Loire. All that remained of the Roman identification was the Romance dialect adopted by the population, although as late as the end of the ninth century it is likely that some areas or northern France were still speaking and understanding Frankish. By the eighth century, so thoroughly had this transformation taken place that it was commonly and erroneously believed that after the conquest by Clovis, the *Romani* of the area had been exterminated, although the Franks had adopted the language of their predecessors. It's a myth but one that nevertheless reveals how deeply the transformation of Gaul had been carried out.

A new kind of Christian barbarian kingdom had been established north of the Alps—one which changed forever the face of the West. With the exception of the Burgundians (whose kingdom would be destroyed and integrated into the Frankish realm by Clovis's sons), the core of the Frankish kingdom had been constituted; a loose confederation of barbarian chieftains had been replaced by a single ruler whose wealth was matched only by his capacity for violence; an uneasy alliance of pagan and Arian barbarians and Christian Romans had been replaced by a kingdom unified culticly under a Christian king recognized by

the emperor in Constantinople and supported by orthodox bishops, the representatives of the Gallo-Roman elite. In spite of
the disunity and internecine violence that characterized the
reigns of Clovis's sons and grandsons, the transformation of the
West would continue along the lines he had begun.

CHAPTER IV

Sixth-Century Francia

Clovis's Successors in the Sixth Century

Although there might be a number of Frankish kings and sub-kingdoms, the Frankish kingdom ruled by Clovis's sons continued to be conceived of as a unity: there was only one *regnum Francorum*. Within this divided kingdom his successors continued the main lines of his policies. In terms of external affairs, this often meant concerted efforts to expand the kingdom at the expense of their neighbors; in terms of internal affairs, it often meant the attempt to eliminate each other as he had eliminated his cousins. The result is a complex and violent political narrative, perhaps more reminiscent of late Roman imperial history than of early Germanic tradition. In their internecine struggles the Merovingians had obviously absorbed much from the Romans.

External Expansion

Under Clovis's sons and grandsons the expansion of the Frankish kingdom was largely completed. After a series of partial successes, the Burgundian kingdom was destroyed and absorbed by 534. The Ostrogoths, desperate for assistance against Justinian's wars to reconquer Italy, allowed the Franks to absorb Provence in return for assistance against the Romans two years later. Campaigns against the remaining Visigothic outposts in Aquitaine resulted in the reduction of the Gothic presence north of the Pyrenees to the strip of coast as far east as Narbonne by 541.

In the east, Theuderic I took advantage of the crisis which the reconquest of Italy was causing not only in Italy itself but in the Alpine regions to the north to bring much of the area under his control. First he conquered the remains of the Ostrogoth's longtime clients, the Thuringians, and brought the Saxons to the north under a weak sort of Frankish control. His son Theudebert I (reigned 534–548) went still further. The Ostrogoth withdrawal from Provence left the Alemanni, who were established east of Burgundy in what is now southeastern Germany and northern Switzerland, isolated, and he added them to his kingdom as well as the Rhaeto-Romans in the Alpine regions such as Chur. Still further east, he established control over the newly formed amalgam of peoples, including Thuringians, Langobards, Erulians, Veti, Alemanni, and others who, set loose by the movement of the Langobards into Italy at the Byzantine invitation, had combined with what was left of the Roman population of Noricum to form the Bavarians. In 539 he used this region as the launching pad for an incursion into Italy where, through shifting alliances and treachery to both Byzantines and Ostrogoths, he managed to bring upper Italy under his control.

Theudebert was no simple barbarian king seeking plunder. With his Roman advisors to educate him, he probably intended to accomplish what other Gallic pretenders had wanted for centuries: to use the West as a base for the conquest of the imperial throne. His plan came to naught, and after his death his son Theudebald I (reigned 548–555) abandoned upper Italy, but Theudebert had demonstrated both the ability and the ambition of Clovis's successors.

Subsequent Byzantine emperors sought, through subsidies, emissaries, and support of various factions and pretenders in the Frankish kingdoms, to use Frankish power to bolster imperial designs in the West, particularly in trying to eliminate the Langobards, who had entered Italy during Justinian's attempt at reconquest. Although largely unsuccessful, such attempts demonstrated both the Byzantine acknowledgment of Frankish superiority in the West and the Franks' continued intimacy with the Empire.

The Merovingians made no attempt to absorb the regions east of the Rhine or even south of the Loire into a thoroughly integrated empire; control of the Frankish heartland was challenge enough. With each conquest, they assured the local inhabitants of their right to live by their own law, barbarian or Roman depending on the region, and in Thuringia, Alemannia, Bavaria, Rhaetia, Provence, and even Aquitaine established Frankish dukes (known in Provence as patricians and in Rhaetia as *praeces* or tribunes) to rule, subject to the king. These dukes or patricians were "Frankish" in the sense that they were appointed by the Franks. In Bavaria, for example, the dukes were from the powerful Agilofing family, which had Burgundian, Frankish, and probably Langobard relations. In Rhaetia, the Frankish commander quickly married into a powerful Roman family of the region, and his descendants continued to monopolize both secular and episcopal office until the end of the eighth century. The same was generally true elsewhere. The dukes either had previous ties or very quickly married into the local elites. As a result, particularly in times of weak Merovingian kings, these regions were likely to become virtually autonomous.

Internal Constitution

Upon the death of Clovis's last surviving son, Chlothar I, in 560, the kingdom was divided once more among his four sons, one of whom died six years later, leaving the kingdom in three major portions. This tradition of dividing the kingdom would continue to be the norm in Francia well into the ninth century. However, subsequent divisions of the kingdom did not result in infinite fragmentation. Instead, by the middle of the sixth century the heart of the kingdom was largely divided into three portions. Although upon each subsequent division the exact boundaries of these portions shifted somewhat, by the next century they were sufficiently well-defined to receive specific names: Austrasia, Neustria, and Burgundy.

While it is tempting to take at face value the name Austrasia ("The East Land"), this would be misleading, since Austrasia included not only the eastern areas between the Rhine and the Meuse rivers and the areas east of the Rhône conquered by Theuderic and his son Theudebert, but also Champagne, the royal residence in Reims, and later Metz and a large portion of central and southern Gaul. Although portions of the region were, in population at least, more "Germanic," Austrasia in the sixth century was a center of Roman culture and influence. We have seen that here were born imperial political ambitions greater than any that Theodoric the Ostrogoth ever envisioned. The court was also a center for Latin letters; from the Austrasian part of Aquitaine the kings welcomed cultured senatorial aristocrats such as Venantius Fortunatus. This Roman cultural exposure affected Frankish aristocrats as well, increasing the amalgamation of the two elites.

The Austrasian kings apparently intended more than the adoption of Roman culture and imperial conquest. Theudebert may have attempted to establish in his eastern lands the same kind of Roman tax system still functioning in parts of his Gallic possessions. Brunechildis, the Visigothic wife of his successor Sigibert I, attempted to continue this Romanization, with the result that an increasing rift developed between the aristocracy and the monarchy, which resulted in a long and bloody series of wars.

Fiscal reforms may have played a measure in this conflict, but such conflicts in Frankish society tended to be conceived of in personal terms and carried out as family feuds. The family feud in this case divided the Merovingian family and brought the Austrasian monarchy to destruction.

Although less extensive, the region richest in fiscal land, in Roman cities (such as Paris, Tours, and Rouen) and in productive population was Neustria, the "New West Lands," with the Merovingian capital in Soissons. The Neustrian king Chilperic (reigned 561–584) spent much of his reign fighting his brother, the Austrasian Sigibert (reigned 561–575), and the latter's widow, Brunechildis, over the extent of his kingdom. This war, ostensibly over conflicting claims to the inheritance of their deceased brother Charibert (died 567), was simultaneously a bitter feud initiated by Chilperic's wife Fredegund and her arch rival Brunechildis. Chilperic was already married to Fredegund (among others) when he took as his second wife the Visigothic princess Galswintha, sister of Brunechildis. As Gregory says of

Chilperic's attitude toward his new bride, "He loved her very dearly, for she had brought a large dowry with her."[1] Egged on by Fredegund and fearful that Galswintha might try to return home with her dowry, he had her killed. His brothers, especially Sigibert, husband of Brunechildis, outraged and eager to seize the opportunity to divide Chilperic's kingdom, attempted to depose him. The result was a three-generation feud that wrecked the Merovingian family and ended only after the deaths of ten kings and the execution of Brunechildis by Chilperic's son Chlothar in 613.

The third section of the kingdom was Burgundy, which included not only the old kingdom of the Burgundians but also a large region of Gaul reaching to the capital of Orléans. This region initially was composed of large populations of Burgundians, Romans, and Franks. Burgundy particularly depended on the important ecclesiastical province of Lyon, which had long been the center of senatorial power. King Gunthchramn (reigned 561–593) depended heavily on these Roman aristocrats in his administration, filling its most important position, that of patrician, with three successive Romans. In a short time the three cultural groups became fused, although the Roman tradition predominated. In response to the significance of the Rhône Romans, in the 570s Gunthchramn moved his court to Chalon, which he developed into a religious as well as political capital.

Although necessarily caught up in the violent feud between the wives of his two brothers, Gunthchromn seems to have been more influenced by a Christian-Roman ideology of government than the others, perhaps resulting from the fact that his kingdom was the most Roman of the three regions. Here not only Roman culture but Roman traditions of justice and Christian ideas of royal obligation could take root. However, as we have seen Roman tradition was every bit as prone to violence as was that of the Franks. A more likely explanation for Gunthchramn's style of rulership was his personal piety—Gregory of Tours portrays him in an extremely favorable light. Still, he remained capable of the violence that was characteristic of late antiquity. To cite but one example, when he suspected his chamberlain of having poached aurochs, a now nearly extinct European buffalo, in the royal forest of the Vosges, he ordered a trial by combat. When the chamberlain's nephew and the accusing forester killed each other in the vicious hand-to-hand fighting, the chamberlain attempted to find sanctuary in a nearby church. The king had him apprehended, tied to a post, and stoned to death. The only difference between his conduct and that of his grandfather Clovis was perhaps that, as Gregory records, he later regretted having a faithful servant killed for so small an offense.

The constant feuding among Clovis's descendants weakened all parties and contributed to the power of the aristocracy, Frankish and Roman, whose help was essential for victory. This power was far from unified, however, even though aristocratic groups might at times coalesce to fight a particularly hated royal official. The violence of the Merovingian family was mirrored in the violent interrelationships in the aristocracy, and in this respect the Romans were no different from the Franks. Private warfare was the rule.

In fact, any distinction between private motives and public ones on the part of Merovingian kings and aristocrats is artificial. An attempt to explain aristocratic opposition groups need not choose between the opposition of the aristocracy to the imposition of Roman taxation and governance and private grievances. Taxation, like feuding, had long been a private affair. If, in the accounts of Gregory one cannot tell public from personal motives, it is because they were indistinguishable. Whether king or aristocrat, one fought for family honor and for independent lordship. However not until the seventh century did the aristocratic role in this struggle become dominant.

The one group retaining something of a traditional sense of the *res publicae,* of the public sphere, was the clergy. Although they too were almost exclusively drawn from the aristocracy, whether Roman or Romanized Frankish, and although they were often deeply involved in violent conflict, they nevertheless managed as a group to maintain and increase their power and authority not only on behalf of themselves and their families but on behalf of their office as well. King Chilperic I once complained that "There is no one with any power left except the bishops."[2] This was of course an exaggeration, but more than anyone else, the episcopacy held the keys to power, both human and divine, in sixth-century Francia.

Much has been written about the Frankish church. In reality, no such thing existed. The religious landscape was composed of a great number of churches, each headed by a bishop and serving as the cultic and political center of the local elite. In the course of the sixth century the Frankish monarchs brought some sense of unity to the episcopate, but ultimately it remained as factious as the Gallo-Roman society which controlled and populated it.

Moreover, in addition to the episcopal church, there existed at least two and ultimately three monastic churches, each with its own traditions, its own relation to the local elites, and its religious focus. These cleavages in turn corresponded to the major cultural regions of Francia, which were in general the region north of the Loire, Aquitaine, and the east, including the Rhône watershed and the Provençal littoral.

Bishops: Noble in Birth and in Faith

The first church in Gaul had been the episcopal church, and its traditions stretched back into the most distant memory of the senatorial aristocracy. In fact, its period of establishment, the late third century, corresponded to the period of the creation of this provincial aristocracy; thus both were born together and formed an inseparable institution.

The great majority of early Merovingian bishops were of aristocratic Gallo-Roman background. This was only to be expected given the role the episcopacy played in late Roman Gaul. In fact, the lives of Merovingian bishop saints, composed in the seventh century, generally begin by describing the noble family from which the bishop had sprung: "he was noble by birth, but still more noble by faith" is repeated with minor variations throughout the literature. The implication is clear—illustrious ancestry was expected of a bishop. This secular preeminance, however, could be supplemented by religious virtue, which in turn reflected on the entire family from which he came.

Statistical examinations of the social origins of the Merovingian episcopacy are extremely dangerous because of the lack of data. As Martin Heinzelmann points out in a study of the 707 bishops whose names are known from the eight ecclesiastical provinces of Tours, Rouen, Sens, Reims, Trier, Metz, Cologne, and Besançon, for example, fully 328 are known only by their names.[3] However, of the 179 bishops who can be assigned to a social rank, only eight were, like Iniuriosus of Tours, who was "of inferior but nevertheless free parentage," definitely not of the senatorial aristocracy. Of course, one can well imagine that given the aristocratic orientation of the sources, the lower the social rank the less likely this information was to have been conveyed. However, even lacking specific biographical information, circumstantial evidence such as important positions held by other members of bishops' families, previous high secular offices held by bishops such as referendary, *maior domus,* or *domesticus,* and the reappearance of the same names in lists of bishops in the same or neighboring sees, all suggest that the great majority of the bishops belonged to powerful and important families.

So much is this the case that one can speak of "episcopal families" that controlled sees for generations. The most famous is that of the historian Gregory of Tours. Both Gregory's mother and father belonged to distinguished families from Auvergne which had provided bishops of Langres, Geneva, Lyon, and of course Tours. Gregory boasted that of the eighteen previous bishops of Tours, all but five had been his kinsmen. His case is probably typical. We know, for example, that at Nantes, Châlons, Paris, Sens, Laon, Metz, Orléans, and Trier, it was normal for sons to succeed fathers or nephews to succeed uncles.

Such episcopal dynasties reflected both the power of bishops to influence the naming of their successors and the networks, often stretching back generations, uniting senatorial families across Gaul. Control of episcopal sees was one of the major goals in family strategies, and the competition between senatorial families could be vicious and deadly. An illuminating example is that between the families of Gregory of Tours and Felix of Nantes (c. 512–582). Felix was a member of one of the most powerful families of Aquitaine. He was energetic in promoting the religious and secular affairs of both his see and his family, which were intimately intertwined. Venantius Fortunatus, who admired him, credits him with having converted the "ferocious race of Saxons," that is, the community of Saxon "pirates" established along the coast and officially recognized by the Merovingians. At Nantes itself, Felix sought to redirect commerce on the Loire towards the right bank to profit his city.[4] Such efforts also benefited his family.

Felix succeeded his father, Eumerius, as bishop of Nantes when the latter died in 549 or 550, and he led the life of a great aristocrat. Fortunatus described his favorite estate, Charcé, which included over 3,000 hectares along the Loire in Poitou, as an ideal aristocratic domain with vineyards and pine-covered hills. The tradition of his family's control of Nantes was probably already old in the late sixth century; Martin Heinzelmann has drawn attention to the appearance of the relatively rare names Eumerius and Nonnechius (the name of Felix's successor and kinsman) as bishops of Nantes in the fourth and fifth centuries.

In contrast to Fortunatus, Gregory had a low estimation of this family in general and of Felix in particular. He characterized him as "a man whose greed and arrogance knew no bounds."[5] Gregory's hatred of him was understandable. Around 580 when the archdeacon Riculf attempted to have Gregory removed from office, probably because he had himself been elected by the local clergy, Felix not only supported Riculf but, when the plot failed, he welcomed the archdeacon in Nantes.

Felix's motives in the affair are unclear, but certainly they had as much to do with familial competition as with ecclesiastical politics. He had accused Gregory's brother Peter, a deacon of the church of Langres, of having murdered his own bishop-elect and kinsman, Silvester, in order to succeed him. The accusation enraged Gregory, perhaps because it may have been too close to the truth. A few years previously Peter had certainly been deeply involved in the condemnation and dismissal of another deacon, Lampadius, and this involvement eventually caused Peter's death. Felix's charge against Peter concerning Silvester may well have been part true. Certainly Gregory's family looked upon Langres as another of "their" sees, and Peter may have thought that he, rather than Silvester, ought to have succeeded Tetricus in 572. Whatever the truth of the affair, Lampadius so stirred up Silvester's son that the latter struck Peter down in the streets of Langres. Obviously Felix did not approve of the manner in which Gregory's family members reached episcopal office.

Gregory felt the same about that of Felix. When the latter lay dying he attempted to name as his successor his nephew Burgundio. Gregory, as Burgundio's metropolitan bishop, was responsible for the young man's tonsure and consecration, and he had the delicious revenge of gravely pointing out the irregularity of Felix's action, sending Burgundio home with the advice to "apply yourself seriously to all that the Church asks of you. It may well be that when God decides that the moment has come to remove your uncle . . . you yourself will be given episcopal rank." After Felix's death Gregory could not prevent a more distant relative of the late bishop, Nonnechius, from being named, but it certainly was not Felix's chosen Burgundio.

Such complex family rivalries focused on the office of bishop because it was a prize worth fighting for. Control of major bishoprics was the key to the continued regional power of the kindred. It also provided great wealth. From the fourth century on, enormous amounts of land had been passing into the hands of the church, and all this was controlled by the bishop. A glimpse of just how this wealth might be used to benefit the family can be seen in the rare testaments left by Frankish bishops, such as that of Remigius of Reims, who named as his heirs his church and his nephews Lupus, bishop of Soissons, Agricola, a priest, and Bertram of Le Mans (died 616). The latter named the church as his sole heir. These testaments dispose of estates, churches, slaves, *coloni,* and movables acquired through family inheritance, royal gifts, purchase, exchange, and confiscation. The continued prosperity of the family demanded that it control bishopric wealth, and after generations of such donations it is little wonder that families came to view episcopal succession as a hereditary right worth killing to defend.

This killing took place indiscriminately in Gallo-Roman and Frankish families, if indeed the two can be distinguished by this time. It is usually stated that the Frankish episcopacy was almost exclusively drawn from the ranks of the Gallo-Roman aristocracy well into the eighth century. In fact, the episcopal office has been seen as the bulwark of the Roman population, and it alone could protect Roman traditions and culture from the barbarian Franks.

Certainly in the early sixth century and, in the south, through much of the seventh and eighth, bishops did come from great senatorial families. However, alliances and intermarriages between Romans and Franks began even before the time of Clovis, and in the course of the sixth century these families began to fuse, uniting the courtly favor and military power of Frankish leaders with the cultural traditions and regional patronage and kin networks of the senatorial aristocracy. Most of the evidence marshaled to demonstrate the contrary is drawn from the occurrence of Roman names in lists of Merovingian bishops, which some scholars have seen as proof of continued domination of the episcopacy by "Roman" families. However, sharp distinctions between Roman and Frankish families, particularly in the north and in Burgundy, are difficult to make, especially on the basis of names. Sons destined for the clergy may have been given Christian or Latin names regardless of family background. But very early on, Germanic names came to predominate in the north, even in families of Roman background, partly because of intermarriage with Franks and partly as a political statement of loyalty to the Frankish kings. By the second half of the sixth century one finds among the descendants of the family of Bishop Remigius of Reims not only Roman names such as Lupus, but also the Frankish names Romulf and quite probably Leudegisel and Attalenus. The same process took place across the Rhine, as the old Roman families in Trier and Cologne merged with the Frankish kindreds with whom they shared power, and in Burgundy, where a developing local aristocracy presented an amalgam of Burgundian, Frankish, and Roman aristocratic traditions. The prize sought was the preservation of family power and autonomy, regardless of the pedigree of the family.

The importance of the prize and the magnitude of the task of controlling the office explains the tradition, already established in antiquity, of electing mature men of proven administrative and political ability. True, some bishops arrived at their positions after a regular career in the clergy, rising from lector through priest to bishop, but this was so much the exception that when it occurred, as in the case of Bishop Nivard of Reims or Heraclius of Angoulême, hagiographers considered it worthy of comment. When Cato was chosen by the clergy and people of Clermont-Ferrand as their candidate to succeed Saint Gaul in 551, he presented his clerical background as evidence of his qualifications:

> I have been promoted through all of the ranks of clerical prefer-
> ment according to canonical precept. I was a lector for ten years;
> for five years I performed the duties of subdeacon; for fifteen years
> I served as deacon; and I have held the dignity of the priesthood
> for the last twenty years. What is left but that I should be ordained
> bishop as the reward for my faithful service?[7]

He didn't get the job.

Many bishops entered their office from secular life and even for those who rose within the clergy, the priesthood was normally not the route to ecclesiastical office.

Young men destined for the episcopacy were normally sent to a close relative who was a bishop to be educated by him. A thorough education was expected of a bishop, who in turn was responsible for the education of his clergy and other young people sent by kin and allies to serve as members of his household. However, since most of these bishops had entered the church late in life, the nature of this education was usually more in the tradition of late Latin letters than of theological or ascetic and spiritual instruction. Minor orders could be quickly acquired, but the position most sought after by ambitious clerics was that of archdeacon. The archdeacon was the most important figure in the bishop's court, controlling the temporals of the diocese and in general administering the diocese for the bishop. Not surprisingly therefore, the archdeacon was in an excellent position to succeed the bishop he served, both because he was widely experienced and, since he controlled the diocesan wealth, he could use it to bribe the king, the rest of the clergy, and the people. Such was the case of Riculf with whom Gregory had had so much trouble. Given the depth of support he found within the clergy of Tours, Riculf may well have been their choice over Gregory, in spite of (or even due to) Gregory's familial tradition and Riculf's relatively humble background.

Those few bishops who did have a solid theological and ascetic background tended to come to their office from the monastic church. Here alone a serious religious education was likely to be available, and when this was combined with the administrative and political skills of a capable abbot, it made a strong candidate for episcopal office indeed. Moreover, many abbots had entered religious life only after a period of active service at court. High-born, well-connected, educated, and experienced, they made ideal bishops from the perspective of their family, the clergy, and the king. The model for such a bishop was Pope Gregory the Great (pope 590–604), a member of an aristocratic Roman family who had been prefect of a city from 579 to 585 and then had retired to a monastery of his own foundation before being forced to assume the papacy. In Gaul, bishops such as Salvinus of Albi, Numeranus of Trier, and Guntharius of Tours followed similar career patterns.

If many bishops held secular office prior to entering monasteries on their way to the episcopal dignity, many more went directly from their secular positions to their sees. The office of bishop thus crowned a *cursus honorum* in the traditional sense. In the fifth and sixth centuries, this career progression often went through the surviving offices of the later Empire or positions as regional administrators; increasingly in the seventh century this meant service at the royal court.

Such a case was that of Gregory of Tours's own great-grandfather, Bishop Gregory of Langres. The earlier Gregory had served for forty years as the count of Autun, roughly from 466 until 506, had married Armentaria, a woman from a similar senatorial family background and probably daughter of Bishop Armentarius of Langres, and had produced a family. After the death of his wife, Gregory "turned to the Lord" and was elected bishop of Langres, in which capacity he served until his death around 540.[8]

In the mid sixth century, such "conversions" became even more common as part of the political-familial rivalries we have discussed above. Thus, for example, after the death of Bishop Ferreolus of Uzès, both Albinus, the prefect of Marseille, and the candidate of the rector of Provence, Dynamius, and the latter's deposed predecessor and rival, Jovinus, wanted to be his successor. Albinus was appointed by Dynamius without the permission of King Gunthchramn. An effort would surely have been made to depose him had he not died shortly after. His timely demise cleared the way for a new appointment, but before Jovinus could be installed Dynamius appointed the deacon Marcellus, a son of his friend Felix, a member of a powerful senatorial family from Marseille. The result was a war, in the course of which Jovinus besieged the city of Uzès before being bribed off by Bishop Marcellus.[9]

In the course of the sixth and seventh centuries, an increasingly common background for bishops was the position of count of the city, the representative of the king in the *civitas*. In some cases, the episcopal dignity may have been seen as the normal crowning of the *cursus honorum* which followed the position of count. The distinction between secular and religious office had become as blurred as that which in the period before Diocletian had separated civil and military careers.

Men of high rank tended to be married, and if the wife, unlike Armentaria, the wife of Bishop Gregory of Langres, had not died before their husbands' elections, they moved into the episcopal residence and into public affairs as the *episcopa,* the bishop's wife. The tradition of clerical celibacy was relatively new and indifferently followed in the Frankish kingdom. Although sexual abstinence had been demanded by various popes from the second half of the fourth century, it became an ideal in the Gallic episcopacy only under the increasing influence of Eastern ascetic tradition which, as we saw in Chapter Two, pervaded the senatorial aristocracy in the fourth century. By the sixth century, it was generally expected that married individuals entering the clergy would retain their wives, but that they would refrain from marital relations and the wives would assist the husbands in their offices. To avoid any hint of scandal, they lived apart, and the bishop's wife was not even allowed into his bedroom, in some cases a sort of episcopal dormitory where he slept surrounded by his clergy.

Progressively in the course of the sixth century, wives of deacons, priests, and bishops became more marginal and their status was decreased by Conciliar enactments. However, through the middle of the century they, and in particular the *episcopa,* played a public role along with their husbands. The most complimentary portrait of an *episcopa* is that presented by Gregory of Tours of the wife of late fifth-century Bishop Namatius of Clermont-Ferrand. She is depicted as undertaking personally the construction of the Church of Saint Stephen. She liked to sit within the church reading edifying "stories of long ago" and telling the workers which of these she wished to see depicted on the church walls.[10] In spite of this positive image, however, Gregory does not deign to mention the woman's name. His image of the wife of Sidonius Apollinaris, who was the daughter of Emperor Avitus, is somewhat negative. After Sidonius's election he was in the habit of handing out the family silver to beggars who appeared at his door. His (likewise unnamed) wife would chide her husband for what she considered his excessive generosity and then seek out the beggars and buy back the silver.[11]

The progressive decline of the ascetic ideal among sixth-century aristocrats may have resulted in a change in the comportment of the *episcopa* along with that of her husband. In any case, Gregory has little good to report about bishops' wives from his own time. More typical, in Gregory's view, was Susanna, the wife of Bishop Priscus of Lyon, who was consecrated in 573. Not only did she actively assist her husband in his persecution of the supporters of his predecessor, the saintly Nicetius, but she and her attendants would visit the living quarters of the bishop. With great satisfaction Gregory reports that ultimately she went mad and, possessed by a demon, ran bare-headed through the streets of Lyon, proclaiming that Nicetius had indeed been a man of God and calling upon him to spare her.[12]

The only potential rival that bishops faced for authority in the city was the count, but with the disappearance of civil government the rivalry was no equal contest. The position of bishop was considered a step up from that of count of the city, with the former office often filled by an aristocrat who had already served as count. The office of count lost progressively in prestige and power to that of bishop in the sixth century, partly due to the higher social background bishops tended to have. While later the church might have provided a path for social mobility denied by secular pursuits, the opposite was largely true in the seventh and eighth centuries. Counts on the other hand, although usually from the same background as bishops, occasionally came from humble origins and if capable or clever, could rise through royal service. This was the case of Leudast, the count of the city of Tours, who was Gregory's greatest enemy. If Gregory can be believed, Leudast's was a classic success story. Born the son of a slave and too delicate even to work in the kitchen, he nevertheless rose in royal favor to become master of the stables and finally count of Tours. Further he could not rise; although he had powerful supporters in some quarters, he was no match for the well-connected bishop. Ultimately he was tortured to death on the orders of Queen Fredegund.[13]

Toward the end of the sixth century the imbalance between the count and bishop became such that the former's appointment needed approval by the latter or else the bishop actually appointed the count. Gregory, for example, had been requested by King Theudebert to reappoint Leudast. Rather than the representative of the king, the count had become an agent in episcopal administration.

The administrative experience acquired by such bishops no doubt prepared them well for the administration of their sees, and their political power made possible their frequent activities as the protectors of their communities against royal demands. If bishops often stood up to kings or their agents in order to resist unusual or excessive taxes, they had a certain advantage as representatives of the local power elite needed by the king. The bishops' protection of the people was often as much a defense of their own largely hereditary lordship as it was of the Lord's faithful.

Birth, learning, and proven administrative ability were necessary for a bishop but they alone were inadequate—a bishop needed election and consecration. Here ecclesiastical custom (one can not yet really speak of ecclesiastical law), royal prerogative, and local power politics could and often did meet to create major crises.

Tradition demanded that the bishop be elected by the "clergy and people" of the diocese. In practice this was probably never how the majority of bishops were selected, although in the isolation of late Roman Gaul, something akin to this formula was probably followed, if by "clergy" one means primarily the archdeacon and by "people" the senatorial aristocracy. Following the establishment of the Frankish kingship, a new element was introduced, or rather reintroduced—the approval of the king. Thus in the sixth century the elements combining to select the new bishop were king, diocesan clergy, and aristocracy. In addition, just over the horizon would be found the *populus* in the sense of the masses, who might on occasion be excited to play a role in a disputed succession. The possible different titrations of this volatile mixture were as numerous as elections.

Because no regular mechanism for an orderly succession existed, the approaching death of a bishop was awaited with a mixture of anxiety and hope on all sides. An episcopal death and interregnum could bring violence, looting, and a time to settle old scores. In fact, such a period of troubles seems to have been expected. When Bishop Theodore of Marseille was captured by his enemy, Dynamius, the delighted clergy of the city pillaged and looted the episcopal residence "just as if the bishop were already dead."[14] In his case, he survived and was even returned to his see. In some instances, the death of the incumbent had been precipitated by those hoping to succeed to the office. This had been the accusation against Gregory's own brother; Gregory accused Bishop Frontonius of Angoulême of having murdered his predecessor Marachar;[15] at Lisieux a priest and the archdeacon conspired to murder Bishop Aetherius, and only the failure of the cleric hired to do the job saved him.[16]

In order to attempt to provide for an orderly succession and to maintain the office in their family, some bishops tried to secure the election and consecration of their successors during their lifetimes. We have seen the attempt on the part of Bishop Felix of Nantes to ensure his nephew's succession. Such practice was contrary to ecclesiastical custom and encountered serious opposition. More frequently the bishop would state his strong preference for his successor, as did the saintly Bishop Mauilio of Cahors, who successfully urged that Queen Ultrogotha's referendary, Ursicinus, be elected in his place.[17] Similarly Bishop Sacerdos of Lyon was succeeded by his choice, Nicetius.[18]

The competition between rival families, royal candidates, and the favorites of local clergy began in earnest as soon as the bishop was dead. Normally, three things had to be secured—election, confirmation by the king, and consecration, the last being the most important. Once an individual had been consecrated, even if scandalously elected or unconfirmed, while he could as a last resort be exiled and even excommunicated, it was extremely difficult to replace him before his death, and in any case he remained a bishop. Bishop Faustianus of Dax, it is true, was deposed at the second council of Mâcon by King Gunthchramn because he had been ordered consecrated by the king's rival, Gundovald, but even then the three bishops who had consecrated him were ordered to provide for him and pay him 100 gold pieces per year.[19] The sacred nature of consecration was such that God's annointed remained a bishop, regardless of how he reached that position. One sees a similar philosophy regarding secular office, particularly that of the later emperors and the king. God worked through the most evil of men, and He alone could remove them, although He might well use other men as His agents.

Better than anything else, the drama surrounding an episcopal election indicates the complexities and ambiguities of political power as they existed in sixth-century Francia. This most highly prized office demanded some sort of consensus or at least that a temporary truce be established among the differing factions. Every case was different, and Gregory of Tours's vivid accounts often obscure more than they enlighten. Why, when Bishop Laban of Eauze died, did Childebert allow himself to be bribed by a layman, Bertram, into confirming Bertram as Laban's successor, and then refuse, upon the latter's death, the bribes of his designated successor, the deacon Waldo, who was probably the godson of Bertram and moreover enjoyed the full support of the citizens of Eauze?[20] Gregory doesn't explain and we cannot guess. In this instance the king, whatever his motivation, was able to enforce his will against a united clergy and populace. In other situations, such as the dispute in Uzès, two successive royal candidates were blocked by powerful local interests. Here one sees the limits of royal power.

Religious Role of the Bishop

The power of the bishop was not reducible to the strength of his support at court, to his family, and to his good relationship with his supporters at home. Essentially he was considered the agent of God's will in his community, and the core of his power lay in this control of the sacred. If this is hard to see through the blood and intrigues of episcopal politics, it is because we fail to share the view of divine providence common to the sixth century.

The model bishop was an administrator both of his clergy and of the monasteries in his diocese, but he was above all a defender of the faith and protector of the poor. Defense of the faith might mean, in rare instances, a theological defense of doctrine against the errors of the Arians or, in even rarer instances, of a Chilperic, a learned Frankish king who attempted to write a treatise on the Trinity. But in reality Francia was largely devoid of real heretics just as it was of real theologians. Somewhat more frequently, it meant attempts to eliminate polytheistic practices within their dioceses, which might mean the kind of syncretistic religious observances carried on no doubt by recently converted Franks. At the Council of Orléans in 533, for example, bishops assembled primarily from northern Aquitaine enacted measures against Catholics who continued to make sacrifices to idols, a measure reaffirmed in the same city at a council eight years later.[21] One must not imagine that paganism was limited to the more barbarian north. Christianity had been largely an affair of the aristocracy in Gaul, and in rural areas throughout Francia paganism was by no means dead and traditional agrarian rituals persisted for centuries. The countryside could not be fully Christianized until the network of parishes extended into every corner of the kingdom, a development which would not take place until the ninth century.

The more essential, if prosaic, role of defending the faith was the instruction of the laity and the clergy, both through sermons and through the fostering of schools. Bishops educated in the

monastic tradition, particularly that of Lérins, were best equipped
for this task, and from the model Merovingian bishop, Caesarius
of Arles, we have a collection of sermons that show his ability to
put his rhetorical education to the task of educating the clergy
and laity of his diocese. Through the sixth century, most bishops
had a good education in Latin letters if not in Christian doctrine, and thus could at least adapt the teaching of Caesarius and
others to their own needs.

The task perceived as more immediate by the episcopate was
to provide discipline in the particularly turbulent and unruly
world in which they lived. This meant both establishing a sense
of unity and purpose within the disparate factions which made
up their communities and the community of bishops, and establishing and maintaining norms of Christian conduct for clergy
and laity alike.

In this world of strong personalities, the primary source of
unity for the competing forces within society was sought in the
personality of the saints. One of the major achievements of recent scholarship, particularly that of Peter Brown, is to elucidate
the absolutely critical social role that saints' cults played in early
medieval society.[22] In these communities, often split by the most
violent and overt kinds of competition, in which no living man
or woman could be assured of unanimous acceptance, the saint
became the rallying point. He (or she) alone was both part of the
supernatural world, and, through his tomb, continued to reside
among and serve the people. He was, then, a tangible, physical
source of authority and power, a sure point within a world of
constantly changing fortunes.

While no Christian doubted the power of saints, at the death
of any individual, some might doubt the sanctity of that particular person. After all, every living man and woman of any note
was caught up in the political struggles already described. Bishop
Priscus of Lyon and his wife Susanna, for example, were not at
all prepared to consider his predecessor Nicetius one of God's
elect. It was then necessary for the community to arrive at a consensus concerning the saint's special status, and this could be directed by the bishop. To this end, the rhetorical training of the
Frankish episcopate was ideal; their task was to persuade, to

show the divided community the unmistakable signs of the saint's power. By interpreting the misfortunes of enemies and the good luck of friends in terms of their comportment relative to the saints, bishops could work to form consensus about the saint, which simultaneously established consensus about the bishop. Bishops and saints were thus mutually dependent on each other for their reputations.

The control of saints by bishops was not granted without challenge by the rest of society or indeed by the saints themselves. The first challenge, which the Western episcopacy faced head-on and largely overcame, was posed by the latter group. If the bishops' greatest source of spiritual power was that of dead saints, their greatest threat was that of living ones. In the East, holy men and women, through their lives of asceticism and detachment, had become a major factor in the balance of power in village, regional, and occasionally, in imperial affairs. Such persons received their power not from the bishop, not from the emperor or his representatives, but directly from acclamation by public opinion as emissaries of God. Such a situation was entirely unacceptable to the episcopal aristocracy of Francia. The story of Vulfolaic the Langobard shows how the episcopate reacted to the threat.[23]

As a small (and presumably Arian) child, Vulfolaic had heard the name of Martin, and without any knowledge of his life or works, developed a great devotion to him. In time, he taught himself to read, became a disciple of Abbot Aredius of Limoges, and finally visited Tours, where he obtained as a relic dust from the tomb of Saint Martin. On his return to Limoges, the dust miraculously expanded, spilling out of the small box in which he carried it around his neck. Inspired by this miracle, he moved to the region of Trier where he found, in the ruins of a temple, a statue of Diana on a pillar, which the locals worshiped. Vulfolaic climbed another pillar and, in imitation of Simeon Stylites, there endured the harshness of a German winter. Soon crowds from the neighboring manors flocked to see this holy man, and from his column he preached against the idol on the neighboring one. Convinced by his words and example and assisted by his prayers, the locals destroyed the statue. As effective as his efforts had been, however, the local bishops objected. Finally they sent him off on an errand and in his absence had his column destroyed. Heartbroken but not daring to disobey the bishops, he took up residence with the local clergy.

To Gregory and his fellow bishops, Vulfolaic had done just about everything wrong that one could, with only one exception, which nevertheless redeemed him in the end.

First, he was a rustic. Vulfolaic was of obscure barbarian parentage—the Langobards in the sixth century were the rudest and least cultivated people within the Roman world. As evidence of his simpleness, he developed his devotion to Martin without the guidance of a properly trained bishop who could instill in him the proper *reverentia,* that deeper, inner intelligence accessible to the trained cleric.

Second, he had allowed the miracle of the expansion of the sacred dust to fill him with pride. Instead of remaining in his monastery, he took this as a sign that he was somehow marked for greater and more public things and set out on his own mission. Gregory explains elsewhere just how this miracle should have been handled. When the grain harvest at a Bordeaux monastery was miraculously saved by the prayers of a young novice, the wise abbot immediately had the youth seized, beaten, and shut up in his cell for a week lest he be inflated with pride at having been an instrument of God's will.[24]

Third, without education or authority, Vulfolaic had begun to preach to the people, a charge reserved to the bishop. Here indeed was the blind leading the blind, and it mattered little that the effects of his preaching were the destruction of the idol and the conversion of the people.

At this point Vulfolaic was within an inch of being cast in with the wandering preachers, miracle workers, and other troublemakers who often ended their days rotting in episcopal prisons. He was saved by his obedience. In the end, he accepted their decision, made no attempt to reestablish the column, and ended his days a deacon, firmly under episcopal authority.

This theme of episcopal control of the saints occurs again and again, both in Gregory's history, his lives of saints, and in Merovingian hagiography generally. It is part of an overall plan to assimilate every possible form of supernatural power to the control of the hierarchy, and to brand what could not be so assimilated as apostasy or paganism. Even in Gregory's accounts of the lives of hermits, the bishop is never far away. When, for example, Friardus, a recluse near Nantes, lay dying, his last wish was to see his bishop, and he died as soon as the latter arrived. Before Saint Patroclus began his career as a hermit, he was careful to first appear before his bishop and request tonsure.[25]

Not only did the episcopal tradition attempt to assimilate the power of Christian saints, but it attempted to assimilate popular beliefs into the Christian tradition as well. Most illuminating in this regard is the account of Saint Marcel of Paris and the dragon, told by Venantius Fortunatus. In brief, a dragon had been terrorizing the outskirts of Paris. Bishop Marcel arrived on the scene, tamed the beast, and ordered it to disappear. The monster complied and was not seen again. As analyzed recently by Jacques Le Goff, this legend takes on the character of a fusion of episcopal authority and popular beliefs.[26] The dragon, who appears across the barbarian and Mediterranean worlds, represents not only the devil but also serves as an ambivalent symbol of earthly and aquatic natural forces, at once dangerous and attractive. In the legend, the bishop is seen as the civilizing force triumphing over the forces of nature, but not destroying them. The fearful dragon was so impressed with Saint Marcel that it lowered its head in supplication and wagged its tail like a small dog. The bishop, in driving the monster away, had acknowledged the forces of nature, in this case the marshy and uninhabitable swamps near the Seine, and brought them into a rational and civilized relationship with humankind. The bishop thus drew his prestige in the community not only from his ability to appropriate traditional Christian power to himself, but from his ability to dominate more ancient, elemental powers as well.

The Monastery

In 811 the great Frankish emperor Charlemagne ordered an investigation:

> Let it be determined whether there were monks in Gaul before the arrival of the Rule of St. Benedict in these ecclesiastical provinces.[27]

By the ninth century, the rule of Benedict had become the norm for monastic life in the West. However, if Charlemagne's researchers did their work properly, they would have had to answer that, not only were there other forms of monastic life in Gaul prior to the introduction of the Benedictine rule, but that Benedictine monasticism was a relative newcomer to Francia. Three forms of monastic traditions preceded it—that of Martin of Tours, that of Lérins, and the Irish tradition of Saint Columbanus. An understanding of the first two are essential to an understanding of sixth-century Francia.

Martin of Tours

The life of Saint Martin presents a microcosm of the Western Empire in the fourth century. Martin was the son of a soldier, born c. 316 in modern Szombathely, Hungary, one of the vital Pannonian military posts defending the Danubian frontier. He moved to Italy when his father, a military tribune, was transferred to Pavia, and there became a catechumen. In accordance with the Roman law tying sons to the professions of their fathers, Martin became a soldier and his unit was transferred to Amiens. There was said to have occurred the famous story of his cloak. Seeing a shivering beggar at the city gates one day, he cut his military cloak in half and gave one half to the poor man. Although his appearance in only half a cloak was met with laughter in the city, that night he had a vision of the Lord, who was wearing the half he had given away. His portion of the cloak in time became the *cappa,* the most important sacred relic of the Frankish kings, guarded and venerated by the clerics in the royal household who made up the *capella* or chapel.

Martin was baptized at Amiens and shortly after, at Worms, was allowed to leave the military. He then went to Bishop Hilarius of Poitiers to perfect himself in his new faith. He soon traveled to Italy to see his parents again, but before he could return to Poitiers he heard that the Arian Visigoths had exiled Hilarius to the East. Unable to return to Gaul, he led for a time a hermitic life on the Isle of Albenga in the Tyrrhenian Sea, his first personal experience with monasticism. When Hilarius was allowed to return to Poitiers in 361, Martin immediately joined him and received from him permission to lead a solitary life at Ligugé, which he had begun at Albenga. Before long, his reputation spread; a community of followers joined him, and he was often called away to preach in central and western Gaul. When Bishop Lidorius of Tours died in 371 the citizens tricked Martin into entering the city and made him their bishop.

Although Martin exercised his office conscientiously, he continued to lead his monastic life in a cell a short distance from the city. Again, a monastic community grew up around him at this new monastery, Marmoutier. From here Martin continued to involve himself in the religious affairs of the West, traveling as far as Trier and even Rome in his role as a major spokesperson for orthodoxy. He died in 397 and was buried in a stone sarcophagus in his monastery, which in time became a major pilgrimage site.

Initially, however, the cult of Saint Martin and his monastic tradition did not spread far beyond the region of his most intense activity. Prior to the adoption of Saint Martin by Clovis as the special patron of his family, his cult was largely limited to the Loire region, Aquitaine, and a few sites in Spain. The monastic tradition he had introduced, a rather eclectic form combining Eastern traditions of asceticism with the life of the Gallic clergy in the West, took no root beyond those areas where he had been most active. One can adduce several reasons for this. Unlike the great aristocratic bishops of Gaul, Martin was an outsider, a soldier (a déclassé profession in the eyes of Roman aristocrats), and above all a strange hybrid of a monk-bishop—an ascetic who nevertheless relentlessly involved himself in the activities of the world. North of the Loire and in the southeast of Gaul, Martin's form of monasticism seems to have held little attraction.

The ultimate popularity of this most unusual man was to a great extent the result of the image drawn of him by his biographer, Sulpicius Severus, an educated and refined follower who, in his account of Martin's life, presented him as the ideal of a new type of bishop—one who could be a great churchman pursuing the life of action traditionally associated with high Roman office and still be able to lead the life of self-renunciation characteristic of monastic observance. Gradually this tale of active and

contemplative life, rewritten in a classic of late Latin prose, attracted Aquitainian churchmen who sought more in religion
than the daily routine of administrative tasks and the constant
threat of political competition.

Still, the determining figure in the development of Martin's
cult was not Sulpicius, the learned Aquitainian monk and aristocrat, but rather Clovis, the newly converted Frank. What he
saw in Martin is not altogether clear—in large part he must have
considered Martin a key ally in his victory over the Visigoths.
Also, since Martin's cult was spreading slowly through the aristocracy of the same region where Clovis made his conquest, his
special attention to Martin was a means of establishing strong
ties with the leading figures of his newly acquired lands. It may
even be that Martin, the Pannonian soldier who came to play
such a leading role in Gaul, was a figure particularly attractive
to Clovis. In spite of Sulpicius's coloring of his life, Martin was
clearly not a great intellectual or man of letters like the majority
of southern bishops Clovis must have encountered. Instead he
was a man of action who knew the sources of real power and how
to wield it. Clovis too was a relative outsider (who also perhaps
considered himself of Pannonian origin, if the legend discussed
earlier was already in currency) and a recent convert who was
likewise making his way in Gaul. Thus Martin and Clovis had
much in common.

In any event, Clovis's patronage transformed Martin from a
patron of the Aquitainian bishops to the patron of the Frankish
kingdom and the symbol of the new Frankish church. The cult,
and with it the attempt to combine an active public life with the
ascetic contemplative tradition, spread north to Paris, Chartres,
Rouen, and Amiens; east to Trier, Strassburg, and Basel; west
to Bayeaux, Avranches, and Le Mans, and south to Saintes, Angoulême, Limoges, and Bordeaux, to name but a few of the major cities where his cult flourished in the sixth century. In the
following century, the cult of Saint Martin traveled with the expansion of the Frankish empire as far north as Utrecht and as
far east as Linz.

The Aquitainian form of monasticism should not be seen as a
systematic movement or even a group of monasteries following a

particular rule or group of rules. Rather it was a series of local initiatives often inspired by the example of Martin but not with any particular institutional connection with Marmoutier. In fact, little is known about the internal organization and discipline of these communities—a problem, as we shall see, for other, more formal monastic traditions.

The example of Martin attracted not only men but also women. However, while communities of men might spring up around a particularly impressive hermit, those of women tended to form around oratories and basilicas where were found the remains of saints to whom the religious felt particular devotion. Communities of women were generally in cities or in their immediate suburbs, where they could be supervised by the local bishop and protected from men. Bride theft was still a normal means of acquiring a wife, and aristocratic convents were convenient locations in which to find a suitable woman who could be stolen, raped, and then married for her inheritance.

The Rhône

The one region in which the cult of Martin barely penetrated was, with Aquitaine, the most profoundly Roman region of Francia—the Rhône watershed. Here developed almost simultaneously a parallel but different from of monasticism, much more aristocratic in its associations, more carefully disciplined, and more directly related to the Eastern monastic tradition. The two traditions and their adherents were wary of each other, and the differences and disagreements may have reflected not only different styles of monastic observance, but also important divisions in the late Gallo-Roman aristocracy of the West.

The first of the great Rhône monasteries, Lérins, was founded between 400 and 410 by Saint Honoratus, a member of a consular family from northern Gaul. As youths, he and his brother devoted themselves to the ascetic life and together undertook a pilgrimage to the East in order to experience Eastern monasticism. After his brother died on the Peloponnesus, Honoratus returned to Gaul and founded on the island of Lerinum a small monastery modeled on those he had known in the East.

At almost the same time that Honoratus was founding Lérins, John Cassian was founding the monastery of Saint Victor at nearby Marseille. Cassian had been a student of John Chrysostom in Constantinople and Pope Leo the Great in Rome, but his most formative experience was the fifteen years he spent among the anchorites in Syria and monastic communities in the Egyptian desert of Scete. Cassian thus imported Eastern monasticism directly into the West, both in the rigorous descriptions of monastic life and discipline in his *Institutes* and in the collection of the wisdom and sayings of the fathers of the Egyptian desert in his *Colloquies*. While the latter are hardly verbatum transcriptions of the Desert Fathers' teachings, they nevertheless record the spirit and vitality of Eastern monasticism and present it as a model to be followed in the West.

The Eastern monasticism introduced by Honoratus and Cassian arrived at exactly the right moment to provide a spiritual and cultural refuge for northern aristocrats displaced by the turbulence of the fifth century. The island monastery of Lérins became in particular a place of refuge for the northern Gallic aristocracy, who, like Honoratus himself, sought a refuge from the political and social upheavals of their homeland. The list of these refugees is long and illustrious: Saint Hilarius, a kinsman of Honoratus and later archbishop of Arles; Caesarius, from Chalon-sur-Saône, who also ended his life as archbishop of Arles; Salvian, who came to Marseille from Cologne or Trier; and Faustus, originally from Armorica, who was abbot at Lérins before becoming bishop of Riez, to name but a few.

Rhône monasticism, unlike that established by Martin, maintained a strongly aristocratic character. This elite tradition is evident in the quality of writing and theological polemic which came from it. Prior to their conversion, these monks had been thoroughly educated in the pagan rhetorical tradition, and although they came to Lérins to practice silence, isolation, abstinence, and prayer, they nevertheless continued to employ their intellectual talents. Thus unlike the monasteries of the Martin tradition, Lérins produced, or perhaps rather influenced, intellectuals. The most significant example of the ascetic influence exerted on fifth-century intellectuals by Lérins was the participation of at least two of its monks, Vincent of Lérins and Faustus of Riez, as well as Cassian himself, in the attack on Augustine's predestinarian teaching. These so-called semi-Pelagians, like other monks dedicated to the importance of the ascetic life and the value of self-mortification and self-control, could not accept as pessimistic a view of the human potential as that of the African bishop. To accept Augustine's resolution of the paradox of inevitability and responsibility seemed to them to destroy responsibility. Not only was Augustine's doctrine of predestination seen as a fatalistic, heretical solution to the problem of divine grace and free will, it was also new. Vincent of Lérins, attacking the novelty of Augustinian theology, formulated what would be the fundamental definition of orthodox consensus: Augustine's predestinarian teaching was unacceptable because it did not conform to what had been believed "everywhere, always, by all" (*ubique semper ab omnibus*).[28] This formulation exemplified a monastic intellectual firmly maintaining the cosmopolitan and universal culture of Christian Roman civilization.

This aristocratic character of Lérins was also clear in the nature of its attraction—it was a desert retreat, but a fruitful and pleasant one where displaced elites, dedicated to the life of the mind and to the pursuit of spiritual perfection, could find solace for a short period or for a lifetime. Upon their departure for the episcopacy, many, like Hilarius, Faustus, and Caesarius, went on to establish similar communities in their cities. Since most of these sees were to be found along the fluvial axis created by the Rhône and Saône, the Lérins model of monastery gradually filtered north to Arles, Lyon, Autun, St. Maurice d'Agaune, to the monasteries of the Jura region, and as far as Troyes.

Although the differences between the traditions of Martin and those of Lérins and Marseille were more of emphasis than content, they were nevertheless deeply felt through the sixth and even seventh centuries. Although little is known about the organization of Martin's monasteries, Rhône monasticism was apparently much closer to Eastern traditions in strictness. Aquitainian (Martin's) monasticism seems to have been more the result of improvisation; a holy man would appear, a group of followers would congregate, and the resulting community would live more as a group of hermits than a regular monastic community. Cassian was aware of this loose form of monastic life and condemned it in his *Institutes* without mentioning Martin by name.

In fact, through the sixth century, proponents of the two traditions seem to have ignored each other, refraining from directly attacking the other tradition but also from mentioning its existence whenever possible. Thus Hilarius of Arles, Eucherius of Lyon, Vincentius of Lérins, Caesarius of Arles, and the other leading proponents of the Rhône monastic tradition never mention Saint Martin. Although in some regions deeply influenced by Lérins, such as the Jura monasteries where his *Life* by Sulpicius was read and venerated, he was simply not considered a part of the same monastic tradition from which Lérins and Marseille originated.

Similarly, Gregory of Tours, the great proponent of Martin's cult in the sixth century, has little to say about the Rhône tradition. In all his accounts of the bishops and saints of Gaul, he never once discusses Caesarius of Arles, Faustus of Riez, Honoratus, Hilarius, or Salvian. He mentions Lérins only in conjunction with the translation of the relics of Saint Hospitius; he says nothing about its ascetic tradition. The two worlds of Gallic monasicism remained divided camps.

And yet, the similarities were greater than the differences. Both had developed from Eastern monastic tradition around the same time. Both involved primarily the clergy. We have seen how closely the bishop was connected to the monastic and hermitic tradition praised by Gregory. In the Rhône area, monasticism was essentially an affair of aristocratic churchmen; it found its support within clerical society, not among the laity. For the most part, the latter remained neutral toward monasteries unless they desired to abandon the world for the cloister. Abbots, unless they left the monastery for an episcopal see, rarely cut an imposing figure in worldly society. Thus the two worlds did not penetrate each other.

During the course of the later fifth and sixth centuries, the two forms of monastic life began to blend. In particular, the more rigorous rules followed in the Rhône valley, such as strict subordination of monks to their abbots and the requirement that monks remain in the location where they had taken their vows rather than traveling about founding new hermitages and cells, began to be demanded of all monks by episcopal synods. The Rhône valley model of monastic life appealed to councils much more than the ad hoc religious life followed in Aquitaine because it made it easier for bishops to control monks. Above all, whether in Aquitaine or the Rhône valley, monasticism was (or was supposed to be) firmly under the control of the bishop. This subordination was emphasized at the first Frankish council held in 511. Canon 19 stated emphatically that "By reason of religious humility, abbots are to remain under the authority of bishops and should they do anything contrary to [their] rule, they are to be corrected by the bishop."[29]

Bishops Against Monks

That this canon had to be repeated at subsequent synods during the sixth century suggests that, while bishops claimed and in theory abbots acknowledged, episcopal authority over religious communities, at times abbots (and abbesses) acted with considerable autonomy, much to the discomfiture of their bishops. Rebelliousness could have social and political origins, as in the case of the revolt in the monastery of the Holy Cross founded by Radagunda, wife of Chlothar I, in Poitiers.[30] After Radagunda's death, nuns who, like her, were of the royal family refused to accept her successor and staged a revolt. Some left the convent for marriage while others, with the assistance of their armed servants, beat up the bishops who came to negotiate with them. This case was, however, exceptional in every respect. The nuns in revolt were Merovingians; Radagunda's successor, Agnes, seems to have been one of the few members of the community not of royal parentage; the bishop of Poitiers, for unexplained reasons, had long refused to supervise the monastery. Such a situation could hardly have been typical.

More common and ominous was a different sort of disobedience. In his *Book in the Glory of the Confessors*, Gregory tells that when Bishop Agricola of Cavillon heard that Desideratus, a recluse living nearby in a religious community that had sprung

up around him, had died, the bishop immediately sent his archdeacon to obtain the body. The monks of the community refused
to surrender it.[31] Here indeed was a potential threat to the bed-
rock of episcopal power. Monastic communities, as we have seen,
tended to grow up either around a hermit known for his piety or
around a basilica or tomb of a reputed holy man. It was from
just such deceased holy persons that bishops could draw their
power, if they could control access to them. If sanctity could escape episcopal control in the West as it had done long before in
the East, the monopoly of religious and political authority of the
bishop, as well as that of his aristocratic Gallo-Roman kinsmen,
could be in jeopardy. This is precisely what happened in the seventh and eighth centuries.

In the face of real and potential threats to their position from
Frankish agents, rival families, disgruntled kinsmen, and free-
lance saints, bishops found support in solidarity. Perhaps in recognition of the precariousness of their existence, the bishops of
Francia were able to set aside their differences sufficiently to meet
in regular regional and national synods at which common problems might be discussed and remedies found. Also, we see them
acting as a group under their metropolitans to deal with problems too complex or too dangerous for any single bishop.

The factious episcopate of Francia can hardly be credited with
the initiative of calling national councils. These began in 511 at
the initiative of Clovis and continued to meet from time to time
at the initiative of the kings. Moreover many councils, including
the first, were not really attended by bishops from all of the
Frankish kingdom; they tended to be regional in scope, although
some, such as the Council of Orléans in 549, really did assemble
bishops or their representatives from the entire Frankish world.

The issues addressed at these assemblies were a combination of
ad hoc problems and more general questions facing the bishops
and the kingdom. Much of the legislation concerns episcopal col-
legiality and the protection of episcopal authority. Annual provincial synods were required in order to encourage "fraternity
and charity" among themselves. Bishops were protected from
each other, from their clergy, and from the interference of the
king.

A second vital area of concern was the discipline of the clergy. Whenever possible, the bishops sought to eliminate ambiguity and foster the sort of Christian asceticism in the secular or diocesan clergy that they admired in the regular or monastic clergy. Progressively, the traditions of Western religious and social practice were subordinated to Eastern ascetic ideals even while monastic communities were required to submit to strict episcopal supervision.

However, in the following century a fundamental challenge was raised to this corporate, episcopal control of the discipline and practice of Frankish religion by a new type of monasticism. It appeared on the Continent in the last years of the sixth century and would spread rapidly during the reigns of the two greatest Merovingians, Chlothar II and Dagobert I. Before considering this challenge, we must first look at Francia under these two great kings.

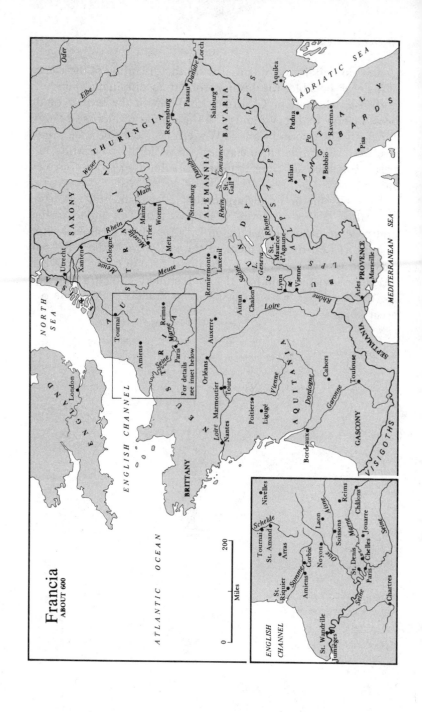

Francia
ABOUT 600

Oder

Elbe

NORTH SEA

THURINGIA

SAXONY

Weser

Main

Mainz

Rhein

Worms

Trier

Cologne

Metz

Xanten

Utrecht

Meuse

Moselle

Danube

Regensburg

Passau

Lorch

Salzburg

BAVARIA

ALPS

Strassburg

Danube

ALEMANNIA

L. Constance

St. Gall

Rhein

Aquilea

ADRIATIC SEA

Padua

Ravenna

LOMBARDS

Milan

Po

ITALY

Bobbio

Pisa

Rhone

St. Maurice d'Agaune

L. Geneva

Lyon

Vienne

Saône

BURGUNDY

Chalon

Autun

ALPS

PROVENCE

Arles

Marseille

MEDITERRANEAN SEA

Luxeuil

Remiremont

Meuse

AUSTRASIA

FRISIA

ENGLAND

London

NORTH SEA

ENGLISH CHANNEL

Tournai

Reims

Marne

Amiens

Seine

Paris

For details see inset below

Oise

NEUSTRIA

Auxerre

Orléans

Loire

Tours

Marmoutier

Poitiers

Ligugé

Loire

Nantes

BRITTANY

Vienne

AQUITANIA

Dordogne

Garonne

Cahors

Toulouse

Bordeaux

GASCONY

VISIGOTHS

SEPTIMANIA

ATLANTIC OCEAN

Miles

0   200

Inset

ENGLISH CHANNEL

Schelde

Nivelles

St. Amand

Tournai

Arras

Somme

Amiens

Corbie

Laon

Aisne

Noyon

Soissons

Oise

Reims

Marne

Châlons

Seine

St. Riquier

St. Denis

Paris

Jouarre

Chelles

Seine

Chartres

St. Wandrille

Jumièges

CHAPTER V

Francia under Chlothar II and Dagobert I

Francia Reunited

Brunechildis was brought before Chlothar who was boiling with fury against her. . . . She was tormented for three days with a diversity of tortures, and then on his orders was led through the ranks on a camel. Finally she was tied by her hair, one arm and one leg to the tail of an unbroken horse, and she was cut to shreds by its hoofs at the pace it went.[1]

The brutal humiliation and dismemberment of Brunechildis was the final dramatic act (613) in the consolidation of the Frankish subkingdoms under Chlothar II (reigned 584–629). The next twenty-five years of his reign and that of his son, Dagobert I (reigned 623–629 with his father, 629–638 alone) would be the most peaceful, prosperous, and significant period of Frankish history since the reign of Clovis. It would also be a period when the aristocratic forces that would ultimately destroy the Merovingian dynasty would come to a new self-awareness, quietly building and consolidating their strength.

Chlothar's victory had been made possible by the cooperation of the Burgundian and Austrasian aristocracy. Gunthchramn, the Burgundian king admired by Gregory, had died childless in 593 and his nephew Childebert II, son of Brunechildis and the Austrasian Sigibert I, acquired the kingdom. After Childebert's death in 596, Brunechildis attempted to control both Austrasia and Burgundy as guardian of her minor grandsons Theudebert II (reigned 596–612) and Theuderic II (reigned 596–613). Chlothar II attempted unsuccessfully to take advantage of their minority to absorb their kingdoms.

In 599 the Austrasian aristocracy, unhappy with her rule, expelled the old queen, who fled to the kingdom of her grandson Theuderic, where she was warmly received. The two brothers initially cooperated in their efforts to eliminate their Neustrian cousin Chlothar and were largely successful in absorbing a large portion of his kingdom. However tensions between the supporters of Brunechildis (largely the aristocracy in the more Romanized regions of the Burgundian kingdom) and her grandson Theuderic, and the Austrasians and Burgundian Franks reached the point that in 612 Theudebert attacked his brother's kingdom. The attack was a disaster, Theudebert was captured, incarcerated at Châlons-sur-Marne, and killed. Theuderic ordered that his infant nephew Merovich have his brains dashed out.

This union of the two kingdoms lasted only a few months. The Austrasian aristocracy, represented by Arnulf of Metz and Pippin of Herstal, invited Chlothar into the kingdom. Theuderic attempted to move against them but he died unexpectedly at Metz. Brunechildis tried to continue her control of Burgundy by making Sigibert, her great-grandson and the eldest son of Theuderic, king of the two regions, but Sigibert and his great-grandmother were betrayed by the Burgundian aristocracy into the hands of Chlothar. Sigibert and his brother Corbus were executed, his other brother, Merovich, the godson of Chlothar, was sent into exile in Neustria, and Brunechildis received the fate described above by the chronicler known as Fredegar.

Chlothar's victory had been a victory of the Austrasian and Burgundian aristocracies, and immediately following the execution of Brunechildis he took steps to confirm the position of those who had made his victory possible. Warnachar, the particular favorite of Theuderic II and Brunechildis, whose defection had made possible the capture of the latter, was immediately named *maior domus* in Burgundy for life—Chlothar swore a solemn oath that he would never remove him from office. In Austrasia Chlothar established as *maior domus* one Rado, who had probably played a similar role in that area.

Shortly after, in Paris, Chlothar issued a 24-article edict that in essence promised that the traditional rights of the aristocracy, the church, and the people would be respected.[2] Hardly novel, these measures were intended to guarantee that abuses which had developed in the years of internal warfare and arbitrary governance by the Visigoth Brunechildis and her descendants would be corrected. It is ironic that, if much of the opposition to Brunechildis resulted from her attempts to reintroduce Roman fiscal traditions, the edict was probably prepared in response to petitions drawn up by southern bishops drawing on Roman and Visigothic legal tradition. Thus Chlothar promised that episcopal elections would be carried out by the clergy and the people, and that the person thus selected, if worthy, would be confirmed by the king; he forbade the practice of bishops naming their successors; he reaffirmed the authority of the bishop over his clergy; and he guaranteed that widows and virgins who had devoted themselves to a religious life either in monasteries or in their own homes could not be forced into marriage. Much of the edict concerned the administration of justice. Except in criminal matters, clerics were to be judged only by ecclesiastical courts; cases involving clerics and laymen were to be judged in the presence of an ecclesiastical provost and a public judge; neither freemen or slaves could be punished or executed without judgment; Jews were not to pursue legal actions against Christians. Chlothar was also concerned with fiscal abuses. Wherever tax rolls had been unjustly raised, formal inquiries were to be made to correct them; no tolls were to be collected that did not date back to the reigns of Gunthchramn, Chilperic, and Sigibert; no royal tax collectors were to infringe on ecclesiastical or private immunities; the property of persons dying intestate was to go to their legitimate heirs and not the king.

Finally, the edict promised to respect the authority and traditions of local powers. In a famous chapter, Chlothar promised that "no judge [presumably royal official] from one province or region shall be appointed in another." Some have taken this as a major departure in royal policy, a guarantee of local autonomy which amounted to a surrender of royal authority to the interests of the local aristocracy. In reality it probably reflects what had by this time become traditional, appointing royal officers by much the same process as in the selection of bishops. Moreover, another chapter forbids lay and ecclesiastical magnates holding estates in more than one region from appointing judges or agents from outside the region. However, while the edict is not the result of a constitutional revolution or the abandonment of royal prerogative into the hands of the aristocracy, it explicitly confirms the intensely local character of Francia. Governance, meaning essentially the collection of taxes and maintenance of justice among consenting freemen, was a local affair within the *civitas* or *pagus* (that is, the administrative district surrounding a town). No attempt, whether by the king, the church, or magnates to introduce outsiders into this system would be tolerated. As a result, the governance of the three regions of Francia, although united under Chlothar, would not be centralized. Instead, each would continue to preserve its own regional power bases and, to an extent, its institutions under Chlothar and his successor Dagobert, whom he associated in his reign in 623, placing him over Austrasia, and who succeeded him in 629 as king of all of Francia. In the course of the seventh century this particularity became even more accented as other regions, such as Bavaria, Thuringia, Frisia, Aquitaine, and Provence, traditionally either divided among the three central kingdoms (as in the cases of Aquitaine and Provence) or controlled by Austrasia, developed into virtually autonomous subkingdoms.

The Regions of Francia

In the wake of the aristocratic-royal cooperation that reunited the kingdoms, the role of royal advisors within each of the regions of Francia became extremely important since they largely determined the extent of royal influence. In Burgundy, where royal officers in the days of Brunechildis had been instruments of royal control, the aristocracy, badly split among the more western "Franks" and the Rhône "Romano-Burgundians," had little interest in seeing a strong central government under a *maior domus*. When Warnachar died in 626/27, the Burgundian aristocracy informed Chlothar that they did not wish any new appointment to be made but that they be allowed to deal directly with the king. This is to say, in all likelihood, that they chose to be ruled directly by themselves. In particular, the more southern region, corresponding most closely to the old Burgundian kingdom, continued to develop separatist tendencies centered around powerful aristocratic families through the remainder of the century.

The extent to which these autonomous tendencies had progressed in less than fifteen years can be judged by the account of Dagobert's judicial visit to Burgundy in 628. According to the chronicle of Fredegar, "The profound alarm that his coming caused among the Burgundian bishops, magnates, and others of consequence was a source of general wonder; but his justice brought great joy to the poor."[3] The presence of the king making his way across Burgundy, administering justice and righting wrongs, certainly had a great effect, but it was only temporary. Local magnates were constantly attempting to strengthen their own local power base and escape royal control. When the *maior domus* Warnachar died in 626, his son Godinus attempted to consolidate the regional power his father had created through marriage alliances by taking the extraordinary step of marrying his father's widow, his stepmother Bertha. Chlothar was so displeased that he had him killed. Later Brodulf, the uncle of Dagobert's half brother Charibert II, whom Chlothar had given only a border kingdom in Aquitaine, became a major source of trouble in Burgundy for Chlothar. Brodulf presumably intended to establish his son-in-law on the throne. Before leaving Burgundy in 628 Dagobert ordered Brodulf's execution. However the king could not always be in Burgundy, and in his absence autonomous tendencies were bound to develop once more.

In Austrasia, which had experienced almost a century of fairly unified governance under Sigibert I and his successors, the aristocracy sought to protect itself through different means. There, Chlothar was pressured to reestablish the kingship under his son Dagobert. Moreover, when Chlothar attempted to reduce the size of the Austrasian kingdom by detaching the Austrasian section of Aquitaine and the area west of the Ardennes and the Vosges, this effort was blocked. When Dagobert protested the division, a group of twelve arbiters were selected to settle the disagreement. Since the most important of these was Arnulf of Metz who, along with Pippin of Herstal was the most powerful representative of the Austrasian aristocracy, it was no surprise that Dagobert was able to retain all of the territory north of the Loire which had previously been part of Austrasia.

This then was the strategy for the preservation of aristocratic control in Austrasia. The region was to remain centralized with its own court, but the whole was to be controlled by Pippin and Arnulf, who had invited Chlothar to enter the kingdom in 613. Later, when Arnulf left the court he was replaced by another Austrasian, Bishop Cunibert of Cologne. The extent of their power was such that they could even force the king to eliminate their rivals, such as Chrodoald, a leading member of the powerful Agilolfing clan whose power spread across Austrasia and into Bavaria and probably Lombardy.

After Dagobert succeeded his father and moved his center of activities to Paris in 629, the influence of the Austrasians on him waned somewhat. Only Pippin stayed with him, but he too fell from favor and his presence in Neustria may have been in part because Dagobert wanted to keep an eye on him. However the strategic position of Austrasia prevented him from ignoring it or alienating its aristocracy. Frankish reversals against the Slavic Wends, led by their Frankish king Samo in 631–633, pressured him to reestablish a reduced Austrasian kingdom and to place at its head his two-year-old son Sigibert. As his tutor, Dagobert appointed an opponent of Arnulf and Pippin, Otto, son of the *domesticus* Urso. But the real power in the kingdom was shared by Bishop Cunibert of Cologne, a close friend of Pippin, and the Duke Adalgisil, who was almost certainly a member of the Arnulfing clan. Thus, despite the king's efforts to the contrary, the Austrasian aristocracy remained in control. This control was consolidated by the alliance of the two leading Austrasian clans with the marriage of Arnulf's son Ansegisel and Pippin's daughter Begga. The new family, termed the Arnulfings or Pippinids, would in time produce the next royal dynasty, the Carolingians.

Neustria had been the center of Chlothar's kingdom, and after 629 Dagobert made it his center as well. Here were found the largest amounts of fiscal land, the important cities of Paris, Soissons, Beauvais, Vermand-Noyon, Amiens, and Rouen, as well as the richest Frankish monasteries. Paris became increasingly the primary royal residence and the center of royal religious and political ideology. The great royal monasteries of St.-Germain-des-Prés and St.-Denis were found just outside the city, and the latter in particular became, under Dagobert, the center of royal cult. Dagobert richly endowed St.-Denis, raised its patron to a position of royal saint equal to that of Saint Martin, and initiated its tradition as the royal burial site, a role it played until the French Revolution.

Beyond the three central Frankish regions, control of the Frankish empire varied enormously. In Aquitaine, Chlothar had established his son Charibert, described as "simple-minded" by the chronicler Pseudo-Fredegar, at the head of a border kingdom. The establishment of the Aquitainian kingdom, like that of Austrasia, was a response to external threats, in this case that of the Gascons or Basques. The Aquitainian kingdom maintained the peace until Charibert's death in 632, but shortly after the Basques again began to menace the region. Dagobert ordered a Burgundian army to occupy and pacify the region, but it met with only partial success. On its return, the contingent led by Duke Arnebert was ambushed in the valley of the Soule and destroyed by the Basques—a defeat which may have created the legend that over a century later would be modified to fit a similar defeat by a Frankish army at Roncevaux, this time under the command of Count Roland.

Dagobert's reverses in Aquitaine were paralleled in Thuringia and in his Slavic campaigns. The Wends had been united by Samo, a Frank who, although described as a merchant, may well have been a Frankish agent sent to organize the Slavic Wends against the Avars, a steppe people who had replaced the Huns in Pannonia and were menacing not only the Byzantine Empire but Italy and Francia. He met with extraordinary success organizing the Slavs and protecting them from the Avars and was made their king, a position he held for some thirty-five years. His kingdom stretched from Bohemia to Carenthia and soon threatened the Frankish zone of influence in Thuringia. Dagobert's attempt to crush them ended in failure, largely because of Austrasian duplicity. As we have seen, this Slavic threat led to the reestablishment of the Austrasian kingdom.

In Thuringia similar problems developed after the reestablishment of the Austrasian kingdom and the appointment of
the Austrasian Radulf as duke. Radulf was successful in defending Thuringia against the Wends, but in the process he
developed Thuringia into a virtually autonomous kingdom.
Later, after Dagobert's death, he successfully revolted against
Sigibert and, after defeating the latter, he went so far as to term
himself "King in Thuringia," a bad omen for the future of the
Merovingian family.[4]

The distant Bavarian duchy created at the end of the sixth
century took shape around the region of the old Roman city of
Ratisbonna, Regensburg. It spread gradually down the Danube
and south into the Alps, filling the vacuum created by the retreat of the Langobards into Italy and the Franks back into Austrasia, and incorporated the various Roman and barbarian peoples in this mountainous region. The threat posed to the duchy
by the Avars, Slavs, and Bulgars had kept Bavaria and its Agilolfing dukes closely dependent on the Frankish king. Around
630 an order of Dagobert, made on the advice of his Frankish
aristocrats, that Bulgar exiles wintering in Bavaria be slaughtered, was sufficient to see 700 men, women, and children murdered in their sleep by their Bavarian hosts in the course of one
night. However, the Agilolfings were too wary to depend entirely
on Dagobert. The death of their kinsman Chrodoald at the instigation of Pippin was evidence of the potential for opposition
at court. Thus they developed both Avar and Langobard connections and in the course of the seventh century married extensively into the royal house of the latter. Although they did not
go as far as Radulf and call themselves kings, their neighbors,
the Langobards, did not hesitate to so designate them. Paul the
Deacon, the eighth-century Langobard historian, wrote that in
593 Tassilo had been ordained king in Bavaria by Childebert.

The Royal Court

Chlothar and Dagobert could not hope to control effectively
the entire Frankish kingdom by sending central agents to fill
positions of authority in each region. Instead they sought to

bring together members of regional elites in their Paris court, where they could be watched, but also educated and indoctrinated into their political and cultural views. By selecting the best and most capable of these for ecclesiastical and secular posts in their home territories, they could then return them, fulfilling their promise to name local men to important positions and still insuring that they would have people in vital offices who could work with the king.

For their part, members of local aristocratic families saw the court as a place to which to send sons and daughters for education, to make contacts, and to secure for their families the kinds of positions needed to perpetuate their family goals. Thus the Neustrian court was a major cultural center for Francia, where young Gallo-Roman aristocrats from Aquitaine, such as Desiderius, the future bishop of Cahors, and Eligius, an aristocrat from Limoges who later became Dagobert's treasurer and bishop of Noyon, formed friendships with northern counterparts such as Audoenus (known as Saint Ouen, Audoin, or Dado), later referendary under Dagobert and bishop of Rouen. Also it was a place where marriages might be arranged, as that between the young Austrasian noble Adalbald from Ostrewant and Rictrudis, a Gallo-Roman from Aquitaine. From even as far away as Northumbria, King Edwin sent his two sons to be raised in Dagobert's court.

The court served a variety of educational roles. Young men of good family had already begun their educations when they arrived, around the age of puberty, and entered the household of the king, possibly even attaching themselves to him by a special oath. It appears that they were raised along with the royal children under the control of the royal tutor or the *maior domus*. Their education probably involved both military training for young men destined for secular office and training in rhetoric and notarial procedure for those likely to enter the royal chancellery. However, the young aristocrats were not simply at court to learn how to become bureaucrats; they were there to develop and continue the complex network of friends, patrons, and royal proximity which could sustain and enrich their families.

The most complete image of how such a cultural, social, and political network developed at the court can be derived from examining the life and correspondence of Bishop Desiderius. He was the son of Salvius and Herchenefreda, both members of the Gallo-Roman aristocracy from Albi. He was one of five children, each of whom carried a Roman name with deep resonances in senatorial tradition—Rusticus, Siagrius, Selina, Avita. First his elder brother Rusticus was drawn to the court of Chlothar, where he served as chaplain and archdeacon before being appointed by the king to the see of Cahors. His second brother Siagrius also went to the Neustrian court where he entered the household of Chlothar, later returning to Albi as count of the city. Ultimately he was appointed patricius of Provence, the Provençal equivalent of duke.

Desiderius too, after studying rhetoric and law, was drawn to court, where he served as treasurer. Here his associates included some of the most important and influential people of the seventh century—the future bishop Paul, of Verdun, Abbo of Metz, Eligius of Noyon, and Audoenus of Rouen. Court life offered a variety of possibilities. The court of Clothar and Dagobert was coming increasingly under clerical influence; bishop courtiers such as Eligius and Audoenus had much more influence than had been common in the sixth century, and a new monastic culture, which we shall examine below, was taking deep root in the Frankish aristocracy at court as well as in the provinces. But the court also offered all of the opportunities for dissipation and seduction that have characterized royal courts everywhere. Particularly after Dagobert set aside his first queen, the childless Gomatrudis, and married Nantechildis around 639, if one can believe the rather hostile Pseudo-Fredegar, the court became notorious for debauchery and, as the king aged and it became increasingly clear that following his death there would be a new division of the kingdom and long minorities, a center of intrigue. Desiderius's mother was certainly aware of its repution. In her extant letters to her son during this period she urges him to avoid both the dangers of court politics and of moral temptations: "Keep charity toward all," she advised, "be cautious in your speech, and above all, preserve your chastity."[5]

Desiderius followed her advice and in 630, after his brother Rusticus had been assassinated, Dagobert appointed him to the see of Cahors and Rusticus's successor. This career pattern was increasingly typical of the early seventh century. In the past it had not been unusual for members of the royal household to be appointed bishops, but now it was quite common. Apparently Dagobert reserved to himself, rather than to his half brother or, later, to his son, the right to appoint or approve bishops for the entire kingdom—a means of maintaining a hold even in Austrasia and southern Aquitaine.

In Cahors, Desiderius served the king in the twin capacities customary for seventh-century bishops—his biographer takes great pains to describe the ecclesiastical building program he undertook, but also praised him for his work constructing fortifications. Not only did he repair the city walls but even constructed towers and fortified gates. He also established a monastery in Cahors, the first in the city, according to his biographer, in which he chose to be buried. In addition, he maintained close contact with the elite group with whom he had been educated and with whom he had served at court. In his extant correspondence one finds letters not only to or from his metropolitan and other bishops in Aquitaine but also, among others, Dagobert, Sigibert III, Grimoald, the *maior domus* in Austrasia, Chlodulf, apparently the son of Arnulf of Metz, Bishop Medoald of Trier, Abbo of Metz, Audoenus of Rouen, Paul of Verdun, Felix of Limoges, Eligius of Noyon, and Palladius of Auxerre. Clearly these wide connections were the result of his years at court and his continuing role in the kingdom. In two letters, one to Abbo of Metz and the other to Audoenus of Rouen, he recalls with fondness the happy days together as companions in the court of Chlothar.

We know quite a lot about Desiderius and his fellow episcopal alumni of the royal court because of their correspondence and the lives composed after their deaths. Much less is known about the secular officers also raised at court, although one can infer that a similar and interconnected network developed among them. Some, like Desiderius's brother Siagrius, were returned to their own regions as counts. Others, like Radulf, were sent as dukes to border regions of Francia where they may have already had, or soon developed, strong local ties. Still others, such as the Austrasian Adalbald who married the Aquitainian Rictrudis, were apparently married to women from sensitive regions in order to create the local connections necessary for effective functioning. Such efforts were often met with resistance, Adalbald was murdered at the instigation of his brothers-in-law. However it appears that during the first quarter of the seventh century numerous Austrasian and Neustrian aristocratic clans established ties in Aquitaine, Provence, Burgundy, and the regions east of the Rhine due to the court policies of the kings, while a corresponding number of Aquitainians, in this case primarily bishops, were established in northern sees.

The court during the reign of Chlothar and Dagobert thus played an essential role in the continuance of royal authority by drawing in, training, and then sending out capable administrators. Although less visible, two other developments were taking place during these decades which would have equally important effects on subsequent European history. The first was the development of the bipartite manor, which became the model for later medieval agriculture; the other, economically facilitated by the first, was the Christianization of royal tradition.

Royal Estates

The imperial fisc confiscated by Clovis in the north of Gaul had always formed the heart of Merovingian wealth. Largely for this reason, in the division of the kingdom that followed his death, each of his sons had received capitals relatively close together between the Rhine and the Loire. The *civitas* of Paris was probably at least three-fourths entirely fiscal land, the most important of which were Chelles, Rueil, and Clichy; at Soissons the vast fiscal lands centered on Bonneuil-sur-Marne, Compiègne, and Nogent-sur-Marne; on the lower Seine fiscal estates were found at Etrépagny, the forest of Bretonne, and on the sites that became the monasteries of Jumièges and St. Wandrille; the most important royal estates around Amiens were centered on the villa Crécy-en-Ponthieu.

These vast royal property holdings underwent continual transformation through the Merovingian period. Portions were given
away to important magnates, and others became the sites of
major monasteries. However, they had certain characteristics
lacking in other areas and in estates held by individuals. First
were the physical and demographic characteristics of the region.
The soil of this gently rolling area was essentially of two types.
The first was sandy uplands that could be worked easily and lent
itself to exploitation by individual peasant families, and the
second, heavy, rich lowlands that could be better exploited by
groups of laborers using heavier, more expensive tools such as
the heavy plough. After the abandonment of the classic Roman
villas, which we discussed earlier, the region experienced fairly
dense Frankish settlement, which resulted in widespread de-
forestation from the beginning of the sixth century and a progressive abandonment of animal husbandry in favor of farming.

Moreover, because much of this land remained in the royal
fisc, it did not figure in the frequent dismemberment of estates
that characterized private allodial landholding by the aristocracy, who engaged constantly in the purchase, sale, and exchange
of land, and whose death normally meant the division of their
lands among heirs. Also, because it was fiscal land, obligations
of the peasants working it, whether free or slave, differed somewhat from those on private estates. In particular, individual
holders of farms were obligated to considerable amounts of work
on the portion of the estate held in reserve for the direct benefit
of the king.

As a result, during the reigns of Chlothar and Dagobert probably a slow process began that resulted in the sort of manor
which typified agrarian organization of the high Middle Ages.
Its structure was essentially bipartite. On the one hand portions
were divided into individual peasant holdings, manses (a term
which first becomes common in the first half of the seventh century), which were worked in return for a fixed rent. These
manses were apparently often created in the course of deforesta-
tion and settled by freemen attached to the fisc or by slaves established as unfree tenant farmers. On the other hand, a considerable portion of the estate formed the reserve, and although

in the seventh century this reserve was still largely worked by gang slaves, peasants holding manses were required to perform a fixed amount of work on the domain or reserve, the profits of which went directly to the king.

Because these estates were part of the fisc, the late Roman tax system, which had become privatized and absorbed into the estate management of magnates, survived longer here as a public, or at least royal, system. The continuity of property holding made possible continued record-keeping and planning, and because these estates were fiscal, no bishops or local magnates were able to stand between royal agents and the peasants to demand a reduction in payments or even, as happened in the sixth century, the destruction of the tax rolls.

Such estates must have been quite profitable and formed an important source of royal wealth with which to support the court and finance the building programs and displays of royal status and largesse required of the kings. Gradually, the model spread out across Francia, penetrating most readily into those regions such as Burgundy, Austrasia, and even distant Bavaria, where soil conditions, population, and availability of fiscal land made it profitable, and less readily into the south where older, Gallo-Roman traditions and a different type of agriculture proved more resistant to restructuring.

Not only the form of estate organization but the estates themselves were coveted by the aristocracy as rewards for service and churches as rewards for intercessory prayers. Although the kings were obligated to show their generosity by granting estates to petitioners, in general they seem to have avoided distributing fiscal property to laymen whenever possible. Thus, while we hear of generous donations of land to various aristocrats, particularly to those who had supported Chlothar against Brunechildis, most of these estates had been confiscated from opponents. Nevertheless kings were obligated to grant fiscal estates, and normally with these grants, solemnized by guarantees of immunity, went the same rights over the dependents and the incomes which had been enjoyed by the king. The long-term effects of such grants, both in terms of royal income, since the taxes went to the owner, and in terms of the erosion of royal power, were ominous.

Chlothar and especially Dagobert were, on the other hand, much more generous in the distribution of fiscal property to the church. This was an old tradition. Clovis had endowed the church of St.-Geneviève, where he was buried, and Childebert I had founded St.-Germain-des-Prés, all on fiscal land. Chlothar and especially Dagobert were particularly interested in St.-Denis, which stood near their favorite villa of Clichy. Dagobert granted the monastery not only confiscations such as those taken from the rebel Aquitainian duke Sadregisel, but also important elements of the fisc from around Paris and from as far away as the Limousin, Le Mans, and Provence.

This dissemination of royal property served specific purposes for Dagobert. In time however, it had an unanticipated, twofold effect. In the long run, it weakened the monarchy in relationship to aristocrats who had either been the recipients of these estates or who had managed to take control of the monasteries which had been so favored by the kings. However, it also helped diffuse the bipartite estate model beyond the confines of the Parisian basin and the royal fisc until, by the late eighth century, it had become the primary model for estate structure.

Neither effect was in Dagobert's mind, however, when he made his grants to St.-Denis and other ecclesiastical institutions. His particular goals were religious and monarchical—he was wedding the royal tradition to a specific form of Christianity, with the intention of strengthening both.

Christianization of Royal Tradition

Frankish kings had had a close working relationship with the churches of their kingdom for over a century. However, under Dagobert this relationship became more systematic, explicit, and far-reaching. Royal interest lay in the development and appointment of bishops like Desiderius whose personal loyalty was unquestioned. But this was only part of the reason for the close relationship between monarch and church; it is anachronistic to suggest that Dagobert was attempting to create a Frankish episcopate as a protection against the lay aristocracy. He was extremely concerned with the spiritual protection of his kingdom and with the firm foundation, the *stabilitas,* which a well-supported church could provide.

Two paths led to this *stabilitas.* First, as Dagobert stated in the introductory harangue of his letter announcing the appointment of Desiderius as bishop of Cahors, "our election and disposition ought to conform in all things with the will of God."[6] This obligation to God comes from the fact that the king's "territories and kingdoms are known to have been given into our power to be governed by the generosity of God." This formula is neither original nor an acknowledgment that Dagobert is king "by the grace of God," a phrase which was later used by the Carolingians, but it is an acknowledgment of the royal dependence on God and the duty that this dependence requires.

This obligation meant appointing God-fearing men such as Desiderius to ecclesiastical and secular office and governing with justice. We have seen both of these concerns translated into action. Whatever their political and social ties, the bishops raised at the royal court and distributed by Dagobert throughout the kingdom stand out as particularly capable and, by the standards of their time, worthy churchmen. Dagobert's concern with justice was seen not only in such royal judicial visits as that which threw Burgundy into consternation in 639, but also in the codification of the laws of the Ripuarian Franks, the Alemanni, and possibly the Bavarians. Unlike the Salic and Burgundian laws, these later codes are not simply records of traditional law drawn up by Roman jurists at the command of the local king. Instead they are imposed laws, the first code having been drawn up for the small Austrasian kingdom ruled by Dagobert's son Sigibert, and the other two Frankish products imposed by a Merovingian king through his appointed dukes.

The second route to *stabilitas* led through almsgiving, and particularly generosity to monasteries. Pseudo-Fredegar, who disapproved of much in Dagobert's later career, nevertheless acknowledged his generosity. He suggested that, had he been even more generous, he might have saved his soul:

he had once been prodigal in his almsgiving; and had this earlier wise almsgiving not foundered through the promptings of cupidity, he would indeed in the end have merited the eternal kingdom.[7]

In reality, Dagobert was exceedingly prodigal in his almsgiving, and even as he lay dying asked that his son confirm his last donations to St.-Denis. We have mentioned this special generosity to St.-Denis before—it was a hallmark of Dagobert's reign. Not only did he endow it with enormous amounts of land and grant it immunity from royal officials, but he gave it great amounts of gold, gems, and precious objects. According to tradition he also established at the monastery the great October fair, which for centuries was a major source of income. And finally he chose St.-Denis as his final resting place.

This generosity was not to be a one-way process. In return Dagobert expected the spiritual assistance of the monks. In particular he established at St.-Denis the liturgical tradition of the *laus perennius,* the perpetual chant on the model of St.-Maurice d'Agaure in which monastic choir followed monastic choir so that at all hours of the day and night prayers were offered to God for the king, his family, and his kingdom. Dagobert took his responsibilities seriously, and he expected his favorite monastery to do the same.

Creation of the Aristocratic Tradition

We don't know what sort of rule the monks at St.-Denis followed in the time of Dagobert. Presumably it was something on the order of the tradition of Saint Martin. After his death, Dagobert's son imposed on the monastery the so-called mixed Benedictine and Columbanian rule. This form of monasticism, increasingly important in the seventh century, was part of a religious and social transformation which in time profoundly restructured the Frankish world and tilted the balance of power away from Merovingian kings and bishops toward Frankish aristocrats and monks.

The aristocratic Frankish kindreds which had developed their independence and force during the troubled last years of the sixth century were not, as was once believed, a new creation.

We have seen that a Frankish aristocracy had existed before Clovis and continued to play an important role under his successors. However, unlike the Gallo-Roman aristocracy, which not only had a strong political and social base but also a religious role as the chief proponents (and monopolizers) of high office in orthodox Christianity, the Frankish aristocracy had no religious role in society after the conversion of the Franks. True, its members may well have continued to enjoy prestige for their *utilitas,* that is, their military skill and political acumen, and in a society not fully Christianized something may have remained of their earlier religious importance. Indeed, Eligius of Noyon encountered near Noyon kinsmen of the Neustrian *maior domus* Erchinoald, who were presiding over summer celebrations including games and dancing which he, at least, considered pagan rituals and which they considered part of the customs handed down from time immemorial.[8] However, with the conversion of Clovis, the aristocracy rapidly became Christian, at least to the extent of acknowledging Christ as the most powerful victory-giving god and of demanding the performance of Christian rituals to assure their well-being and that of their families.

However, prior to the last quarter of the sixth century, no means of direct involvement in the growing Christian cult was readily available to the Frankish aristocracy. To become a bishop meant to adopt the cultural and social traditions of the senatorial aristocracy of the south, and while this was done by some Frankish families in the sixth century, it was rare. To become a monk was likewise unusual for a Frankish noble. As we have seen, monasteries were largely episcopal foundations, supported and closely controlled by them. True, Lérins offered aristocrats a type of monastic existence, but this was once more a Roman cultural and religious tradition attracting mostly aristocratic clerics who had already chosen the religious life. The more northern aristocrats had little involvement in such monasteries that were deeply rooted in Gallo-Roman cultural tradition and firmly supervised by the bishops recruited from the old elite. All this began to change with the introduction of a figure as extraordinary and as alien to sixth-century Gaul as Martin had been to that of the fourth—the Irish monk Columbanus.

Columbanus

Irish society and the form of Christianity which it developed were radically different from anything known on the Continent. Alone of all the regions of the West which converted readily to the new religion, Ireland had never formed part of the Roman Empire. It remained an isolated and archaic Celtic society. It was, in a very technical sense, uncivilized, that is, the city, that primary element of classical social and cultural organization, was completely unknown prior to the Viking raids that would begin in the eighth century. Moreover, it was radically decentralized, being organized into petty kingdoms or tribes which were in turn composed of kindreds called septs, the equivalent of the Germanic *Sippe*.

Just when Christianity first reached Ireland is much disputed, but linguistic evidence indicates that some Irish were Christian already in the late fourth or early fifth century. Nevertheless there existed no bishops or diocesan organization prior to the first half of the fifth century, when first Bishop Palladius and then shortly after Patrick arrived and began to organize a church modeled on the Gallic church they had known on the Continent. However, while Patrick's system won support in the north, elsewhere in Ireland, the older, pre-episcopal form of Christian life continued, and after his death much of his administrative organization disappeared even in those areas where he had been most successful. Lacking the tradition of Roman cities and provincial organization, Ireland was hardly an ideal area for the development of an episcopal church, and in the sixth century the Irish church became a federation of monastic communities, each corresponding roughly to a tribe and each under the jurisdiction of the "heir" of the founding saint of the region.

These monasteries owed much to the Eastern monastic tradition probably introduced into Ireland via Lérins but radically altered to conform with Irish culture. Their administration was firmly under the control of the abbot, a hereditary office within the ruling sept. When new monasteries were founded by members of existing monasteries, they remained under the authority of the abbot of the original foundation. Within the monastery was often found a bishop, but his function was liturgical and cultic, not administrative. Unlike monasteries on the Continent, which were communities of men or women determined to escape the world, these Irish monasteries were the centers of Christian life and the primary religious institutions around which lay religious practice focused and on which it was modeled. They were also centers of considerable Latin letters and learning, if of a fairly esoteric sort, in part since the Latin language in Ireland was entirely divorced from that of daily life. More importantly, they were also extremely rigorous centers of ascetic practice, some cenobitic, others consisting of cells of solitaries.

A primary characteristic of Irish monasticism was the predilection of its monks for traveling abroad. This was not pilgrimage in the more modern sense of a journey to a specific shrine and back, but rather an attempt to live out the image of the Christian life as a journey in an alien land between birth and death. Thus many Irish monks set out to separate themselves from all that was familiar and, either alone or with a few companions, traveled to Scotland, Iceland, and the Continent, not with a goal of conducting missionary work but simply of living as a monastic pilgrim among an alien people. Of these pilgrims who reached the Continent, the most important was Columbanus, who arrived in Gaul from Scotland around 590.

Columbanus and his companions made their way to the court of Gunthchramn of Burgundy, the king most admired by Gregory of Tours, who received them well and allowed them to establish themselves in a ruined fortress at Annegray in the Vosges mountains. Their peculiarly rigorous lifestyle attracted a large following, and Columbanus soon obtained from Gunthchramn another ruin, where he established the monastery of Luxeuil. Not long after, he added a third at Fontaines. For twenty years he remained in Burgundy, but in time the increasing popularity of his form of monastic life and observance created antagonism within the episcopacy. Some of these objections were based on the forms of ritual observance practiced in his communities, and in particular the fact that he celebrated Easter according to the Irish, rather than the Continental, calendar. More important was the relationship between his communities and the episcopacy. Gallic monasteries were supposed to be strictly subordinate to the local bishop. However, in the Irish tradition, Columbanus controlled his monasteries and wanted only to be left in peace by the Burgundian bishops. Instead of bowing to episcopal authority, he appealed to Pope Gregory the Great (pope 590–604) in Rome to be allowed to continue unhindered in his Celtic tradition, a step virtually unheard of in Gaul. Gregory, however, died before the appeal reached him.

Before the dispute could be resolved, Columbanus ran afoul of Queen Brunechildis and her son Theuderic, whose polygyny he had had the audacity to attack directly. Ultimately he was expelled from the kingdom and made his way to the Neustrian court of Childeric. Here he was extremely well received, as he was in the Austrasian kingdom of Theudebert. He traveled into Alemannia, where he found some remnants of Christian observance mixed with local polytheism and established a new community at Bregenz on Lake Constance. However local opposition drove him over the Alps into the Langobard kingdom, where King Agilulf received him and granted him a site for a new monastery at Bobbio between Milan and Genoa, where he established his final monastery. After Chlothar's victory over Brunechildis, the king invited him to return to Luxeuil, but by then he was too old and thus remained in Bobbio until his death in 615.

A Christian Frankish Aristocracy

The impact of Columbanus on the Frankish aristocracy can scarcely be overestimated. Here was a form of rigorous and fearless Christianity which was not an expression of Gallo-Roman culture and was not a creature of the episcopacy. Moreover, it was propagated by a saint who did not cut himself off from the secular world but who maintained close connections with powerful families across the north of Francia. These connections were particularly strong in Neustria among the court aristocracy and can be traced in the account of the life of Columbanus written by Jonas, a native of Susa and monk in Bobbio under the founder's immediate successor. In fact, Columbanus and his monastic tradition provided the common ground around which networks of northern aristocrats could unite, finding a religious basis for their social and political standing.

The list of aristocrats influenced by Columbanus reads like a Who's Who of the Frankish aristocracy. For example, Columbanus was well received near the valley of the Marne by Agneric, who had been close to Theudebert and after the death of the latter joined the group of Austrasians favorable to Chlothar II. His son, Burgundofaro, became the referendary of Dagobert and later a bishop; his daughter, Burgundofara, became an abbess. In the same region Columbanus was also received by Autharius and his three sons Audo, Audoenus (Dado), and Rado, the first of whom later founded his own monastery of Jouarre. The second, who founded a monastery at Rebais, became a referendary under Dagobert, and finally ended his life as bishop of Rouen. In Austrasia Columbanus was in contact with the supporters of Chlothar II, especially with Romaricus, who later went to Luxeuil and then founded Remiremont, which became a major aristocracy monastery in the next centuries. Bertulf, a kinsman of Arnulf of Metz, entered Luxeuil and later followed Columbanus to Bobbio, where he eventually became abbot. In Burgundy Columbanus's strongest contacts were with the family of the dux Waldelenus, whose kin were found as far south as Provence and east to Susa. Two of this kindred, Eustathius and Waldebert, in time became abbots of Luxeuil.

All of these Frankish families shared certain common traits. First, all had one or more members who were strongly attracted to this new monasticism and either visited or entered Luxeuil as monks. Second, they founded monasteries themselves on family property. These monasteries followed in general the rule which Columbanus had prepared for his Burgundian monasteries, although in the course of the seventh century this rule was merged with that of Benedict, which began to influence Frankish monasticism, resulting in what is called the Iro-Frankish monastic tradition. This mixed rule preserved much of the independence of Columbanus's rule while tempering the extremes of Irish asceticism. Third, these monasteries took on a new meaning in society. Not only were they centers of religious devotion, but they became spiritual centers for the small political units of family control. They were integrated into the political and social life of the families that had established them. The members of these families who founded these monasteries and served as their first abbots or abbesses came in time to be revered as saints, thus adding a family tradition of supernatural power and prestige to that of traditional lordship.

Gone was the rude, primitive image of the Gallic monastery of Martin's time. Instead, the monasteries founded by the Frankish aristocracy were more in keeping with their noble status. These were great monasteries with richly decorated churches in which aristocratic men and women could continue a noble lifestyle even while dedicating themselves to God. Something of this wealth can be seen in the testament of Burgundofara, daughter of Columbanus's supporter Agneric.[9] She was the abbess of a monastery founded on her father's estates near Meaux, known later as Faremoutiers, but she had not given up her wealth upon entering the convent. In her testament composed in 633 or 634 she made her foundation her principal heir. The donations included property she had inherited from her father or had acquired from a variety of persons, and consisted of rural *villae,* vineyards, mills on the Marne and the Aubetin, and houses and land within the city of Meaux and its suburbs. This was clearly no rustic hermitage but a wealthy institution integrated through personal and propery ties with the founder's family. Nor did such ties end with Burgundofara's death; the monastery continued under family control, forming a family necropolis and spiritual center.

The best example of such a family necropolis is the church of St. Paul at Jouarre, founded, as discussed earlier, by Audo, the son of Columbanus's supporter Autharius. Here are still found, among others, the tombs of Audo, Theodochilda, the first abbess of Jouarre, and her brother Agilbert, who spent the first part of his career as a missionary in England and was made bishop of Wessex before returning to the Continent as bishop of Paris. In addition the crypt contains the tombs of Agilberta, Theodochilda's cousin; Balda, a Bavarian who was the aunt of

Agilberta and Theodochilda; and Moda, Balda's cousin and wife of Autharius. Since in time all of these persons came to be venerated as saints, the family tomb was also a center of spiritual power and prestige for its members.

Probably related to the development of such family mortuary chapels is the transformation of Frankish burial practice which took place around this same time. Since the fourth century, Frankish burials had normally taken place in rural cemeteries such as Lavoye, where the dead were laid to rest fully clothed and supplied with weapons, utensils, and jewelry. Conversion had not affected this practice. Such burials were not statements of religious belief but of social and cultural continuity—solidarity with their ancestors who had been so interred.

However, beginning in the second half of the sixth century, such burial traditions began to be replaced by burials within or around churches. This had long been a Gallo-Roman custom, and as early as Clovis the Frankish royal family had opted for church burial. Now this began to be the rule rather than the exception, and families sought burial at or near saints' tombs. If the family had its own monastery and produced its own saints, as was the case for the descendants of Autharius, so much the better. In other cases, instead of beginning a new burial site, a mortuary chapel would be constructed on the site of the old row cemetery. At Mazerny in the Ardennes, for example, the burials from the sixth century are arranged in the traditional manner, in roughly parallel rows oriented north-south. However a roughly rectangular group of seventh-century burials in the cemetery seem at first glance to be disoriented—some fourteen are oriented east-west. The archaeologist Bailey Young has suggested that these were originally enclosed in a wooden chapel and formed a family group around tombs of a man and a woman. The rich grave articles in these two tombs suggest persons of high social rank and were probably the founders of the chapel, which served as their family necropolis until the entire cemetery was abandoned, possibly in the later eighth century.[10]

In still other cases, as at Flonheim in the Rhineland and Arlon in the Belgian province of Luxembourg, chapels apparently were built over the tombs of men and women who died in the early sixth or even late fifth centuries. In these cases, it appears that their descendants wished to provide their ancestors, some of whom were probably pagan, a means of sharing in the benefits of the new move toward the sanctification of the aristocratic family.

As with the family of Autharius, integrally connected with this development of family monasteries that were not tied to the local bishop but to the founding family was the parallel development of new concepts of sanctity, which transformed the image of the aristocracy. We examined in Chapter Four the model of sanctity elaborated by the Gallo-Roman episcopacy. The saints were either men of senatorial background who pursued the active life of a bishop, or else they were holy men and women who fled the world to become monks or recluses, cutting themselves off from the world but remaining carefully under the authority and direction of the bishop. Increasingly in the seventh century a new type of saint emerged—the aristocrat who served actively in the royal court before going on to found monasteries, serve as bishops, and undertake missionary activities, but always stayed in close relationship to the world. Far from being men and women who fled the evils of their day, they in general maintained good relationships with kings and other nobles. After their conversion to religious life they even continued to participate in secular politics. The hagiographers who composed their *vitae* were careful to present them in this light, recalling Matthew 22, 21, "Render unto Caesar that which is Caesar's and unto God that which is God's."[11] In the hagiography of the seventh century, the part of Caesar was not forgotten—seldom have saints been presented as having such a comfortable relationship with kings, a particularly remarkable situation when one thinks of the accusations made concerning the immorality at Dagobert's court. Audo's brother, Saint Audoenus of Rouen, for example, was a saint in royal service whom, we are told, Dagobert loved above all of his other courtiers. Saint Wandregisel was a noble Austrasian who served in the royal administration and even after receiving tonsure, traveled to court on horseback, the aristocratic mode of transportation par excellence. The most famous of these new saints was Arnulf of Metz, close counselor and agent of the king and also one of the leading figures in the Austrasian aristocracy.

Of course, many of the earlier senatorial bishops had also held important civil offices—we have seen that they had achieved their sees as a culmination of a late classical *cursus honorum*. However, in the hagiography of the fifth and sixth centuries, their earlier careers had been passed over quickly, almost apologetically. The decisive break between their lives in the world and their later religious careers was emphasized, and in some cases they were portrayed as having only symbolically carried out worldly office after their conversion. Sulpicius Severus had presented Martin of Tours as having given up warfare even before formally leaving the Roman army. The lives of saints of the seventh century, on the other hand, dwell in detail on the subjects' lives before their conversion; they describe their families, the excellent marriages they made, their duties at court, and the power and prestige that they enjoyed. In contrast to Sulpicius's depiction of Martin as a pacific soldier-monk, the author of the life of Arnulf of Metz even praises Arnulf's extraordinary skill with arms. Merovingian hagiography only stopped short of presenting saints who continued after their conversion to serve the Lord as warriors. The saint of the seventh century never abandoned his family or his social niveau. Rather, his sanctity was reflected back on them; the family and its social stratum was thereby sanctified.

This change in presentation does not indicate simply the transformation of a literary tradition. Hagiography was essentially a form of propaganda, and these accounts of noble saints were part of a program, developing both at court and, increasingly, in the power centers of the northern aristocracy, to celebrate, justify, and promote the formation of a self-conscious Christian Frankish elite charcterized by a distinctive cultural tradition that spread out from Neustria to all parts of the Frankish world.

To say that the new type of saint and the Iro-Frankish monasticism with which it was identified served the needs of the elite is not to imply that it was merely a political ploy on the part of the aristocracy. In fact, this new political sanctity probably was more effective in the Christianization of Francia than had been the older Gallo-Roman tradition. Christianity had long remained an urban phenomenon, and even in the most Romanized areas of the West, the degree of its penetration into the countryside had been minimal. The more active involvement of the northern Frankish aristocracy as well as that of wandering Irish monks such as Columbanus began to introduce Christian observance and cult into the countryside. Religious cult and political power were understood as inseparable, whether at the level of Dagobert or at the local level of Frankish aristocrats who sought to introduce uniformity in cult in their areas of power. Thus it was in the interest of the aristocracy to assist in the implantation of Christianity. For example, the family of Gundoin, who was duke in Alsace in the first half of the seventh century, was responsible for founding monasteries in Alsace as well as in northern Burgundy and for introducing there the cult of Saint Odilia. That Odilia was a member of the family was of course not incidental, but neither was the family's close involvement with Columbanus. Likewise the family of Rodulf, the duke in Thuringia, was involved in Christianization, disseminating the cult from its residences in Erfurt and Würzburg. For such aristocrats, cult and lordship were inseparable.

Some of the most important missionary activities were undertaken by royal bishops educated at the Neustrian court who worked closely with Dagobert. Amandus, an Aquitainian with royal support, was largely responsible for the establishment of monasteries across Flanders, especially at Elnone (later St.-Amand), Ghent, and Antwerp. From Noyon, Acharius and his successors Eligius and Mummolinus were heavily involved in missionary activities, as was Audomar of Thérouanne. All of these activities were supported by the king, particularly through enormous grants of land from the fisc.

This activity was an attempt to establish a Christian and Frankish presence in the north, especially in Frisia which, during the reigns of Childeric, Dagobert, and their immediate successors, was becoming increasingly important to the Frankish kingdom because of its vital role in trade and the exchange routes between Paris, London, Cologne, and the regions be-

tween the Scheldt and the Weser. The intimate connection
between Christian expansion and royal involvement in this trade
can be seen in the establishment of a church in Utrecht.[12] The
importance of the mouth of the Rhine for trade with Cologne
was beginning to increase around 600; gold coins minted around
that date by the Frisians imitating Merovingian coins have been
found in southeast England, on the western coast of Jütland
from the mouth of the Elbe to Limfjord, and up the Rhine
as far as Coblenz and even Lake Constance. By 630 Duurstede,
located slightly south of Utrecht, had become the center of
Frisian trade. At this time Dagobert established the church of
Utrecht under the control of Bishop Cunibert of Cologne, to
whom he donated the fort at Utrecht on the condition that he
would evangelize the Frisians. At the same time he also transferred two coiners, Madelinus and Rimoaldus, from the mint at
Maastricht to Duurstede in order to take charge of and to benefit from the commercial exchanges increasingly taking place in
the region. The evangelization of the region and the control of
its economic activities were closely related.

The effects of the Iro-Frankish religious movement were not
limited to the king, the Neustrian court, and the northern aristocracy. Southerners, such as Desiderius of Cahors, raised at
court were also deeply affected by it and, as the amalgamation
of the various aristocratic traditions in Francia became more
pronounced, the movement spread south and east as well as
north. Although individual Gallo-Roman bishops had often
taken seriously their responsibility to Christianize the rural populations of their dioceses, the first half of the seventh century
saw, in the areas north and south of the Loire as well as east of
the Rhine, the first serious, concerted, and systematic attempt to
spread Chrisianity not only within the elite but throughout
society. For the first time in Western history, the tide of religious
culture had reversed. After centuries of the Mediterranean forms
of Christianity gradually penetrating north, a new and vigorous
form of Christianity, closely tied to royal and aristocratic interests and power bases, was spreading out from the north and
gradually transforming the Romanized south.

CHAPTER VI

Merovingian Obsolescence

Dagobert's Successors

> From Chalon where he continued his work for justice, he next traveled to Auxerre by way of Autun, and then went on through Sens to Paris; and here, leaving Queen Gomatrudis at the villa of Reuille on the advice of the Franks because she was sterile, he married Nantechildis, a most beautiful girl, and made her his queen.[1]

This description of Dagobert's second marriage, taken from the *Gesta Dagoberti* written long after the event, reflects the hindsight with which later generations viewed Dagobert's decision to abandon Gomatrudis. Pseudo-Fredegar, the source for the *Gesta*, mentions no reason for the divorce, saying only that it had been at Reuille that he had married Gomatrudis, and says nothing about Nantechildis's beauty, only that she had been a mere serving girl before her marriage.[2] As we have seen, Merovingians did not usually consider it necessary to put away one wife before taking another. However in this case Dagobert may have had several reasons: Gomatrudis was the sister of his stepmother Sichildis, whom he had married at his father's command. Thus she may have been the aunt of his stepbrother Charibert and sister of Brodulf, whom he had just had executed for plotting against him on behalf of Charibert. Divorcing his wife was the logical step to rid himself of the final influence of this family whose alliance with the royal family had been orchestrated by his father.

However, the later tradition ascribing the divorce due to her sterility is understandable. By 629 Dagobert must have been desperate for heirs, and if he was not, surely "the Franks," that is to say, the aristocracy, was. Since the beginning of the dynasty, failure to leave an adult heir had normally meant trouble—a long interregnum characterized by vicious fighting for control over the future king or kings, an opportunity for aristocratic factions to increase their power, and overthrow of the *stabilitas* that Dagobert so desired. He had been able to capitalize on the consolidations made by his father because he had been associated in the reign six years prior to his father's death. Joint rulership proved the surest means of providing royal continuity. Thus by 629 he was under pressure to provide an heir or heirs, from himself as well as from the aristocracy. While the nobles would not tolerate an autocrat, a weak king was to no one's advantage. Periods of weak contral power normally meant confusion, the outbreak of old feuds, and violent competition among the magnates. A strong kingdom needed a strong king, and for this he needed a son. This remarriage was not his only attempt to produce an heir. In the following year an Austrasian woman, Ragnetrudis, bore him a son, Sigibert III. In about 633 Nantechildis provided him with a second, Clovis II.

Still, it was not enough. Dagobert died in 637, leaving his sons too young to provide the kind of continuity necessary to sustain the tradition of their father and grandfather. This proved the pattern for most of the next century. Sigibert III died young, leaving a young son, Dagobert II, who was tonsured and sent into monastic exile in Ireland, to return twenty years later; Clovis II, after a two-year interregnum and long minority, reigned until 657, when he died, leaving still more minor sons— Childeric II in Austrasia, Chlothar III in Neustria, and Theuderic III, who succeeded his brother Chlothar in 673. Thus for almost forty years, the Merovingian family would be unable to provide any continuity to the central administration of the kingdom.

These Merovingians, however, were not all the *rois fainéants,* or "do-nothing kings," of popular legend. Childeric II of Austrasia, for example, attempted to recover royal authority and direct his administration; he was murdered for his efforts. His brother Theuderic was likewise not content to merely reign but, after the death of the *maior domus* Ebroin, reunited the kingdom and actually managed for a brief time to rule, although he was defeated in the battle of Tertry (687) by Pippin II and kept under firm control until his death in 690/91. Upon his death, the cycle repeated itself; he left as heir a small son, Clovis III. Thus from 691 the Merovingian kings were once more thoroughly under the control of the various aristocratic groups who were now the central actors in the struggle for political hegemony. The members of the royal family were useful symbols around which to organize support, but they played no independent role. Even the exact kinship connections among the later Merovingians is unclear. Contemporaries did not consider them of sufficient interest to bother to note the exact relationship between the last Merovingian king, Childeric III (reigned 743–751), and the more illustrious descendants of Clovis.

Thus the long series of minorities, more than any other single factor, contributed to the decline of royal power. This circumstance, rather than the myth of hereditary degeneracy, which we shall examine in the next chapter, led to the dynasty's fall. However it is insufficient to explain completely what happened. Other royal families have survived long minorities and recovered their control of government. The loss of Merovingian power was part of a much more complex transformation of the Frankish world in the seventh and early eighth centuries. While these transformations grew out of the political, social, economic, and religious traditions already forming in the reign of Chlothar II and Dagobert, they were not such as to inevitably lead to the obsolescence of Merovingian kingship, but combined with the series of minorities, they proved fatal.

Within Neustria-Burgundy and Austrasia, aristocratic groups fought each other for control over the fisc, the monastic network, and the office of *maior domus*. In the peripheral regions of Frisia, Thuringia, Alemannia, Bavaria, Provence, and Aquitaine, local dukes established themselves as princes of autonomous principalities.

In this struggle, the balance between reform monasticism and royal service was lost, and the Frankish episcopacy adopted more than ever the characteristics of secular lordship as bishops looked not only to governing their *civitates* and acting as advisors to kings, but became directly involved in the struggle for control over the sections of Francia. The educational traditions inherited by the church from the Gallo-Roman aristocracy suffered irreparable damage during this same time. The decline of letters so evident in Francia by the mid-eighth century was probably less than a century old.

The loss of Frisia and thus the northern port of Duurstede and the temporary disruptions in Provence, hobbling its Mediterranean ports of Fos and Marseille, interfered with both ends of the long-distance commercial relations of the kingdom. The internal disturbances also ended the regular plunder of neighboring kingdoms, cutting the supply of booty and tribute which had been the primary source of specie with which to carry on this commerce. In place of gold coinage designed for display and international trade, new, local silver coinages appeared, which, while testifying to vigorous local exchange networks, probably indicate a decrease in long-distance commerce.

And yet this period also saw important missionary activities, the consolidation of the Iro-Frankish monastic movement, the progressive expansion of the Benedictine rule across much of Francia, and the emergence of those geographical units which, in the long run, proved more stable than the Frankish empire itself. We must consider each of these changes.

Neustria-Burgundy

Although the Austrasian aristocracy had hoped that Dagobert might pass a unified kingdom on to his elder son Sigibert III, four years before his death Dagobert specified that Sigibert was to inherit only Austrasia, while his younger son Clovis II should receive Neustria and Burgundy. In addition, Sigibert received one-third of Dagobert's treasure, the cities of Poitiers, Clermont, Rodez, and Cahors in Aquitaine, Marseille in Provence, and other cities south of the Loire. The remaining two-thirds of the royal treasure were divided equally between Dagobert's widow Nantechildis, and Clovis, who was probably around four years old at the time of his father's death.

Dagobert had named Aega, a leading member of the Neustrian

aristocracy and a faithful supporter of the royal house, as *maior domus* and regent (639–641). He and Nantechildis directed the royal household as well as the kingdom. When Aega died in 642 he was succeeded by Erchinoald (regent 641–658), another Neustrian magnate related to Dagobert's mother Haldetrud. His lands were centered on the lower Seine in the area of Jumièges and St.-Wandrille as well as in the region of Noyon-St.-Quentin and on the Marne and Somme rivers.

Erchinoald seems to have belonged to a large and powerful clan in Neustria that attempted to dominate Neustria for much of the seventh century. The process by which he and his kin worked to solidify and expand their political and social position illustrates the transformation of the Neustrian aristocracy in the generations following the death of Dagobert. Although after Erchinoald's death, the Neustrian magnates elected Ebroin as *maior,* the first to be selected by the aristocracy rather than appointed by the king or his regent, Erchinoald's son was chosen *maior domus* in 658. Circumstantial evidence suggests that the later *maiores,* Waratto (680–686), his son Ghislemarus (680), and son-in-law Bercharius (686–688) may also have been related to him. After Pippin II defeated Bercharius at Tertry in 687 and presumably had him executed a year later, he arranged a marriage between his own son Drogo and Anstrudis, the widow of Bercharius and daughter of Waratto. The kin network and the property amassed by this family through the seventh century were considered important enough to incorporate into the family of the Pippinids.

Erchinoald was intimately connected with the Iro-Frankish monastic movement. He initially welcomed Irish pilgrims such as the wandering abbot Furseus, who arrived in Neustria around 641 after having founded communities in Ireland and in East Anglia. Erchinoald assisted Furseus in founding monasteries at Lagny and on his own estates at Péronne. He also ceded the estates of Wandregisel, where Furseus founded the monastery of Fontenelle.

This involvement in the monastic movement was part of the process by which Erchinoald built his family fortunes, which were increasingly independent of the royal household. Furseus in particular was the religious figure around whom Erchinoald constructed his family cult. The Irish abbot had been asked by Erchinoald to stand as his son's godfather, and to this end had invited him to Péronne. Spiritual kinship thus bound Furseus and Erchinoald's descendants. Although the estates at Péronne offered to Furseus for a monastery had been acquired from the royal fisc, according to the nearly contemporary *Virtues of Saint Furseus,* after the saint had selected the site, Erchinoald attributed them not to royal largesse but to divine favor: "I give thanks to God who gave me this property where you have decided to establish your dwelling."[3] The foundation of Péronne and the presence of the saint were clearly to reflect on Erchinoald, and he considered both his property. After Furseus died at Mézerolles, a small monastery in the Somme which he had founded on the estates of the duke Haimo, the *maior domus* arrived and demanded, "Give me my monk." According to the *Virtues,* the issue was decided by a sort of trial by ordeal. Two wild bulls were hitched to a cart bearing the body of the saint and allowed to go wherever God determined. The bulls went straight to Péronne and there Furseus was buried.

The care with which Erchinoald nurtured his relationship with Furseus, both during and after the saint's lifetime, did not mean that he was an unconditional supporter of the Irish monastic tradition. After Furseus died Erchinoald expelled the Irish monks from Péronne, presumably replacing them with Franks. Ominously for the future of Erchinoald's family fortunes, the monks found refuge with Iduberga, wife of Pippin of Herstal, and thus a member of the highest circles of the Austrasian aristocracy.

Nantechildis and Erchinoald exercised little power in Burgundy, where since the time of Chlothar II there had been no royal *maior domus* to control the region. In 642, Nantechildis traveled to Orléans in the kingdom of Burgundy and there reestablished the office. She wished to increase her direct authority in the region and managed to convince a portion of the aristocracy to select as *maior domus* Flaochad, a man with close ties to Neustria and especially to Nantechildis, whose niece he married. Erchinoald apparently saw this as an occasion to find outside support for his own position, since he entered into an agreement with Flaochad in which each promised the other support in his office. Although Flaochad had promised loyalty to the magnates and bishops of the kingdom, he soon faced major opposition from the aristocracy, led by the Burgundian patrician Willibad. He had been one of the three loyal supporters of Dagobert responsible for killing Brodulf almost fifteen years before. Flaochad and Willibad apparently had previously been allies, but Flaochad's new position had turned them into personal enemies.

The reasons for Willibad's opposition provide considerable insight into the Burgundian kingdom in the mid-seventh century. It has been seen as a Burgundian-Roman hostility to the "Frank" Flaochad, as an attempt to maintain local autonomy, or even as simply a private feud between the *patricius* and the *maior*. The reasons were probably rather complex. Since the time of the last *maior domus*, Willibad had been one of the Burgundians to profit most from the benign neglect the region had been subjected to. From his control of the regions of Lyon, Vienne, and Valence, he had become extremely wealthy and powerful. Others, particularly in the area around Chalon, the old center of the Burgundian kingdom, had also profited, and the establishment of a *maior domus* with close ties to Frankish Neustria clearly meant that this independence was threatened.

However, Willibad was hardly the leader of a united Burgundy. Other Burgundian aristocrats, including Duke Chramnelenus of Besançon and Duke Wandalbertus of Chambly, both of the clan of Waldelenus, the supporter of Columbanus, and Duke Amalgar of Dijon, supported Flaochad. The reason is probably not so much that they were ethnic Romans or Franks opposing ethnic Burgundians in a last struggle for autonomy as that they represented the other major clans in Burgundy which had long been in competition with Willibad and may have been feuding with his family in the past. The arrival of a Neustrian-backed *maior* gave them a strong outside ally to use in their fight against Willibad, a fight which culminated in a bloody battle at Autun involving only the principals and their closest allies. Pseudo-Fredegar records that the remainder of the Neustrians and Burgundians simply stood by, evidence that, to most present, the fight was not one of ethnic or national resistance or of public revolt but rather a private feud.[4] Thus the conflict was both internal, pitting the major families in Burgundy against each other, and external, involving the Burgundian patricians, as opposed to Neustrian authority.

The long-term results of the effort to reintroduce the office of *maior* and affirm Neustrian control in the region were minimal. Willibad was killed along with his close supporters, but Flaochad was unable to follow up his victory; he died of a fever eleven days after the battle. Nantechildis, who had begun the whole project, had died a few months before the final confrontation. The Burgundian office of *maior domus* apparently continued in the person of one Radobertus until around 662, when the palaces of the two kingdoms were definitively united under the Neustrian *maior* Ebroin. The real winners of the contest were probably the clan of Waldelenus. In the next decades they would spread their authority south of Besançon into lower Burgundy and Provence.

In addition to the status Erchinoald had by his kinship with Clovis II's grandmother, his office of *maior domus,* the wealth he had inherited or acquired from the fisc, and the spiritual prestige he enjoyed as the "owner" of a fine collection of Irish monks, Erchinoald enjoyed yet another source of power: he had provided his young king Clovis with a wife from among his slaves. Baldechildis had arrived in Francia as an Anglo-Saxon slave purchased by Erchinoald who, according to the author of her *vita,* was so taken by her beauty, intelligence, and strong character that he intended to make her his wife (or at least a concubine). Instead she became the wife of his king.

Marrying women of low birth was, as we have seen, a common practice for Merovingian kings ever since Charibert I (reigned 561–567), who had married two sisters in his wife's service, Merofled and Marcoveifa. Later Chilperic I (reigned 560/61–584) married one of his wife's servants, Fredegund. Two of Theudebert II's wives, Bilichildis and Theudechild, had been slaves, as was Dagobert's wife Nantechildis. Such marriages made considerable political sense. A marriage with the daughter of an aristocrat necessarily meant contracting an alliance with the wife's family and raising her male kin to favored positions. This could in turn alienate other aristocratic groups and create powerful opposition centering around the queen's kin should her sons not be favored in any future divisions of the kingdom. The complications caused Dagobert by the kin of his wife Gomatrudis shows how serious this threat could be. Slaves and lowborn women, on the other hand, did not represent powerful aristocratic parties, and if they failed to produce sons or fell out of favor they could be put aside. If, on the other hand, they did produce male heirs and show themselves capable and intelligent, as did Nantechildis and Baldechildis, they could rise to considerable prominence.

Lacking powerful male kin, such queens tended to turn to ecclesiastics for support, and in turn proved among the most important founders of monasteries and supporters of missionary activity. This was true of Baldechildis, who established particularly important relationships with bishops Chrodobert of Paris and Audoenus of Rouen and with abbots Waldabert of Luxeuil, Theudefrid of Corbie (a monastery she founded), and Filibert of Jumièges. After the death of her husband Clovis in 657, she assumed the regency for his minor son Chlothar III (lived 657–683) with the support of her ecclesiastical advisors. Her enormous generosity toward religious foundations helped transform the region of Paris from a largely fiscal region to an ecclesiastical one, a policy which for a time won her and her sons important support but which eventually provided the Arnulfings with the means to insert themselves into a powerful position in Neustria. But this effect was no doubt far from her mind at the time.

Her active involvement in monastic foundation and reform included founding Corbie and Chelles, introducing the mixed rule into St.-Denis, guaranteeing this institution ecclesiastical immunity by the bishop and secular immunity by the king, as well as the support and enrichment of numerous other basilicas and monasteries. Her purposes were not simply to gain the political support of these institutions. The program of religious reform was a continuation of that concern for the "stability of the kingdom" already expressed by Dagobert, and was particularly a way to enhance royal prestige. The basilicas she and other Merovingian kings and queens supported were to a great extent royal necropolises, equivalent to the smaller monasteries such as Jouarre founded by aristocratic families. The reform and regulation of these institutions' liturgical commemoration of the dead was closely tied to the development of the royal cult; Baldechildis united previous Merovingians with her own sons. As the author of Baldechildis's *vita* expressed it, in a phrase almost certainly borrowed from one of the royal privileges for such institutions, these grants were made so that "it might be more pleasing to them [the monks] to petition the clemency of Christ the highest king on behalf of the king and for peace."[5]

At this time, the use of the saints traditionally associated with the royal family took a new turn. Baldechildis, her husband before his death, and her sons, in an effort to surround themselves with the power of these special dead, began to draw together a collection of relics in the royal palace. Not content to venerate the saints in their traditional locations, which constituted the sacred geography of Francia, they began to assemble them around the king. Thus Clovis II had already removed the arm of Saint Denis from its basicila; shortly after the *cappa* of Saint Martin, which had been venerated for centuries in Tours, was added to the royal collection, which in time came to be the center of the chapel, the very name of which comes from *cappa*.

In 658 Erchinoald died and Baldechildis, presumably not wishing to strengthen her former owner's family, along with the "Franks," selected as his successor Ebroin, an aristocrat from the area of Soissons who had already been part of the royal household. Ebroin and Baldechildis resumed the policy of merging the Neustrian and Burgundian palaces and attempting to reassert their authority in the name of Chlothar throughout the two regions. The result, of course, was violent opposition in Neustria and Burgundy.

The first attempt against Ebroin was an abortive assassination plot led by Ragnebert, son of Duke Radebert, a Neustrian probably related to the Burgundian *maior domus*, Radobertus, who was replaced by Ebroin. Ragnebert and his accomplices were caught, and he was sent into monastic exile in Burgundy, where Ebroin had him killed.

This attempt was representative of the opposition Ebroin and Baldechildis met. Ragnebert was commemorated in the diocese of Lyon as a martyr, just as was Willibad, who had also died at the hands of Neustrians. However the real issue during the second half of the seventh century was not really Burgundian autonomy from Neustrian hegemony, but the individual power of Neustrian and Burgundian magnates. Private interests were taking precedence over regional ones, and even ecclesiastical magnates were increasingly transforming their territories into independent lordships, establishing mints, and conducting affairs autonomously. Baldechildis and Ebroin attempted to curb this by appointing loyal bishops who had been raised and educated at the palace and were proponents of Iro-Frankish monasticism. This meant breaking the tradition formalized by Chlothar II of naming only local men to office. They faced tremendous opposition to this new policy from such families as that of Bishop Aunemund of Lyon and his brother Dalfinus, the count of the city, who had together transformed Lyon and the surrounding area into an autonomous principality. Aunemund's leadership of the opposition in Burgundy led to his execution. The *Life* of the Anglo-Saxon Wilfrid accused Baldechildis of having ordered the deaths of nine bishops—this was her only means of ending autonomous episcopal-aristocratic enclaves. In Lyon she replaced Aunemund with her faithful supporter and almoner Genesius. She also appointed a monk from St.-Wandrille, Erembert, bishop of Toulouse, and another supporter, Leodegar, whose brother Warinus was count of Paris, bishop of Autun.

As long as Baldechildis was regent, these ecclesiastics remained firm supporters of the program she and Ebroin were directing. However when in 664 or 665 she was forced into retirement at her monastery at Chelles, they joined the opposition, with Leodegar at its head. In 673 Chlothar III suddenly died, and Ebroin raised Chlothar's younger brother Theuderic III to the throne. The reaction of the Neustrian and Burgundian aristocracy was to shift their support to Theuderic's brother, Childeric

II, who had been made king in Austrasia. Abandoned, Ebroin had no choice but to accept monastic exile to Luxeuil while his puppet Theuderic was exiled to St.-Denis.

The reunification of Neustria and Burgundy did not last. Soon Leodegar fell into disfavor with Childeric II and was also sent to Luxeuil. In 675 Childeric was murdered by assassins probably connected to both Ebroin and Leodegar, and the result was civil war. Ebroin and Leodegar returned from exile, the latter rallying around Theuderic III, who was removed from St.-Denis. Leodegar's forces elected Erchinoald's son, Leudesius, as *maior,* while Ebroin joined with Austrasians who rallied around an alleged son of Childeric, Clovis III. Ebroin was victorious, killed both Leodegar and Leudesius, and managed to reunite Neustria-Burgundy for another five years. However, when Ebroin attempted to extend his power over Austrasia as well, he met opposition in the form of a descendant of Arnulf of Metz and Pippin of Herstal, Pippin II. In 680 Ebroin was murdered by a Neustrian magnate who then fled to Pippin for refuge.

Austrasia

The long series of minorities and resulting internecine rivalries in the Neustrian-Burgundian kingdom tore apart the synthesis achieved by Dagobert, although how this happened can only be inferred, as many of the details are extremely sketchy. Our knowledge of Austrasia during this period is even more tantalizingly obscure. For the first time since Clovis, someone who may not have been of royal blood apparently ruled a Frankish subkingdom.

Sigibert III, whom Dagobert had appointed to rule Austrasia, died in 656, leaving a son, Dagobert II. What happened next is the subject of enormous and probably endless debate. The only near contemporary narrative source to speak of it, the *Liber Historiae Francorum,* says:

> When King Sigibert died Grimoald had his small son Dagobert tonsured and sent him and Bishop Dido of Poitiers on pilgrimage to Ireland and established his own son in the kingdom. The Franks, who were extremely angry because of this prepared a trap for him

and having caught him they took him before Clovis, king of the Franks. He was imprisoned in Paris where he was bound and tortured and, deserving death because he had harassed his lord, he was tortured to death.[6]

The Grimoald in question was the *maior domus* Grimoald I, son of Pippin I the Elder, and his son referred to was Childebert, who apparently did reign for a time in Austrasia. It thus appears that the family which in the next century would replace the Merovingians had made a preliminary, abortive attempt to do so in the 650s, and were thwarted by the Neustrian aristocracy. But it is entirely unclear if this is what happened, although certainly the significance of royal succession was being tested against aristocratic power.

Like so much Merovingian history, the actual series of events and their chronology defy exact determination, although there is no lack of scholarly argument defending one or another theory. If one takes the above account at face value, it seems that the attempted usurpation was abortive. Since Sigibert III died in 656 and his brother Clovis II in 657, it might appear that the usurpation lasted at most a year before Grimoald was betrayed to the Neustrians and executed. However evidence from a charter that Grimoald was alive in 661 introduced a change in this theory. Dagobert II was presumed to have reigned until 661, when Grimoald exiled him to Ireland and placed his son Childebert on the throne. To support this theory, it was suggested that a scribe copying the above passage wrote "Chlodoveo" (Clovis) by error instead of "Chlothario" and that thus Grimoald's execution actually took place under Chlothar III around 661 or 662. But yet another charter dated "in the sixth year of King Childebert" suggested that the usurpation must have taken place even earlier, and that Grimoald's son was accepted in Austrasia and Neustria as a legitimate king from the death of Sigibert until Childebert's own death in 661; only after this was his father betrayed and executed. Others have speculated that actually there was no usurpation as such, but that Grimoald was the descendant of a Merovingian daughter and therefore had some right to give his son a Merovingian name and have him succeed Sigibert. It may even be that Dagobert II had been exiled not by the ambitious Grimoald but by the Neustrians. The whole idea of a usurpation would then be a later reinterpretation of events from the Neustrian perspective. We will never know for sure.

Whatever the actual events were in Austrasia, the whole confusing episode indicates highly significant attitude shifts concerning the relationship of the region to the Merovingian kingship. Presumably, when Grimoald's son was adopted as king, Sigibert III's son Dagobert II had not yet been born. Thus the kingdom may have faced the likelihood that upon the king's death, his brother Clovis II would succeed him, thus reuniting the entire kingdom under Neustrian control. Apparently this was unacceptable in Austrasia, a region which, as we have seen, had a longer tradition of unity and autonomy than either Neustria or Burgundy. Under both Chlothar II and Dagobert, Austrasia's identity had been protected by the elevation of its own king with his own palace and central court. Whatever the circumstances were surrounding Childebert's ascension, the hostility of the Austrasians to Neustrian control was clearly the foremost consideration.

This hostility was not based on any sort of "ethnic" opposition between East and West, Germanic or Roman. In the seventh century, Austrasia included not only the eastern regions around Metz and Trier, but such old Roman cities as Reims, Chalons, and Laon. No linguistic boundary separated the regions, and families had ties in both areas. The magnates thought of themselves as Franks. The primary considerations were spheres of influence and local political traditions.

Whatever Grimoald's ancestry or the nature of his son's rise to the throne, his destruction was a severe blow to his family's aspirations, although the fact that this blow did not permanently end the clan's future indicates how well-established it was. But in the short run, the aspirations of the family and their authority in Austrasia underwent an eclipse. After Childebert's death, Baldechildis and Ebroin managed to place her minor son, the Neustrian king Chlothar III, on the Austrasian throne. In this arrangement the opponents of Grimoald, led by Chimnechild, the widow of Sigibert, and the Austrasian duke Wulfoald, seem to have taken a leading part, and in the next year they arranged a compromise whereby the young brother of Chlothar, Childeric II, would marry his cousin, who was the daughter of Sigibert III and Chimnechild and brother of the exiled Dagobert II. Chimnechild undertook the regency of the young Childeric, thus maintaining Austrasian control of the palace.

In a society in which kinship was traced exclusively or even primarily through the male line, Grimoald's defeat would have meant the end of his family. However, because of the fluid nature of aristocratic *Sippe* in the early Middle Ages, even such a severe reversal could not eradicate Pippin's clan. Grimoald's own line apparently ended with the death of Childebert, but the alliance of his father's family with that of Arnulf of Metz, contracted through the marriage of Grimoald's sister Begga to Ansegisel, a son of Arnulf, assured the continuation of the kindred. Of this family, one hears nothing for the next twenty years. However in time the Pippinid tradition would return in the person of Pippin II and even Grimoald would be remembered in the person of Grimoald II, *maior domus* in the early eighth century.

One of the reasons for the survival of this kindred was the religious significance acquired by some of the family, particularly Arnulf of Metz and Gertrudis of Nivelles. The body of Arnulf, who was initially buried in Remiremont, was translated by his successor to the Church of the Apostles in Metz, where his cult was fostered and developed by his descendants. The extraordinary role played by Arnulf in the developing self-perception of this family is indicated by the fact that, in contrast with the usual hagiographical tradition which calls for the parents of the saint to be named, Arnulf's seventh-century *vita* does not identify his parents, nor have any subsequent attempts to discover their identities proven successful. Arnulf is, like some mythical hero, the founder of the family, but has himself no identifiable ancestry.

Gertrudis was the sister of Grimoald and abbess of the Pippinid family monastery of Nivelles. Although early attempts to see Gertrudis as a "Germanic Isis" are certainly distortions, the growth of the cult of this woman, who rejected a political marriage at the court of Dagobert II for a life in the family monastery, became an important element in the sanctification of the descendants of her sister Begga, who married Ansegisel.

These two cults provided a sacred legitimization of the family, in direct opposition to the growing royal cult begun by Dagobert I and continued and developed by Baldechildis. By the end of the century, Arnulf and Gertrudis had developed a following that extended far beyond the Arnulfing kindred and their dependents. Both cults spread across a Francia soon to be governed by their descendants.

Reunification under the Arnulfings

As we have seen, the death of the Neustrian Chlothar III in 673 and the reaction of the Neustrian-Burgundian aristocracy against Ebroin led to the invitation to Childeric II to assume the kingship in Neustria. However, in order to protect themselves from the introduction of Austrasian control, he was required to guarantee what amounted to the provisions of Chlothar II's Edict of Paris forbidding the appointment of *rectores* from outside the various regions of the reunited kingdom. When the king attempted to renege on this agreement and appoint the Austrasian duke Wulfoald *maior* of the entire kingdom, he was assassinated along with his pregnant wife.

The resulting civil war paved the way for a return of the family of Grimoald in the person of Pippin II, who, as duke in Austrasia apparently made an alliance with Ebroin against Wulfoald and Dagobert II, who had returned from Ireland in 676 and had begun a serious attempt to regain control of Austrasia. In 679 Dagobert II was assassinated, presumably for the same reason as Childeric—the great magnates of both kingdoms had no use for a Merovingian who wanted to rule as well as reign. The assassination of Ebroin himself in 680 showed that Austrasia, under the leadership of Pippin (Wulfoald died the same year), would not be dominated by Neustria.

For six years the new Neustrian *maior*, Waratto, kept peace with the Austrasians, but only with difficulty. After his death in 686, Pippin moved against Waratto's successor and son-in-law Bercharius, and at the battle of Tertry-sur-Somme defeated the

Neustrians. Pippin acquired access to Theuderic III, who had kept himself alive by being accommodating to Ebroin, Waratto, and Bercharius. Pippin now had a chance to make himself not the duke or *maior* but, in the words of later annalists, the *princeps* or ruler of all Francia.

After Tertry

He had acquired the chance, but not yet the reality. After 686 Pippin began the most serious and difficult aspect of consolidating power in Neustria. Military conquest alone was not sufficient, nor the heavy-handed suppression of the aristocracy that Ebroin had attempted. Another aristocratic rebellion would have taken place, another assassin would have appeared, and Pippin would have gone the way of so many others. Instead, in 688 he returned to Austrasia, leaving his agent Nordebertus and presumably, his son Drogo, to consolidate his family among the power structures in Neustria—the kin networks that had been the source of Waratto's power, the royal court, and the patronage of the church.

The first was the most easily and readily accomplished. Bercharius died soon after Tertry, at the hands, it was said, of his mother-in-law, although Pippin could not have been too saddened by his death, and Bercharius's widow Anstrudis married Drogo, Pippin's elder son. As discussed earlier, the kindred of Waratto may well have had connections to the family of Erchinoald, and through him to the mother of Dagobert I. By arranging the marriage of Drogo and Anstrudis, Pippin thus absorbed the Neustrian party of Erchinoald. Rather than alienating the powerful Neustrian *Sippe,* it became part of the foundation of Arnulfing power.

This kinship with the old Neustrian *maior* family gave Pippin access to the second pillar of Neustrian power, the Merovingian court. We have seen that since Dagobert I, rendering justice had been a major function of the Merovingian kings. With the exercise of political leadership through the appointment of counts and bishops long denied them, the Merovingian court of justice had become their single most important contribution to the

Frankish realm. To the king's court came magnates from throughout Francia. With the king, or his *maior* or count of the palace acting as chair, cases of major importance involving the laity and ecclesiastical powers of the realm were debated and decided. While the king was hardly in a position to mete out the kind of fearsome justice for which Dagobert had been famous, and in fact these later Merovingians may often not even have been present, these assemblies provided aristocrats a structure in which to participate in nonviolent but nonetheless vital competition.

Acquiring this power base proved more slow, as the process was more delicate. A consensus among the magnates had to be formed; enemies had to be defeated in the court of public opinion and according to the rules of Frankish customary law. This was not always easy, as two cases will serve to illustrate. The first case involves Pippin's confiscating the property of a former supporter of Ebroin, Amalbert. Amalbert had been accused of having unjustly taken the property of an orphan. The accused failed to appear. When Amalbert's son Amalricus attempted to speak in his father's defense, it was determined that he had no authority from his father to do so. The case was decided in favor of the orphan, the property returned, and Amalbert was forced to pay a fine. One should not be misled by the formal description of the proceedings to think that the case was simply decided by the magnates present simply on its technical merits—the language hides the real maneuvering of the Pippinids for their cause. This begins to be evident when one realizes that the guardian of the orphan was none other than Pippin's agent Nordebertus, and this judgment was the final act of a long series of court appearances in which the Pippinids had pursued their old enemy. The victory, as Paul Fouracre has pointed out, was a triumph of Pippin's ability to mobilize collective magnate power against an individual. Participating in this court were some twelve bishops and forty secular magnates.[7]

The royal court was not always a tool of Arnulfing policy. It was still possible for the other magnates at the royal court to deal them an occasional setback. Such a defeat can be seen in a second court decision. In 697 Drogo appeared before the court of King Childebert III (694/95–711) at Compiègne, the royal villa which had largely replaced Paris as the Merovingian's favorite residence, to face an accusation by the abbot of the monastery of Tussonval concerning an estate at Noisy. The abbot produced a diploma of King Theuderic III confirming the monastery's right to the estate and claimed that Drogo had unjustly seized it. Drogo replied that the estate had come to him through his wife by means of a contract of exchange. It thus appears that he was attempting to acquire the former estates of Waratto's family. The abbot admitted that an exchange had been planned, but asserted that it had not taken place. When Drogo could not produce documentary evidence of the exchange, the case was decided in favor of the abbot.

Once more, procedure and legal merits provided the formal structure within which conflicts over broader issues were fought out. Among the "bishops and magnates" assembled to hear the case were Pippin himself, Grimoald, Pippin's son and successor (designated as *maior*), and Bishop Constantine of Beauvais, a loyal supporter of Pippin. But also present were Bishop Savaric of Auxerre, and Agneric, *patricius* of Provence or lower Burgundy, both of whom were apparently extending their own lordships in the later seventh century at the expense of the kingdom. The court proceeding was thus probably a confrontation between Pippinid and anti-Pippinid magnates, and in this instance the latter won.

The third foundation of Pippin's power in Neustria was the church. We have seen how the Neustrian kings, queens, and aristocrats had taken a leading role in the establishment of religious foundations as a principal basis for their power, in the process transforming many of the old fiscal lands into church lands. Pippin and his successors systematically insinuated themselves as protectors of these institutions, thereby coming to control enormous power in the region. Again, the merger of his family into that of Waratto was a key to this policy. In the last years of the seventh century and the beginning of the eighth Pippin solidified his control over the church in the region of Rouen, where the bulk of the estates of Erchinoald and Waratto had been. The key institutions in this process were the monasteries of St.-Wandrille and Jumièges and the Rouen episcopacy. He had early acquired patronage of the small religious foundation of Fleury-en-Vexin, which he enlarged and reformed with the assistance of monks from St.-Wandrille. Most importantly, he took the monastery under his own protection and that of his family, a form of immunity that did not involve the king and thus established the institution under his direct control. Gradually, he and his successors undertook the protection and patronage of St.-Wandrille and Jumièges. Because of the authority exercised by the bishop of Rouen over these institutions, it was necessary to exile Bishop Ansbert, a supporter of the older Neustrian party. This made it possible to place Godinus, probably the bishop of Lyon and a supporter of Pippin, as abbot of Jumièges. Pippin similarly established Bishop Bainus of Thérouanne, previously associated with Fleury-en-Vexin, in a similar position at St.-Wandrille.

Control of these enormously wealthy institutions established a firm position in the lower Seine from which to extend family influence elsewhere in the reunited kingdom. In the dioceses of Nantes, Châlons, and Soissons, for example, essentially the same process was followed: monasteries were reformed and enlarged, new monks, often from St.-Wandrille, were introduced, abbots and bishops who were members of or loyal to the Pippin family were installed, and the key institutions were taken under the family protection.

These three measures—mergers with regional aristocratic families, manipulation of the royal court, and control of ecclesiastical institutions—solidified Pippin's power throughout the kingdom. However, his preoccupation with Austrasia and Neustria provided the dukes in the more peripheral areas of Francia the opportunity to attempt the same process of control and consolidation in their areas. Moreover, his death in 714 and that of his son Grimoald II opened the way for a violent conflict among the members of his family for succession, threatening to tear down the entire edifice he had so carefully constructed over the preceding three decades.

In early 714 Pippin, sensing that he was nearing the end of his life, sent for Grimoald, his son and designated successor as *maior domus*. On his way to see his father at Jupille, Grimoald was assassinated in the Basilica of St. Lambert in Liège. Pippin himself died a few months later, leaving a disputed succession and the last opportunity the anti-Pippinid faction would have to assert its independence. The result was three years of war followed by six years of desperate political maneuvering, during which the three-pronged power base constructed by Pippin largely collapsed, to be replaced by his eventual successor, Charles Martel.

Pippin left three possible successors. Pippin's own choice was Theudoald, the minor son of Grimoald, whom Pippin had entrusted to his widow, Plectrude. Second, there were the sons of Pippin's son Drogo, who had died in 708, including Hugo, who by 714 was a priest, Arnulf, Pippin, and Godefrid, the latter two minors. Finally there was Charles, known to history as Martel ("the hammer"), the only adult surviving son of Pippin. However he was not the son of Plectrude but of one of Pippin's concubines, or perhaps an additional wife in the Frankish tradition. In any case, Plectrude imprisoned Charles and established Theudoald as *maior* in Neustria and Arnulf as duke in the area of Metz.

Within a short time, Neustrian aristocrats seized the opportunity to revolt, rallying around Childebert III's son Dagobert III (711–715). They defeated the Pippinids near Compiègne, putting Theudoald to flight. He died shortly after the battle, and the Neustrians elected one of their own, Ragamfred, as *maior*. Ragamfred concluded alliances with the Frisians to the north and the Aquitainian duke Eudo in order to crush the Pippinids and move east toward Metz. Charles escaped the captivity of his stepmother and began to organize his Austrasian supporters in his defense against the Neustrians. Dagobert in the meantime died and the Neustrians found a son of Childeric II, a cleric named Daniel, and made him king under the name Chilperic II. For his part, Charles found his own Merovingian, Chlothar IV.

Supporters flocked to the Neustrians from throughout Francia, from the area of Rouen, Amiens, Cambrai, the Paris region, upper Burgundy, Alemannia, and from as far away as Provence and Bavaria. Chilperic II's court became a gathering place for all groups which sought to check Pippinid ambition, more to protect their own autonomy than to support the Merovingian dynasty.

Charles had to fight against both Plectrude and the Neustrians. However in 717 he was able to defeat his stepmother and the following year overcame the Neustrians at Soissons. At last Charles was able to move into Neustria and begin the process of consolidating his family's power.

This reconsolidation required roughly five years and was a painstaking process, reestablishing control city by city across Neustria and Burgundy. The primary means by which he accomplished this was through his use of monastic and episcopal offices. The result was not only a firmly established *princeps* in the kingdom, but a new kind of church and a new culture. Perhaps this, more than anything else, marked a break with late antique traditions of local control and would come to characterize the Carolingian age. However, before we examine the cultural and religious transformations under Charles we must turn to the changes of the other regions of Francia during this period of political unrest.

Formation of Territorial Kingdoms

When the *maior domus* Bercharius had been killed Pippin the younger, son of Ansegisel, came from Austrasia and succeeded him in the office [principatum] of *maior domus*. From this time forth the kings began to have the [royal] name but not the dignity [honorem]. . . . At that time Godafred, duke of the Alemanni and certain other dukes around him refused to obey the dukes of the Franks, because they were no longer able to serve the Merovingian kings as they were formerly accustomed to do, and therefore each kept to himself.[8]

The ninth-century author who penned this portrayed the relationship between the Pippinids and the other dukes of Francia perhaps more accurately than he knew. The office of *maior* had indeed become a princely position. Prior to the seventh century, the term *princeps* had referred only to imperial or royal office. Now increasingly *maiores* were claiming sovereignty. However, the same diminishing of royal power combined with the consolidation of regional power that pushed the *maiores* of Neustria and Austrasia toward quasiroyal status was having the same effect on dukes in other areas. In Thuringia, Frisia, Aquitaine, Alemannia, and Bavaria the *maiores* were becoming more independent. By the early eighth century, even bishops were exercising a *principatum* in their territories. As their common bond, a relationship with a powerful Merovingian king, disappeared, such independent lords felt no similar allegiance to the Pippinids, who were at best their equals, and in many cases their social inferiors.

Each of the peripheral regions of the Frankish world had its own particular social and political organization, and each related to the center in different ways. We shall examine three of the most important—Aquitaine, Provence, and Bavaria—as examples of the process taking place across Francia.

Aquitaine

Aquitaine was the region with the greatest continuity of Roman culture and society. It was also the richest region of Francia, and its geographic position bordering the Visigothic kingdom and the Basques made it of vital strategic importance.

The links with Roman society and culture were extremely strong in Aquitaine, where language, social organization, and religious culture continued much as they had in the sixth century. The great estates populated by slaves and *coloni,* which had characterized the agrarian and social organization of the region since the fifth century, continued without major interruption. Estimates of the size of some of these estates, termed *fundus,* have them almost as large as a modern French department; smaller ones might still reach the size of a modern commune. In the course of the seventh century, these estates if anything gained in size, as magnates expanded their holdings through purchase, exchange, and inheritance.

At the same time, Aquitaine continued to have smaller free tenures. During the sixth century, plague, introduced through the port of Marseille, had ravaged the region as far north as

Orléans before subsiding. Its effects had been severe depopulation and the loss of arable land due to the lack of labor. Now,
in the later seventh century, the population slowly began to
rise, and peasants were encouraged to cultivate abandoned land
belonging to the fisc, to magnates, and to the ecclesiastical institutions. The arrangements with these free peasants were such that
they could return land to cultivation and thereby obtain part
of it as their own. As a result, the agrarian wealth of the region
was slowly growing, providing a basis on which to develop autonomy and making Aquitaine a prize worth fighting for.

The riches of Aquitaine, not only its agricultural produce but
also its salt, wood, furs, marble, lead, iron, and silver mines, had
long made it a valued Frankish possession. We have seen that
at every division of the kingdom, each king had received a portion of Aquitaine. In turn, these kings had been extremely
generous to the great monasteries and churches of the north
with grants of property, incomes, and tariff exemptions in the
region. Le Mans, Metz, Cologne, Reims, Paris, and Châlons,
among other northern bishoprics, had extensive holdings in
Aquitaine, as did monasteries such as St.-Wandrille, St.-Denis,
Corbie, and Stavelot. This northern presence in the south insured constant interaction between the laity and ecclesiastical
magnates of both regions.

The northern presence in the south was paralleled by a
strong Aquitainian presence in the north. Since Clovis, southern
senatorial aristocrats had played key roles in the courts of Merovingians, had provided important bishops to the north, and had
made political and marriage alliances throughout Francia. Thus,
without denying the peculiar character of the region and its
essential *Romanitas,* one can place too much emphasis on the
Roman character of the region's aristocracy. While the smaller
and middling landholders no doubt looked to their local traditions, the great aristocracy was part of both worlds, moving freely
from one to the other and able to use their wide connections to
participate in the political and cultural movements of the entire
Frankish kingdom. True, they were "Romans," but primarily in
the same sense that the people north of the Loire, regardless of
"ethnic" ancestry, had come to consider themselves and to be
considered Franks. Just as "Frank" had become a geographic

description, "Roman" tended to mean an inhabitant of the south. From the first third of the seventh century, these "Romans" sought increasingly the same sort of autonomy desired in other regions of Francia.

This desire for autonomy was aided by the continuing need for security from the Basques or Gascons. We have seen that Dagobert had established his half brother Charibert II in a small Aquitainian kingdom as an outpost from which to control the Basques. Ebroin did essentially the same around 650, when he apparently established an aristocrat from Toulouse named Felix as patrician and gave him the *principatum* "over all the cities as far as the Pyrenees and over that most evil people, the Basques."[9] In effect, he reestablished the border kingdom of Charibert with a nonroyal official holding the *principatum*. After the death of Felix, his successor, Lupus, in the midst of the confusion following the death of Childeric II, claimed sovereignty and even a royal throne.

Although Lupus apparently died a year later, it appears that the de facto autonomy of Aquitaine continued well into the eighth century. The next Aquitainian duke we hear of is Eudo, styled "prince of the Aquitainians." Nothing is known of his origins or background. His name suggests a Neustrian origin however, and it is quite likely that he had both Neustrian and Aquitainian connections on which to build and consolidate his position. This is typical of independent "princes" of the time across Francia. During the period of gradual Pippinid consolidation in the north and the fight over Pippin's succession that followed his death in 714, Eudo was able to expand his independent principality north and east. Neustrian opponents of the Pippinids, led by the *maior* Ragamfred and his Merovingian Chilperic II, found an ally in Eudo. As long as he was facing only Basques to the southwest, a divided Gothic kingdom to the southeast, and a disordered Frankish world to the north, he could maintain virtual independence. This equilibrium was destroyed by the sudden collapse of Visigothic Spain before the Islamic invasion of 710–711.

The collapse of Spain was rapid and complete. After the destruction of King Rodrigas at the battle of Guadaleta in 711, resistance disintegrated across the country. By 719 Septimania had fallen, and by 721 a Moslem army was besieging Toulouse. Here it was stopped by Eudo and his Aquitainians, reinforced by Basque contingents, who effected a crushing defeat on the Moslem army. Eudo seems to have received for this victory recognition from Pope Gregory II, who was looking for alliances with important princes outside Italy both to protect the West from Islam and, possibly more important, as potential allies against the Langobards. Then followed a period of consolidation and peace, during which time Eudo apparently contracted a treaty with the rebellious Berber commander of the strategic Cardagne region, giving the Berber his daughter in marriage. Presumably he realized that in the future his major threat might come from the north and he needed Moslem neutrality, if not support.

Ten years later, Pippin II's son and successor, Charles Martel, had established his position in the north sufficiently to allow him to look to the other subkingdoms and independent territories of the Frankish world. In 731 he invaded Aquitaine and carried off a great amount of booty. This left Eudo in an impossible position. His ally in the Cerdagne had previously been eliminated by the governor of Spain, leaving him without Moslem support. The following year the governor of Spain, Abd ar-Rahmān, taking advantage of Aquitaine's exposed position, invaded Gascony and Aquitaine, raiding as far north as Bordeaux and Poitiers. When Eudo attempted to stop him, the Aquitainian army was destroyed, and he was forced to ask Charles Martel for assistance. The resulting Frankish victory between Poitiers and Tours not only checked the Moslem advance north of the Pyrenees, but meant the beginning of the end of Aquitainian independence. Eudo was reduced to the position of Charles's client, and subsequent attempts by his sons and successors to reassert their independence following Charles's death in 741 and that of his son Pippin III in 768 were brutally crushed.

Provence

The pattern, as in Aquitaine, of aristocrats with at once local and Frankish connections taking advantage of the disintegration of central authority to establish independent lordships, the use of a Merovingian as a figure around whom to rally "loyalist" support, and alliance with powers outside Francia for protection against the Pippinids, was repeated across the perimeter of Francia. In Provence, the same process developed in the last third of the seventh century.

Here the patricians Antenor and Maurontus, the latter quite possibly a distant kinsman of the Neustrian *maior* Waratto, were able to take advantage of the situation to establish themselves in autonomous positions vis-à-vis the Pippinids. However, this independence apparently did not extend to the Merovingians themselves, especially Childebert III. Antenor was one of the magnates present at Childebert's court in 697 when Drogo was defeated in his attempt to use his marriage connections to increase his family property. Childebert seems to have been a rallying point for anti-Pippinid opposition throughout Francia. As we shall see, not only did the Provençal rebel attend his court and assist in defeating the Pippinids, but members of his court would later be found in areas hostile to Pippin and his successors.

This ostensible Merovingian support seems to have continued to a limited extent under Childebert's successor Chilperic II, who managed for a short time to organize opposition to Charles Martel. Even during the periods of apparent rebellion, Chilperic apparently maintained some influence over customs officers in Marseille and Fos and was able to guarantee the traditional immunities that St.-Denis enjoyed there. These Provençal patricians seem to have wanted to establish independent lordships along the same model as that of the Pippinids themselves—they pledged their loyalty to the legitimate Merovingian king, attended his court, and recognized his authority over some important aspects of the fisc. On the other hand, they were no more ready than was Pippin or later, Charles Martel, to accept Merovingian rule.

Princes such as Antenor and Maurontus based their power both on their local ties in society and on their control of ecclesiastical and secular offices. Marriages, inheritances, and land transactions over the decades had established such men in con-

trol of vast estates througout the regions in which they were
active. These estates, often consisting, in the Rhône valley, of
relatively isolated farmsteads as well as larger *fundus,* were
worked by slaves under the control and direction of *coloni* who
themselves were often freedmen, that is, former slaves or the
descendants of slaves who had been emancipated by their masters. Such freedpersons seem to have been the key to local control. While the status of freedperson in the classical period had
been an intermediate position and the children born of freedpersons were considered free, by the seventh century the status
had become a permanent, inheritable one. Descendants of emancipated slaves, usually established on a plot of land or even
given several such plots to cultivate with the assistance of slaves,
continued under considerable financial and moral obligations to
the families of their former masters. Although technically free
in relation to others, they risked being reduced once more to
slavery if they did not meet their special obligations to their
masters. Thus they were particularly suited for the management of great landholders' estates, for conducting their business,
and in general for providing that direct link between their patrons and the general society.

At the other end of the social spectrum, magnates controlled
offices such as those of count and duke or patrician, as well as
local offices that had originated in particular provincial civic tradition. They also controlled episcopal offices, with rival families
competing city by city for episcopal control and willing to assas-
sinate incumbents if necessary to achieve their ends. Churches
and monasteries were particularly important as sources of wealth
to divide among their followers in order to secure their loyalty.
In Marseille, Antenor confiscated the estates of the monastery of
St.-Victor and ordered the abbot to place on the high altar all
the records of landholdings so that these could be burned, thus
preventing any attempt by subsequent abbots to reassert their
rights to the property. Charles Martel's much-discussed policy
of confiscating church lands to reward his supporters was but
the continuation of a strategy employed by many of the "princes"
of the early eighth century.

This competition within Provence, as within other regions, worked ultimately to the advantage of Pippin and Charles Martel. If Antenor and Maurontus sought to establish themselves as princes, this would have to be at the expense of other local magnates, and thus they found themselves facing not only the Pippinids but also local rivals, often equally well-connected regionally and internationally. In Provence, the competition came from the clan of the Burgundian-Juran Waldelenus, discussed earlier, from the region of Besançon. By the late seventh century this group, with close ties to Austrasia, had married into the family which controlled the important Alpine passes into Italy centered on Susa, Gap, and Embrun. In the first third of the eighth century the head of this family, Abbo, led the local opposition to Maurontus.

These local rivalries resulted in feuds carried out over generations, and in time each party looked for external allies to help them tip the balance in their favor. In the 720s and 730s, Maurontus looked to the Moslems of Septimania and invited the Wali of Narbonne into Provence to assist him, while Abbo cooperated with Charles Martel, who conducted a series of expeditions into the lower Rhône. As in Spain and in Aquitaine, the Moslems quickly attempted to push aside their erstwhile allies and occupy the region. Charles used the situation to present himself as the champion of Christianity, expel the Septimanian Moslems, and assume control of the region, establishing his local ally Abbo as *patricius,* and strengthening Abbo's position with property confiscated from his opponents, termed rebels in the pro-Carolingian sources.

However, Charles was not content to establish an ally and then allow him to begin again the process which might lead to yet another separatist movement. Abbo, who may have allied fairly late with Charles, was perhaps allowed to become *patricius* because he had no legitimate heirs. Upon his death, he left all of his estates, the accumulated wealth of generations of family strategists as well as the rewards of faithful service to Charles, to his family monastery, Novalesa, in the area now known as the Italian Piedmont. With Abbo's death, this monastery passed, like the great Neustrian monasteries would do, under the direct control of the Carolingians, placing them at the pinnacle of regional power.

BAVARIA

The one major region not absorbed into the Pippinid orbit in the early eighth century was Bavaria. Bavaria, located at the crucial intersection of the Frankish, Langobard, Slavic and Avar worlds, had long been developing into an autonomous region under its Agilolfing dukes. The ability of the Agilolfings to expand their territory and act autonomously depended to a great extent on their ability to maintain an equilibrium with their neighbors and to unite the disparate peoples in their "kingdom." At times of strong central Frankish power, as under Dagobert I, Bavaria had no choice but to submit to Merovingian authority, especially because of the threat posed by the Slavic kingdom of Samo, and the Avars, successors to the Huns in Pannonia. When these neighbors were weak, as after the death of Samo (c. 660), the Bavarians were quick to take advantage of the situation by extending their control as far as the Vienna woods. But when the neighbors were strong, as was the Langobard duke of Trent twenty years later, the Bavarians were forced to retreat, in this instance from the region of Bosen in south Tyrol. Likewise, the Avars, freed from the threat of Samo's kingdom, were able to push as far as Lorsch on the Inns River, leaving the region between the Inns and the Vienna woods a sort of Avar-patrolled no-man's-land.

The Agilolfings based their growing autonomy in part on their control of the surviving fiscal lands, which seem in some regions of Bavaria to have survived from late antiquity, and on the remains of Roman administrative organization. This is most clearly seen in their court at Regensburg, which they established in the former Roman *pretorium,* or governor's residence, of that city.

The territorial expansion and political unification of the polyethnic population was closely related to its religious unification, and competition for the lead in missionary activity and political hegemony went hand in hand. At the beginning of the seventh century, the population of the region included not only Alpine Romans who had remained orthodox Christians, but also pagan Celts and Slavs and Arian Germanic groups. The strategies of conversion were as diverse as the peoples to be converted.

First, isolated Christian communities, such as Salzburg, provided continuity with late antique Christianity. The extent of this continuity is difficult to determine, but unlike other Germanic regions, the conversion of Bavaria was not entirely an imported phenomenon but rather had indigenous roots.

The second unique aspect of Bavarian Christianity was its ancient connections with northern Italy, especially with Verona. These connections, too, dated to late antiquity, and instead of destroying them by establishing the Bavarian duchy under the Franks, the early Frankish conquests in northern Italy actually strengthened these ties. Under the Agilolfings, the duke's close familial ties to the Langobard royal family ensured that these connections continued.

Iro-Frankish monasticism entered Bavaria via Luxeuil. The first representatives of the tradition were Abbot Eustasius and the monk Agrestius, who undertook missionary activities in Bavaria during the first third of the seventh century. Their activities and those of others, such as Saint Emmeran, were, just as in the West, part of a Frankish effort to establish not simply Christianity but a society firmly tied to Francia. The Bavarian dukes needed this form of Christianity for their own consolidation. However they continued to fear it, with reason, as a "fifth column" that threatened to undermine their autonomy because of the continuing strong ties of these clerics and the institutions they founded with the West, particularly with Austrasia.

Not surprisingly then, when, in the early eighth century the Bavarian duke Theodo began to take advantage of the power vacuum in Francia to structure his duchy into a centralized monarchy, he looked not to the West for assistance in organizing a church but to the south. In 716 he visited Rome and sought the assistance of Pope Gregory II to organize a regular ecclesiastical hierarchy. This Bavarian-papal alliance prefigured both that of Eudo of Aquitaine and Charles Martel.

Not only was Bavaria becoming a truly independent subking-dom, but in the late seventh century it was increasingly a center of refuge for the enemies of the Pippinids. The most significant of these was Bishop Rupert of Worms, who apparently exiled himself around 694 from the Merovingian court and went to Regensburg, where he was received by Theodo and granted the right to establish an episcopal see in the old Roman town of Salzburg. Later Rupert returned to the West, presumably to participate in the short-lived opposition formed around Chil-peric II.

Unlike the other independent kingdoms of the late seventh and early eighth centuries, Bavaria maintained its independence into the reign of Charlemagne. The reasons for this were the distance of Bavaria from the center of Carolingian power, the successful manner in which the dukes maintained their alliances with the Langobards and at times with the Avars, and the other more pressing problems which faced Pippin and his successors.

The other regions of Francia generally followed the pattern of Aquitaine and Provence, rather than of Bavaria. The Frisians, Alemanni, and Thuringians were all brought under the lord-ship of Charles Martel. The long process had been costly and destructive. In Aquitaine, Burgundy, and Provence the physical effects of Charles's conquest were felt for generations. But in the cultural transformation of European society, the effects were felt even longer.

Effects on Society

The West had known episcopal lordships since antiquity, when bishops such as the fifth-century Germanus of Auxerre had proven more capable than the local Bagaudae in protecting the community from an often hostile and indifferent world. However, between 700 and 730 the nature of episcopal lordship had been radically transformed. Consider the brief account con-tained in the near-contemporary history of the bishops of Auxerre of the life of Germanus's successor, bishop Savaric, discussed previously:

Savaric . . . was, as it is reported, of very high birth. He began to turn aside a little from the status of his order and to covet secular cares more than was appropriate for a bishop to such an extent that he subjected to himself by force of arms the districts of Orléans, Nevers, Tonnerre, and the Avallonais. Putting aside the episcopal dignity this bishop raised a great army, but when he marched on Lyon to conquer it by force of arms he was struck down by divine lightning and died instantly.[10]

At least Savaric had been a bishop. His successor Hainmar, termed *vocatus episcopus,* apparently never bothered with ordination or consecration. He is said to have held his *principatum* for fifteen years before his "martyrdom" when attempting to escape from Charles Martel, whom he had been accused of betraying in a conspiracy with Eudo of Aquitaine. These warrior-bishops, or more appropriately, warriors who held bishoprics, were a far cry from the political bishops of the sixth century or even those such as Arnulf of Metz and Leodegar of Autun.

The radical change in the episcopacy was not that bishops had become key figures in the struggle for political dominance or that their sees were seen as private property and used as bulwarks for family territorial organization. Nor was their willingness to take active roles in the bloody fighting of the eighth century novel. All of this was part of the long tradition of the episcopacy and stands condemned only in the anachronistic perceptions of later ecclesiastical propagandists. Episcopal dynasties existed even in the fifth and sixth centuries, and bishops had been deeply involved in politics before the arrival of the Franks.

What was radically new was that in contrast to earlier episcopal power, which had been based not only on secular connections but also and always on the bishop's role as representative and custodian of divine power, the new type of bishop was primarily or even exclusively a secular magnate. The power of earlier bishops came from their control of access to sacred places and objects as well as from family wealth and connections, and they embodied late Roman cultural traditions, assuming such traditional civic duties as social relief and the maintenance of peace within their communities. But the new bishops' power and prestige came exclusively from their control of the material resources of one or more dioceses.

Savaric and Hainmar were not exceptions. In the first third of the eighth century, the bishop, the most fundamental institution of late antiquity and the primary representative of *Romanitas,* was rapidly being transformed almost beyond recognition. And no party made greater use of this than Charles Martel. His own cousin Hugo was simultaneously bishop of Rouen, Bayeaux, and Paris, as well as, quite probably, Lisieux, Avranches, and Evreux, while holding offices of abbot of St.-Wandrille, St.-Dennis, and Jumièges. Pluralism of this sort became increasingly common. At Trier a son succeeded his father as bishop not only of that city but of Laon and Reims as well, although it is unclear whether either had been ordained. After Hugo's death, the process of secularization of episcopal and monastic office advanced even further. His successors in Rouen and St.-Wandrille were not even literate.

Charles's use of the episcopacy and of monasteries was the hallmark of his process of consolidation in Neustria. His father's methods of solidifying his position—absorption of other clans into his, the manipulation of the royal court, and the assumption of protection over the monastic church—had been insufficient. Attempts to absorb the Neustrian maioral family and its allies had proven in the long run unsuccessful. The royal court had turned vicious as Merovingians had proved themselves capable of still acting independently and making common cause with the opposition; thus their courts could no longer be a stage for political maneuvering. The church would therefore be the focus of Charles's new consolidation, but not in the way his father had attempted. It would be a new church, controlled by his kinsmen and most trusted associates, without regard for religious or educational formation, local cultural traditions, and the niceties of episcopal election or consecration.

The one institution Charles treated with respect and caution was St.-Denis. The enormous holdings of the basilica were the key to the control of Neustria, as he was well aware. St.-Denis had supported Ragamfred against Charles, and after 717 he moved cautiously to secure it, making his nephew Hugo its abbot, but also protecting its far-flung property rights from others and enriching it with the grant of the remaining portions of the great Merovingian villa of Clichy-Ruvray, an estate estimated at over 2,000 hectares. This grant made St.-Denis by far the largest property holder in the region of Paris. Of course, by this time, it pertained as well to Charles as to St.-Denis—so close was the connection between him and the monastery that he had his son Pippin III educated there and was himself buried under the porch of the basilica when he died in 741.

This new religious situation, certainly not initiated by Charles but promoted by him, was decisive for the cultural and religious life of Francia. The destructive wars of pacification and the transformation of the episcopacy eliminated the cultivation of letters that had so long been associated with episcopal culture. Ravaged by the armies of Charles and his son Pippin III, Aquitaine ceased to be a center of learning, as did Provence. The tradition of literate laymen virtually died out, as did their role in the royal and maioral chancelleries. Writing became a virtual monopoly of the clergy, and as a result the use of writing, so important throughout Merovingian history, decreased accordingly.

Viewed from the perspective of Roman cultural tradition and Gallo-Roman civic identity, the results were no doubt disastrous. However, in effect Charles Martel accomplished what no other secular power had been able to do in the previous two centuries. By his manipulation of ecclesiastical office, by the confiscation of the wealth it controlled, and by the appointment of ignorant and entirely worldly lay supporters, he finally succeeded in destroying the religious basis on which had long rested the independent power of the Frankish episcopate. Henceforth medieval bishops would be powerful lords, at times rivaling in power dukes, counts, and even kings. They would never again command that particular power as monopolists of the sacred as they had in previous centuries. This role, along with the lead in cultural life, would pass to monasteries.

From the tabula rasa of early eighth-century religious culture, Charles and his successors built a new kind of episcopal and monastic edifice and simultaneously a new religious basis for their own lordship. The pillars of this edifice were Anglo-Saxon missionaries and the Roman pope.

The Anglo-Saxon Missions

The early seventh century had been the great period of Irish influence on the Continent, due to the efforts of Columbanus and many less famous Irish pilgrims who found their way to the Continent after him and helped extend Iro-Frankish Christianity, in close cooperation with the aristocracy. Now, beginning in the lifetime of Pippin II, Anglo-Saxons came increasingly to replace the Irish as the most active missionaries and reformers in Francia. A world of difference separated these two groups. First, by the later seventh century, England had a firmly established episcopal hierarchy imposed by papal agents, rather than either the monastic, decentralized church of Ireland (itself waning by this time) or an indigenous tradition of local churches as was the case in Francia. Second, the Anglo-Saxon church had been established in close cooperation with Anglo-Saxon kings. The bishops and abbots were accustomed to close cooperation with and control by the kings of the territories in which they worked. Finally, Anglo-Saxon monasticism was essentially Benedictine. Augustine of Canterbury and many of his companions had been monks, and the spread of Roman episcopal Christianity in the island had been intimately connected to the Benedictine monastic expansion, reinforced by Benedict Biscop in his great monasteries of Wearmouth and Jarrow. It was this Roman Benedicine form of Christianity that the Anglo-Saxon missionaries introduced to the Continent.

The earliest Anglo-Saxon missionaries, Wilfrid and Willibrord, concentrated on Frisia, establishing the essential political character of theirs and subsequent missions. Wilfrid, bishop of York, had been deposed by the archbishop of Canterbury Theodore for objecting to the division of Wilfrid's huge diocese, and was on his way to Rome via the Rhineland (his assistance in arranging the return of Dagobert II had made him persona non grata in Neustria) when he first arrived among the Frisians. His successor Willibrord arrived in 690 and began his work under

the protection of Pippin in those areas that had been reccon-
quered by the Franks. One of the first things he did was to travel
to Rome to obtain papal sanction for his activities. This would
have been unthinkable for a Frankish clergyman, but seemed
only natural to Anglo-Saxons.

The process of Christianizing the Frisians and subduing them
militarily went hand in hand. Conversion meant conversion to
Frankish Christianity and thus a radical break with their own
autonomous social and political past. The Frisians understood
this well. The story was told that Duke Radbod was taking religious instruction and nearing the point to be baptized when
he asked Willibrord whether his ancestors were in heaven or
hell. The orthodox response was that they were surely in hell
because they had been pagans, but the duke would no doubt
achieve heaven after baptism. On hearing this Radbod refused
baptism, saying he could not do without the company of his
ancestors in the next life.[11]

Willibrord lived to be over eighty, dying in 739. In theory
he had become the head of an autonomous metropolitan see
directly under the pope. Pippin had sent him to Rome to be
consecrated archbishop of the Frisians, and thus he established
a new metropolitan see on the model of the English church. He
had envisioned a vast missionary project extending throughout
Frisia and into Denmark and Saxony. In reality, he was only successful where Pippin and later Charles controlled the territory.
Elsewhere he met with total failure. Moreover, after his death,
his ecclesiastical province was swallowed up into the Frankish
church.

Willibrord's more famous successor and countryman, Wynfrid,
known as Boniface, the name given him by the pope, met the
same limits on his efforts. Although he first focused on Frisia,
Boniface soon found his calling east of the Rhine. Like Willibrord, he traveled to Rome to secure papal authorization for his
mission and in 719 was commissioned to preach to "the gentiles,"
presumably meaning the Thuringians. After initial successes
there, he returned to Rome in 722 to be consecrated bishop, and
again in 738 to receive the commission to organize the church
in Bavaria and Alemannia. Although known as "The Apostle

to the Germans," much of Boniface's missionary work took place in regions already Christian for generations. Iro-Frankish missionaries, wandering bishops, and aristocrats from across the Rhine had already established Christian communities in large parts of Alemannia, Thuringia, and especially in Bavaria. But these were not organized into a single church and they did not all follow Roman tradition. Boniface sought to change this. In addition, these churches were not instruments of Carolingian political control. Although this last issue was not of paramount importance to Boniface, it was to his Carolingian supporters.

These changes did not meet with universal approval, especially from such perfectly orthodox if non-Roman churchmen as Bishop Virgil of Salzburg, a brilliant Irishman who stubbornly resisted being forced into Roman conformity. In every instance, Boniface was eager to enforce a strict interpretation of Roman institutional structure and Roman moral and religious tradition on the areas of his mandate. The results, where enforced by Charles Martel or, after his death, by Pippin III and Carlomann, were considerable, although this secular assistance was brought to bear more often against autonomous opponents than against immoral, unqualified, or unworthy bishops who had been appointed by the Carolingians themselves.

Boniface's genuine concern for his mission and his tremendous organizational skills proved fruitful. He established Benedictine monasteries as points of acculturation and bishoprics as centers of ecclesiastical control in Hesse, Thuringia, and Franconia. The value of his form of centralized church was even appreciated by the still-independent Duke Odilo of Bavaria, who invited him to organize the Bavarian church. When Willibrord died his province was incorporated into Boniface's area of jurisdiction. By 742 he was recognized as the "Archbishop of the East," metropolitan of an enormous, well-organized, and increasingly reform-minded hierarchical system.

The extent to which this organizational activity benefited Charles and his successors was considerable. By 742 it was possible to call a council of all the bishops of the Austrasian regions under the authority of Charles's son Carlomann. This council, which met to establish a strict hierarchical order within the church, set the style for future church assemblies. Called in the spring to coincide with the annual military muster or "May-field," participants included not only bishops but secular mag-nates as well. Moreover, the decrees of the synods were promul-gated, not in the names of the bishops themselves as had been the tradition since antiquity, but in the name of Carlomann. This pattern was soon followed by a synod in the West held in 744 at which a similar program was enacted and the groundwork was laid for the construction of a Western church on the Aus-trasian model. In 745 and 747 councils of the whole Frankish church were held under similar conditions. Through their sup-port of the missionary bishop, the Carolingians had gained con-trol of a well-disciplined, effective instrument of central control.

Along with the work of reforming the episcopal church, Boni-face, a lifelong devotee of Benedictine monasticism, worked to found monasteries and reform others in which the rule of Saint Benedict rather than the Iro-Frankish or Gallo-Roman traditions prevailed. Here too he received enormous support from Charles and his sons. The extent of the spread of Benedictine monasti-cism at the expense of the older forms marked the growing range of Carolingian control in the Frankish world.

However, for all his service to the Carolingians, he was not simply their creature. Had he been, his effect could not have been so great. In 742, when he was recognized as archbishop of the East, he was termed *missus Sancti Petri*, the ambassador of Saint Peter.[12] It was from Rome that he derived his charisma, and it was this charisma that he sought to give to his church.

Unlike the old Merovingian episcopacy, the new religious foundation of the Frankish episcopacy was not founded in the local traditions of aristocratic control or even in the patronage of the local saints. For Charles's political bishops, it was clear they needed nothing but the *maior*'s support. But Boniface and his suffragens were still outsiders, appointed by the pope or chosen by the Anglo-Saxon missionary monk; they could not look to indigenous sacred traditions. They had to import them, primarily from Rome.

Thus the eighth century saw not just the establishment of Roman-style bishops and monasteries throughout Francia, but also the wholesale importation of Roman saints' relics into these new churches. The initiative for this came largely from Rome. In 739 Pope Gregory III sent Charles Martel the keys of the tomb of Saint Peter and a portion of the saint's chain. These gifts made a great impression in Francia: "Such things had never been seen or heard of before," comments the later writer of the Fredegar Chronicle.[13] He was wrong. Gifts of keys and fetters from the tomb of Saint Peter had been traditional long before, particularly in England, which the pope sought to firmly attach to the Roman church. Now the same process was being used to chain the Frankish church to Rome. In the process the sacred geography of Western Europe began to change. No longer were the tombs of Gallic martyrs, saintly bishops, or even saintly noble ancestors the central points of contact between heaven and earth. Now these points could be anywhere, they could be moved about, and their power came from Rome.

The New Monarchy

The newly constituted Frankish church was thus built on a sacred foundation radically different from that of its Merovingian predecessor. The transformation of royal sacredness was almost an afterthought. Since 718/19 Charles and successors were firmly in control. The testament of Abbo, written in 739, was even dated "in the twenty-first year that the illustrious Charles has governed the Frankish kingdoms."[14] Several long periods had passed when there had not even been a Merovingian to serve as a figurehead. Before, these figureheads had been necessary, or at least useful, in maintaining the Frankish realm. They embodied and represented the unity of the kingdom and the tradition of Frankish legitimacy within a context of late antiquity.

By the mid century this kind of identity and legitimacy was an anachronism, although it was perhaps still used as an excuse for peripheral magnates to oppose Carolingian rule, as had been the case under Pippin II. But this tradition had never made much sense to the Romans and Anglo-Saxons who had come to transform Francia, and increasingly their alien view of kingship, namely that kings not only reigned but ruled, were coming to be held by the elite of Francia as well. The Carolingian ecclesiastical system was based on imported Roman sacrality; it was only a matter of time before their own political position would be as well.

The development was gradual, natural, and mutually advantageous to pope and *princeps* alike. Since the early eighth century the popes had been casting about for outside support of their increasingly independent and precarious position vis-à-vis the Langobards in central Italy. The Eastern Empire could no longer provide any serious support, and in any case the popes were not eager for effective control from Constantinople. They had looked to the Bavarians and the Aquitainians, but neither had been as effective as they had hoped. Thus in 739 Pope Gregory III appealed to Charles Martel for assistance, sending him at the same time the relics mentioned above. Gregory's plan was probably for an independent Roman lordship in central Italy under the protection of a distant Frankish prince. Although little came of these initial overtures, they began the long and complex relationship between popes and Carolingians.

In a bit more than a decade, Charles's son Pippin needed papal assistance. After his father's death and his brother's decision in 747 to enter religious life, first in Rome and then at Monte Cassino, Pippin found himself the sole ruler of Francia but not the sole claimant to that position. His half brother Grifo, who had been excluded from the succession, was no less a potential prince than Pippin and was constantly the focus of opposition groups in the peripheral regions of the kingdom. Carlomann had left sons when he entered the monastery who might, in time, threaten Pippin's own heirs. Pippin needed a source of authority distinct from mere political power and superior to that of other Frankish magnates and even his own kinsmen. This he found in the same place that his church had found its sanctity, in Rome.

Thus in 749 or 750 he sent Bishop Burchard of Würzburg and Fulrad, later abbot of St.-Denis, where Pippin had been raised, to ask Pope Zachary, "Was it right or not that the king of the Franks at that time had absolutely no power but nevertheless possessed the royal office?"[15] This was not a Frankish question but a Roman one, and the response was a foregone conclusion. Thus in 751, "on the command of" Pope Zachary, Pippin was elected king "according to the Frankish custom" and anointed by either Boniface or Frankish bishops. This rite, with its Biblical, Gothic, Irish, and Anglo-Saxon precedents, was an innovation in Francia—never before had a king been confirmed in his office by ecclesiastical ritual. Merovingian blood and the symbolism of their long hair had been enough. The last Merovingian, Childeric III, no longer useful even as an anachronistic symbol, was tonsured and removed to a monastery, where he spent the remainder of his life.

CHAPTER VII

The Legacy of
Merovingian Europe

The descendants of Clovis had lost the inheritance of
his martial and ferocious spirit; and their misfortune
or demerit has affixed the epithet of *lazy* to the last
kings of the Merovingian race. They ascended the
throne without power, and sunk into the grave without a name. A country palace, in the neighborhood of
Compiègne, was allotted for their residence or prison:
but each year, in the month of March or May, they
were conducted in a wagon drawn by oxen to the assembly of the Franks, to give audience to foreign ambassadors and to ratify the acts of the mayor of the
palace.

Thus Edward Gibbon described the last Merovingians in his
great *History of the Decline and Fall of the Roman Empire*.[1]
He was being kind: traditionally most historians have suggested
that the decline of the Merovingians was due largely to their
personal depravity, congential degeneracy, or both. The glorious
brutality and faithless cruelty of Clovis and his successors was
seen to have been followed by the impotence, passivity, and incompetence of his last heirs. The family has not gained much
favorable appreciation in the past 1,200 years. Moreover, the
whole period from the victory at Soissons to the anointing of
Pippin has been an epoch with which heirs of the European
tradition have been acutely uncomfortable.

While every country in the West seems eager to claim Charles
the Great (Charlemagne, Karl der Grosse, Carlo magno) as their
own, and pan-Europeanists term him the "Father of Europe,"
Clovis and even Dagobert are largely unclaimed. In Germany,
generations of study of the tribal duchies and their origins have

sought continuity between the migration period and the duchies which emerged with the dissolution of the Carolingian Empire. Scholars have tended to forget that these tribal duchies were artificial creations of the Merovingians and their agents.

In France, national memory jumps from the Gallo-Roman period of Syagrius (or perhaps even before, from the time of Asterix) to the glory of Charlemagne. A long tradition, nourished by three disastrous Franco-German wars, has encouraged the French to forget that before there was a "douce France" there was a "Frankono lant," and that this Frankish land was centered in the lower Seine. "Les Francs sont-ils nos ancêtres?"* reads the title of the lead article in a recent issue of the popular French journal *Histoire et Archeologie*.[2] Through most of European history, the general desire on both sides of the Rhine has been to answer "no."

This disinclination to acknowlodge the continuity between the Merovingian period and later European history is the result of a variety of factors. The first and most obvious is the tendency to accept in an uncritical manner the anti-Merovingian propaganda created and disseminated by the Carolingians and their supporters, which was intended to undermine the prestige of the Merovingian royal family. Too often this unflattering view of the Merovingians has been taken at face value and accepted as an accurate assessment of the dynasty and, in particular, its inglorious end.

This portrait of the Merovingian family explains why subsequent dynasties did not wish to be associated with it, but does not explain the negative view of the entire period. Perhaps a reason is offered by the peculiar nature of the society, culture, and institutions of the Merovingian period. The world we have been examining was at all times deeply rooted in late antiquity, a world little understood in comparison with earlier or subsequent periods. We must examine both of these factors in order to understand the negative image of the Merovingian period in European history.

* Are the Franks our Ancestors?

The Rois Fainéants

Gibbon's description of the last Merovingians was largely derived from that of Einhard, the biographer of Charlemagne who began his life of the great emperor with a description of the Merovingians, dismissing them by trivializing them. According to Einhard, long before Childeric III's deposition, the family had lost all power and no longer possessed anything of importance but the title of king. Childeric's duties were to

> sit on the throne, with his hair long and his beard flowing, and act the part of a ruler, giving audience to the ambassadors who arrived from foreign parts and then, when their time of departure came, charging them with answers which seemed to be of his own devising but in which he had in reality been coached or even directed. . . . Whenever he needed to travel, he went in a cart which was drawn in country style by yoked oxen, with a cowherd to drive them. In this fashion he would go to the palace and to the general assembly of his people, which was held each year to settle the affairs of the kingdom, and in this fashion he would return home again.[3]

This image had long been presented by historians of the early eighth century favorable to the rising Carolingians. Already the first continuer of the Chronicle of Fredegar was concerned with reworking the *Liber Historiae Francorum,* a Neustrian chronicle completed in 727 in a way that presented an Austrasian and hence Carolingian perspective. The second continuation, prepared under orders of Charles Martel's half brother Count Childebrand, is even more closely associated with the Carolingian tradition. In these texts we begin to see the characterizations of the Merovingians as they would carry for centuries. Childeric II for example was "altogether too light and frivolous. The scandal and contempt that he aroused stirred up sedition among the Frankish people."[4] This image is not of a particularly dangerous king or a tyrant, but rather of a king who inspires scorn. This frivolity contrasts with the characterizations of men such as Grimoald, "the mildest of men, full of kindness and gentleness; and he was generous in almsgiving and constant in prayer,"[5] and Charles Martel, "that shrewdest of commanders."[6]

This tradition, which culminated in Einhard, dismisses the Merovigians as ridiculous anachronisms. They are not so much troublesome as they are useless. Of course, one might well dispute this judgment without disputing the essential accuracy of the image. The king with his archaic hairstyle and his ritual oxcart, receiving ambassadors and appearing as a symbol of the unity of Francia at the annual assembly, cannot but remind modern readers of the British monarch in gilded coach, receiving ambassadors and reading annual speeches to Parliament written by the governing party. Symbolic personifications of the kingdom can be extremely useful and important to societies, in spite of the fact that they do not govern, but precisely because their role is outside of politics. Childeric represented the Franks and the Frankish tradition before the Franks and others both in his appearance and no doubt in the manner in which he presided over the annual assembly. Even the oxcart, far from being a sign of rusticity, was an ancient symbol of Frankish identity—since the time of our first-century cattle trader Stelus, Germanic religious and political life had been intimately tied up with livestock. However, appreciation of such a role requires a more subtle understanding of tradition and its role in government than the Carolingians and their increasingly Romanized advisors were capable of.

Their reason for replacing the Merovingians was thus based on a novel and in the long run extremely potent justification. Childeric was not deposed for tyranny, evil, injustice, or any other vice; he was deposed for simple incompetence. Thus, as Edward Peters has pointed out, a new and important category of kingship was introduced into the traditional dichotomy between the just king and the tyrant, that of the useless king, the *rex inutilis*.[7] As the epitome of the useless king, the Merovingians would be remembered through history, not with the fear and loathing which a royal dynasty can accept, but rather with scorn. This scorn for the last Merovingians reflected back upon their predecessors, even the great king Dagobert. The French nursery song, "Le bon Roi Dagobert," conveys the image of a king at once stupid, impotent, and cowardly, who needs his faithful advisor, in this case Saint Eloi (Eligius of Noyon) to take care of him:

> Le bon roi Dagobert
> Avait sa culotte à l'envers
> Le grand Saint Eloi lui dit: "O mon roi!
> Votre Majesté est mal culottée."
> "C'est vrai," lui dit le roi
> "Je vais la remettre à l'endroit."

> Le bon roi Dagobert
> Chassait dans la plaine d'Anvers
> Le grand Saint Eloi lui dit: "O mon roi!
> Votre majesté est bien essoufflée!
> "C'est vrai," lui dit le roi
> "Un lapin courait après moi."[8]

A king who cannot even put on his pants without assistance and who runs in terror from rabbits is hardly one to be remembered with respect.

The Carolingian historiographers were extremely successful in creating an image of the preceding dynasty that has been accepted for centuries. Subsequent political apologists could use the image of a dynasty that lost power through incompetence. If a Merovingian could be deposed and sent to a monastery, and a new king elected and consecrated in his place, so too could a Carolingian. In less than a century, this happened to Louis the Pious, Charlemagne's son. More importantly, by the tenth century the replacement of the Carolingian dynasty by the Saxon and particularly by the Capetian dynasties was justified by the same standards applied to the Merovingians. They too were seen as having become *fainéants* and could thus be superseded. Within France and subsequently in England, the tradition of opposition to kings based not only on tyranny but on incompetence would continue well into the seventeenth and eighteenth centuries, although by the end of that century Louis XVI, a *fainéant* par excellence, would be sent not to the monastery but to the guillotine.

The negative image of the Merovingians, created by the Carolingians and constantly renewed for political purposes, explains the bad light in which the dynasty is viewed, but it is insufficient to explain why the sixth and seventh centuries, those formative periods of Western history, are as little appreciated as Dagobert and Childeric. This attitude is best explained by the alien character of this world and that of late antiquity which produced it. By way of conclusion, we shall examine some of the salient characteristics of this Frankish society.

The Uniqueness of Early Frankish Society

Merovingian civilization lived and died within the framework of late antiquity. Its characteristic political structure remained the kingdom of the imperial German military commander who, by absorbing the mechanism of provincial Roman administration, was able to establish his royal family as the legitimate rulers of the western provinces north of the Pyrenees and the Alps. His rule consisted primarily of rendering justice, that is, of enforcing Roman law and Romanized barbarian law where possible or appropriate within the tradition of his people, and of commanding the Frankish army. The economic basis for his power was on the one hand the vast Roman fisc and on the other the continuing mechanism of Roman taxation. The broader organization of society continued to be based on small communities, the late classical cities, with their local power structures virtually intact. Wherever possible, in the north of Gaul around Soissons, in the Rhineland of Trier and Cologne, or in distant Regensburg and Salzburg, the Merovingians and their agents integrated themselves into these existing Roman structures and derived their power and legitimacy from them. In a relatively short period of time, the warrior bands which had made up the mobile forces of the imperial Germanic commanders became territorially established and integrated into their corresponding indigenous populations. The distinguishing characteristic of this society as opposed to the Goths in Italy and Spain was its adherence to the orthodox Christianity of the indigenous population, making possible the rapid amalgamation of the various communities in Europe. By the eighth century this process was so complete that it not only had produced a new world but rendered the past virtually opaque to subsequent generations.

An essential characteristic of Francia was the fluidity of the political and cultural identities of its inhabitants. To many modern French, who identify with the Roman cultural tradition as opposed to Germanic conquest and occupation, the Gallo-Roman aristocracy of the Merovingian period were a disappointing lot. Gallo-Romans were ready to defend their Roman cultural tradition even while opposing any attempt by Roman imperial government to interfere with their local control. Thus they willingly and easily made common cause with any barbarian rulers who were prepared to accept them on their own terms. From Caesarius of Arles and Remigius of Reims through Eligius of Noyon and beyond, Romance identity was quite separate from political autonomy. In the political sphere, Aquitainian and Provençal elites acted exactly like their northern counterparts, stubbornly refusing to fit into modern categories of regional political structures based on cultural and ethnic identity and marrying into other elites without any hesitation. In short, in spite of sporadic attempts to portray the south as a region of heroic resistance to Germanic Frankish barbarity, the area's elites appear to the modern French like nothing so much as a society of collaborators.

The Franks of the north are even more perplexing, a curious blend of Germanic-speaking warriors governing through the institutions of a subclassical Roman administration whose primary characteristics, including even kingship, were the product of Roman military and civil tradition. Their pride in being Franks was only matched by their eagerness to serve the Roman state religion, orthodox Christianity, and to win recognition of their legitimacy in the eyes of the Roman emperor in Constantinople. The political fortunes of the Byzantine Empire fill almost as many pages of Merovingian chronicles as do those of Francia. The ease with which the Franks established themselves within a world of Roman cities, international commerce, literate government, written law, and Latin letters without abandoning their cherished feuds, kinship structures, and personal alliances is profoundly disturbing to those who expect the Franks to act like the Germanic tribes of Tacitus. Small wonder, then, that when Germans of the nineteenth and early twentieth centuries looked back to find their ancient past, they largely bypassed these Roman Franks in favor of the myth of more authentic Germanic peoples east of the Rhine.

In reality, of course, both the Romanized kingdoms of Gaul and western Germany and the "tribal" duchies east of the Rhine were the creations of the Merovingian world. In both areas, the intensely local interests at the end of the fifth century developed first into personal units around individual leaders or influential families, and then, in the course of the seventh century, these personal groupings, largely established for military purposes (for example, to counter the Basques in Aquitaine or the Slavs in Thuringia), evolved into territorial units that used the vocabulary of ethnic and cultural solidarity for political purposes. Thus the units of political organization which came to characterize Europe in the tenth and eleventh centuries—Aquitaine, Burgundy, Provence, "France," in the West; Bavaria, Alemannia, Thuringia, Saxony, in the East—first appeared in the Merovingian period. Although these areas took their names from preexisting geographical units or personal groups, they received their institutions, their geographical confines, and their leadership in the course of the seventh century. The Carolingian period would be but a hiatus in the development of the regionalism of the late Merovingian world.

This profound localism was characteristic of the Merovingian period because its primary actors, "Frankish" and "Roman" alike, had been formed within the structures of Gallo-Roman antiquity and particularly within the provincial city. The shift of the center of cultural and political focus from city to countryside coincided with the disappearance of the Merovingian world. To a great extent, this also meant the shift in religious authority from the urban world of bishops to the rural monastery, a process already begun in the sixth century but carried to fruition by Irish and then Anglo-Saxon monks in the seventh and eighth. The ruralization of the Western Church was paralleled by the decay of the city as an economic and political center. With the decline in international commerce and the increasing importance of monasteries in the economic life of the West, towns lost their significance as commercial centers to monasteries, of which St.-Denis, with its great fair, is the most important example. Also, the great monasteries such as Corbie, St. Bavon, and Fulda, the monastery of Boniface, became the principal centers for artisanal production and agents of distribution of both primary and manufactured goods. As the political importance of towns decreased, kings and their agents took up principal residence in rural villas rather than in the cities favored by Clovis and his successors. The last Merovingians resided principally at Compiègne, while the Carolingians would spend most of their time at one or another favored rural estate until Charlemagne selected Aachen, an insignificant rural spa, as his primary residence.

The power centers of the Roman Empire had been progressively neglecting the West, a situation that largely suited its population. The language and ritual of international Roman culture was used to emphasize local concerns. This was particularly true in the essential elements of Merovingian power—saints, bishops, kings, and aristocrats. In late antiquity and in the Merovingian period, each of these derived its authority from local, indigenous roots. When these again became dependent on a wider order, the result was a new world.

In the sixth century, religious power was rooted in the local holy man, or even better in his relics. When a young girl from Toulouse possessed by demons was brought to St. Peter's in Rome for exorcism, the demon refused to leave her: it insisted that it could be exorcised only by Remigius of Reims.[9] As Raymond Van Dam has pointed out, Gaul was presented as a direct rival to Rome in the force of its indigenous martyrs and special patrons.[10] The West was prepared to look to its own devices in the religious as well as in the political sphere. By the eighth and early ninth century, Rome was again looking at the West. In the early ninth century a young girl from Aquitaine who was mute and deaf arrived at Seligenstadt, a monastery founded by Einhard in the Rhineland, where her father had brought her after unsuccessfully seeking a cure at many other sanctuaries. Upon entering the basilica, she was seized with violent convulsions, blood flowed from her mouth and ears, and she fell to the ground. When she was raised up she could speak and hear, and she announced that she had been cured by the saints venerated in the church, Marcellinus and Peter, Roman martyrs whose relics had been recently brought to Francia from Rome.[11]

These two miracles indicate the shift in religious power from the Merovingian to Carolingian worlds. In both cases divine power is manifested through holy men, and in both the location of this action is north of the Alps. However by the end of the Merovingian period this power is mediated through Rome. Marcellinus and Peter had been transplanted to the north, and not to a city but to a rural monastery named paradoxically "the City of the Saints."

This transformation is paralleled, as discussed in the previous chapter, by the transfer of authority from Rome to the bishops of Francia appointed and supervised by Boniface and the Carolingians. The reestablishment of metropolitan sees, and the introduction of Roman usage and norms in the place of indigenous Gallo-Roman and Iro-Frankish ones tied the power of bishops to central rather than to local sources.

The Merovingians had been preeminently the embodiment of local authority. Never needing election or consecration, they were kings by their very nature, quite apart from any external religious or secular authority. The election and anointment of Pippin upon papal approval or even, according to some traditions, papal directive, fundamentally altered the nature of kingship, tying it to a particular religious and institutional tradition quite apart from the old Gallo-Roman and Frankish worlds.

Finally, along with the Carolingians, rose a new "imperial aristocracy" composed of nobles from many different backgrounds. Many were from old Austrasian families; others were from regional elites who had made the Carolingians secure in the various areas of Francia; still others had risen through service to the Carolingians or even to their predecessors but who had joined forces with the winning side at an early date. From this relatively small group of families the Carolingians drew their bishops and counts, whom they sent throughout the empire. Owing their positions to royal favor rather than primarily to local ties, these families, no less than Roman saints, Anglo-Saxon bishops, or Carolingian kings, depended on external sources of authority and power. Only after some time would these families intermarry, put down local roots in the areas into which they had been introduced, and produce the regional aristocracies of the High Middle Ages.

Although these transformations had been accomplished in the name of Roman tradition, by the end of the eighth century, when these new elements were firmly in place, little remained of the authentic late Roman West. The Rome that had sponsored Boniface was itself a new, artificial creation, as were the traditions of Latin letters and imperial destiny cultivated in Carolingian circles. And yet the transformed barbarian world so badly needed a Roman imperial tradition, even more than it had in the sixth century, that on Christmas Day in 800 Charles Martel's grandson received the title of emperor and Augustus. The barbarian world, that creature of Rome, had become its creator.

APPENDIX A

The Merovingian Genealogy

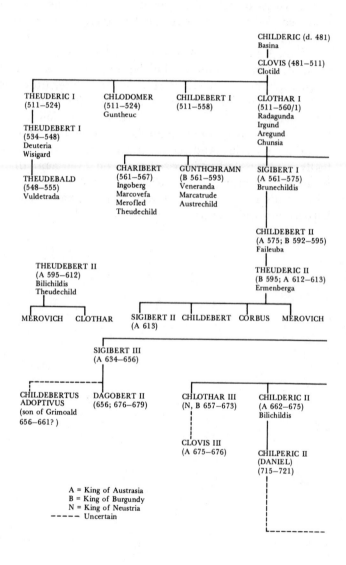

CHILDERIC (d. 481)
Basina

CLOVIS (481–511)
Clotild

THEUDERIC I
(511–524)

THEUDEBERT I
(534–548)
Deuteria
Wisigard

THEUDEBALD
(548–555)
Vuldetrada

CHLODOMER
(511–524)
Guntheuc

CHILDEBERT I
(511–558)

CLOTHAR I
(511–560/1)
Radagunda
Irgund
Aregund
Chunsia

CHARIBERT
(561–567)
Ingoberg
Marcovefa
Merofled
Theudechild

GUNTHCHRAMN
(B 561–593)
Veneranda
Marcatrude
Austrechild

SIGIBERT I
(A 561–575)
Brunechildis

CHILDEBERT II
(A 575; B 592–595)
Faileuba

THEUDERIC II
(B 595; A 612–613)
Ermenberga

THEUDEBERT II
(A 595–612)
Bilichildis
Theudechild

MEROVICH   CLOTHAR

SIGIBERT II   CHILDEBERT   CORBUS   MEROVICH
(A 613)

SIGIBERT III
(A 634–656)

CHILDEBERTUS
ADOPTIVUS
(son of Grimoald
656–661?)

DAGOBERT II
(656; 676–679)

CHLOTHAR III
(N, B 657–673)

CLOVIS III
(A 675–676)

CHILDERIC II
(A 662–675)
Bilichildis

CHILPERIC II
(DANIEL)
(715–721)

A = King of Austrasia
B = King of Burgundy
N = King of Neustria
----- Uncertain

232

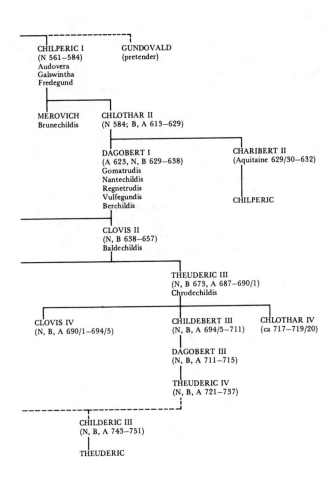

CHILPERIC I
(N 561–584)
Audovera
Galswintha
Fredegund

GUNDOVALD
(pretender)

MEROVICH
Brunechildis

CHLOTHAR II
(N 584; B, A 613–629)

DAGOBERT I
(A 623, N, B 629–638)
Gomatrudis
Nantechildis
Regnetrudis
Vulfegundis
Berchildis

CHARIBERT II
(Aquitaine 629/30–632)

CHILPERIC

CLOVIS II
(N, B 638–657)
Baldechildis

THEUDERIC III
(N, B 673, A 687–690/1)
Chrodechildis

CLOVIS IV
(N, B, A 690/1–694/5)

CHILDEBERT III
(N, B, A 694/5–711)

CHLOTHAR IV
(ca 717–719/20)

DAGOBERT III
(N, B, A 711–715)

THEUDERIC IV
(N, B, A 721–737)

CHILDERIC III
(N, B, A 743–751)

THEUDERIC

APPENDIX B

A Note on Names

The bewildering variety of spellings encountered for early medieval names results from contemporary scribal variations, from internal transformations of early medieval languages between the fifth and ninth centuries, and from the tendency of modern scholars to reproduce medieval names according to modern equivalents. The result can be bewildering for students, since, for example, the name of the victor at Soissons appears at various times as Chlodovic, Chlodovicus, Chlodowech, and Clovis, all of which are equivalent to the modern Ludwig, Luigi, Louis, and Lewis, while the great Ostrogothic king's name which passed into the Merovingian family can be found as Theodoricus, Theuderic, Thodoric, Theoderic, and Thierry. Gunthchramn became in time Guntram, Sigibert also appears as Sigebert, and Brunechildis is transformed into Brunichild, Brunehaut, and Brunhilda. Rather than projecting back onto the period modern name forms (which subtly transform their bearers into French or Germans), I have attempted to use one consistent, contemporary spelling for each of the names with the exception of Chlodovic, who is so well known today as Clovis.

Notes

Preface

1. Florus of Lyons, *Opuscula adversus Amalarium*, PL 119.82a.

Chapter I

1. P. C. J. A. Boeles, *Friesland tot de elfde eeuw* (S'Gravenhage: Martinus Nijhoff, 1951), 130, plate 16.

2. Eugippius, *Vita Severini* 21, *Monumenta Germaniae Historica* (hereafter MGH) *Auctores Antiquissimi* (hereafter AA) vol. I posterior, p. 19.

3. Walter Goffart, *Barbarians and Romans A.D. 418–584: The Techniques of Accommodation* (Princeton: Princeton University Press: 1980).

4. Walter Goffart, *Caput and Colonate: Towards a History of Late Roman Taxation* (Toronto: University of Toronto Press: 1974).

5. *Vita patrum Iurensium Romani, Lupicini, Eugendi*, II, 10, MGH *Scriptores rerum Merovingicarum* (hereafter SSRM) 3 p. 149.

6. Martin Heinzelmann, *Bischofsherrschaft in Gallien: Zur Kontinuität römischer Führungsschichten vom 4. bis zum 7. Jahrhundert. Soziale, prosopographische und bildungsgeschichtliche Aspekte, Beihefte der Francia* 5 (Munich: Artemis Verlag, 1976).

7. Raymond Van Dam, *Leadership and Community in Late Antique Gaul* (Berkeley: University of California Press, 1985), 51–56.

Chapter II

1. *Germania*, 46. tr. H. Mattingly, (Harmondsworth, U.K.: Penguin Books, 1948), 140.

2. Here and elsewhere in this chapter the author draws on Bruno Krüger, ed. *Die Germanen: Geschichte und Kultur der germanischen*

Stämme im Mitteleurope. Bd. I *Von den Anfängen bis zum 2. Jahrhundert unserer Zeitrechnung* 2. berichtigte Auflage (Berlin: Akademie-Verlag, 1978).

3. Plinius Maior, *Naturalis historia,* ed. C. Mayhoff (Leipzig: Teubner, 1892), 18, 44.

4. Julius Caesar, *Bellicum Gallicum,* ed. Otto Seel (Leipzig: Teubner, 1961), 6, 22.

5. Böhme, Horst Wolfgang, *Germanische Grabefunde des 4. bis 5. Jahrhunderts zwischen unterer Elbe und Loire: Studien zur Chronologie und Bevölkerungsgeschichte* 2 vols. *Münchner Beiträge zur Vor- und Frühgeschichte,* Bd. 19 (Munich: C.C.H. Beck'sche Verlags Buchhandlung: 1974).

6. The following depends largely on Herwig Wolfram, *History of the Goths* (Berkeley: University of California Press, in press).

7. Hans Zeiss, "Fürstengrab und Reihengräbersitte," *Forschungen und Fortschritte 12* (1936, 302–303, reprinted in Franz Petri, ed. *Siedlung, Sprache, und Bevölkerungsstruktur im Frankenreich, Wege der Forschung* 49 (Darmstadt: Wissenschaftliche Buchgesellschaft, 1973), 282.

Chapter III

1. Gregory of Tours, *Historia Francorum* (hereafter HF 2, 9. Throughout the author has frequently used or adapted the translation by Lewis Thorpe (Harmondsworth, U. K.: Penguin Classics, 1974).

2. *Chronicarum quae dicuntur Fredegarii scholastici Liber III,* 2. *MGH SSRM* 2, 93.

3. Cited in Joachim Werner, "Zur Entstehung der Reihengräberzivilisation: Ein Beitrag zur Methode der frühgeschichtlichen Archäologie," *Archaeologia Geographica 1* 1950, 23–32. Reprinted in Petri, *Siedlung, Sprache und Bevölkerungsstruktur,* p. 294.

4. *MGH Epistolae* 3, 113.

5. Ian Wood, "Gregory of Tours and Clovis," *Revue belge de philologie et d'histoire* 63 (1985), 249–272; Friedrich Prinz, *Grundlagen und Anfänge: Deutschland bis 1056. Neue Deutsche Geschichte,* ed. Peter Moraw, Volker Press, Wolfrang Schieder, vol. 1. (Munich: C. H. Beck Verlag, 1985), pp. 63–64.

6. HF 2, 37.

7. HF 2, 37.

8. HF 2, 42.

9. *Lex Salica* Prologue 2, *MGH Legum Sectio* I, IV, 2, p. 4.

10. *Lex Salica* 82, 2, p. 142. I am grateful to Professor Poly for allow-

ing me to consult his study of the Salic Law, which is to appear shortly.

11. The author follows here Ian Wood, "Kings, Kingdoms and Consent," in *Early Medieval Kingship*, P. H. Sawyer and Ian Wood, eds. (Leeds: University of Leeds, 1977), 6–29.

12. *Concilium Epaonense anno 517*, canon 8, *MGH Concilia* I, 21.

13. HF 3, 34.

14. HF 10, 26.

15. René Joffroy, *Le cimetière de Lavoye: Nécropole mérovingienne* (Paris: Éditions A. & J. Picard, 1974).

16. Jean Chapelot and Robert Fossier, *The Village and House in the Middle Ages* (Berkeley: University of California Press, 1985), 54–55.

17. H. Ament, *Fränkische Adelsgräber von Flonheim in Rheinhessen*, *Germanische Denkmäler der Völkerwanderungszeit* 5 (Berlin: 1970), 157.

18. Heike Grahn-Hoek, *Die fränkische Oberschicht im 6. Jahrhundert: Studien zu ihrer rechtlichen und politischen Stellung*, *Vorträge und Forschungen Sonderband* 21 (Sigmaringen: Jan Thorbecke Verlag, 1976).

19. Franz Irsigler, *Untersuchungen zur Geschichte des frühfränkischen Adels. Rheinisches Archiv, Veröffentlichungen des Instituts für geschichtliche Landeskunde der Rheinlande an der Universität Bonn* no. 70 (Bonn: Ludwig Röhrscheid Verlag, 1969).

20. Karl Bosl, "Freiheit und Unfreiheit: Zur Entwicklung der Unterschichten in Deutschland und Frankreich während des Mittelalters," *Vierteljahresschrift für Sozial- und Wirtschaftsgeschichte* 44 (1957), 193–219, reprinted *Frühformen der Gesellschaft im mittelalterlichen Europa* (Munich: R. Oldenbourg, 1964), 180–203.

Chapter IV

1. HF 4, 28.

2. HF 6, 46.

3. Martin Heinzelmann, "L'aristocratie et les évêchés entre Loire et Rhin jusqu'à la fin du VIIe siècle," *Revue d'histoire de l'église de France* 62 (1975), 75–90.

4. Venantius Fortunatus, *Carmina* 4–10, *MGH AA* 4/1.

5. HF 5, 5.

6. HF 6, 15.

7. HF 4, 6.

8. Gregory of Tours, *Liber vitae Patrum* (hereafter L.V.P.) 7 *MGH SSRM* 1, 686–690.

9. HF 6, 7.

10. HF 2, 17.

11. HF 2, 22.

12. HF 4, 36.

13. HF 5, 48.

14. HF 6, 11.

15. HF 5, 36.

16. HF 6, 36.

17. HF 5, 42.

18. HF 4, 36.

19. HF 8, 20.

20. HF 8, 22.

21. *Concilium Aurelianense, anno 533,* canon 20, and *Concilium Aurelianense, anno 541,* canon 15 *MGH Concilia* 1, 64 and 90.

22. Especially "Relics and Social Status in the Age of Gregory of Tours," in Peter Brown, *Society and the Holy in Late Antiquity* (Berkeley: University of California Press, 1982), 222–250.

23. HF 8, 15.

24. HF 4, 34.

25. L.V.P. 10, 705–709.

26. Jacques Le Goff, *Time, Work and Culture in the Middle Ages,* (Chicago: University of Chicago Press, 1980), 153–158.

27. *Capitula tractanda cum comitibus episcopis et abbatibus,* 12, *MGH Capitularia* 1, 162.

28. Vincent of Lérins, *Commonitorium* 2, 3, ed. R. S. Moxon (Cambridge: Cambridge University Press, 1915), 10.

29. *Concilium Aurelianense,* 19, *MGH concilium* 1, 7.

30. HF 9, 39.

31. *Liber in Gloria Confessorum,* 85, *MGH SSRM* 1, 802–803.

Chapter V

1. *Fredegarii Chronicorum Liber Quartus cum Continuationibus* (hereafter CF), J. M. Wallace-Hadrill, ed. and tr. (London: Thomas Nelson and Sons Ltd., 1960), 35.

2. *Childeberti secundi decretio, MGH Capitularia* 1, 15–23.

3. CF, 48.

4. CF, 74.

5. *Vita Desiderii Cadurcae urbis episcopi, MGH SSRM* 4, 569.

6. *Vita Desiderii,* 571–572.

7. CF, 50.

8. *Vitae Eligii episcopi Noviomagensis liber* II, 20, *MGH SSRM* 4, 712.

9. J. Guerout, "Le testament de Sainte Fare: matériaux pour l'étude et l'édition critique de ce document," *Revue d'histoire ecclésiastique* 60 (1965), 761–821.

10. Bailey K. Young, "Exemple aristocratique et mode funéraire dans la Gaule mérovingienne," *Annales ESC* 41 (1986), 396–401.

11. *Vita Audoini episcopi Rotomagensis, MGH SSRM* 5, 555.

12. Stéphane Lebecq, "Dans l'Europe du nord des VIIe–IXe siècles: Commerce frison ou commerce franco-frison?" *Annales ESC* 41 (1986), 361–377.

Chapter VI

1. *Gesta Dagoberti I. regis Francorum, MGH SSRM* 2, 408.

2. CF, 49.

3. *Virtutes Fursei abbatis Latiniacensis, MGH SSRM* 4, 444.

4. CF, 78–79; J. M. Wallace-Hadrill, *The Long-haired Kings and Other Studies in Frankish History* (New York: Barnes & Noble Inc., 1962), 142–143.

5. *Vita Sanctae Balthildis, MGH SSRM* 2, 493–494.

6. *Liber Historiae Francorum* 43, *MGH SSRM* 2, 316.

7. Paul J. Fouracre, "Observations on the Outgrowth of Pippinid Influence in the 'Regnum Francorum' after the Battle of Tertry (687–715)," *Medieval Prosopography* 5 (1984), 1–31.

8. *Erchanberti Brevarium, MGH Scriptores* (hereafter SS), 2, 328.

9. *Miracula Martialis*, 3 *MGH SS* 15, 280.

10. *Ex Gestis episcoporum Autisiodorensium, MGH SS* 13, 394.

11. *Vita Vulframni, MGH SSRM* 5, 668.

12. *Concilium in Austrasia habitum q.d. Germanicum, 742, MGH Legum* III, II, pars prior, 3.

13. CF, 96.

14. "Testamentum," ed. by Patrick J. Geary in his *Aristocracy in Provence: The Rhône Basin at the Dawn of the Carolingian Age* (Philadelphia: University of Pennsylvania Press, 1985), 40–41.

15. *Annales regni Francorum*, 749, ed. F. Kurze, *Scriptores rerum Germanicarum in usum scholarum* (Hannover: 1895).

Chapter VII

1. Book 6, Chapter 62.

2. No. 56 (September 1981).

3. *Vita Karoli*, 1. tr. Lewis Thorpe, Einhard and Notker the Stam-

merer, *Two Lives of Charlemagne* (Harmondsworth: Penguin, 1969), 55.

4. CF, 81.

5. CF, 86.

6. CF, 18.

7. Edward Peters, *The Shadow King: 'Rex Inutilis' in Medieval Law and Literature 751–1327* (New Haven: Yale University Press, 1970).

8. Jean-Edel Berthier, *1000 Chants 2* (Paris: Les Presses d'Ile-de-France, 1975), 50.

9. Fortunatus, *Vita Remedii, MGH AA* 4, 12–23.

10. *Leadership and Community*, 171.

11. Einhard, *Translatio et miracula SS Marcellini et Petri*, 3, 5 *MGH SS* 15, 249–250.

Suggestions for Further Reading

Until quite recently, virtually all of the fundamental work on Merovingian history has been done in German and French and little has been translated. The following recommendations are intended as a first introduction for an English-reading audience; however the essential works of continental scholarship are included as well.

1. Sources

The standard commentary on the sources of Merovingian history is Wattenbach-Levison, *Deutschlands Geschichtsquellen im Mittelalter: Vorzeit und Karolinger*, 5 parts (Weimar: Herman Böhlaus Nachfolger, 1952–73). Only the narrative sources have been translated: Gregory of Tours, *History of the Franks*, L. Thorpe, tr. (Harmondsworth: Penguin, 1974); *The Fourth Book of the Chronicle of Fredegar with its Continuations*, J. M. Wallace-Harrill, ed. and tr. (London: Thomas Nelson and Sons Ltd., 1960); and *Liber Historiae Francorum*, Bernard S. Bachrach, tr. (Lawrence, Kansas: Coronado Press, 1973). Lives of Martin of Tours and Germanus of Auxerre and Honoratus of Arles are translated in F. R. Hoare, ed. and tr., *The Western Fathers* (New York: Sheed and Ward, 1954). Additional texts are found in Edward Peters, ed., *Monks, Bishops and Pagans: Christian Culture in Gaul and Italy, 500–700* (Philadelphia: University of Pennsylvania Press, 1975) and in J. N. Hillgarth, ed., *Christianity and Paganism, 350–750: The Conversion of Western Europe* (Philadelphia: University of Pennsylvania Press, 1986). Jo Ann McNamara, John E. Halborg, and Gordon Whatleg have translated the lives of all of the Merovingian female saints in *Sainted Women of the Dark Ages*, forthcoming.

2. General

Four general surveys of the entire Frankish period have recently appeared, with useful sections on the Merovingian centuries: Edward James, *The Origins of France: From Clovis to the Capetians, 500–1000* (London: Macmillan Press, 1982) (with a very useful bibliography); Friedrich Prinz, *Grundlagen und Anfänge: Deutschland bis 1056, Neue deutsche Geschichte*, Peter Moraw, Volker Press, Wolfrang Schieder, ed., vol. 1 (Munich: C. H. Beck Verlag, 1985); Karl Ferdinand Werner, *Histoire de France*, vol. 1. *Les origines (Avant l'an mil)*, (Paris: Fayard, 1984); and Patrick Périn and Laure-Charlotte Feffer, *Les Francs:* vol. 1., *A la conquête de la Gaule*, and vol. 2, *A l'origine de la France* (Paris: Armand Colin, 1987). An essential survey with bibliography is found in Gebhardt, ed. *Handbuch der Deutschen Geschichte*, vol. 1 (Stuttgart: Ernst Klett Verlag, 1970).

CHAPTER I

The most abundant literature in English concerns the late Roman period. The standard work, Arnold Hugh Martin Jones, *The Later Roman Empire*, 3 vols. (Oxford: Basil Blackwell, 1964), is now available in paperback from Johns Hopkins University Press. Other important works include Peter Brown's *Religion and Society in the Age of Saint Augustine* (Berkeley: University of California Press, 1969); his *The World of Late Antiquity A.D. 150–750* (New York: Harcourt Brace Jovanovich, Inc., 1971); his *The Cult of the Saints: Its Rise and Function in Latin Christianity* (Chicago: University of Chicago Press, 1981); his *Society and the Holy in Late Antiquity* (Berkeley: University of California Press, 1982); and Ramsay MacMullen, *Soldier and Civilian in the Later Roman Empire* (Cambridge, Mass: Harvard University Press, 1963). The standard study of Gallo-Roman aristocratic families remains Karl Friedrich Stroheker, *Der senatorische Adel im spätantiken Gallien* (Reutlingen: Alma Mater Verlag, 1948). An impressive recent study of Gaul is Raymond Van Dam, *Leadership and Community in Late Antique Gaul* (Berkeley: University of California Press, 1985). The continuity of Roman political ideology East and West is traced in Michael McCormick, *Eternal Victory: Triumphal Rulership in Late Antiquity, Byzantium and the Early Medieval West* (Cambridge: Cambridge University Press, 1986).

CHAPTER II

The most important work in English on the barbarians is that of E. A. Thompson, especially *Romans and Barbarians: The Decline of the*

Western Empire (Madison: University of Wisconsin Press, 1982). Still useful is J. M. Wallace-Hadrill's summary, *The Barbarian West: The Early Middle Ages A.D. 400–1000* (London: Hutchinson and Company, Ltd., 1962). Also important are Walter Goffart, *Barbarians and Romans A.D. 418–584: The Techniques of Accommodation* (Princeton: Princeton University Press, 1980); Lucien Musset, *The Germanic Invasions* (Pittsburg: Pennsylvania State University Press, 1975); and Alexander C. Murray, *Germanic Kinship Structure. Studies in Law and Society in Antiquity and the Early Middle Ages* (Toronto: Pontifical Institute of Mediaeval Studies, 1983). The fundamental study from a methodological perspective is Reinhard Wenskus, *Stammesbildung und Verfassung: Das Werden der frühmittelalterlichen gentes* (Vienna–Cologne: Böhlau, 1977). On the Goths, Herwig Wolfram's *History of the Goths* (Berkeley: University of California Press, in press) is extremely valuable both substantively and methodologically, as is his "The Shaping of the Early Medieval Principality as a Type of Non-Royal Rulership," *Viator* 2 (1971), 33–51. On the later Ostrogoths, see Thomas Burns, *The Ostrogoths* (Bloomington: Indiana University Press, 1984) The archeological evidence is summarized in Bruno Krüger, ed., *Die Germanen: Geschichte und Kultur der germanischen Stämme im Mitteleuropa. Bd. I. Von den Anfängen bis zum 2. Jahrhundert unserer Zeitrechnung*, 2nd edition (Berlin: Akademie-Verlag, 1978). Additional essential works are Joachim Werner's "Zur Entstehung der Reihengräberzivilisation" in Franz Petri, ed., *Siedlung, Sprache und Bevölkerungsstruktur im Frankenreich. Wege der Forschung*, vol. 49 (Darmstadt: Wissenschaftliche Buchgesellschaft, 1973), 285–325; and Horst Wolfgang Böhme, *Germanische Grabefunde des 4. bis 5. Jahrhunderts zwischen unterer Elbe und Loire: Studien sur Chronologie und Bevölkerungsgeschichte*, 2 vols., Münchner Beiträge zur Vor- und Frühgeschichte Bd. 19 (Munich: C.C.H. Beck'sche Verlags Buchhandlung, 1974); and his "Archäologische Zeugnisse zur Geschichte der Markomannenkriege (166–180 N. CHR.)," *Jahrbuch des Römischen-Germanischen Zentralmuseums* 22 (1975), 153–217. On the peoples of the Danubian region, see most recently Herwig Wolfram and Falko Daim, *Die Völker an der mittleren und unteren Donau im fünften und sechsten Jahrhundert* (Vienna: Verlag der österreichischen Akademie der Wissenschaften, 1980).

CHAPTER III

The fundamental study of the early Franks is Erich Zöllner *Geschichte der Franken Bis zur Mitte des 6. Jahrhunderts* (Munich: C. H. Beck Verlag, 1970). The work of Eugen Ewig is basic for all Merovingian history and much of it has been collected in *Spätantikes und fränkisches Gallien. Gesammelte Schriften (1952–1973)* Beihefte der *Francia* 3, ed. Hartmut Atsma. 2 vols. (Munich: Artemis Verlag, 1976–1979). Also important are the essays by J. M. Wallace-Hadrill in *The Long-Haired Kings and Other Studies in Frankish History* (New York: Barnes & Noble, Inc., 1962). On Merovingian archaeology see in particular Patrick Périn, *La datation des tombes mérovingiennes: Historique—Méthodes—Applications* (Geneva: Librairie Droz, 1980). In recent years, a number of younger British historians, trained largely by Wallace-Hadrill, have begun to make important contributions to Merovingian history. Among the collections in which their work appears are: Wendy Davies and Paul Fouracre, *The Settlement of Disputes in Early Medieval Europe* (Cambridge: Cambridge University Press, 1986), P. H. Sawyer and I. N. Wood, *Early Medieval Kingship* (Leeds: University of Leeds Press, 1977); and Patrick Wormald, Donald Bullough, and Roger Collins, eds., *Ideal and Reality in Frankish and Anglo-Saxon Society: Studies presented to J. M. Wallace-Hadrill* (Oxford: Basil Blackwell, 1983).

On the household and society see David Herlihy, *Medieval Households* (Cambridge, Mass: Harvard University Press, 1985) and Suzanne Fonay Wemple, *Women in Frankish Society: Marriage and the Cloister 500–900* (Philadelphia: University of Pennsylvania Press, 1981). On Merovingian economy see Renée Doehaerd, *The Early Middle Ages in the West: Economy and Society* (Amsterdam: North-Holland Publishing Company, 1978); Robert Latouche, *The Birth of Western Economy: Economic aspects of the Dark Ages* (New York: Barnes & Noble, 1961); Georges Duby, *The Early Growth of the European Economy: Warriors and Peasants from the Seventh to the Twelfth Century* (Ithaca: Cornell University Press, 1974).

CHAPTER IV

On the political and institutional history of the sixth century see Herwig Wolfram, *Intitulatio I, Lateinisches Königs-und Fürstentitel bis zum Ende des 8. Jahrhunderts, Mitteilungen des Instituts für österreichische Geschichtsforschung* Ergänzungsband 21 (Vienna: Hermann Böhlaus Nachf., 1967); Ewig, "Die fränkischen Teilungen und Teilreiche *(511–613)* in *Spätantikes und fränkisches Gallien,* 114–170; and J. M. Wallace-Hadrill, *The Long-haired Kings,* 148–206. Useful are Bernard Bachrach, *Merovingian Military Organization 481–751* (Minneapolis: University of Minnesota Press, 1972); and Archibald R. Lewis, "The Dukes in the "Regnum Francorum" A.D. 550–751," *Speculum* 51

(1976), 381–410. On Frankish-Byzantine relations see Walter Goffart, "Byzantine Policy in the West under Tiberius II and Maurice: The Pretenders Hermenegild and Gundovald (579–585)," *Traditio* 13 (1957), 73–118.

J. M. Wallace-Hadrill's *The Frankish Church* (Oxford: Clarendon Press, 1983) contains important chapters on the church. A very useful introduction in English is the translations of volume two of the *Handbuch der Kirchengeschichte,* which contains essays on the early medieval church by Eugen Ewig and others in Hubert Jedin and John Dolan, eds., *Handbook of Church History,* vol. 2, *The Imperial Church from Constantine to the Early Middle Ages* (New York: Herder and Herder, 1980. On the episcopate see Martin Heinzelmann, *Bischofsherrschaft in Gallien: Zur Kontinuität römischer Führungsschichten vom 4. bis zum 7. Jahrhundert. Soziale, prosopographische und bildungsgeschichtliche Aspekte, Beihefte der Francia 5* (Munich: Artemis Verlag, 1976); and Georg Scheibelreiter, *Der Bishof in merowingischer Zeit, Veröffentlichungen des Instituts für österreichische Geschichtsforschung* vol. 27 (Vienna: Hermann Böhlaus Nachf., 1983). On Martin of Tours see Clare Stancliffe, *St. Martin and His Hagiographer: History and Miracle in Sulpicius Severus* (Oxford: Clarendon Press, 1983). The classic study of Merovingian monasticism remains Friedrich Prinz, *Frühes Mönchtum im Frankenreich* (Munich: 1965), a new and revised version of which is in press. Prinz has also edited a collection of essential articles on monasticism and society: *Mönchtum und Gesellschaft im Frühmittelalter* (Darmstadt: Wissenschaftliche Buchgesellschaft, 1976). The major examination of Merovingian hagiography and society is František Graus, *Volk Herrscher und Heiliger im Reich der Merowinger: Studien zur Hagiographie der Merowingerzeit* (Prague: Nakladatelství Československé akademie věd, 1965).

CHAPTER V

On the dynastic history of the later sixth and early seventh centuries see Ewig, "Die Frankischen Teilreiche im 7. Jahrhundert (613–714)," in *Spätantikes und fränkisches Gallien,* 172–201; and J. M. Wallace-Hadrill, *The Long-Haired Kings,* 206–231. The standard reference for Merovingian secular officials is Horst Ebling, *Prosopographie der Amtsträger des Merowingerreiches von Chlothar II (613) bis Karl Martell (741),* Beihefte der *Francia* 2 (Munich: Wilhelm Fink Verlag, 1974). Concerning estates and estate management see above all John Percival, "Seigneurial aspects of Late Roman Estate Management," *The English Historical Review* 332 (1969), 449–473; Walter Goffart's "From

Roman Taxation to Mediaeval Seigneurie: Three Notes," *Speculum* 47 (1972), 165–187 and 373–394; his "Old and New in Merovingian Taxation," *Past and Present* 96 (1982), 3–21; and Adriaan Verhulst, "La genèse du régime domanial classique en France au haute moyen âge," *Agricoltura e mondo rurale in occidente nell'alto medioevo, Settimane di studio del centro italiano di studi sull'alto medioevo* 13 (Spoleto: 1966), 135–160.

On Columbanus and Frankish monasticism see the essays in H. B. Clarke and M. Brenna, eds., *Columbanus and Merovingian Monasticism*, British Archeological Reports s-113. (Oxford: 1981); as well as the fundamental works by Prinz in *Frühes Mönchtum* and in "Heiligenkult und Adelsherrschaft im Spiegel merowingischer Hagiographie," *Historisches Zeitschrift* 204 (1967), 529–544; R. Sprandel, *Der merowingische Adel und die Gebiete östlich des Rheines* (Freiburg: 1957); and Sprandel's "Struktur und Geschichte des merowingischen Adels," *Historisches Zeitschrift* 193 (1961), 33–71. On the development of aristocratic and clerical culture see Pierre Riché, *Education and Culture in the Barbarian West, Sixth through Eighth Centuries* (Columbia, S.C.: South Carolina University Press, 1976); and M. L. W. Laistner, *Thought and Letters in Western Europe A.D. 500–900* (Ithaca: Cornell University Press, 1957); as well as Franz Irsigler, *Untersuchungen zur Geschichte des frühfränkischen Adels. Rheinisches Archiv, Veröffentlichungen des Instituts für geschtliche Landeskunde der Rheinlande an der Universität Bonn* no. 70 (Bonn: Ludwig Röhrscheid Verlag, 1969), a portion of which has been translated in Timothy Reuter, ed. and tr., *The Medieval Nobility: Studies on the ruling classes of France and Germany from the sixth to the twelfth century* (Amsterdam: North-Holland Publishing Company, 1978), as "On the aristocratic character of early Frankish society," 106–136. On missionary activity see Karl Ferdinand Werner, "Le rôle de l'aristocratie dans la christianisation du nord-est de la Gaule," *Revue de l'historie de l'église de France* 62 (1976), 45–73; C. E. Stancliffe, "From Town to Country: The Christianisation of the Touraine, 370–600," *Studies in Church History* 16 (1979), 43–59; Ian N. Wood, "Early Merovingian Devotion in Town and Country," ibid., 61–76; and Paul Fouracre, "The work of Audoenus of Rouen and Eligius of Noyon in Extending Episcopal Influence from the Town to the Country in Seventh-Century Neustria," ibid., 77–91.

CHAPTER VI

On the regions of Francia in the later seventh and eighth centuries see, in addition to the essays by Ewig noted above, his "Volkstum und

Volksbewusstsein im Frankenreich des 7. Jahrhunderts," *Spätantikes und Fränkisches Gallien* 1, 231–273 (although the author differs with some of his conclusions); Erich Zöllner, *Die politische Stellung der Völker im Frankenreich* (Vienna: Hermann Böhlaus Nachf., 1950); and Karl Ferdinand Werner, "Les principautés périphériques dans le monde Franc du VIIIe siècle," *I problemi dell'Occidente nel secolo VIII, Settimane di studio del Centro italiano di studi sull'alto medioevo* 20 (Spoleto: 1973), 483–532. On specific areas see Edward James, *The Merovingian Archaeology of South-West Gaul*, 2 vols. British Archaeological Reports Supplementary Series 25(i) (Oxford: 1977); Michel Rouche, *L'Aquitaine des Wisigoths aux Arabes 418–781: naissance d'une région* (Paris: Éditions Jean Touzot, 1979); Patrick J. Geary, *Aristocracy in Provence: The Rhône Basin at the Dawn of the Carolingian Age* (Philadelphia: University of Pennsylvania Press, 1985); A. Joris, "On the Edge of Two Worlds in the Heart of the New Empire: The Romance Regions of Northern Gaul during the Merovingian Period," *Studies in Medieval and Renaissance History* 3 (1966), 3–52; Matthias Werner, *Der Lütticher Raum in frühkarolingischer Zeit* (Göttingen: Vandenhoeck & Ruprecht, 1980); Herwig Wolfram, "Der heilige Rupert und die antikarolingische Adelsopposition," *Mitteilungen des Instituts für österreichische Geschichtsforschung* 80 (1972), 4–34; Otto Gerhard Oexle, "Die Karolinger und die Stadt des heiligen Arnulf," *Frühmittelalterliche Studien* 1 (1967), 250–364; and Herwig Wolfram, *Die Geburt Mitteleuropas: Geschichte Österreichs vor seiner Entstehung 378–907* (Vienna: Kremayr & Scheriau, 1987).

On Merovingian queens see Janet L. Nelson, "Queens as Jezebels: The Careers of Brunhild and Balthild in Merovingian History," *Medieval Women,* Derek Baker, ed. (Oxford: Basil Blackwell, 1978), 31–77. And most recently Pauline Stafford, *Queens, Concubines and Dowagers: The King's Wife in the Early Middle Ages* (London: Batsford Academic and Educational Ltd., 1983). On the confusing history of Griomoald and Childebert see Eugen Ewig, "Noch einmal zum 'Staatsstreich' Grimoalds, *Spätantikes und Fränkisches Gallien* 1, 573–577; and Heinz Thomas, "Die Namenliste des Diptychon Barberini und der Sturz des Hausmeiers Grimoald," *Deutsches Archiv* 25 (1969), 17–63. On the rise of the Carolingians see Paul J. Fouracre, "Observations on the Outgrowth of Pippinid Influence in the 'Regnum Francorum' after the Battle of Tertry (687–715)," *Medieval Prosopography* 5 (1984), 1–31; and Josef Semmler, "Zur pippinidisch-karolingischen Sukzessionskrise 714–723," *Deutsches Archiv* 33 (1977), 1–36. On the Anglo-Saxon missionaries on the Continent the fundamental work remains Wilhelm

Levison, *England and the Continent in the Eighth Century* (Oxford: Clarendon Press, 1946). On the papacy of the eighth century see Thomas F. X. Noble, *The Republic of St. Peter: The Birth of the Papal State, 680–825* (Philadelphia: University of Pennsylvania Press, 1984). On Charles Martel and the early Carolingians see, in addition to Semmler, Rosamond McKitterick, *The Frankish Kingdoms under the Carolingians 751–987* (London: Longman, 1983). The literature on the coronation of Pepin is vast. Most recently in English is Michael J. Enright, *Iona, Tara and Soissons: The Origin of the Royal Anointing Ritual, Arbeiten zur Frühmittelalterforschung* 17 (Berlin: Walter de Gruyter, 1985).

CHAPTER VII

Edward Peter's *The Shadow King: Rex Inutilis in Medieval Law and Literature 751–1327* (New Haven: Yale University Press, 1970) remains the essential examination of the formation of the traditional attitude toward the Merovingians. On Einhard's image of the Merovingians see Adolf Grauert, "Noch einmal Einhard und die letzten Merowinger," in Lutz Frenske et al., *Institutionen, Kultur und Gesellschaft im Mittelalter. Festschrift für Josef Fleckenstein zu seinem 65. Geburtstag* (Sigmaringen: Jan Thorbecke Verlag, 1984), 59–72. Karl Ferdinand Werner has worked for years to reform attitudes in France and Germany concerning Frankish history. See in particular the first essay in his *Vom Frankenreich zur Entfaltung Deutschlands und Frankreichs: Ursprünge—Strukturen—Beziehungen. Ausgewählte Beiträge* (Sigmaringen: Jan Thorbecke Verlag, 1984), "En guise d'introduction: Conquête franque de la Gaule ou changement de régime?" 1–11.

Index

* This index includes only the principal persons and places figuring in the text.